W.P. Wiles

THE LAST BLADE PRIEST

A NOVEL

ANGRY
ROBOT

ANGRY ROBOT
An imprint of Watkins Media Ltd

Unit 11, Shepperton House
89 Shepperton Road
London N1 3DF
UK

angryrobotbooks.com
twitter.com/angryrobotbooks
Blades For Days

An Angry Robot paperback original, 2022

Cover by Alice Coleman
Edited by Simon Spanton and Andrew Hook
Set in Meridien

ISBN 978 0 85766 982 7
Ebook ISBN 978 0 85766 983 4

Printed and bound in the United Kingdom by TJ Books Ltd.

9 8 7 6 5 4 3 2 1

MIX
Paper from
responsible sources
FSC® C013056

BOOK ONE OF
The Holy Mountain

INAR

Stone was not alive, he knew. But it had moods, it had needs, it had desires. And it often wanted to kill him.

This morning it was a corbel that had murder in mind. It resembled a heavy stone beam, almost as tall as a man but only a couple of hand-breadths wide. Laid across the top of the wall with many others like it, it would help support a platform from where defenders could drop heavy objects and unpleasant substances on assaulting soldiers. This morning it was the heavy object that dropped, and Inar was playing the part of the unlucky soldier beneath.

The work team had been winching corbels to the top of the rebuilt wall since first light, and Inar's heart had never stopped pounding. The equipment was inadequate and the men would rather throw away their lives than listen to a simple instruction. Twice, someone had nearly fallen from the wall; it was the Mountain's work that they had not seen a dozen broken feet and two dozen smashed hands. What good is a mason whose hand is a bleeding bag of splinters? And men were so scarce.

Only half of these bastards could wield hammer and chisel with skill. But none of them, it appeared, could tie a straight knot. Long and heavy, the corbels needed to be lashed at both ends to avoid swinging dangerously on the rope or slipping from its grasp altogether. Halfway up the wall, one of the bindings on this corbel had slipped towards the middle of the stone, and it had begun to sag and swing. Inar ordered the man at the pulley-rope to raise his pace; he had to order Lott, standing atop the tower, to hold back, not to lean out into space to try to grab the swaying weight. Cursing had followed. The pulley creaked and groaned – a certain looseness had come into its actions over the course of the morning, and Inar now feared for its security.

Kneeling on the unfinished top of the wall thirty feet above Inar, Lott had managed to get his hand on one of the corbel's bindings and was guiding it closer to the wall. The pulley block shuddered. Inar shouted at him, again, that he should leave it alone until it was above the top of the wall. As he did so, unthinking, he moved closer to the bottom of the wall, beneath the winch arm. And then he realised that, if the pulley really was weakening, the last thing Lott should do was let go – that would cause the corbel to swing out, away from the wall, greatly adding to the stress on the ropes and wooden wheels that were allowing it to temporarily defy gravity.

Lott let go. He had taken his eyes off the stone, and his mind off the job, distracted by something behind Inar. The corbel swung away from him like a battering ram. He lunged for it, almost following it into space, then, fearing it might swing back and strike him, he scrambled backwards onto the scaffold.

The corbel never swung back. When it had swung as far from the wall as the rope would allow, the pulleys and the crane-arm supporting them shattered in a starburst of splinters.

It moved so slowly. The corbel executed a lazy turn in the cool morning air, hardly really falling at all as far as Inar could see. But it was falling, trailing loops of rope – falling towards Inar.

Inar leaped backwards, an action that came entirely from the darkness of instinct. His heel struck something hard and he sprawled onto a pile of rubble, left elbow twisting underneath him with an ugly pain, and a hard point jabbing into his right shoulder with the force of a battle blow. He cried out, without words. The corbel hit the ground point-on with a deep, solid boom, and for an idiotic instant Inar forgot his own safety and that of his men and instead hoped for the safety of the stone, issuing a prayer to the Mountain that this well-carved block should not break. It didn't, and instead impaled itself a hand's-length deep into the soft earth, remaining drunkenly upright like an ancient menhir.

The pain from his shoulder snatched Inar back to attention, followed by the realisation that the danger was far from over. Again moving mysteriously slowly, the remnants of the pulleys and the crane-arm were breaking away from the scaffold, and for a leisurely moment of horror Inar feared that a chain of collapse might have been set in motion, that the whole structure atop the wall might simply unravel before his eyes, taking half a dozen men and at least a month of work with it. But it held as the timbers and ropes of the crane clattered noisily to the ground, planting a garden of broken timber around the fallen corbel.

Dust rose, and there was a beat of quiet. Inar tried to raise himself from the heap he had fallen into, wincing again at the pain – but he was not bleeding, and nothing was broken. Just pain, which Inar now felt the need to spread around.

"Lott!" he screamed. "What are you thinking?! You could have killed us!"

But Lott still wasn't paying attention. Instead he was gawping out over the fields beyond the city, where the lane that led to the Lowgate wound between broken dry-stone walls and farm-folk tending to spring planting. Inar turned to look.

There were horsemen approaching, not in any hurry. At the head of the small, sedate procession was a League knight, who, Inar noted with surprise, was also a woman. Flanking her were a younger girl and an older man, and following them were four more League knights in armour, one bearing a standard from which fluttered a pennant: three cascades, in white, on a blue background.

Inar had never hated a symbol more.

"I didn't think the League had a Queen," Falde said. He had arrived at Inar's side unseen.

"They've got classy whores," Lott shouted from the top of the wall, and a few of the Stull men laughed, not hiding their nervousness.

"Mountain's silent, Lott!" Inar barked. But he did not take his eyes from the Leaguer woman, and she did not take her eyes from his. Hopefully, she did not speak Mishigo. She wore the padded leather armour traditional to the lowlands, but worked to a much higher quality than Inar had seen in battle-dress: shaped subtly to her form, covered in embossed decorations, highlighted with hints of silver thread. Such armour of this kind that Inar had seen before was brown, its colour chosen by the cow, but this was deep midnight blue. It was an outfit that spoke of the highest rank or the most unimaginable wealth, but the woman's dark brown hair was cut short, like a peasant's. The girl beside her was pale and distracted, like a noble's poorly daughter dragged from her sickbed for an afternoon's ride. The older man was stout, dressed in plain city clothing all in black, and he frowned up at the wall.

"Inar?" the armoured woman asked in practised Mirolingua. "Inar, the son of Astar?"

Inar straightened, in an instant painfully aware that the visitor must have witnessed the deadly farce of breaking timber and falling stone seconds earlier. He was reluctant to lay ownership to this shambles, but the truth could not be averted.

"I am Inar," he said. "May I ask…?"

The woman smiled. "I am merite Anzola Stiyitta, surveyor-general of the League of Free Cities. We are in the same trade, Inar."

A woman, dressed as a warrior, who claimed to be a builder. Inar found he had little to say. "Oh?"

Merite Anzola dismounted from her horse in a single smooth movement, and walked across the rough ground of the filled-in moat towards Inar's works.

"I saw the accident. What do you suppose went wrong?"

Inar bristled. He had no desire to chitchat with a Leaguer of any kind, but for this chameleon of a woman to start to advise him on his business was intolerable. "Well, what happened is, this gang of leather-wearing arseholes from the mudflats came and knocked down this wall, and we're trying to rebuild it. Only we're short on men, and money, and keep getting interrupted while we're trying to work." This raised a grunt of mirth from Falde, and from the wall Lott shouted agreement. Inar turned to glare at the apprentice, who suddenly found a reason to get his head down and start dismantling the wrecked crane.

"I know you don't have any reason to love the League," merite Anzola said. She did not appear to be offended by his words, maintaining an expression of sunny enthusiasm. But Inar could also see the rest of her party: the miserable girl, the surly man in black, the stern-faced knights. "You or any of your men," Anzola continued. "The war was an awful affair, awful – one we did not seek, remember. But our nations are friends now, and this friend would like to assist you."

Friends? Master and servant was more like it, Inar thought, or perhaps landlord and serf. He said nothing.

"I saw the mechanism you had set up," Anzola said. She had passed Inar and was inspecting the tangled wreckage at the foot of the wall. "Multiple pulleys, so a single man can lift a great weight – it's very intelligent. Your design?"

Inar felt trapped, or at least as if he was standing at the edge of a trap and a wrong step might trigger it. For all her cordiality, this woman was dangerous. He was dealing with a puzzle made out of snakes. They all had to smile and agree with the League, the whole land, but he knew how the King's court felt about anyone who might harbour actual loyalty towards their conquerors, especially if that anyone was already under suspicion. "No. I read about it in a book. Nothing clever."

"It was intelligent to look for a better way of doing things, and it was intelligent to apply this design," Anzola said kindly. "We think alike, Inar. As it happens we use something similar on the docks at Pallestra."

Think alike? That sounded neither accurate nor praiseful to Inar. "It would work better if I could forge iron parts. But iron is in short supply around here."

Anzola shrugged. Nothing appeared to alter her pleasant mood, not even mention of the high price the League had asked in exchange for peace. "The demands of war, sadly."

"War's over."

"One war is over," Anzola said. "The next..." Still smiling, she turned away from Inar and began to walk back to her entourage. "Delightful to meet you, Inar. I look forward to seeing you again."

If a party of Leaguer knights had ridden up and cursed at him, Inar would have been less concerned. It would fit in with how he saw the world. But for them to compliment and encourage him – that left him unmoored, and troubled in ways he could not describe. He watched as the noblewoman mounted her horse and spurred it back down the road, followed by the rest of her party, as grand a display as they had made when they approached. None of them looked back at him, apart from the pale young girl. She was frowning, mirroring his own furrowed brow, as if he presented a puzzle, or a disappointment. Disturbed by her silent attention, Inar broke his gaze and turned back to his men.

"Show's over," he said. "Let's get on with it."

Mishig-Tenh: the name meant "land of the late dawn". To the east and south of the kingdom, the Shield Mountains rose, a curtain of rock thousands of feet high, and the sun took its time to climb above their clawing peaks. The rays of dawn reached places to the west of Mishig-Tenh before the sun rose high enough to surpass the mountains and shine down into the kingdom itself. The breaking of day was always slow, and in the winter felt as if it might never come at all. It was preceded by a long hinterland of quarter-light and half-light, the shepherd's night.

It was in this time that the king's men came for Inar Astarsson.

When they had come for his father and his brother two years ago, they had been as loud as battle. They had broken in the thick wooden door of the keep even as servants rushed to open it. They had overturned every loose piece of furniture they saw, and dragged out Astar and Essian with curses and blows.

This morning, the chief builder never heard them enter. Inar awoke in a grey dimness to find Cilma, the Lord Chancellor, standing at the foot of his bed, watching, still. Behind, in the doorway, a cluster of armour and weapons and hard eyes.

"My Lord," Inar gasped, scrambling to sit up. He felt as if a trapdoor had opened within his bed, the worst kind of falling dream. His bladder was full and he feared for his mastery of it.

"What do they want, Inar?" Cilma asked, as calm as if he were asking if the young man had eaten breakfast yet. Even without force behind it, the question slashed to Inar's innards.

"What?"

"What. Do. They. Want." The dark brown cloak at the foot of the bed stirred ever so slightly.

"My lord," Inar said. Any moment now the men behind Cilma would enter, and the next time he saw daylight of any kind would be at his execution. If he was lucky.

"Don't make me ask again," Cilma said, searching the room with his eyes, finding shadows that sharpened as the light clarified. "In the normal course, the second time and third time I ask a question, the man answering it is in great pain."

"What do who want?" Inar said, somehow.

"You know very well *who*," Cilma said. "The League."

"I spoke briefly with the League Lady," Inar said, almost babbling. He lacked a precise answer to Cilma's question and felt that the least dangerous course was to give a full account of everything that had happened the previous day, as quickly as possible. "She didn't ask for anything. She praised my work. I insulted her. She went on her way."

Cilma straightened and ceased to look into the half-light, fixing his grey eyes instead upon Inar. The chancellor had lost his own son on the field at Halsk Trun. Even before then, he had been the most severe figure at court. But after, that severity was honed with a terrible quality – more terrible, even, than his unopposed power. He had nothing to lose. It was in every hard line of that granite face of his. Nothing to lose, and so he gave everything – a berserker in the service of a shaky crown, impervious to civility, uninterested in precedent, indifferent to blood.

Inar's room occupied half of the second floor of the keep, separated from the other half by a partition of wood panels. Through the connecting door, Inar could see the soldiers waiting in the stair. He could hear the floorboards creak under their shifting weight, the scuff of their boots, metal notes of armour and weapons. At any time the word could be given, and in they would come. Cilma saw the builder's eyes fixing on the men, and he waved at them to close the door.

Now that they were alone, Cilma continued. "When a plot is exposed, you arrest the plotters, naturally," he said, and something about the way he said *arrest* made it synonymous with *kill*. "And you arrest anyone who knew about the plot, and failed to do anything about it, because they are little better than plotters. And you must arrest anyone who stood to benefit from the plot. Nine times out of ten, they knew about the plot as well. But then there's that one time out of ten when the beneficiary of a plot is unaware – an infant or dunce whose half-witted relatives want to put them on the throne. Are they innocent?"

To Inar, this appeared to be a rare occasion when it was safer to not give an answer. He was certain that Cilma had an answer ready. The chancellor was not a man to weigh on the one hand *this*, on the other hand *that*. There was only ever one hand, and it always came crashing down.

"In truth, innocence doesn't matter," Cilma continued. "You arrest them. Benefiting is culpability enough. And it discourages others. There'll be fewer willing to elevate their six-year-old nephew if they know that his innocent head will join theirs in the sawdust all the same. But, you know…" Cilma sighed, and in doing so seemed suddenly his true age, and capable of doubt, perhaps even fallible. "You know, sometimes you just want to arrest *everyone*, and you can't. You have to stop somewhere. And that leaves the possibility that you've made a mistake."

He crossed the room, running an eye over the few books piled on the writing-desk under the south window, the carvings Inar used to weigh his papers, and then looking through the window itself. Dawn, at last – the sun was over the Shields. Good strong light, the harbinger of a bright spring day. From that window, Cilma would have a view of the mouth of the Sojonost Pass. Inar's keep stood on moorland above the valley – worse for planting, but fine for views. On a clear day, by the east window, you could see God.

"After the betrayal of Stull, we were thorough," Cilma continued. "Your father confessed freely. Your brother knew of the plot, and as your father's heir stood to benefit from any preferment. Guilty twice over. But you – both claimed you knew nothing, even when the question was put with considerable force. Your death set no example. Enough blood had been spilt. And you had the makings of a great builder. You were an ideal candidate for mercy."

Inar swallowed, and put some words together. If the decision had been made, he did not imagine that there was anything he could say that would save him; but if it had not, he wished to avoid condemning himself. "I will always be grateful to the crown for its mercy," he said. "I desire only to be its loyal servant."

Cilma smiled sourly – more a grimace than anything pleasant. "Hmm. And so you have been. But now the League have come, and *they* desire your service. Our filthy treaty with them means they can levy anyone they like, but for *you* they offer riches. Why is that, do you think?"

Inar could not give an answer. He was too surprised. But he did not get the chance to say anything, as Cilma swooped back across the room, moving fast and silent and certain, his countenance again terrible.

"Perhaps," he said, his voice low and venomous, "it is the pay-off of a treacherous little bargain made by your traitor father? Which would make you a beneficiary of treason."

Then, as if the effort of this threat had wearied him, Cilma sank onto the stool that stood by the work table. "Get dressed," he snarled.

So this was it – the end. Arrest, and death. One always led to the other.

He could not make himself move. What did one wear to prison? Or to torture? It was an unnatural courtesy to be given the chance to dress.

Highly unnatural. A faint outline of possibility – too faint to be called hope – had formed.

"Where are we going?" he asked, daring.

"I am going nowhere," Lord Cilma said. "You are going to serve the League."

Inar blinked at him. "My lord, I hate the League," he said, and he was not forcing a show of fealty. The words came easily.

Cilma shrugged, a distinctly un-Cilma thing to do. "So do we all. But when they are here, they rule over us, and they are here. You'll need to pack for travel, too, and ready a horse.

Warm clothes, furs, and whatever you need for sleeping in the field. You are going to Sojonost."

"What?" Inar said. Only just past sunrise, and already the day had exhausted him.

"The League Merite is coming," Cilma said. He shot Inar a look, one Inar had never seen before – one of confidence. "An impressive lady, yes? She has impressed our king. Consequently, you are a League levy now, young Inar. You'll go with them and do as they say."

"My lord, this is not…"

"You listen to me," Cilma said. He leaned in, his eyes as hard as dungeon stones. "You will be in their service, but you work for me. The builder becomes the spy. You will tell me everything. What are they doing at Sojonost? What are their plans? Will there be another war? Are they moving against Miroline? I want to know every detail you learn, and you will be eager in your learnings, you will ask questions and pursue answers. Do you understand that?"

"Yes, my lord."

Cilma looked away. "Perform well, and there's a good deal to be gained. The restoration of a few confiscated holdings, perhaps; perhaps even a path to the title that was promised your father…" He turned back, and again the severity was there. "If, however, I detect disloyalty, either to the crown or to me personally, I may decide that I showed too much leniency when dealing with your father's treason. Do you understand?"

"My lord." The words all made sense to Inar, yes. But he understood nothing.

The morning had passed in a storm of preparation. Inar had two servants, an elderly couple who were the last remnant of his father's household. He tried to reassure them that he was only going to Sojonost, and that he would be back soon, but they were unwilling to meet his eye, and clearly expected not to see him again. The lingering presence of Lord Cilma, executioner of their previous employer, did not help. It was the lord chancellor who gave most of the orders, with Inar hardly knowing what to say.

Later, waiting on the Stull road for the League to come, Inar felt giddy from the speed of events. Lord Cilma had insisted that they meet the League with some ceremony, so he and his men had stayed in attendance, and Inar wore his best cape. They made a handsome group, and Inar even felt a little proud of the kingdom and of himself. But most of the prestige emanated from Cilma, astride a magnificent black charger, straight-backed and wrapped in robes and black furs like a column of smoke. To either side were the armoured guards, one of whom bore the royal standard, which turned and folded on itself in the light spring breeze.

There was no sign of the League. They were organisers, Inar thought, devoted to clocks and reckoning, trying to put all the world in their ledgers. He had expected them to be early. But they were not. In the distance, smoke rose among the black spires of Stull, and Inar could make out the neat line of towers that marked the line of the new fortifications, and the flat-topped pyramid of the shiel. Behind was the tower of the citadel, on the scarp that formed the city's northern boundary. Nearer at hand, between the city and their waiting-place, was the akouy shiel, where the dead were united with heaven, and around it wheeled the black specks of birds.

"Eyes open, ears open, remember," Cilma said.

"Yes, my lord," Inar said obediently. "But how should I report to you?"

"Where are all our men?" Cilma replied. "Levied by the League, that's where. They are using Mishigo and Oriri labourers and mercenaries. There are loyal men at Sojonost, they will contact you."

"If you already have loyal men at Sojonost, why do you need me to spy?"

"Besides your obvious wish to serve your king and prove your fealty?" Cilma said, with a note of danger. "Because, young Inar, this woman, this *merite*, is a big beast. One of the biggest, in the top half-dozen or so people in their whole government. And you'll be working for her directly, not digging holes. That's why. *Goff*! That is a royal standard, not a stick for knocking apples out of trees! Upright and steady, you imbecile!"

Few other travellers used the road while they waited – a small straggling group of old peasant women, who kept their heads down and steered a wide course around Cilma's men; a young shaven-headed man who might have been taken for the cutpurse if he had not been wearing the black robe of an acolyte of the Mountain; and an old man steering an empty horse and cart away from the city. Of the fields on either side of the road, maybe one in four had been tended recently. The rest were choked with two summers of overgrown neglect, made brown and matted by the winter, now returning to tangled, useless life. Dry stone walls tipped into the filling ditches. A brick chimney stack rose from the weeds – the house it had warmed had collapsed or burned. Only the old worked the farms – the young men were in the mines and quarries, paying the League's price for peace, or had been levied. Rightly, this road should be busy with farmers and merchants, heading south to Miroline and west to the League, and pilgrims heading towards the pass – but there was no one using it now, bar one underfed horse and its scruffy-looking rider.

They were familiar, that horse and rider. Inar squinted at them at they drew closer.

"Oh, no."

"Oh, yes," Cilma said, amused. "The League advised that you take an attendant, and really only one man was suited to the job."

Inar stared at Cilma. Was he capable of pranks? He did not seem the sort. But an inscrutable joke was clearly being played.

"Only one man?!" Inar asked, still unable to believe his eyes. "I have my own servants..."

"Too old, wouldn't you say, for a perilous journey into the mountains?"

"Falde..."

"Falde is needed here, completing *your* work, builder."

"Any number of men..."

"All needed. But I found I could spare one."

"Good morning!" Lott cried from the road.

The League approached with the same majesty as they had the day before, blue pennant fluttering, the merite Anzola leading the party beside a League knight standard-bearer. Behind her were the older man and the quiet, sickly girl. The remaining three League-knights brought up the rear. Lord Cilma had been wise – if Inar had been on his own, waiting at the side of the road for this stately party, he would have felt shabby indeed. Even worse if Lott had been with him, slumped in his saddle, picking at his filthy nails.

The chancellor placed Inar in the service of Anzola with no more than a dozen words of basic courtesy. Then he turned and spurred his stallion back towards Stull, soldiers thundering behind him, one gripping the royal standard with white knuckles.

2

ANTON

Anton wondered if he was sufficiently terrifying. What more could he do to strike fear? The robes and the mask did not leave much scope for acting. Perhaps there was a way of walking, or something he could do with his arms or his hands. But he feared that trying to stride or prowl like a monster would make him look more like one of the absurd ribbon-strewn players who went from village to village earning coins by scaring children. Maybe that was fitting – maybe that was his purpose, to be a player and play the monster. Better than being the monster.

The trouble was that he had no practice at being a monster, and for that he was glad. He did not particularly want to see, through the eye-slits of his mask, the visitors made afraid by the sight of him. But the alternatives were little better. Curiosity he could tolerate. What he dreaded was pity. A born monster, in an age that had no need of them.

He sighed and flexed his shoulders. They had been waiting a while. Benches at the sides of the antechamber provided for the older altzans, but there was no room for him and Elecy, the two anomalous youths. It would be disrespectful to sit with Ving, Dionny and the others on the same narrow seat – and of course there was no question of sitting on the other side of the room. So they stood in a corner. It was a high-ceilinged, long room, with a large double door at each end, and it had been built for precisely this purpose: a place for altzans to wait, discreetly, before the beginning of a ritual. Nearby, perhaps beneath their feet, there were other, smaller chambers, less grand in their materials and proportions, where the ritual's other participants would wait. Rooms with iron doors and guards. Not today. The temple itself was very ancient, from long before the age of Miroline, its central space lined by columns built of vast cubes of brown stone. Its flagstone floor had been worn down by generations of human feet, and the stone steps at the entrance sagged like melted butter. But here in the antechamber, many fewer had trod. The floor was sea-green Mirolinian marble and, combined with the pale light that came from small, high windows, it was like waiting in a water cistern. Four braziers stood in the corners, but only two were lit.

The mask was heavy, its sharp beak pulling his head forward, and the leather straps dug into Anton's scalp and the back of his neck. Despite the chill, sweat and his hot breath made his face slick. There was no sign that they were needed yet, so he lifted the mask and wiped his brow and neck with the sleeve of his robe, enjoying the relief of the cool air.

Elecy turned to him. The beaks did have an unnerving effect, Anton had to admit. It was like being noticed by a predator.

"You should not remove your mask," she said in a whisper.

Anton could not see her face, but he could picture her scowl.

"We can do as we please," he replied softly.

"I did not say *could not*," Elecy said, straightening. "I said should not."

"You must be uncomfortable. Lift your mask a moment. We have time."

The beak swung away, and the eyes that Anton had seen glittering through their slits were lost in shadow. "I am perfectly comfortable."

Yes, that made sense.

The tall door nearest Anton and Elecy opened with a sharp crack, ancient wood on under-used hinges. In came altzan Dreyff, Ramnie's secretary, a man who needed no lessons in striking fear with his stride. He did not acknowledge Anton, or anyone on that side of the chamber – instead he went directly to the altzan-al and bent to whisper in the old man's ear. Ramnie nodded, and mouthed a reply.

Dreyff drew himself to his full height, dwarfing the ancient priests around him – only Anton was taller, and by only a little. He acknowledged his colleagues, and then turned to address the other side of the chamber, where Ving and his followers sat and Anton and Elecy stood.

"The delegations have assembled," he said. "Make ready."

He spoke with icy formality, but without courtesy or deference, despite the seniority of the priests seated before him. Anton could sense Ving's indignation surging, as clear as if a gong had been struck. Dreyff displayed not the slightest emotion of any kind, but his eyes flicked for the tiniest moment to regard Anton. Not Anton and Elecy, who were generally treated as an indivisible legion, but just Anton. The mask – Anton hurriedly pulled it back over his face.

Acolytes rushed into the chamber, one to each altzan, and began to fuss about, helping the elderly to their feet, adjusting robes, taking away anything not needed in the ceremony. The novice assigned to Anton, a boy of perhaps twelve or thirteen, kept his head bowed as he tucked and arranged Anton's robe, preferring to contort himself than to look up at the mask or catch a glimpse of the eyes that lay behind it. Anton wondered if there was anything he could say or do that might put the lad at ease, but nothing came to mind. No one else was speaking – it did not seem to be an appropriate moment for pleasantries or attempts at wit. "Thank you," Anton said when the youth was finished, but he had not stopped to hear. The doors at the far end of the antechamber had opened, and from beyond came the gentle sound of hundreds of people gathered in silence.

* * *

The altzans entered first, Ramnie at their head. The factional divide that had dictated their seats in the waiting-place was now invisible – their order reflected only their rank within the leadership of the Tzanate. They took up positions in front of the altar, facing a line of Zealot soldiery. Behind those sentinels stood... many hundreds more tzans and altzans. The temple was filled with priests, priests from every part of the world where the Mountain was worshipped.

Anton and Elecy entered last. They alone wore robes of white, and they alone took up positions behind the altar. All the other altzans wore robes of black and grey, although at a glance Anton saw dozens of variations of region, rite and rank. Some of the vestments were little more than rags, stained from the road, perhaps always stained. Others were inky black silk, accented with threads of silver, draped over well-fed bellies.

Around them, the interior of the temple was a rainbow of fabric. Normally this vast space would be open to the sky, but prayer-printed banners in multiple colours had been draped across the peristyle, giving shelter from the winds that whipped across the plateau and trapping the thick clouds of incense that poured from burners in niches. Standards were hung between the columns, sighing and snapping against their cords. And behind the altar was a single vast sheet of crimson, painted with a human heart, superimposed on a stylised outline of the Mountain. All around was colourful movement, as if the ancient, massive masonry was the living breathing thing, and the priests within the stone statues. The heart that dominated them all appeared to beat, caught like a sail by the mistral across the lake.

Why hide the lake, and the Mountain, like that, Anton wondered? The whole high temple had been built to align with Craithe, so that pilgrims would see the object of their journey rising above the azure waters of Hleng, directly behind the altar of the Gift. It was strange – impious, even – to see that it had been hidden behind a curtain.

Perhaps it was this puzzle that distracted him, and caused him to do what he did. He simply forgot himself, forgot where he was, what he was doing, who he was supposed to be. As he and Elecy approached the altar, he had spotted an imperfection in its surface. He reached out a hand and ran his fingertips along the smooth, hard stone, and found it: a mark made by the point of a knife.

The temple held its breath. Even the canvas heart behind him missed a beat. Every eye was on his unrobed hand, its fingers trailing along the altar like a man brushing dust from a bookshelf. On the killing slab.

Trying to avoid unseemly hurry, Anton withdrew his hand and wrapped it once again in the robe.

Not everyone had seen – fortunately, Ramnie, Ving and the others stood with their backs to Anton and Elecy, and while they undoubtedly detected the change in atmosphere, decorum forbade them from turning to see the cause. The moment passed, and eased. The great heart beat again.

A mark made by the point of a knife. It would not be the only one, but it was more recent than most. Anton wondered if it had been made the first time he had stood in this space, the day he had seen a man killed here. Then, he had been standing on the other side of the altar, but only a yard away, no distance. Their eyes had met, wide with terror. What had the man thought, in those final moments? He was frightened, of course – but did he believe himself to be important? To be useful? Did he think his death was in the service of a greater purpose? Or was it just another futile, violent incident in a life filled with futility and violence? Which was better?

Or – he had seen Anton and Elecy – had he died thinking, *Why are there children here?*

Elecy had seen him touch the altar. She stood impossibly still, and he wondered what she was thinking. Memories of that first time? It was all so clear – the falling blade, the harsh movements of Vertzan and Giftmeat, the gouts of red against pure white, the stink of slaughter, the beating of wings – he could not turn away, because he was held, and they would know if he closed his eyes, so he raised them instead and tried to look at the Mountain itself, thinking this might appear suitably pious. And he asked the Mountain, is this truly what you want?

It did not say no.

Censers had been lit in concealed niches and the air was hazed with scented smoke; the harsh sun of the plateau, filtered through crimson and purple fabric, was stained a bruised pink. All the altzans in the audience had travelled long distances, some extremely long, by ship and trail, through war-crossed and uncertain lands. It had been sixty years since the last such gathering. Anton hoped that the scene that greeted them was sufficient reward for their hardships, that it lent proper gravity to the gathering. Again, he wondered why God had been blocked from sight.

The altzan-al was speaking, illuminating the rarity of a full Conclave and the crucial importance of the next few days. He spelled out a few facts of schoolboy theology – the impossibility of error and schism within the Tzanate, which served a single, visible God. He smiled and praised and even ventured into wry humour; it was a marvellous performance, a reminder of the skills and qualities that had helped Ramnie to his supreme rank and maintained him within it for decades. But even in its fullest flow, Anton saw the glances that came towards him and Elecy, the last two blade-priests.

How did they appear, Anton wondered? The imposing, inscrutable bearers of a ghastly sacrament? Or young and disappointing, nothing special, an anticlimax after weeks on the road?

A novelty, anyway. A sign that this was indeed the place – the epicentre of the faith. At the last meeting of the Conclave, this ceremony would have included the giving of the Gift. Today, it would not. After much discussion, it had been decided that Anton and Elecy should not carry blades. They would be blade-priests in name only – and, depending on the events of the next few days, they would be the last. Elecy had been furious at the decision, and Anton joined her in a few protests for the sake of appearances, but he was profoundly glad that he did not have a weapon as well as a mask. By Augardine's Tomb, the strap at the back of his skull was a trial. He should have taken more time in replacing the mask, to make sure it was comfortable, but Dreyff's glance had put the fear into him. Never mind the blade, the hard leather was going to take the top of his head right off. Thankfully, the bulk of the altzans were in their elder years, which placed certain constraints on the ceremonials. They had rehearsed four times. Ramnie would make his remarks, conduct a short blessing, and they would retire while altzan Yisho emptied the temple and began the immense job of ferrying everyone to the Brink.

That had been the plan, but Anton sensed deviation. Yisho, the Tzanate's strategos, was nowhere to be seen, when she should have been on the stage with the rest of the leadership. An emergency? Anton rarely left the Brink, and he had to admit that being outside the walls of the vast fortress made him uneasy, even though they were well inside a natural fortress of far vaster proportions. Nevertheless, there it was, a sparkle of concern. The Tzanate, so magnificently lonely for so long, played host to many strangers this day, and in front of him was the top echelon of the whole religion. Thousands of Zealots ringed the alshiel Hleng and, beyond them, thousands more. Gathering and protecting the Conclave had been the largest military endeavour conducted by the Tzanate in decades. But such efforts only reflected how high the stakes were, and the risks.

Deviation. Ramnie was ending his remarks. "The age of Augardine has passed," the altzan-al said. "He is gone, his

successors are gone. We can wish for another age of greatness
to emerge from Miroline, but we cannot wait for it. We must
remember that Augardine did not found our faith, he refounded
it; we can be reborn again. We must remember what endures
and will always endure, and place our trust in it."

The Mountain, Anton thought, apt words. And they might
have made a fine introduction to the blessing that would
conclude proceedings. But no blessing came. Instead, altzan
Ving rose stiffly to his feet, leaning on his cane, and took
the few steps towards the altzan-al. Anton held his breath,
unable to imagine what Ving was doing, interrupting such an
important moment. But Ramnie was not dismayed, or even
surprised.

"Altzan Ving, my friend," he said. "My brother." He held
out his hand to his ancient doctrinal enemy, and the two men,
who had dissolved decades in mutual hate, embraced.

No one spoke, or applauded. The leaders of the Tzanate's
two factions, men who had not shared a civil word in many
years, now stood hand in hand on the stage. Their heads were
held high, and they smiled warmly on the hundreds of faces
turned to them. Slippered feet shuffled against the flagstones,
a tzan tried to stifle a cough. The banners sagged against their
lines, suddenly slack, abandoned by the wind.

A chill entered the air – not a chill felt on the skin, but in
the soul. A winter in the part of a person that is warmed by the
presence of other people.

Anton knew what approached. He knew why the banner
had been hung between them and the Mountain. He need
not have worried about making the delegations afraid, fear
was coming. They never approached in sight, always hidden.
Predator instincts. He briefly wondered if he should say
something to Elecy, but if he had detected the change, surely
she would as well. Anyway, there was no time.

Behind them, the crimson heart billowed, and sprouted
talons. In a blur of movement, the canvas was slashed left and

right, up and down, its tatters blown into the temple by the thumping of wings. On that blast of air came the scent of death.

With the utmost effort of mind and body, Anton prevented himself from crying out or falling to the ground. He had learned that much at least, he was not the child that screamed in terror, not any more. Very few others held their composure. The assembly swayed like a field of grass under a strong wind, and emitted a collective howl of astonishment and fear. A few voices proclaimed praise to the Mountain, although it was not clear if they were giving thanks for what they saw, or pleading to be protected from it.

Claws scraped onto the altar, pushing aside remnants of the banner entangled in them, and Anton saw that not all the marks in the stone had been made by the point of a knife.

A Custodian had arrived.

3

INAR

"Have you ever actually *seen* a knome, though?"

"No."

"What do they look like?"

"What? I said I'd never seen one."

"Yeah, and if you know you've never seen one, then you must know something of what they look like, so you know what you have seen isn't one of them."

Not for the first time, Inar felt dizzy, as if so overcome with weariness that he might simply slide from his saddle and fall to the ground, dead. Perhaps that wouldn't be so bad. He wouldn't have to listen to Lott any more.

But they'd stop, wouldn't they? They'd pick him up and revive him, the inconsiderate bastards.

"I am sure I have never seen a knome," he said, tired. It was their third day on the road.

"Shepherds say they've seen them," Lott said. Unusually for the son of a builder, he had never been to Sojonost before, and as they climbed from the moors into the foothills of the Shield Range, he had started to bubble with mountain lore. It had been Custodians this morning, and now it was knomes.

"Shepherds say a lot of things, Lott," Inar said. "They're superstitious folk."

"On account of being alone so much," Lott said. "That's what

24

being alone does to you." He added a meaningful, warning
look.

"It hasn't done that to me," Inar said.

"You talk to them, the shepherds," Lott continued. "They
talk about knomes?"

"Almost as much as you do," Inar said. He knew there would
just be another question on the way, so he dredged up some
more tidbits to give Lott. "I've been shown sheep – the remains
of sheep – that they say were killed by knomes."

Lott gawped at him. "Really?"

"Yes. No. That's what they say, yes, but it could have been
wolves. No mystery. There are plenty of hungry wolves."

Lott narrowed his brows. Inar knew that he was deciding,
now and forever, that knomes had killed those sheep.
Whatever it had been, the shepherds were getting more wary
about entering even the lower hills of the Shields. Why take
the risk, when there was grazing to spare on the moors, and
even in the valleys? They had told Inar about the lost and
mutilated sheep by way of warning, as they saw him walking
out early in the day, seeking time alone among the peaks. His
pretext, always, was that he was looking for carving-stones,
which in truth could be found much nearer at hand. But the
stones around the keep were quiet. The ones in the cairns
of the Shields had more to say – they suggested new and
interesting forms to him.

Though the stream of questions could be tiring, Inar was
not unhappy at Lott's presence. He would have felt lonely if
he had been the only Mishigo in the League party. The merite
Anzola made much effort to be friendly, riding alongside
them often and making smiling small talk, though the talk
stayed very small and formal. She had also introduced them
to the others. Kielo, the portly older man, was her secretary,
and she spent long hours in serious conversation with him.
He treated Inar and Lott with courtesy, but remained aloof.
The four knights were merrier, but enjoyed each other's

company more than that of anyone else; only Anzola was admitted to their camaraderie, as a sort of honorary soldier. Inar was told their names but they were all mumbo, jumbo, rumbo Leaguer names and he could never remember which was which.

The young girl, Duna, was the real mystery of the group. Inar had at first assumed her to be Anzola's daughter, or maybe a niece, but Anzola had laughed this away, saying only that Duna was her ward. Which was ordinary enough, but she was still out of place on a military inspection. And although she never complained, Duna looked miserable morning and night – her desire to be elsewhere was written clearly in her permanent frown and the faraway look she had in the saddle. In this, Inar could sympathise, and he might have felt kindly disposed towards her, were it not for the unnerving aura that clung to her. More than once, he had caught her staring intensely at him, as if she harboured a secret grudge. They had interacted so little that at first he had assumed she spoke no Mirolingua – it was not Inar's first language either, but none of the Leaguers spoke Mishigo and he had no Palla or Wenodari, so they all used the ancient world-speech of the old empire. But on the second day, Duna had asked Inar a couple of stilted questions about the nature of the stone in the Shield Range, and how it was cut in the quarries. Even this was done with reluctance, and she had asked only after some whispered prodding from Anzola.

Anzola indulged Duna like the soldiers indulged Anzola. "Miss Duna would like to stop a while" had become a familiar phrase on their journey, heralding a roadside break. Far from resting, the girl would often disappear during those stops, leaving Kielo kicking stones and grumbling about lost daylight. But Anzola was never visibly annoyed by these absences, or even questioning about them. Duna would reappear, and they would set off again without a word being spoken.

* * *

All the way to Sojonost, they passed work and workers. There were carts going both ways, carrying stripped tree-trunks and bales of supplies to the fortress, and coming back empty. And gangs of olive-clad labourers were working on the road itself, filling in ruts and runnels, hardening its surface, restoring the camber and the roadside ditches, replaced packed dirt with good cobbles. Inar doubted that the road had seen such improvement since the Mirolinians themselves had built it. But the wayposts that now stood every mile were painted the bright blue of the League, and gave the distance to Matchfalls and Pallestra, with no mention of Miroline or Stull. Inar supposed that he should feel glad that at least some parts of the world showed signs of improvement, but he could not. He thought sourly of the pitted and mired state of the Stull Road, and the lack of men and materials when the League had so much.

For all the prosperity and progress on display, the work gangs had a dejected air, and they laboured under the eye of League soldiers. As they passed one gang, Anzola and Kielo had paused to exchange words with the overseeing soldier, and Inar had lingered to try and catch what was said, but it was in Palla.

"I didn't think the League had slaves," Inar said when they set off again. He was annoyed. They might have reached Sojonost the previous evening, and spared themselves a night on the road, but Anzola had tarried and called an early halt, saying that she preferred to arrive in the morning.

Anzola tensed and Kielo scowled.

"They are not slaves," Kielo said firmly. "These men are Oriritheni. They are earning League citizenship and the chance of a better life. They are volunteers."

Oriritheni, Inar reflected. Erstwhile brothers-in-arms of the Mishigo – and the bigger brothers, at that. It was Oririthen that had attacked the League, and its confidence in a swift victory had inspired the late king of the Land of the Late Dawn to join the war as well. And now look at them. Mishig-Tenh might be an unhappy land, but it had only been defeated. Oririthen had been devastated.

"The League does not subjugate," Anzola said. "Its power is its openness. It does not see Pallestran and Mishigo, or lord and commoner. It sees only ability. Anyone can earn citizenship, and more. You are a builder of great skill, Inar. You could join us, and one day you could be a merite yourself."

"What is a merite, anyway?" he asked.

"It's a lordship, Inar, but one awarded for talent, not passed on by birth. Anyone appointed to a League high office becomes a merite, and is given a vote within the Convention. Merites vote to decide the duzh, and are eligible to become duzh. The League, in a small way, belongs to us. It is in our trust, and as such we give our best for it. It is the greatest honour."

There are some material rewards, too, Inar thought, casting his eye again over the gold trim on Anzola's armour, and her rich velvet cloak.

"Mishig-Tenh," Anzola said to herself. "*Land of the Late Dawn.* Your people have quite a poetic way with names, Inar. What is the other one, the Hidden Land?"

"Elith-Tenh," Inar said. He knew that he was being steered off a subject, but had decided not to resist. "Because only the followers of the Mountain knew it was there, before Miroline came. Sometimes it's Tzan-Tenh, land of the priests."

"It's Elizhen in Palla," Anzola said. "One of the words we take from the mountain languages. 'Hidden Land' – surely 'forbidden land' is more apt? If only priests are allowed there."

"That's not quite true, pilgrims are allowed," Inar said. Temper prickled within him. "*Were* allowed. It's forbidden now, by the League. You closed the pass."

"A temporary measure," Anzola said, more sternly than usual. "Why would we invest so much effort in improving a road, only to forbid its use?"

If you were using it to move an army, Inar thought, but he kept it to himself.

As they drew closer to Sojonost, he saw that his suspicion had been correct – and Lord Cilma had been well informed. The wide pass that lay before the ancient fortress had become a vast camp. Huge groups of men, mostly wearing the drab olive vests of the labourers they had seen on the road, toiled within this new town, sawing, hammering, forging, building. There were cookhouses, bathhouses, storehouses and a city of canvas. And everywhere there were soldiers – League knights, armoured men-at-arms, and footsoldiers in drab orange tunics.

All this activity was still made insignificant by the fortress itself, a spear of stone rising above all, exceeded only by the mountains on every side. Sojonost stood where this wide, steep valley branched into two narrower ravines. Between these two deep, V-shaped gouges in the mountainside was an immense blade of rock, like the head of a giant's axe. The ancient fortress was the blunt cutting edge of this blade, built into the rock itself on one side. As it had been rebuilt over the centuries, it had come to overhang the small ledge that had been its first foundation, so at times it looked almost precarious, a clutch of towers perched on a toe-hold – but few places in the world were so secure.

This security had been its gift to Mishig-Tenh – the whole country had been built on it. The two valleys that met here were the mouths of two of the most important passes through the mountains, one leading south-east to Elith-Tenh, the other south to Mal Nulalus, Tarch and – ultimately, after many hundreds of miles – Miroline. To hold Sojonost was to secure a frontier hundreds of miles long, the whole southern and eastern flank of the Land of the Late Dawn. When the Elves had ravaged the world, Sojonost had kept Mishig-Tenh safe. Sojonost was the reason Miroline treated Mishigo kings almost as equals. And it had long been the last resort of those kings, the comfort they kept at the back of their minds: if facing defeat, retreat to Sojonost and let enemies break themselves in this miserable valley.

As it happened, the League overcame the kingdom so quickly that the war never reached Sojonost. On the bright spring morning that Anzola and her companions climbed the stony valley towards the ancient fortress, it looked unusually colourful: bright blue banners, each bearing the threefold cascade symbol of the League, had been hung from its highest ramparts.

Anzola had ridden to the head of the party, with all four knights, and they had raised their own standard high. Kielo and Duna hung back, almost sulkily, with Inar and Lott. Laughter from the knights, and shouted agreement, split the air, all in gibberish Palla.

"Now we see the reason to approach in daylight," Kielo said, a mocking note in his words. Was he sharing a joke with Inar? A barb at his employer, her fondness for display?

"Knights and soldiers treat her as one of them," Inar said.

"She *is* one of them, builder," Kielo said, looking towards Anzola. "The surveyor-general began as a military office. It is still."

They were close, and the sun had risen high enough to clear the topmost peaks of the Shield Mountains and bring its light to the valley floor. It was behind the fortress, in Inar's eyes, but he could see men on the battlements, many men, and pikes and pennants, an armourer's forest. There were men in the valley too, watching them approach. Noise came down, shouting, cheers.

Anzola had spurred her horse and opened up a lead on the rest of them, sitting straight and proud in the saddle, her cape flying. Three of the knight escort, those not holding the standard, unsheathed their swords and waved them above their heads.

"I might never have taken her for a soldier," Inar said above the growing racket, "but she looks well in the role."

Kielo stared ahead, his cynicism gone, replaced with his own aura of pride. "Oh, she is more than a soldier, Inar."

The shouting from the top of the fortress had become clearer. Many cacophonous voices had joined together, and begun to chant a single word.

AN-ZO-LA! AN-ZO-LA! AN-ZO-LA!

"She is a *hero*."

The rest of the party did not hurry, and let their mounts climb the steep, narrow path to Sojonost's only gate at their own pace. Before long they had dismounted in the castle's small, dark courtyard, forever cast in shadow by high walls and the cliff face, and their horses had been led away. Anzola was nowhere to be seen. All around was an uproar of activity. Every free inch was taken up with stacked barrels and bales, and League men rushing to and fro. The gates never closed.

"Am I in the same room as last time?" Duna asked, stretching.

"Yes, but I understand the merite wishes to begin immediately, Miss Duna," Kielo said. His total courtesy was hesitant, even apologetic, as if he feared the reply.

"We've been on the road for three nights," Duna said icily. "I would like to bathe."

Kielo raised his hands apologetically. "As would I, Miss Duna. I understand there will be time before dinner."

Duna rolled her eyes, and annoyance radiated hotly from her, but she made no further objection.

Inar had the odd sensation of being invisible. "And us?" he asked. "Should we attend?"

Kielo bit his lip, momentarily stumped. "No," he said. "We'll send word. Banqueting tonight, that'll be fun." He added this last information with a doubtful frown, before apprehending a passing boy – a youngster of eleven or twelve, in the tabard of a League squire – and speaking some words of Palla to him.

"This, this, come this," the boy said timidly and in terrible schoolhouse Mirolingua, and he led them into the castle.

Inar had been to Sojonost before, with his father. He remembered it as a grim, eerie place, filled with exhausting stairs and windowless rooms that managed to be both cold and stuffy.

In two years, it had changed dramatically. Not its stone fabric, of course – but Inar was struck how completely a place could change even though its walls and rooms remained in the same places and at the same dimensions. For a start, the League had covered every interior stone surface with whitewash – an effort, Inar imagined, to relieve its permanent inner gloom. This effort wasn't wholly successful, and it must have taken an ocean of whitewash, but he was impressed that it had been tried. And the League had been busy with black paint, too. Every door had been given a number – at every junction and on every passage from every stairwell, there were arrows pointing where groups of room numbers could be found. Twice, Inar saw the squire take a thin ticket of white wood from his pocket and refer to the writing on it: a directory, Inar assumed.

These improvements gave Inar much satisfaction. This was precisely the sort of thing that he would do if anyone ever gave him a free hand. It was the way that he wanted the world: orderly, practical, rational. It was only whitewash and black numbers, but it struck Inar as being profoundly beautiful. Mishig-Tenh never worked this way. Inar's father was an intelligent and skilled man, but he valued learning as a way of knowing the world as it was. What the League had done was to make this labyrinth explicable, to *reduce* the amount of learning needed to find one's way around, so that even an untutored boy from hundreds of miles away could find a room.

The other great change in Sojonost was its population. The stairs rang with boots. They passed room after room crowded with beds and hammocks. The kitchens were adjacent to the entry courtyard – they were a storm of steam and noise. There were soldiers, knights, and the green-tunic bonded labourers, all of whom could be identified by sight. Inar also saw many men, and even a couple of women, dressed similarly to Kielo: plain, dark robes, unostentatious, but nevertheless finer linen than anything Inar owned. Anzola was not the only merite present, Inar understood, there were a couple of others, most importantly an army chief called Ernesto.

"Room," the boy said once they had climbed what felt like a hundred flights of stairs. "Room here. Rest here, you." And he was gone.

Inar knew at once where they were in the fortress, as he would have known even without the League's paint. He could read the stone. A small room high in the main tower. Although they would kill themselves with stairs, the room had advantages, such as a fair-sized window. But it was cramped. A bunk bed, new-made, filled most of the space, and a washstand and chest had been squeezed into what remained.

"What do we do now?" Lott asked, and it was exactly the thought that had occurred to Inar. Were they supposed to wait in this room together – for how long? Without even the distractions of the ride and the road, Inar anticipated that it wouldn't take Lott long to get on his nerves.

"I don't know," Inar said. "I thought they'd have work for us to do." He went to the window and pushed it open. Above a tiny jumble of buildings and courts on a ledge, Sojonost was, almost, a tower. If it stood alone on a plain, it might be the greatest tower in the world. But it only stood at all because its lowest levels were built up against the rock of the mountain, and only the top stood alone. Inar's window looked inwards, towards the mountain, rather than out at the valley or either of the passes. If he craned his neck out, he would be able to see down into the little courtyard they had entered through, far beneath. Closer was the steep pitched roof of the feast-hall, between tower and mountain, and – a little distance away – the ridge of the blade of rock itself, disorientingly *below* where Inar stood now. It rose as it joined the higher peaks behind.

Lott was lying on the lower bed, humming tunelessly. "It's almost lunch time," Inar said. "Why don't you go down to the kitchen and get something to eat? I'll find you if we're needed."

"You'll never find me. We ought to stick together."

"I'll find you." Inar smiled.

Lott swung his legs off the bed and came close to bumping his head on the upper bunk. "I won't say no to something to eat."

"Get some rest too," Inar said. "Once they call us, we might be kept busy."

"Yeah," Lott said. He looked at Inar, an unusual shrewdness in his eyes. "Our own room, huh? They must like us."

"I suppose so."

"They must like *you*, in any case." And he ambled out through the open door, humming again.

Inar was able to do as he pleased for the first time in days. When he and Lott had been led to this high-up room, he had remembered the one feature of Sojonost that he truly loved – its compact but excellent library, only a short flight of steps away. (In his mind's eye, Inar saw the fortress, imagined it as a shape he could turn in his hands like one of his carvings, sensing its weight flow through it towards the ground, and he knew why the library, with its heavy books, was placed where it was, on a stone floor, supported by an arch beneath that was distributing the load between the tower and the feast-hall... it was all so clear to him.)

The library was no more than a couple of stacks in a middle-sized chamber, but it was a delight. And what Inar liked best about it was the delicious sense that its existence was a secret only he knew. Before the League came, most wardens of Sojonost preferred to stay in Stull spending the stipend that came with the appointment. Nevertheless, as Miroline retreated and chaos engulfed the world, a few liked to imagine improvements to the fortress, and bought books to help them plan: titles on war and siegecraft, but also building and architecture.

Nobles are always better at buying books than reading them, and building up here in the mountains was difficult and tiresome. Bastions, turrets and bridges sprouted much easier in the imagination, by a fireside down in the valley, with a glass of wine in the hand. When Inar discovered the two shelves of heavy codices on building, engineering, siegecraft and machines, they were topped with half an inch of dust. Opening a volume on bridges and aqueducts, fetched all the way from Miroline's legendary book market, fine white sand poured from between the pages. It had been left there by the copyists to dry their ink, and had never been disturbed.

As chief builder, Inar's father visited Sojonost at least once a year, usually in the spring, to see what damage had been done by the mountain winter. He took his sons with him. When not patching mortar and tiling roofs, Inar would come to the library, and stay until the oil went from the lamps. His father complained non-stop that clerks and acolytes lost their eyesight young, and that a week of reading was barely worth an hour of practical experience, but took no action to obstruct him. It was in these books that Inar had learned the technique of gearing pulleys, and much else. He regretted not one minute spent here. But there was something he was looking for, that forever eluded him. The men that had written these texts were builders, and they knew builders – men like him. But none of them were *exactly* like him. He expected to find, described on these pages, a particular quality, a particular ability, peculiar to builders. A talent he experienced every day. And yet it was never mentioned. It was as if it was unknown to them. But surely that couldn't be true?

When he asked his father, he was told that the unsaid was almost always unsaid for a reason, and best forgotten. But he had known what his son was talking about. Did all these ancient builders know as well, and leave it unsaid, or were they ignorant of it? He read of methods for calculating the load borne by columns. Why did they need such calculations? Did they not *know*?

But he left it unsaid.

He had spoken of it with his brother once, and Essian had responded with a blow just behind Inar's ear that made his head ring even as he remembered it, years later, his brother and his father dead in the dishonoured ground.

There was unexpected treasure waiting in the library – new books. Not just books that were new to Inar, but *new* new, made in the past couple of years, with crisp, clean pages and bindings that creaked when they were opened. A whole crate of them, a crate of pale, fresh wood, daubed with the triple-cascade of the League and the stamp of the surveyor-general. More new books than Inar had seen in his whole life.

Most of them had been composed in an unfamiliar way, with uniform little black letters. Many were in Palla, and thus of limited use to him. But a few were in Mirolingua. Engineering was not their sole province – indeed, about half were histories. There were two editions of the *Augardiniad*, one in each language, which made Inar shake his head. They might as well have brought snow to the mountains, as the library already had several copies of the single most important text of both religion and empire. There was a Palla edition of Klintoe, too, and the library had Mirolingua and Mishigo editions of that as well. But it was evidence, he supposed, of the League making an effort to understand the region and its faith, and he could not object to that. The *Augardiniad* and Klintoe's *Lords of the Wing* both told the same story, that of the emperor Augardine's war against the Elves, his perilous journey into the Hidden Land, his conversion to the Mountain faith and return to victory as living god. The *Augardiniad* was an immense first-hand pseudo-history, a good deal of it dictated by the emperor himself. Klintoe had been a later scholar of this monumental text and the folklore around it. In his time, a century after Augardine's fall, with the empire spanning the world and encompassing many unbelievers, he retold the story in more digestible form: a verse epic, intended to enchant, inspire and convert.

Both stories took as their backdrop the Elf-War, and Inar found three other books on that subject in the box. And someone had been going through the stacks, gathering up books on the Elves and grouping them together: descriptions of their bloodthirsty rituals, tales of their cults and conquests, scholarly tomes on the Elfcap, the poison mushroom that was the source of their sickness. This was not reading for general interest. The League was learning about an enemy. In its meticulous, rational way, it was preparing for war.

Soon Inar found contentment in the unlikely form of a book about defensive ditches. It was just hole-digging, the crudest form of building he could imagine, but Inar was transported into its world: the correct number and distribution of men for the most rapid excavation, sharpened stakes artfully concealed to impale cavalry, ways to disguise archery positions, methods for making ditches invisible, how to divert streams to improvise a moat. He had no sense of how much time had passed – a couple of hours, at least, as the bell for middle meal had long past when the messenger boy burst in, breathless.

"No room?" the boy demanded, the words slurred in a Pallestran accent.

Inar frowned at him. "No room?"

"Room!" the boy repeated, red-faced with exertion, written over with frustration at the inadequate Mirolingua he was forced to use. "Stay room." He muttered some words of Palla. "Merite, Anzola merite. She need."

"The merite wants to see me? Is she... in room?" For emphasis, Inar pointed upwards, through the ceiling.

The boy shook his head. "She... tower?" He stepped over Inar, to the window, and pointed out of it. "She there."

Inar stood, his joints stiff from being on the hard floor. He followed where the boy was pointing, across the courtyard, out of the castle, to the ridge beyond. "There?" he asked. "Why would she be over there?" He could hardly believe it, imagining that a mistake had been made, that an instruction had been mangled in between messengers and languages. But as he squinted at the peak, his eye caught a white point of light, the afternoon sun caught on a shining metal instrument. They were where heaven met the world.

4

ANTON

The Custodian settled itself on the altar and spread out its wings, a salute to the tzans and altzans who cowered before it. It was a fearful creature, standing a foot higher than Anton, who was a clear six feet tall. But this height was in its stooped shoulders, the bony peaks of its folded wings. Its head was held lower, supported by a neck shaggy with grey-black feathers. Its wings, lined with charcoal feathers as long as a man's arm, had a greasy look, and as they stretched out they cast a gloom over the temple, blocking much of the light that now flooded in from lake Hleng. Untidy plumage made the beast seem wrapped in rags – a child could have deduced where the tzans drew inspiration for their sombre robes. But what was always seen first, and remembered longest, was its beak, long and proud, a crow's beak made with the dimensions and danger of a broadsword.

A word of warning must have circulated among the leaders of the Tzanate, and not shared with Anton or Elecy, because they retained their calm as the Custodian tore its way into the temple. They turned to face the altar, and kneeled before the creature that stood there. Shakily, the rest of the assembly joined them, as even the most afraid found reverence and overcame terror. Some prostrated themselves, some were already on the floor, having fainted dead away, and others were in the throes of their first wakemares. It made for a disorderly spectacle and Anton felt a pang of species embarrassment as he too sank to his knee. Not that the Custodian was unworthy of veneration, but a more regimented display of it would have been more courteous. The creature valued the element of surprise.

No one was closer to the Custodian than Anton and Elecy. Their faces were inches from the long feathers of its tail. It smelled of dead things, the unmistakable reek of flesh separated from life. But not corrupt, not lost to decay. Cultivated death, death made obedient. The air was thicker around it, richer – it was charged with an unfamiliar quality, a hidden potential made detectable.

Behind them, Anton knew, the Mountain was now exposed. He could feel it, like the sun on the back of his neck. He longed to turn and look at it.

"*Tzaaans*," the Custodian hissed, furling its wings. In this, it used its own language – man had adopted that particular word, emulating it as best as possible with soft lips.

"Tzans, always arguing," it continued, croaking in Mirolingua. "You live such short lives, and you waste them so. We do not dictate your affairs. But we entrust to you one paramount duty: defend the Craithe. Defend the Mountain. Defend your living God. And instead you argue." A ghastly rasp of contempt arose in the Custodian's throat. "We tell you that we no longer wish to receive the Gift, and you argue. We tell you that the power of Miroline has failed, and you argue. And we tell you that your ancient enemy has returned, and still you argue."

Again, it raised its wings. "*You must be as one*," it hissed, lifting itself into the air with a downwards stroke that almost knocked Anton off balance. The stench of raw magic was making Anton woozy. "The Craithe demands one voice!" the Custodian declared, beating its wings harder, before pirouetting in a weightless way quite at odds with its size and disappearing out into the blue brightness.

An aeon passed while a drop of sweat ran from the nape of Anton's neck to the small of his back. The temple was not silent – there were utterings and shiftings, and whispered prayers. Fearing that he would be left abased on the floor long after everyone else had resumed their feet, Anton stood, only to find that he was the first. Seeing him rise behind the altar, Ramnie, Ving and the others followed, and the audience followed them. Another slip – he should have waited. But it was so difficult to tell what was going on from behind the killing slab, and he had been so concerned about missing his cue he had accidentally pre-empted it.

With a shocking crack on its ancient, under-used hinges, the tall side door opened again, and Ramnie walked out, with the rest of the leadership falling into line after him. Behind them, the assembled tzans and altzans hardly moved, stunned at what they had seen.

The Custodians tended to their solitude like humanity tended its crops and commerce. Anton was vertzan, a rank equivalent to the highest altzans, and a resident of the Brink, but in his nineteen years he had seen them on fewer than ten occasions. That included the three times he had witnessed the Giving of the Gift, when a Custodian would swoop in at the climax to receive the bloody fruit the previous vertzan had plucked from the chest of the Giver. On rare, significant days, a Custodian had attended one of the Tzanate's other solemnities – most memorably, when they announced to the aghast priests that they no longer wished to receive the Gift. Human sacrifice was to cease at last. Anton counted this as one of the happiest days of his life, as if he had been one of the souls lingering in the dungeons waiting to Give themselves, but he kept that secret joy locked up tight. The blade-priest Leass had been struck mad that day and the Tzanate had fallen into bitter schism. Sometimes Custodians could be seen circling about

their terrible windowless roost on the Shoulder of God –
always alone. Anton had never seen two of the creatures
at once. There were murals and tapestries within the Brink
that showed flocks of them, feasting on heaped Gifts from
defeated armies, honouring Mirolinian Emperors, attending
Conclaves. It was as alien as seeing more than one sun in
the sky.

In the antechamber, acolytes sprang from corners like bandits
and relieved Anton and Elecy of their masks. They ushered
the blade-priests to sit, and gave each a cup of warmed wine –
courtesies designed for the elderly altzans and extended to the
two teenagers by the unthinking mechanisms of protocol. Very
soon they were alone, their seniors having retired to private
vestries, exhausted by the ceremony.

Elecy ran her fingers through her clipped, dark hair,
massaging the parts of the scalp where the straps had dug in.
She was grinning – more than that, she radiated joy.

"Magnificent!" was the first thing she said. "Wasn't that
magnificent? Oh, they'll remember that! That took them out
of their cities and their palaces and put them where we want
them! Magnificent!"

In general, if Elecy was in a fit of religious enthusiasm,
Anton preferred to be elsewhere. But he found that he shared
some of her elation, and he wanted to enjoy it. It was better
than the scolding he had half-expected. The unshielded power
of the Custodian and the Mountain together was terrifying,
but it was also thrilling.

"Magnificent," he agreed. "You're right – none will forget that
in a hurry. But I was more surprised by what happened before."

"What?" Elecy said, frowning with incomprehension. Then
she remembered, and the frown deepened a little. "Oh, yes –
Ving and Ramnie. That was unexpected. Well, I daresay Ving
knows what he is doing."

"I daresay," Anton echoed. "There is clearly a great deal we have not been told. They must have agreed on something." The more he reflected on the embrace between the moderniser and the traditionalist, the more it troubled him. It suggested a rare, miraculous, change in heart on the part of the fanatic Ving.

As he ruminated, Anton had neglected to keep up the conversation. He now found a comforting hand placed on his shoulder. "Anton, please, do not doubt," Elecy said. "We have right on our side. Ving would not suddenly change his beliefs, would he? Whatever has changed, must be in our favour. And–" she nodded to the temple doors "– soon we will be here again, giving the Gift."

"With no one to receive it," Anton said.

"There is no end to the Custodians' hunger," Elecy said. "And while I would never claim to understand their thinking, I understand that hunger."

She swilled the wine in her silver cup and drained it in a gulp. A red droplet stained the corner of her mouth. Anton smiled at her. He disliked Elecy's piety, but not Elecy. The world was brighter to her, its shadows darker, its colours more alive. She might have some puritan tastes, but if either of them was an ascetic, it was Anton.

"You can be proud today, Elecy," he said. "Our guests will have expected to see ferocious defenders of the Mountain's traditions, and you have always performed that role well. In you they will have seen a true vertzan."

"And you, Anton!" Elecy said, delighted at the praise. "We can both be pleased."

"Really?" Anton asked. Until the Custodian arrived, he had been certain that Elecy was appalled by his performance. "I kept forgetting myself…"

"You did?" Elecy said. "Your every action was so confident – the way you drew their attention to the altar at the start, I would never have thought of that. You had men and women three times your age quaking. We are the future of this church, not them. They will know that today."

Anton raised an eyebrow, but said nothing and sipped his wine. What good would it do to say anything? Whether he was quiet or loud, brash or thoughtful, right or wrong, people just saw a blade-priest. Everything he did and said was interpreted as coming from the deepest and darkest sacraments. If only they all knew the froth of doubt that lay within.

Acolytes waited with riding cloaks. "Thank you," Anton said as the fur was placed across his shoulders, but the youngster scurried away without saying a word.

Horses, like all intelligent animals, shunned the Elith-Tenh, that vast emptiness of broken rock, devoid of good grazing. But the Brink kept a small stable, bred for hardiness, and several of these were being prepared in a secluded mews adjoining the high temple.

Spring had come, but the sun brought no warmth and the snowpiles in the shaded corners of the yard showed no sign of melting. Nevertheless, all around were signs of renewed life. Slates that had never felt a blizzard shone on the roofs, somewhere hammer tapped busily against chisel against stone, and Anton smelled sawdust, a scent as rare as spice in this treeless land. When every nation had turned its sight towards the Mountain, the temple on the shore of Hleng had been a destination for thousands of pilgrims. Over the centuries it had grown to resemble a small town, surrounded by a labyrinth of accommodation, courtyards, side-temples, barracks and kitchens. But as the faith had faltered, and the protection of Miroline had receded, the pilgrims had ceased to come. The devotional pass from the lands to the north had been closed since the war between the League and the loyal mountain kingdoms, and the Augardinian Way to the south had become hazardous. There was another pass, but few dared tread there. Assembling the Conclave had only been possible with vast armoured columns of Zealots, ferrying parties of tzans from the imperial outpost at Cassodar to the Gull Gates.

The altzan-al and the senior leadership were already on horseback when Anton and Elecy arrived in the mews, their factions keeping to opposite sides of the cobbled expanse. But there was evidently a delay. Altzan Yisho, still afoot, was speaking earnestly with Ramnie, accompanied by a half-dozen Zealots. The remaining score or so altzans waited in varying airs of boredom, their horses breathing smoke and toeing the ground.

Mounts had just been produced for Anton and Elecy when Yisho broke off her discussion with the altzan-al and strode across to Ving's group. Anton saw that Ramnie and Dreyff were dismounting.

"Captain Lypre is here, and has requested an urgent conference with the altzan-al," Yisho said, addressing Ving.

"Is it the…?" Ving asked, completing the question with a raised eyebrow.

Yisho answered with a military nod, and did not elaborate.

Ving sighed theatrically. "Very well then, I…"

"The altzan-al has requested that vertzan Anton attend the conference," said Yisho, speaking over the ancient priest without a blink of hesitation. The strategos was an Estami, tall and brown-skinned, trained as a Zealot first and an altzan second. Conversation was not her manner. She was relaying a command.

"Oh, he has, has he?" Ving said, with a poisonous edge on his words. He glanced down at Anton, his expression first full of resentment. But then it turned more indulgent, and somehow Anton did not like the change at all. "So the young man's education begins. Tzan Anton, find me the instant you return to the Brink. I hope our noble leader does not detain you too long."

* * *

The altzan-al, high priest of Craithe, supreme authority of the Tzanate, man's ambassador to the Custodians of God, was a tiny man. No one knew his true age, but it was said that he had been present the last time a Mirolinian Emperor visited the Brink, and that was almost a century ago. Though his vigour was unfaded – much to Ving's disappointment – he appeared to be getting smaller with age. At the head of a long, scarred wooden table in a disused refectory, he resembled a child: a wizened, white-haired child. Dreyff, who stood behind the altzan-al's right shoulder, might have been one of the temple columns in comparison.

"Yisho, splendid, splendid," Ramnie said cheerfully as he saw the strategos enter with Anton. "I do hope you'll forgive my sitting, tzan Anton, but it has been a very long day."

Anton bowed stiffly as response, stunned to have been directly addressed at all. He had guessed why Ramnie had asked for him specifically – he would stay quiet, whereas Ving could be relied upon to carp. Yisho and Dreyff stayed on their feet, and he followed their example. There were others present: a score of Zealots, helmeted and in armour, including an officer, who carried his helm under an arm. After the heady ceremony of the temple, this unexpected assembly had a hasty, improvised air that made Anton deeply uneasy.

"Tzan Anton, this is Captain Lypre, who is known to us," Ramnie said breezily, beckoning the officer forward. "Captain, we are whole, you may proceed."

The captain bowed his head sharply and took a step forward. "Your excellency, your graces – it is my duty to report the loss of thirty-two Zealots. A scouting party of eight, and a company of twenty-four sent after them."

It took Anton a moment to grasp what the captain said. Loss? Loss? The word did not describe anything at first, and it was with a sickening lurch that he realised that the men were dead. The breath went from him, as if by a hidden puncture, and his jaw fell slack. He looked at the other altzans to see their reactions to this horrifying news, imagining rage or fear. But Yisho and Dreyff were as silent as marble. Ramnie closed his eyes and nodded, once, in recognition of what he had heard.

"Thirty-two," he echoed, a hollowness in his voice. "And the bodies...?"

"Twenty-four have been returned to Mal Nulalus," the captain said. "The first eight were burned."

Anton closed his eyes and issued a silent prayer to the Mountain. The Tzanate disposed of its dead by union with heaven – the exposure of the bodies to the sky and the birds in devotional towers. Denying the soul this union was a terrible dishonour.

"It was the pyre that drew the attention of the second company, seeking the first," the captain continued. "They made haste into the forest and, I am sorry to say, hurried into a trap."

Ramnie nodded again. It appeared to Anton that he had met the news of this disaster with great, almost excessive, equanimity. He promptly learned the reason.

"So the total stands at ninety-three," Ramnie said.

"Yes, your excellency," Lypre said.

"Twenty-four in a single encounter, though," the altzan-al said, putting his head in his hands. "That's..." He trailed off.

"It suggests that they are becoming bolder," Lypre said. "Or at least more numerous. They might be preparing to attack our parties on the road."

Ramnie raised his head. "We must not mistake a terrible mischance for an omen," he replied. "Twenty-four is a heavy toll, but it took a carefully laid trap, well within Tarch. I do not believe they would be willing to strike at twenty-four or more Zealots on the road, not to mention the altzans' own retinues."

The captain grimaced, as if he had tasted something sour. "Excellency, I appreciate your confidence, but my men are disturbed, and I am concerned about our ability to protect the honoured delegations when the time comes for their return."

"I know what it is that you want, captain, and I cannot..." Ramnie began.

"We must reinforce Mal Nulalus from the garrisons at the Brink and the Gull Gates," the captain continued, and Anton's stomach lurched with astonishment – he had talked right across the altzan-al, as if the ancient priest wasn't even speaking. "Our numbers must be doubled if we are to guarantee the safety of the caravans. The enemy–"

Anton could stand it no longer. The captain's shocking insolence to the altzan-al had given him a sudden realisation of the bizarre nature of the whole gathering: fresh from a moment of solemnity that was unnerving enough in its own way, he had been dropped in the middle of a small war, the existence of which had hitherto been unknown to him. He could stomach the disjunction no longer.

"What enemy?" he found himself asking, feeling his voice too clear, too young in the tense atmosphere of the refectory. "Bandits?"

Even as he said the word, he knew it was an error, a foolish idea. The Augardinian Way was a lawless and dangerous road, he knew that, they all did. Miroline had withdrawn its legions from the garrison town of Mal Nulalus decades ago, leaving it in the hands of a terrified local militia, and its citadel had been a near-ruin before that. Bandits might easily prey on traders, pilgrims and gutless peasants armed with pitchforks – but eight Zealots? Twenty-four Zealots? Ninety-three Zealots?

Dreyff glared at Anton, and although Anton dared not look, he felt Yisho's eyes on him as well. It had been his place to listen and report, not to speak. But how could he report when he understood only one-third of what he was hearing? Whatever the pique in Dreyff's eye, at least he did not have to look at it every day – he could hardly imagine Ving's reaction if he returned with a garbled account of ninety-three dead Zealots and no answers to the obvious questions.

The altzan-al, at least, did not appear annoyed, but perhaps he was simply more of a diplomat. "Captain," he said, "this is vertzan Anton, who is kindly representing the, ah, corpus of the Tzanate who favour resumption of the Gift. Now that we are at last able to resolve our doctrinal differences, Ving's followers will henceforth be more involved in military matters."

"The vertzan needs no introduction," Lypre said, directing a precise bow at Anton, a courtesy Anton reflexively returned. He had never met the captain, but he need not have. He and Elecy had flanked the altzans on enough occasions, and acolytes and Zealots had been pointing him out and whispering about him for most of his life.

"Anton," Ramnie said. "Rumours already fly among the novices and the servants, and in the delegations. We have reached the stage where concealment is more damaging than candour. Ving already knows. It is not bandits attacking our men – it is the Elves."

5

INAR

The tower was not a place that Inar had visited before but, with his sense for the fortress, he found his way there without trouble. Behind the feast-hall, where others might have thought there was only solid stone, lay a jumble of discreet passages. One of these led to a guard's station and a black, ancient door surrounded by carved knome-wards and superstitious runes. A League soldier stood at this door, and opened it for the builder. Inar found himself outside, the cold a slap to the face after hours in the relative warmth of the library. He was at the bottom of a narrow crevice, a deep fracture in the rock, dark despite the slit of sunlight above. The natural floor had been carved into steps by long-dead hands, and these steps had been worn down by long-dead feet. Oily niches in the rock walls marked where candles could be placed, and devotional carvings could be seen here and there, all older than Miroline.

Inar climbed. The narrow chasm rose into a V-shaped valley, its bottom cluttered with frost-broken stone. Turning, he found that he could not see Sojonost, and realised that the whole of this path must be hidden from the view of the fortress – a discreet route for tzans to come and go as they pleased. Ahead was the tower. Its sloping sides gave it the appearance of a pyramid missing its top; it was faced in dark basalt, as close to black as possible, in emulation of the Holy Mountain itself

– not because the Mountain was black, but because it lacked any colour, and the flat darkness of the basalt best described that impossible hole in perception. The League's fools had raised a flagpole there, where the flag of Miroline or Mishig-Tenh would never have flown, because *it did not belong to them*. Though he had drifted far from the faith, Inar tutted; contempt for the foreigners flooded back. The pole was gaudy, painted in red and white stripes. The ostentation was maddening.

The door at the tower's base stood open and was not in good condition – Inar guessed that no one had come to this place since the League had taken Sojonost, and, even before then, it had probably not been in regular use for many years.

No lights were lit within the tower, and only a little sunlight filtered down from the upper level. As Inar waited for his eyes to adjust he called out, and received a faint, cheerful reply from above. Some of the features of the interior revealed themselves: a large chamber filling the base of the tower, niches lining the walls, and a fat, square central column around which bent a flight of steps. Inar climbed them with care. He could hear birds stirring in the darkness. He hoped they were birds.

He had been in the dark less than a minute, but the sun still dazzled him as he stepped out onto the tower's upper platform. His head thudded – the mountain light could be exhausting, and at this height even the gentle climb it had taken to get here was a trial.

Anzola, Duna and Kielo were gathered around a wooden tripod, which was topped with a brass spyglass of unfamiliar and intricate design. The merite was looking through this apparatus and Kielo was making notes with a bone pen on a wax pad. Duna, uninvolved in this operation, looked deeply bored, and cold, although like the others she was wearing thick white furs.

"You called for me," he said.

Anzola nodded. "Take a moment, builder. The climb up here

is more ferocious than it looks. We all had to rest a while when we got here."

Inar leaned against the parapet, grateful for the instruction. "The higher one rises in the mountains," he said, "the more effort must be put into every action. Men tire faster, and can become quite ill."

"We have observed this," Kielo said, eagerly. "It has been a drag on our works, we feared that sickness was among the men. Is it a quality of the air? A vapour? Emitted by mountains?" He sniffed, cautiously.

"Miners complain of vapours seeping from the rock in their tunnels," Anzola said, frowning at this puzzle. "But those are trapped, deep places – I would not have thought it possible up here, in the open sky, scoured by the wind…"

Inar shrugged. "A vapour, I don't know. I have always felt it to be more like starvation than contamination. Perhaps it is the absence of green life."

"Even the air tells us we should not be here," Duna said, pulling her fur around her shoulders and shivering theatrically.

Anzola shot a scowl over her shoulder at the young girl, but did not respond to this remark. "We have noticed that Mishigo are less affected by the sickness than Leaguers," she said. "See, already you are restored, but we were quite exhausted."

"We were carrying the equipment," Kielo said, with a faint air of wounded pride.

Inar shrugged again. "We are born into the heights, I suppose. I think it may come with time. The Tzanate takes in men and women from every part of the world, and the sickness does not seem to trouble them long."

"They see things, though, don't they?" Duna asked. Mention of this had wiped away some of her glumness, and replaced it with a fearful fascination.

"The mountain sickness, at its most serious, can cause delusions and madness," Inar said. "It can be very dangerous, on a long climb or march. Men can disappear wearing only their vests, believing themselves in a wheatfield in summer, when they are atop an ice-bound pass."

Duna had fixed her pale blue eyes on Inar. His answer was insufficient. "There's other ways to see things, though, aren't there. Sights in the mind, terrible sights."

"Wakemares," Inar said with a nod. "That's different. They are caused by the Mountain. The Mountain-God, I mean." He glanced to the east – there it was, clear above the line of even the highest peaks, a blaze of distortion against blue. "We are too far, here."

Anzola clapped her gloved hands together, and spoke brightly. "Well, if one is wrapped up warm, it is a beautiful place to be. The mountains shine so. I can see why such a landscape invites tales of magic and gods. Truly 'a meeting-place of heaven'."

"You know its purpose, then?" Inar asked.

"Naturally," Anzola said with a smile. "We have them in the League, although we have closed some. Miroline brought the Mountain faith to us, remember, and many still hold to it."

"You mean this is…?" Duna began, her lip curled in disgust.

"An akouy shiel," Inar said. "A temple for the dead. The birds come here and join the dead with the sky. In the past, the Custodians would have come here. We are given to God, we achieve union with heaven, with the Mountain." He could not stop himself thinking of his brother and his father, dumped in the ground like trash, barred from this final honour as traitors.

Head down, Duna charged past Inar, towards the steps. The others did nothing to stop her or call her back.

"Are we blaspheming by being here, Inar?" Anzola asked, voice honeyed with concern. "Would a tzan be angered?"

Inar creased his brow at the question. Young travelling tzans, who earned their bread by gathering crowds and rousing them up, might make a stink of it. But they would condemn the League for getting out of bed in the morning (up to no good!) and going to bed at night (idleness!). Resentment was their trade. Inar kept a careful boundary on his answer: "People care less and less about these things."

The muscles in Anzola's jaw tightened. "Was this... Did they ever... Bring living people here?"

For a moment, Inar did not understand what she meant. Then he did. "You mean for *sacrifice*?" He felt a flash of anger that this foreigner should mention the Gift, but it passed. Why be angry? The Gift had never been a secret, it was a prominent part of the faith's history. But it had been stopped, the altzan of Stull said. The Custodians themselves had stopped it. Inar had been glad it had been stopped. He realised that his anger had come from embarrassment, that his faith of birth should perform such deeds, that people from other lands and other faiths should look at him the way that Anzola and Kielo were looking at him now. Like a savage.

"No, never!" he said, spirit high. He cast around for evidence, keen to disprove the idea. "There's no altar! They haven't done it in public my whole life, my father's whole life. They've stopped, anyway! Even before then, it was only criminals, maybe twice a year, only at the Brink – but they've stopped, it'll never happen again. The Custodians say so."

"It's all right, Inar," Anzola said. She had stepped towards him, and laid a hand on his shoulder. "We know it's a practice of the past. I didn't mean to upset you. Anyway–" she looked up at the sky, tracking the sun "– we must get to work, before this beautiful light goes. We did bring you here for a reason."

Duna was waiting at the base of the tower, as sullen as ever. She had picked up a fist-sized rock from the ground and was staring at it as if imagining the pretty curve it would make in the sky before it connected with Anzola's head, or Inar's. The merite and she locked eyes for a second, and she trudged behind the party.

They walked around the base of the tower to its southern side, which faced away from Sojonost.

"The tower is damaged," Anzola said plainly. "I need to know if it is still safe, or if it will fall."

He looked where Anzola indicated. A crack ran straight up the sloping southern side of the tower, reaching from near the ground to near the parapet. Winter's work? No, more recent – this crack was new, its sides sharp and fresh, no dust gathered within it. And it was not the structure settling or shifting, running around the edges of stones, separating along mortar lines. It was straight, and ran right through all the heavy, flat building stones it touched. The wall was four feet thick if it was an inch, and yet it looked as if it was a sheet slashed by a sharp knife.

"What happened?" Inar asked. He thought he was familiar with every ill that could befall a building, and yet this was odd. "An earthquake?" They were rare, but not unknown.

"No," Anzola said. Then she added, hastily: "Well, maybe. Will it bring down the tower?"

Inar studied the fissure. He *listened* to it. "No. The structure hasn't been weakened, not significantly. But you should fill it in before winter – ice can do more damage than any siege weapon." He looked over his shoulder at Anzola, suspicious. "Were you testing a siege weapon? One of those mangonels on the battery tower?" But he knew that was not it – this had not been caused by a rock hitting the wall, there was no impact, no fragments.

"It's safe?" Anzola asked. "It won't fall? You can tell that just by looking?"

Not *just* looking, not really, thought Inar, but he thought it sensible to put on a show. He approached the crack and ran his fingers along its edge. It was remarkably straight and neat. Splitting a stone was as familiar an act to Inar as tearing a loaf of bread. It happened around him, on his building sites, every day. Large irregular chunks of hewn stone were brought from the quarry, and a mason would find the right seam and carve a small hole in it. Into this hole he would hammer a wedge, and the stone would split along the sediment line. This gave a good flat surface for building. This could have been one of those splits – but it ran through many stones, many layers, and mortar too, against every grain. It ran through granite and basalt: very hard, durable materials. It wasn't *right*. But he could understand the overall state of the tower from a glance. Its weight flowed around the break, and was not working to widen it. The tower was sound.

Nevertheless, the damage made him uneasy.

"There's no danger," he said. "Just make sure it's filled before water gets in."

"See to it," Anzola said to Kielo. Kielo nodded, and the merite turned to Duna. "How are you feeling, my dear?"

The girl dropped the handful of gravel she had been toying with, brushed dirt from her gloves, and shrugged. "Fine. Tired."

She and Anzola held eyes for a moment – a communication passing between them, its content impossible for Inar to pick up. Then the merite turned to the builder and smiled. "That's enough for today, I should think. Inar, thank you for your help, marvellous work."

"That's all?" Inar said, unable to keep the surprise from his voice.

"Oh yes," Anzola said. "Very helpful. Go and get some rest. Banqueting tonight, with the merite Ernesto. You must impress him as you have impressed me."

Neglected again, Inar returned to the library. His mind still continued to turn over the damage to the akouy shiel, as if that hard-edged fissure was right behind his eyes. He found a book of the construction of the funerary towers, and read. They had originated in the mountains, in mountain conditions, starting as simple stone cairns. They could withstand blizzard and tremor. A crack like that was... an anomaly. Inar, who could speak the language of tone, found it offensively silent.

As the dinner hour approached and the light waned, Lott came to find Inar.

"Banquet time," he said. "The man, the secretary, said you should dress as well as possible. 'As well as possible', those were his words." Lott evidently understood the implication, and did not care for it.

"I didn't bring much in the way of lace or silk," Inar said, rolling his eyes. "A clean shirt will have to do. They are clearly expecting mountain savages, it would be a pity to disappoint them."

Lott smiled at this, but it was not an entirely happy smile. "It rubs me the wrong way to have to suck up to them," he said.

"I know," Inar said, feeling a wash of fellow feeling with the apprentice, who was only slightly his junior. "But what could I do? To refuse would have been to refuse Lord Cilma, to refuse the king. They insisted." He considered telling Lott about the job Cilma had given him, to report on the League's activities. But he could not be certain that Lott would keep that to himself. "It will help us, in the long run, to understand the League a little better."

"Was that what your father thought?" Lott asked.

He had not meant those words to sting. Calculated efforts to hurt were not in Lott's nature. But Inar was stung.

"All my father wanted was to avoid a siege. The war was already lost." *Your brother was already dead, at Halsk Trun,* he did not add.

Lott seemed to take this on board, albeit sullenly. It was not the first time the topic had come up. "Well," he said, after a pause to pick his nails in deep thought, "there are ways to rebel. Let's run down their stores by eating as much as possible."

Nothing they could have worn would have equalled the splendour they found in the feast-hall. The hall itself was impressive enough, with tall stained glass windows along one wall. Facing that glass was a wall carved into the living stone of the mountain itself; it was lined with niches, containing likenesses of Mishig-Tenh's kings. Essian the second had not yet been added, nor had Essian the third, nor Inar the fourth, nor Eric, whose number the builder Inar could not remember. The third Essian and his immediate successors would not make impressive statues: a nine-year-old, a three-year-old and a babe-in-arms, who had reigned a collective twenty minutes or so as their uncle stalked his way from bedchamber to bedchamber, bloodily making himself Inar the fifth. That Inar – not for the first time, Inar, son of Astar, cursed his father's decision to call his sons after members of the royal family – had not made it through the night. League soldiers were already pouring through the breach in the city's walls. Lord Cilma and the other high nobles, those that had survived the butchery at Halsk Trun, did not warm to their king's proposals for renewed struggle and sacrifice. Inar the fifth was promptly added to the regicidal tally. An elderly uncle of the late Essian the second became Otto the sixth, and surrendered to the League. It was called the Night of Six Kings. Seven, really, as it was really Cilma who had taken the throne. If you run the king's spies, decide the king's enemies, command the king's armies and govern the king's expenditure, then the king is just a man holding your seat for you.

Tonight the ancient kings of Mishig-Tenh seemed to have each taken a half-step back into the shadows of their niches, astonished at the stellar new age that had erupted before their cold, grey eyes. The high table was covered in linen, set with silver plate, and blazing with candlelight. The great hanging candle-wheels had been lowered on their chains, and they too were thick with candles, brilliant haloes of fire. Never had Inar seen anything so extravagant, and so beautiful. They must have used every candle in a hundred miles. More would have been spent showing the food than on buying it.

The lower tables of the hall seated scores of knights in fine livery, many attended by individual squires. Blossoming boughs had been brought in to decorate the tables – brought in, Inar calculated, from at least as far as Matchfalls, as the buds had yet to break in Stull. More unthinkable expense. How many knights were present? Each one would have his own company of men and his following of horses and servants – added to the companies of regular soldiery that Inar had counted, he estimated that thousands of fighting men must already be gathered around the fortress, with thousands more serving and supporting them.

Kielo had met Lott and Inar at the door of the hall. The secretary noticed the Mishigos' wide eyes as he led them towards the high table. "Extravagant, yes," he said, sombrely. "I advised against this display. She – the merite – argued that the men had been brought far from home, and deprived of much luxury, and the coming months may be hard – that they deserved a golden memory." He gritted his teeth – something in this explanation did not agree with him. "There is the merite Ernesto to consider, as well. He must be impressed. Here, please, sit here." He directed Inar and Lott into two high-backed chairs at the far end of the long high table, and then swept away. Only one other place was occupied, at the opposite end, by a bulky, angry-looking man whose balding forehead was balanced by eyebrows of majestic bushiness. Inar admired the silver plate, the goblets. On each setting was a folded square of white linen.

"What are these?" Lott asked, unfolding his square – it made a bigger square, not revealing anything like a function. "Blowing your nose?"

"No, no," Inar said. He doubted that a cultured people would encourage anything so crude at the table. "It must be for the chair." He unfolded his own square and spread it across the seat. Lott copied him.

The other man at the table laughed – a harsh, yukking laugh that somehow did nothing to make him look less angry. "They

will take you for fools, Tenhe," he said. "The cloth is for your
lap. It keeps gravy off your Leagueish silk breeches, yuh?"

Inar snatched the cloth from his chair. "You speak Mishigo,"
he said.

The man shrugged lazily. "Oriri. Mishigo is easy. We are
Tenhe, yeah?"

"We've seen many Oriri here," Inar said. "Well met, Tenhe."

"When we were coming here, we saw…" Lott said, before
Inar jabbed him in the ribs to shut him up.

It was too late, however – the man had guessed what he was
referring to. "Yeah, well, we must all serve our new masters in
our own ways. Better the silk-breeches gang than the Elves,
that's the way I look at it. I am Solbey Neathe, captain of the
Company of Caenon." They were too far for a handshake, and
Solbey had not risen from his seat as they spoke.

"I am Inar, and this is Lott," Inar said. He omitted his
surname – if this man had fought the League in the war, he
might not take kindly to it.

"You're the native guides, right?" Solbey said. "The
mountain men."

Inar never really thought of himself as a mountain man – he
and Solbey were both "Tenhe", members of the loose family of
peoples spread along the chain of mountains that curved all
the way from the land of the auroras to the coast south of the
League. But Oririthen, at the south-westernmost extremity of
this chain, looked more to the sea and the fields than the peaks,
and its people regarded Mishig-Tenh as high and as remote as
the Elith-Tenh.

"Guides?" Inar said. "We are builders."

But there was no time to ask Neathe what he had meant.
A fanfare had sounded at the far end of the hall, and benches
scraped back as the knights rose together. The merites Anzola
and Ernesto entered together, hand in hand, accompanied
by other dignitaries, Duna and Kielo among them. It took
Inar a second to recognise Anzola: for the first time in their

acquaintance, she was wearing a dress, one of League-blue silk with a stiff bodice, and her short hair was disguised by a circlet of silver wire. It was as close to ladylike as he had seen her, and yet still she managed to give the ensemble an air of business, or authority – the bodice was tooled blue leather, and the dress had been stripped of many of the encumbrances that aristocratic ladies had to bear. Ernesto was, if anything, more decorated. He was a man of middling height, and had perhaps once been physically powerful – but his frame was losing its final battle, with puddings. He wore a refined version of the leather armour favoured by the League, in a near-black shade of blue, and plainly made for sitting and talking rather than riding and fighting. As if to advertise its inability to stop a blade, it was in places slashed, revealing scarlet silk. On his shoulders hung a golden chain of office.

The pair advanced on the high table at speed, and Inar noticed them decoupling their hands a moment sooner than was entirely seemly. Ernesto went straight to the King's Chair, and sat, without a word – Anzola was left standing, stitching together the social niceties. No one else sat.

"Inar, Lott, I have not yet had the pleasure of introducing the merite Ernesto Hapa, High Commander of the Armies of the League of Free Cities, Protector of Sojonost…" She stalled.

"Go on," Ernesto said, smiling without warmth.

"… Conqueror of the Mountain Lands."

Inar inclined his head, surprising himself – surprise doubled when he noticed that Lott had done the same. "My lord," he said.

"'Your grace', Inar," Ernesto said. "So you are our costly Mishigo assistants?"

"We are at your service, your grace," Inar said, as the word *costly* banged around inside his head.

The Conqueror had moved on. "Be seated," he said, with some grandeur, to the hall, and there was a din of moving benches and resumed conversation. Anzola finished introductions at speed – Neathe and another Oriri mercenary captain, Sojonost's castellan and marshal, and a third League merite, called Szymon, older than Anzola and Ernesto but seemingly less important.

The castellan was seated next to Inar, quite deliberately, and spent the entire meal consulting him on Sojonost's labyrinthine layout and the difficulty of running it with a largely foreign (to him) staff. He was a thin man with only wisps remaining on his freckled scalp, although, as he explained his difficulties managing the fortress, Inar formed the impression that he might have left Matchfalls with a full head of hair. In the gaps in this fraught discussion, Inar became aware that the atmosphere along the table was not exactly jolly. At one point, Ernesto and Anzola argued in hisses, while the rest of the table pretended not to listen. As it was in Palla, Inar could not understand a word. The castellan caught his look.

"The merite Anzola and the merite Ernesto have never agreed on how to divide credit for our victory in the war," he said, with care. "They are allies, you see." He slapped his fist into his other hand and gripped it tight. "Very close. But closeness does not always make for friendship."

He took a sip of wine and glanced towards the bickering nobles. "The last war came as a surprise to us. We did not desire it – you may doubt that, but it's the truth – and no one expected that victory would be so swift, or so thorough. It has given them the impression of invincibility, that wealth and reason can together achieve anything. Every day I hear 'we are the League, we can do anything we want', and I have to say, no, it's more difficult... I wish they could see that all their plans to reshape the world rest on the world as it is, not the world they wish."

Inar mulled this over. "Reason has no place at the heart of the world," he said. "Miroline used to think of itself as a place of reason and philosophy, until it went to war in Tarch, until it crossed the mountains."

The castellan grimaced. "We should not be here," he said. "Forgive me, I know you are Mishigo, I know this is home for you, but… this place. I do not like this place."

Inar shook his head. "No one calls *this* place home," he said, indicating Sojonost's hall with a wave of the hand. "Not even the Mishigo."

Once the eating was done, but before the childish sweet dishes and the hot, bitter black drink that the Leaguers wanted after every meal, the merite Ernesto rose to speak. He spoke in Palla, so Inar could not understand what he said, but his tone was serious, perhaps even grave, and his measured delivery became steadily more insistent. The castellan whispered some cursory translation in Mirolingua for Inar and Lott: "He is praising the men… He says they must enjoy this comfort because difficulties lie ahead… Sojonost is at a fork in the pass and the League is at a fork in its story, its history… He says that many of them want to know what will happen next and very soon this will be revealed… He has praised the merite Anzola… He says every city of the League awaits the result of Anzola's activities… Again, he says that difficulties lie ahead, but also greatness, and they will all be remembered when the histories are written. He wishes Anzola, and yourselves, good luck on your departure."

"Departure?"

"We're going home?" Lott said, brightening out of a food-induced stupor.

Inar leaned forward, wanting to catch Anzola's eye, to see if an answer could be found there. He discovered that she was already looking back at him, smiling nervously, eyes full of apology and plea. That was not the answer he was looking for.

The feasting was followed by singing. Anzola took advantage of the noise to leave her seat and approach Inar and Lott. "Come with me," she said. Inar felt the rebellion that had been brewing inside him dissipate – her tone was warm and reassuring, but did not give much promise that disagreement would be entertained.

They left the feast-hall by a rear door and found themselves in a much smaller room, hung with tapestries showing scenes of hunting and victory. There were Mirolinian day-beds covered in fine linen and cushions and the floor was covered with a thick Estami carpet. Inar had never seen this room before, and found it a startling contrast to the spartan interiors of the rest of the fortress. His first thought was to curse the League for bringing so much luxury with them, but none of the furnishings were new. Private royal quarters, then, for private pleasures.

The merite ushered the two builders to sit. They perched awkwardly on the edge of day-beds that were more suited to lounging. Inar expected her to speak, but instead she remained standing.

Seconds later they heard the heavy door open again, and a surge of song from the feast hall. Then the door slammed, and the heavy curtain screening it was pulled back, revealing Ernesto.

"So, does everyone know what we're doing?" he asked, gruffly.

"I was about to explain," Anzola replied.

"Really?" the other merite said, raising an eyebrow. "You've had days."

"Secrecy first," Anzola said, irritably. "And I know how you like to be included."

Inar, himself a little irritable at being a prop in someone else's squabble, cut in. "Where are we going?" he asked.

Anzola sat daintily on the edge of a day bed, and then stared at Ernesto until he sat as well – dropping onto his seat as if trying to defeat it in combat.

"We intend to survey the pass," Anzola said. "We need guides who know the mountains."

Inar nodded. "The Augardinian Way? That's easy. The

Mirolinian road is mostly intact. You could have told us."

Anzola's expression was grim. "No. The other pass. We want to survey the pilgrim route into Elith-Tenh. To see if we can pass an army that way."

Inar was silent. He was dimly aware of Lott slowly turning his way, eyes wide, disbelieving. "Oh." He smiled. "Well, that's even easier. We don't even have to leave this room. You can't. It's impossible."

"Why not?" Ernesto demanded. Inar was surprised – he had expected the objection to come from Anzola. "People go that way. Pilgrims. Priests. Why not an army?"

"You can't move supply carts, or horses, through. Even mules struggle. It is not a road. Pilgrims go *because* it is a hard way to go, to show their faith. Traders – when they were allowed – went via Mal Nulalus and the Gull Gates, scores of miles longer but vastly easier. Even if you forget about supplies and horses and siege weapons, and just move men, you will have a column thirty miles long, moving very slowly, utterly exposed to attack."

He found himself laughing at the idea. "Look, if you'd like me to show you this in person, I'd do so gladly. But there's the other problem: the Tzanate. Unbelievers are forbidden."

Anzola brightened, which Inar had not expected. "That is not the problem that you imagine. They are expecting us."

Inar felt the day-bed calling to him, and he wondered how the others would react if he simply lay down and went to sleep. It had been a long day, the evening meal had been rich, and it now seemed that his addled mind was playing tricks. "How is that?" he said.

Anzola and Ernesto exchanged a look. "We are very close to an agreement with the Tzanate. To cooperate."

"How?"

"We need to destroy the Elves," Ernesto said. "They are becoming a plague in the west. We might be able to defeat them there, only to have them shrink back into Tarch and regather their strength. Their homelands must be destroyed. And we cannot send an army from here into Tarch while the Tzanate is hostile to us. So – that must be addressed."

"Your grace, I can see why an agreement with the Tzanate is desirable to you," Inar said. Perhaps if he were less tired, he would have been less blunt to the nobleman, the conqueror, but as it was Ernesto was listening with more courtesy than Inar had yet seen. "What I cannot understand is why the Tzanate would agree."

"Well, they haven't," Ernesto said.

Anzola scowled at him. "Not yet. They will. The closure of the passes since the war has starved them, and their supply route from Mal Nulalus and Cassodar is threatened by the Elves. And they are more open to change than you might think. The heart-gouging days are over. The altzan-al is a reformer. He has called a Conclave, a great meeting of priests, to get consent for the alliance. But there are hardliners in his hierarchy, fanatics and cultists, who might make things difficult."

"And you might want to move in men to back him up."

"Precisely." Again, she exchanged glances with Ernesto. "We do understand the significance of the Elith-Tenh, Inar. We have no desire to rouse the faithful against us. We would be acting with the support of the proper religious authorities."

"And what of Miroline?"

In their brief acquaintance, Inar had never suspected Ernesto capable of jollity. But now he emitted a terrific bellow of a laugh, and Inar saw a completely different man to the imperious, arrogant commander: a gladhander, the light of a room. This eruption of mirth he thought might be met with disapproval from Anzola, but she was smiling too – either enjoying Ernesto's merriment, or sharing in the humour of Inar's words, humour Inar could not see.

"What of Miroline?" Ernesto echoed. "Well, what of Miroline? What of the cham of Estam? What of far Benzig? What of the Shergine kingdoms? Distant places, all. Emperors of Miroline have been entertained in this very room, boy. And tonight *we* are here, not them."

"Miroline is not what it was," Anzola agreed. She leaned forward. Her eyes sparkled in the firelight. "We embark on a great enterprise, Inar, for the good of the world. Will you help us?"

"I will show you that you cannot move an army through the pass," Inar said. He shook his head and sighed. "It is obvious that you will only understand the reality of the mountains when you see it for yourselves. And, obviously, the Mountain has cursed me with the task of showing you."

"Excellent!" Anzola said, as if he had agreed with every word she had spoken.

6

ANTON

Night was no time to travel in the Hidden Land. The flatness of the plateau could be deceptive – even those who had spent their lives here could forget they were in the mountains and set out too late on a journey. Then the weather would change in the dark, flooding the world with fog or slapping down a storm, and they would never be seen again. Even if the weather didn't change, they might never be seen again.

The meeting with Lypre had lasted two hours, and once it had concluded Yisho advised that it was too late to depart for the Brink. They would stay at Hleng and depart in the morning. Anton found himself back in the room he had shared with Elecy the night before, this time alone. He had been brought food and wine, but had not been invited to dine with the others. All the other tzans and altzans had departed on completion of the ceremony of welcome, a vast procession to the Brink for the Conclave, and only servants and soldiers remained.

It was a comfortable room, far more so than the tents and barracks that many esteemed altzans would have to share over the next few days. Again, as so often, he was treated better than most, and it troubled him. Peat was burning in the brazier, and the windows and doors out onto the terrace were draped with furs. The ceiling was painted like a sky, a

Mirolinian sky, Elecy said, though he struggled to see what made it so. In centuries past it would have comforted wealthy pilgrims or visiting altzans. But the flame of the oil lamp had receded to the dimmest orange spark, and the painting was lost in gloom. So was Anton. He was thinking about the Elves.

The Elves were the ancient enemy. They had come close to overwhelming the world, before Augardine journeyed into the Hidden Land and made his pact with the Mountain. Then, ablaze with the Mountain's shrouding light, Augardine had destroyed them and made a waste of their homeland, making them the stuff of tales and legends.

If only they had stayed in tales. Two years ago, the League had smashed Oririthen's armies and carved off many choice parts of King Murro's fledgeling empire. The remainder had collapsed. That had been startling enough, but, not long after, an army of about ten thousand Elves had emerged from Tarch. They overran the vestiges of Oririthen, including the royal city of Caenon, which they had named Mestiell and made a centre of their vile faith in an orgy of blood and mutilation.

A tragedy, but the astonishment these events caused within the Tzanate was tempered by a sense of design. The League had turned its back on the Mountain faith, and so it stood to reason that its great victory should be accompanied by the resurgence of the very evil that Augardine had banished. In any case, a thousand miles of forest and moor stood between Caenon – *Mestiell* – and the gates of Elith-Tenh. The Elves were the League's problem. They were so fond of account-books, let them balance *that* debt. Let them try to sail their big fat ships into Tarch, and see how far they get. Eventually they would again be on their knees before the Mountain.

Not even two years – the League's victory had been at the end of summer, and it was spring. A year and a half, and the Elves were here as well. What did that say about Tarch? Was it infested, end to end? Where was the "design" now that Elves were burning Zealots? They were crazed creatures, the Elves, erratic as individuals and unspeakably dangerous in numbers, propelled by collective frenzy. So everyone knew. But they had planned an ambush, and carried it out.

The altzan-al had, eventually, agreed to most of captain Lypre's requests. Mal Nulalus and its surroundings would be reinforced while the Tzanate continued its repair of the fortress. This struck Anton as wise – more than wise, it seemed essential – but it would mean more of the Tzanate's army was beyond the Gull Gates, outside the land it was meant to protect. And meanwhile every senior tzan and altzan who could make the journey had been gathered for the Conclave. How could they be safely returned to the imperial outpost at Cassodar?

It did not make for easy sleep. So Anton lay awake, mind divided between the arithmetic of men and garrisons, and more lurid visions of shapeless bloodlust and horror in a green maze.

Eventually, lying down seemed to require an unreasonable amount of effort. Unable to bear it any longer, Anton rose from his bed and put on his thick winter boots. The cot that Elecy had slept in the previous night was still in the room, but it had been stripped of bedding – otherwise there was precious little to divert him, just an oil lamp and a chest. The walls pushed in and the air thickened. It would be icy outside, but he felt compelled to go out anyway, to feel the cold, to let it into him. He took his furs from the chest and, once he had wrapped himself in them, he pushed through the hangings and out into the open air.

His room was one of twenty or so that opened onto a wide terrace which ran along the shore of Hleng. This was part of a long wing projecting from the main temple complex, built many centuries ago by a young, rich, conquering faith. They were raised above the surface of the lake, on an embankment that contained a warren of stores, stables and servants' quarters, the hidden world that made all this elegant emptiness possible. Anton crossed a wide expanse of pink granite slabs – made uneven underfoot by neglect for a score of violent winters – to the pale line of the marble balustrade.

Hleng was a black stillness containing a river of stars. And the Mountain. The vast ranges that enclosed Elith-Tenh were visible only as an absence, a line cut across the arch of heaven above. But they were just mountains. Craithe, the Mountain, was different. It rose above the range at its highest point, supreme and luminous – no, not luminous, for it did not make light, it swallowed it up, but it *radiated*. The stars that came close to it fizzed and recoiled and twisted into many colours. They seemed to skid across its face, or behind or through it, splitting into rainbows. But it was never possible to watch its splintering, maddening effects for too long because it forced the eyes away, like the unshaded sun. Anton instead looked for its reflection in the lake, where it was calm, a shifting wound at the edge of the starfield, a lightless opening that contained all colour.

It winked from view, and reappeared, split and scattered by a flurry of ripples.

The wind picked up, and then died.

Anton looked about. He was alone. Where were the guards? Keeping to warmer corners, he supposed. What was there that could threaten the altzans up here? Only that which came from above.

Despite the cold, Anton felt sweat on his brow. Again, he looked around. The moon and its maids were the only illumination, and while the outline of roofs and buildings could be seen, their doorways were impenetrable blocks of shadow.

A sound – the lapping of lake water against stone, or the beat of a wing? And another, a scrape of talon.

"I know you're there," Anton said, hoping his voice was free of fear. "You can show yourself."

No figure, human or otherwise, stepped forth, and Anton felt ridiculous for having spoken. It had been too long a day. What did he expect, a Custodian skulking on the roof of the guest lodgings like a pigeon? If the Custodians had one truly reliable feature, it was that they favoured obscurity.

"Stupid," he told himself. A gust off the lake caught him and he shivered. It had been foolish to come outside, into this cold. He wanted nothing more than to be back under the covers.

The room felt far warmer now that he had tried the open air. But the relative warmth caused him to realise how cold he had become outside. Anton draped his cloak on top of the furs already on the bed and climbed back in. Though the bedding had not lost the heat it had gained from his body, he found himself shaking with cold, and icy in the hands and feet. The peat-scented air of the room was stifling. His teeth chattered. He stared up at the painted clouds on the ceiling, imagining the bounteous Mirolinian sun.

The trunk of a vast stone figure lay on the floor of the plateau, near the road to the Brink. Headless, armless, legless, and covered in scars and gouges, it might be taken for a natural feature were it not for the fact that it was the wrong colour: a sickly orange, quite unlike any of the broken rocks littered around it. And there was something about the way it lay, face down, broken neck pointed at the road. Care had been taken to make it look careless, and to give it an aspect of abjection. It was the remnant of a dead religion, torn from a long-burned fane in the south and dragged all the way here.

Several of these trophies marked the approach to the Brink, although most were sinking into unrecognisable ruin and junk. Nearby was Anton's favourite, a concave brass disc like a giant's soup-bowl. Although tarnished and torn by centuries of exposure to ice and snow, it could still catch light from the sun it had been made to emulate.

Anton reined his horse and stood at the side of the road, looking for the disc, letting the thin column of Zealots trickle past him. Why was he looking? None of the others did. His predecessors, who had gone to great trouble to bring these fruits of conquest back to this fastness, must have had some aim beyond simply impressing on defeated peoples the totality of their destruction. Armies of slaves would have dragged these trophies, and would then have been Given as the Gift. Some lesson, that the pupil learns for so short a time. Another purpose, surely.

"Vertzan Anton."

He had tarried too long, and one of the others in the party had returned to fetch him. But he did not recognise the voice – or rather, he recognised it, and the small fur-wrapped form on horseback that approached, but he could not believe that they had stooped to the lowly work of messenger.

"Altzan-al. I beg your forgiveness. I was taking a moment to rest."

He would have spurred his horse into movement, but the high priest had blocked his path.

"You were looking for something. The great mirror of the Vosians? It's over there."

A bony finger emerged from under its wrappings, indicating an unexpected direction. Anton saw the dented rim of the dish outlined against a patch of snow. None of its original brilliance was left, replaced with black and flares of white corrosion.

"I'm used to seeing it from the Brink," Anton said, trying to justify his mistake. "We should return. I'm sorry to have delayed you."

"I will have to spend days sitting on a ghastly throne, listening to speeches," Ramnie said. "I am glad of any reason to stay in the outdoors. What is it that interests you about the mirror?"

"Nothing really. I was thinking about our forebears. Those who destroyed the Vosians and brought their mirror here, and all these other trophies. They must have meant for me to feel something when I looked upon them. What was it? Pride? Gratitude? Vindication? Bloodlust?"

"Do you feel any of those?"

"No."

"What do you feel?"

Anton shrugged. "Cold."

The altzan-al laughed – a pleasant sound, and one of those laughs that the listener wishes to hear more often. "When I read their writings, I do not get the impression that they were very interested in the opinions of generations to come. After the work of conquering the world, they seem to imagine shining phalanxes of grateful altzans marching without end, not a thought in their haloed heads."

He smiled into the wasteland. "How disappointed they must be."

The last of the Zealots had marched by, other than a rearguard of six who stood, bored and cold, a respectful distance away. They would not move until the altzan-al did.

"We should return, altzan-al," Anton said.

"Yes," Ramnie replied. "But ride alongside. We'll talk a while, until Dreyff glares at me."

They did not talk – not at first. Anton simply could not think of anything to say. The entire idea of making conversation with the high priest was disturbing to him. What would he say?

So it was Ramnie who broke the silence. "We used to talk often," he said. "When you were to be the blade-priest – in more than name, I mean. Do you recall? I miss those times. The talking, I mean, before the schism. I could even take the time of day with altzan Ving."

"The division saddens me as well," Anton said carefully. "I was encouraged to see you with Ving yesterday."

"Ving and I are old men," Ramnie said. "It is wearisome, all this arguing and plotting. I have no desire to spend my last years playing this game, and it seems he feels the same way. Have you been practising?"

For a couple of yards of road, Anton was unable to answer, because he had no idea what the altzan-al meant. Practising?

Practising what? He did not sing or play an instrument, he did not observe the martial arts of the Zealots.

The thought of physical combat, of swordplay, triggered him in the realisation of what Ramnie was talking about. And he could not answer, because he had no answer.

"The master of animals says he has not seen you," Ramnie said. "Vertzan Elecy, oh yes, once a week. She's the reason we eat so much bacon. But not vertzan Anton, not once, in five years."

"We are not obligated, altzan-al," Anton said. He had been forced to practise wielding the ver and Giving the Gift, before its cessation. Pigs were used instead of prisoners. Everything about those occasions disgusted him, and he felt nothing but shame when he looked back on them. "Altzan Ving made no rule. He said we were free to choose."

"And you choose to forego the experience, while Elecy bathes in blood once a week. You'd never think it, to look at her, would you? Such an enthusiastic killer."

Anton frowned. "I don't believe tzan Elecy enjoys killing, altzan-al, you do her wrong," he said. "She is simply doing as she has been told she is born to do, told since infancy."

Ramnie nodded. "It's strange, is it not? We take two of our orphans, the same age, very similar circumstances, and raise them to believe they have a singular purpose of utmost importance, which governs every aspect of their raising. And then, when they are within months of fulfilling that purpose, we say it will not be required. Times have changed. And your responses are completely different. One becomes the soul of introspection and doubt. The other a fanatic as hard-edged and volatile as anything produced here since the Monize Crusade. Ving's whole philosophy is that if you stamp the right doctrine into the young with sufficient force you will get uniform results, and every day he has the refutation of that sitting right under his nose."

It had been a pleasant surprise to be able to pass the time

with the genial high priest, after so long when he had hardly been allowed to be in the same room as him. But this criticism of Ving, however mild and well-observed, stung Anton back into caution. He would not be drawn into disloyalty to those closest to him, no matter how much he differed from them and their doctrine.

"Altzan Ving is my father in the faith, and Elecy my sister," he said. He wished not to be having the conversation, and to be spared the discomfort of having to listen to that deep-dungeoned part of him screaming that he hated the Gift and wanted no part of it. He was no killer, and never would be. He did not desire to see the faith restored to its ancient bloody glory. He wanted... well, he didn't know, but it certainly was not what Ving and Elecy wanted.

"Yes, of course," Ramnie said. "Well said."

They rode on in silence. Before them lay the Brink, unusually gaudy, decked with banners and pennants to greet the Conclave. The great fortress-monastery of the Tzanate was still a fair distance away but was vast enough to seem quite close. A mighty defensive wall stretched across a gap in the mountains, and behind the wall rose a clutch of glittering towers. It might have dominated the road ahead and commanded the gaze, were it not for the true master of the horizon: Craithe, the Mountain, which made even the mundane peaks around it seem trivial and toylike. It filled the prospect, yet still drove the eye away, a wall of up-trickling impossibility.

"They worshipped false gods, and when their lands fell, they were made to drag their fetishes and idols here, to the threshold of the true God," Ramnie said, returning to the subject of the trophies. "I'm sure you're right, the intention was to cow them, to impress upon them that their history had come to an end. But, you know, I can't help but draw a different lesson: Religions die. They go from the world."

"Not ours," Anton said, with a vehemence that came as a surprise to both priests. "Forgive me, altzan-al, but you can't possibly mean that the Tzanate might die? Doesn't the refutation of that idea lie before *you*?" He raised his arm to indicate the Mountain, taking care not to look at it. He needed no reminders of its existence.

"Oh, of course," Ramnie said. "But the sun is still above us, and there are no Vosians to worship it."

"The sun is…" Anton stopped. He was disturbed by a sudden vision of the Elith-Tenh emptied, the Mountain shunned, the Custodians left alone with their God. It had been that way, once, before Augardine: a secret place, its savage population little more than livestock for the Custodians, a tiny and vicious priesthood trying to give slaughter the lustre of religion.

"My dear boy, you've gone quite grey," Ramnie said. "I'm sorry. First I embarrass you with my impertinence about your friend Elecy, then I upset you with melancholy reflections. It is one of the ill-effects of great age and rank, I'm afraid – one thinks less before speaking."

"It's nothing, altzan-al," Anton said. He was struck by an urge to comfort the old man. "It has been a great privilege to speak with you at all."

Ramnie nodded courteously. "Well, we must make another opportunity, if you can stand it. If the Vosians interest you, I have a book you might enjoy: Xirco's *Southern Travels*. He was a vertzan under the emperor Prull, and when Jemestia fell to Miroline he helped bring the faith there, and encountered Vosians when there were still Vosians to encounter. He was an unimpeachable servant of the Mountain, Ving won't mind you reading him."

Ving might mind if he knew where the book came from, Anton thought. But he also had the distinct impression that this was not an offer that could be declined.

"Most kind of you, altzan-al," he said.

"Come by tomorrow, after Ving's opening address," Ramnie said. "Everyone will be busy making ready for the Conclave, including Dreyff."

A meeting hidden from Ving and hidden from Dreyff? It suggested more than the innocent loan of a book, and Anton prickled with caution. But a foul magic had been worked in mentioning Ramnie's lieutenant, for there he was, waiting on his horse in the middle of the road ahead, surrounded by a knot of bored Zealots.

"Ah," Ramnie said quietly. "It appears I am in for a mighty frowning."

Anton found himself laughing, though the sound died on his lips when he caught Dreyff's eye.

7

INAR

"Almost like being on a quest, isn't it?" said Lott. "Crossing the mountains, like Augardine. Like in Klintoe."

"Almost," Inar said. "Except they were trying to save the world. We're just trying to stop some rich idiots from killing themselves." He looked back at the rest of the expedition. All day they had struggled, mule-step by mule-step, up a path that was no more than a ledge in the side of a jagged canyon, in places as narrow as a bookshelf. They were climbing, steadily but not smoothly: the way did not rise in a slope, but in abrupt and uneven steps, some waist high. It had snowed all day, a grainy snow of tiny hard particles that stung like salt crystals. Scouring wind mostly swept the pass clear, but in sheltered turns drifts had formed and had to be shovelled away. Every step ran the risk of encountering polished ice. A roughly level stretch of pass, as wide as a man's arm and as long as a table, felt as vast and accommodating as the plains of Wenodar. The worst, though, the absolute worst, were the places in which they had to descend in order to move forward, and all sense of mounting the pass was lost.

The valley itself was not deep, but its sides were steep, and at its bottom was a raging torrent of spring meltwater, more like liquid rock than water, a thrashing brown serpent that roared and boomed without pause. As they zigzagged their way up, the party periodically had to cross the furious little tributaries of this stream, which cut across their route – of course, those gaps and traps were the iciest patches.

Some distance back, Inar could see Anzola, Kielo and Duna at the outermost point of one of these zigs, a blunt ridge between streams. They were no more than a few score yards away, if one drew a straight line through the snow-specked air, but their path to where Inar and Lott stood, at the outer point of the next ridge, was several times longer, a long V into one of the corrugations of the valley-side, with a stream to forge at its apex. They had stopped, as they had at almost every single one of these outer points, to set up their tripod and other equipment, and take measurements.

In between them and Inar, strung down and up the V of path, were the six knights accompanying the expedition – tall, well-fed Leaguers, splendid in fur-lined leather armour, rather grand for their task of leading stumbling, angry mules. There were twenty animals in total, roped together, and the knights were trying to coax them along the path and across the torrent without losing any over the edge. Inar had hardly believed his eyes when he had seen the herd of mules at Sojonost that morning. "You'll be grateful for them soon enough," Anzola said. "We've more than enough for all the provisions, and a riding rotation." But just as Inar had predicted – noisily, at length – they had been more burden than assistance. Riding was mostly impossible, so half of them were under-loaded. Two of them carried nothing but fodder for the others. If any one of them should lose its footing entirely and disappear into the valley, it was possible that the rest would follow – and Inar found he could see as much good as bad in that possibility. As it was, he intended to propose slaughtering at least two of the animals at the soonest opportunity.

"We need to push on," Inar called out to the nearest knight, one of the two that spoke Mirolingua. His name was Miroslo. "Tell the merite she needs to pack up and move."

"You tell her!" Miroslo called back, with a pained smile. "They say they're almost done."

"The light won't last," Inar said. His throat was raw from shouting instructions down the pass all day. "With snow in the sky it'll get dark quick. We can't stop here and we can't move when it's dark."

Miroslo frowned. "How much further is it?"

"I don't know," Inar said. He had come this way, once, when much younger – he knew there was a wider, flatter portion of valley ahead, a vale of stone, but they had moved so haltingly that he feared it was hours away. They would have to camp – to try to camp – on the path itself, eleven people and twenty mules stretched out in a line, perched on a lip of uneven, freezing stone above a deafening torrent with more of the characteristics of a meat-grinder than a brook.

"It *is* a bit like Klintoe," Lott said. "The Elves have returned. That part's like Klintoe."

"Yeah, but when I read Klintoe," Inar said, "I'm not half-hoping that the Elves win."

The light failed, and they were obliged to spend the night on the ledge. The canvas and rope that should have been their tents was used to restrain the unhappy mules on the rock face, and the complicated and dangerous work to truss them there had to take place in near-total darkness, lit only by hand-held oil lamps, which shed just enough light to remind them that they were almost blind. By no more than a miracle, no men or animals went over the edge, but the toll on lamps and other equipment was great: bundles of firewood, slabs of canvas, wooden boxes and sacks of food all managed to crash into the canyon. Firewood, but no room for a fire. Inar and Lott weathered the darkness huddled together, backs against the rock face, a line at their waists as a precaution against falling. They had several blankets and furs – here the League's generosity with provisions was welcome – but the stone-funnelled wind meant they felt as thin as fine lace. Sleep was not only improbable, Inar thought it might be deadly, and he fretted about the others as he listened to the gnashing of the torrent, the piteous complaints of the mules and the whistling of the wind.

All day, the hardships and frustrations of their slow passage into the mountains had been sugared by the sense that he was proving a point. He had told the merites that the pass could not be used by an army, they had asked to be shown, and he was showing them. His eagerness to be proved correct had led him to make an error almost as bad as theirs. He had let himself be placed at the head of this expedition, when he was grievously unqualified. At first he had believed that the League's arrogance would kill people; now he feared that his own arrogance might kill them all.

When the grey line of dawn split the jagged mountains from the sky, Inar had made up his mind: he would recommend that they turn back towards Sojonost, with the military uselessness of the pass well proven. He even dared imagine that there would be little resistance from the merite, that a miserable night clinging to the edge of an icy mountain would soften her views. Two entwined thoughts warmed him as the sky lightened and the first rays of sun picked out the snowcaps on the peaks opposite: he had survived the night, and there would not be another like it.

Once it was light enough to consider moving safely down the path, over the men and animals lashed to it, Inar began to stir, massaging feeling back into his muscles and joints, shifting the weight of the dozing Lott away from him. But he had not yet stood when he heard a scattering of pebbles from towards the rear. He raised himself to see Anzola picking her way past the second-nearest mule.

"Good morning," Anzola said, as if encountering him at the breakfast table at Sojonost. For a moment, Inar was seized by the certainty that she had reached the same conclusion as he, and his hopes surged, an inner dawn. It did not last. "We should get moving as soon as possible. It looks like it might be a beautiful day."

"You want to continue?" Inar croaked. Anzola did not look unrested – though the previous day's work had left her as dirty and untidy as the others, there was pink in her cheeks and a shine in her eyes. She, Duna and Kielo were dressed similarly – sheepskin coats and pants, perhaps derived from the costume of the people of the land of the auroras, re-imagined by Pallestran artisans more accustomed to aristocratic riding gear. Though it was not unlike Inar and Lott's own sheepskins, they made the Mishigo feel a hide-clad barbarian or knome in comparison. Each of them topped the ensemble with a white fur, taken from an ice-bear.

"Naturally I want to continue," Anzola said. "We have work to do."

"The case is made," Inar said. "You can't get an army through this pass."

"We are managing it," Anzola retorted. She was unusually sharp with him, perhaps the only indication of a poor night's sleep. "Really, Inar. I thought mountain people were made a little more rugged than this. One uncomfortable night is not such a sacrifice."

"Even if you can move the men," Inar said, conscious of the fact that he was repeating himself, "you can move very little in the way of supplies, and certainly no siege weapons. Do you know what Elith-Tenh is? A vast, treeless plateau. Little grows there. No food, no firewood. And at its far end, once you've fought through tens of thousands of starvation-trained Zealots, backed with *bindlings and titans*, there's a fortress reputed to make Sojonost look like a pigsty."

"Craithe's Brink," Anzola said, almost wistfully. "You've seen it?"

"From a distance," Inar said. "From a great distance."

Once again, he had the agonising sense that nothing he said to Anzola really stuck with her, that it was like the hard, dry snow that fell the day before, and just pattered off her coat.

"I want to see it myself. We have to get to the Sight of God. Do you know where that is?"

"Yes." Of course Inar knew where it was. It was the destination for nine out of ten of the pilgrims who came this way – it gave the faithful the chance to gaze upon their God without actually entering Elith-Tenh.

"We need to be there for the day of Spring Rout," Anzola said, naming a minor festival four nights hence. "Is that possible?"

"Yes, it's possible, but not if we move as slowly as we did yesterday." He rubbed his eyes. "Can you see the difficulties? We might be able to make it, but an army could not. Imagine this, but facing an enemy – suicide."

"Even if we do have to bring through a force, it will be with the assistance of the Tzanate," Anzola said. "Anyway, it doesn't matter. There are things we must do. Let's rouse the rest of the company and get the animals on their feet. I want to be ready to move as soon as Duna gets back."

"Gets back? Where is she?"

But Anzola was not listening. She was staring into the canyon, at the frothing brown water below. "Such a pity there's no room for a fire."

All of the Leaguers agreed that it was a pity about the fire. They seemed more chagrined about it than they had the previous night, when it might have meant the difference between life and death. But Inar then recalled the journey from Sojonost; how, each morning, the company had been unable to move until a hot, black drink had been prepared, the same they drank after the meals. While they were drinking it they all had a conversation about how good and hot and welcome the black drink was. Inar and Lott had both tried the drink. Though it smelled good, it tasted bitter, and they did not understand how the Leaguers could not only enjoy it, but treat it as essential as bread or beer. Meltwater was plentiful, but clearly not as comforting.

None of the mules had died, but one had become lame and it was agreed that it should be killed. A knight would stay behind with it, and do the deed once the expedition had moved some distance, so as not to disturb the other animals.

"What should he do with the carcass?" Miroslo asked Inar, translating for the knight given the task, whose name was Timo.

Inar shrugged. "It's a shame we can't butcher it. We might be grateful for that meat in a few days. Tell Timo to push it into the canyon, if he can. The birds will come for it."

"Of course," Miroslo said, with a badly concealed look of disgust. "I forgot where we are."

Inar shrugged, doing his best to play the part of the sturdy, unsentimental mountain-man. They had not seen any vultures in the snow the day before, but now they were above, three or four of them, circling in the sun-warmed air. "We eat it, they eat it. Prepared differently."

"I do prefer mine cooked," Miroslo said. "By the tide, I wish we had a fire."

The expedition moved a little faster on the second day. There was less chatter and no more endless circling of questions and instructions. Each of the party had a better idea of their particular role, and settled into it. Even Anzola was more helpful, suggesting that Lott and Inar simply keep moving when her rearguard stopped to make measurements. But, given his responsibility for the group's safe passage, Inar did not like to leave sight of the merite and her companions until he knew they were moving.

As a consequence, Inar spent a great deal of the day standing at the outer point of each ridge between side-valleys, looking back at the previous ridge, waiting for the others to pack up and move on. And he noticed that making measurements was not all that they were doing.

Every time they stopped at one of these natural vantages, with clear sight up and down the canyon, at first they would set up the tripod and look back at their last location, where a striped pole had been left. Then they would look around, pointing the spyglass upwards – finding recognisable points among the peaks, Inar assumed. But why? To take measurements? Establishing a straight-line distance was an exercise in pure reason where practical conditions were much more important. What does it matter, knowing that it is a straight one hundred yards between points, when one must walk a zigzagging goat-trail instead? But he was thinking in his father's voice, he realised.

Once they had finished the measurements, and Kielo put his pocket book back in his coat, they were never *entirely* finished. Duna always accompanied them, but didn't do much measuring. She would dawdle around, sometimes helping, but mostly looking cold, kicking stones and staring up at the walls of the canyon all around. At the end of each stop, however, Anzola and Kielo would converse with her. Even though the words could never be heard, even in the clear air of the mountains, the format was plain. Anzola would question Duna. Duna would give her opinion on something, gesturing at the surrounding terrain. Once – and this, for Inar, was the telling sign – she made a point by taking off her gloves and laying her white hands on the surface of the canyon wall.

Inar knew the scene. He had watched kings and generals and nobles asking his father's views on how to arrange a camp or a quarry or a system of defences. And he had seen his father giving his view. Duna was not a builder. From their contact over the past days, Inar had learned that she knew a little about stoneworks and architecture, picked up from spending her life in Anzola's company. But the merite wasn't training her, she was *consulting* her.

Then, during one such stop, the three Leaguers noticed Inar watching them. A more intense and secretive huddle ensued, during which Duna actually gestured towards Inar. A short time later, Miroslo caught up with Inar. "The merite is keen to make better time," he said. "They will be making fewer stops. We are instructed to keep moving."

Inar had not attributed much importance to the huddle – it had just been of mild interest to him, a distraction on a cold, tiring, repetitive day of trudging up a rocky path. But once this instruction came back, he realised that he had seen something of note. He had seen something that he was not supposed to have seen.

8

ANTON

"Forgive me, father librarian, but have you lost your mind?"

Anton thought he had seen the extremes of disgust and horror that could form on a human face – he was a blade priest, after all, and his life's work was meant to produce those expressions – but this morning was providing some novelties. Altzan Ikkosh's features, never very pleasant, were contorted with rage. Altzan Strang, who had spoken, was as pale as sour milk and looked ready to throw up. Even altzan Dionny, normally the most sanguine of the group, was grim. Elecy was sat beside him, and he could not bring himself to look at her face, but she gripped his hand so tight it pained him, her fingers white with the effort.

Altzan Ving, the Brink's chief librarian, arbiter of scripture, defender of traditions, second in rank to the altzan-al, was the object of this disbelief and dismay. And he was taking it with unnatural calm. Ving had been in sole charge of Anton and Elecy's instruction since the day that vertzan Leass was struck mad. While his knowledge of the Mountain faith's rites and practices was of unrivalled depth, the shallowness of his good humour was even more famous. Yelling for a day and then sulking for a week was his usual pattern; he had grudges older than anyone else in the room. But, accused of treachery and idiocy by his closest lieutenants, he was keeping a grip on his temper. In fact, a grip wasn't even needed – he was simply composed. He leaned forward, elbows resting on the blackened ebony surface of his desk, one hand held in the other, regarding his councillors evenly. No fury flickered in those drooping grey eyes.

"Believe me, Strang, I am seeing more clearly than I have in years," he said.

"Are you?" Ikkosh snarled. "Embracing Ramnie, that's one thing, a bit of political theatre, but embracing the League? This is blasphemy!"

For a moment Ving looked ready to reply, but he had seen altzan Dionny motioning to speak, and indicated she should go first. Passing up his turn to speak? This behaviour exceeded unnatural, Anton thought – it was positively eerie.

"I don't believe that any of us are opposed to a reconciliation with the altzan-al's party," Dionny said, the strain of tact sounding in her every word. The way that altzan Ikkosh flinched at this careful statement suggested that it might be more than an exaggeration, but she was allowed to continue. "But alliance with the League heathens is a very different matter. We do not doubt that you have your reasons for going along with this perverse plan of the altzan-al's, but we are impatient to hear them."

"Thank you for crediting me with reason, at least," Ving said, raising his bushy eyebrows and showing a little of his customary spikiness. The traditionalist priests had gathered in Ving's study, in the library tower, for a meeting that would have been to discuss their Conclave strategy, if they had not just learned that their leader had agreed to all of their enemy's demands. "First, brothers and sisters, you must acquaint yourselves with our defeat. The Conclave has not yet begun, and it is finished already. Our cause is lost." He delivered this news without obvious pain or regret.

"Father librarian, we always knew that our task here would be a difficult one," Strang said, "but I thought that we were agreed, at least, to make our case – and that many tzans and altzans in the church beyond this land share our disquiet at the reforms undertaken by the altzan-al, the abandonment of our traditional allies, the suspension of the terrible and glorious sacrament of the Gift…" He glanced nervously at Anton and Elecy, and Anton did his best to appear aloof, holy and terrible.

Ving was waving away Strang's remarks. "The world has changed," he said, a profoundly un-Ving statement. "The Elves have changed it. As brother Anton has just reported to us, they are killing our Zealots and threatening our safety. We expected that the Conclave would discuss the threat posed by the League, now that they hold Sojonost and have closed the passes to trade and pilgrims. The Elves, we thought, were fattening themselves in the west. But no – they are here, and closer every day. Do they frighten you at all, altzan Strang?"

Strang's double chin wobbled slightly. "Of course!" he said. "Who does not…"

"They frighten me as well, altzan Strang," Ving continued, "and I sit here in the midst of the world's greatest fortress, surrounded by thousands of Zealots, behind the further protection of hundreds of miles of wasteland *and* the Gull Gates, not to mention the Mirolinian fortress at Mal Nulalus, which is now in our hands – and I have no intention of moving from this spot! But our brothers and sisters from across the world, who have come here for this Conclave, will have to venture outside those defences, and return through hundreds of miles of wild road with Elven berserkers lining up behind every tree. How frightened do you imagine they are?"

"Very, I expect," Strang squeaked.

"Very!" Ving agreed. "And a frightened man will agree to anything. I don't agree with Ramnie's proposed alliance, of course I don't, but I do admire it as politics. He takes one enemy and uses it to defeat another. And uses it to defeat us, for that matter. He has forged a shining opportunity out of the fires of the world." His eyes widened as he reflected on the master-stroke of his old rival. "Worst of all, he's not even wrong! The Elves exceed anything else we face! The wolves of Tarch are at our gate once again! Their extermination is our greatest and most urgent religious duty, we must all agree. The Mountain will surely forgive a temporary arrangement made in the service of its security and sanctity."

"Temporary!" Ikkosh spat. Of all of the traditionalist altzans in Ving's circle, Anton liked Ikkosh the least. Dionny was warm and pragmatic, almost a moderate; Strang was a nervous but decent man, more terrified of change than opposed to it. Ikkosh, however, was a sour old bigot, made of twisted wire, who delighted in the bloodiest aspects of the Tzanate's past.

"The arrangement may be temporary but the dishonour is permanent," he continued. "What will Miroline make of this? And what about our supporters in the church? What will they think when they see us nodding along to this depraved pact!"

"Well, Miroline is not what it was," Ving said, a little sadly. Then he shook off this shadow and seemed filled with a sudden excess of energy, rising from his chair and pacing into the room, flanking his audience of priests. "Brother Ikkosh, I don't expect you to nod along with anything. You may speak your piece in the Conclave if you desire, you all may. Your disquiet will make my achievement as peacemaker all the more impressive."

"*What* have you achieved?" Ikkosh said. "Surrender might bring peace, but it's hardly an achievement!"

For a second Anton feared that the priest was crossing a line, that his rage was tipping over into insubordination and might puncture Ving's rare good humour. But it did not.

"Ikkosh, calm yourself," Ving said, pleasantly, laying a hand on the priest's shoulder as he passed. He skirted the bookshelves that lined one side of the room, looking without seeing, and then came to rest in front of a painted panel depicting the Emperor Augardine as lawgiver. "Remember, we will be defeated at this Conclave whatever we do. If we are intransigent, if we resist and reject and moan and wail, we will forfeit what little influence we have. But if we bend a little, if we allow Ramnie his united front, his gratitude will keep us in the heart of power. Do you understand?"

"What good will that do, if we have already given up everything?" Ikkosh asked. The hard edge of his anger had softened a little, Anton noted – he was wavering. His eyes, strangely, were not on Ving's, but instead on the painted panel that Ving's hand rested against.

Ving patted the image of Augardine absent-mindedly. "Friends, do you imagine I would embark on this reconciliation with the altzan-al if it did not serve our interests?" he said. "The pact with the League will be temporary – I will see to it. What is also temporary is Ramnie's time as altzan-al. We have been readmitted to the Tzanate's military council, and we have a path clear to a greater prize: the throne itself." With this, he smiled, eyes wide and glittering. He was more than composed, he was exultant.

"Opportunity, that's the thing," he said, quickly retracing his steps to his desk. "Using a moment to maximum advantage. That is what Ramnie has done, the old fox, and that is what we must do."

"And what of the Gift?" Ikkosh said. "What of the blood sacrament? Are we to concede that our most ancient rite is at an end?"

This caused them all to turn their gaze on Anton and Elecy, the two youngsters in a room of aged priests. Anton glanced at his sister in the faith, but she was looking squarely at Ving, waiting on his answer with precious, fragile hope etched all over her.

"For the time being, we must accept the altzan-al's judgement there," Ving said, with a mournful inclination of the head. "The League have made it a condition of the alliance."

Elecy's grip on Anton's hand slackened. She sagged in her seat, and although her eyes were now tightly closed, a tear escaped. Anton hated that her hopes had to be crushed for his to flourish, and he tried to look grim, squeezing her hand as she had clasped his.

"Anton, Elecy, I know that this is a bitter disappointment to you both," Ving said kindly. "I am certain that one day the sickle will be raised again. If you desire to make a protest at the Conclave, and be excused attendance, you have my blessing."

"Thank you, father librarian," Anton said. "That's very thoughtful of you."

Very thoughtful indeed. Uncharacteristically so.

The Craithe Hall, grandest of all the grand chambers of the Brink, was full to capacity. Tzans and altzans sat shoulder to shoulder and the air was warm and stale with their combined breath. More thronged the galleries above. Ving was coming to the end of what the schedule called "a service of welcome and a selection of traditional readings". Anton felt as if he had just sat through a wakemare, crossed with watching Elecy practising the blade on an unlucky pig.

"... The skin stripped from their living bodies and cut into flogging strips that lashed them while they bled into the open mouths of the foul ones that watched!" Ving screamed into the ashen faces of his audience. "Of lashes, the Elf-lord Ujhill was known to break the teeth from living victims in order to add them as spurs on his battle-flail – at Tassenodar, Ujhill was reputed..."

It was a traditional reading, Anton supposed. It came from Filcrid's *Deeds of the Elves*, one of the more graphic and unlikely accounts of the Elf-war – a book mostly ignored in the Brink's history curriculum and instead clandestinely passed around by acolytes looking for a cheap thrill. Anton had read it, of course – who had not? – and was fairly sure that Ving was embellishing an already gaudy text.

Disreputable the text might be, but the effect on the audience was undeniable – they were rigid with alarm. Elecy, by contrast, hardly seemed to be listening at all. The blade-priests had been seated in a niche behind the speakers' dais, where the assembled Conclave could see them at all times, baleful in their robes and masks. Anton's companion had said nothing since the meeting that morning, and misery radiated from her. Between the mask and the shapeless coil of white robes, she might have been taken for something inanimate – a disused marionette, perhaps. The only indications of the humanity within were a patch of pale neck between the mask's straps and the robe's top, and a faint glimmer behind the eye-slit.

The masks had one advantage – they could converse without being noticed. Anton leaned towards his sister. "A little much, don't you think?" he said softly. "I know it serves Ramnie to scare them, but if Ving keeps this up they won't want to go home at all."

Elecy did not move. "I really don't think jokes are appropriate."

"You seem very unhappy, sister," Anton said with tenderness. "I hoped to make you smile."

"*Smile*?" Now the mask turned to him, ghastly in aspect, and there was certainly no smile behind it. Belatedly Anton remembered that his sister was armed. So was he, but she knew how to use hers. "You desire me to *smile*? After what has happened this morning?" The beak swung back to face the audience. "Sometimes you mystify me, Anton. Sometimes I think you don't want to be a blade priest at all."

For a ghastly moment, Anton thought his mask might have slipped – not the ridiculous contraption of wood and leather on his head, but his real mask, the one he wore all day and night. He could never quite believe that the priests around him didn't already know – the thought hammered so loudly in his head, at all times, he fancied it must be audible on the outside, or could be read in his eyes, in gilded capitals. He didn't want the Gift to resume. He didn't want to tear the beating heart from a victim and feed it to a demigod. Maybe it was necessary, part of the mechanics of the universe, as the altzans around him believed and he pretended to believe. Even if that were true, he didn't see why he should have to be the one to do it. He would prefer to do anything else. That day, five years ago, when the altzan-al had announced that the Custodians no longer wished to receive the Gift, when he had been robbed of all purpose and meaning and had been turned into a curiosity and an embarrassment, had been the happiest of his life.

"Of course I do," he said.

Elecy was silent. Though he could not see it, Anton could picture her pinched brow. He did not mind the inflexibility of his sister's faith – they were surrounded by militants, this was Brink – but it sometimes caused her such palpable distress, which saddened him. So she was tormented by certainties, and he by doubts. Was there no comfortable way to bear faith of their intensity? His secret wish, his most intense desire, was granted, sparing him from a life of murder – but it condemned Elecy to a life of disappointment. What could he do to soften that blow?

"We don't have to be here," he said. "Altzan Ving said we were free to protest, to absent ourselves. We know what will happen here, and we cannot change that outcome. Let's have no part of it."

Elecy's head sunk a little, but she did not respond.

Action, then, Anton thought. Do not wait for her agreement. He rose to his feet, with all the poise and dignity he could muster. In the atmosphere of tension that Ving's oratory had created, the movement was immediately noticed by the audience. For the second time in three days, he felt as if every priest in the world was watching him. Ving faltered mid-sentence, turning to see the cause of the shift in attention. Ramnie, watching from his throne in another niche, had also leaned out to see.

Anton walked at a stately pace towards the nearest door. His face burned behind his mask, and he listened to the creak of his feet on the boards of the dais, fearing at every step that he might seem petulant rather than dignified, or ridiculous rather than noble. But he heard a noise that put him at ease: a second set of footsteps behind his own. Elecy was following.

So they passed from public sight – for good, Anton hoped. While the circus of the Conclave took over most of the monastery-palace, the older altzans had urged the young blade-priests to be discreet. They were only to be seen in public masked and robed during the formal sessions, in their peculiar niche behind the stage. But no one in the Tzanate, regardless of their factional persuasion, wanted them to be seen in informal settings. They were told to eat and bathe privately and to be careful of the routes they chose, shunning the more public areas.

The Tzanate was unusually united in this edict. The altzans who wanted to resume the giving of the Gift also wanted to maintain the mystique of the vertzans, and they evidently feared that the sight of two nineteen-year-olds eating noodles rather than standing over the steaming entrails of a sacrificial victim would fatally undermine the prestige and dignity of the thousand-year sacrament they wished to restore. This, Anton realised, was a refined form of embarrassment – a preference for dealing with the whole business of the Gift as an idea, a glorious myth, and to quietly forget the messy business of a person tearing the heart from the living body of another person. And the reformers were simply embarrassed about them, and the Gift, and many other aspects of the Tzanate's mystery and flummery. Altzans like Dreyff were in a constant low-level cringe at what the rest of the world thought of the isolated community at the Brink, surrounded by relics and ruins conducting bloody rites for arcane and magical reasons.

In spite of being barred from public areas, Anton and Elecy could still move around the Brink with relative ease.

The Tzanate's leaders had long valued discretion, and the importance of ritual theatre – they liked to be able to appear in rooms without being seen to move. Perhaps it was another habit they had picked up from the Custodians. In any case, the fortress was riddled with hidden ways to get around. A term like "secret passages" seemed childish to Anton, as these routes hadn't always been built with secrecy in mind. The sprawling fortress-monastery had been rebuilt, reorganised and extended so many times that it also had a fair share of corridors, attics and undercrofts that had simply been forgotten, and could now be used to quietly slip from one chamber to another without being noticed.

These were the tricks of the senior altzans, which included the blade-priests, despite their youth. A paradox of great rank: it wasn't all marble and teak, one spent a surprising amount of time in dusty back stairs, brick vaults and storerooms where even servants preferred not to venture. Anton and Elecy had eaten their middle meal together in the small scriptorium that adjoined their quarters. Though they spoke little, Elecy's mood was much restored, and she showed no sign of suspicion when, some time after eating, he made his excuses and slipped away. Now he feared he was running early for his assignation. His path from the library tower to the altzan-al's office took him through a gallery overlooking Augardine's mausoleum, and, knowing no one else would come that way, he paused to take in the scene.

The Brink had been transformed by Augardine, just as he had transformed the faith, the Empire, and the world. He had found a haphazard fortress spanning the only pass between the Elith-Tenh and Craithe – formidable, but miserable. It was he who turned it into a palace and a city, one better suited to the world-conquering religion he had created. And the centrepiece of this new Brink was to be a vast processional hall stretching from one end of the complex to the other, with an immense window framing the Mountain at the far end.

It was imagined as a terminus for the web of roads he was carving through the lands he had subdued, a physical link between the Mountain and Miroline. The unity of Empire and Craithe made manifest.

As such, the processional hall was a slice of the distant south: a floor of green Mirolinian marble, sparkling white columns of Vellene quartz, a barrel-vaulted roof lined with Estami gold leaf. How those materials must sparkle under the southern sun, Anton wondered – how dull they were in the bowels of Elith-Tenh and the Brink. Neither sun nor Mountain illuminated the arcade – there was no great window at its end. Instead, the last stretch of the processional was sealed with slabs of black basalt, thickly inlaid with Custodian runes. Behind three feet of basalt was another enclosure, built in a hurry from rougher stones and mortar composed by arcane and forbidden methods. Behind that lay the corpse of Augardine, pinned to the marble floor by the helling-blade that had been forged especially to kill him, surrounded by bindling bones and the wreckage of battle. The Emperor's duel with the Custodians had been such a frenzied outburst of contradictory magic that it had permanently tainted the fabric around it. The Brink itself might have been made uninhabitable were it not for the frantic effort to build this sarcophagus. Traces of foulness still lingered – there were sealed chambers, and regions of the fortress that had never been rebuilt. No written records of wakemares existed from before Augardine's death. They began after.

Here ended the great experiment. Never again would the Custodians raise a man or a woman to their level. Not far away, altzans were speaking of the Holy Alliance between the Empire and the Tzanate as something that had lapsed only recently, when Miroline withdrew its legions from Mal Nulalus. That was true, in a sense. But the union that Augardine had founded, the original Holy Alliance, when man and Custodian had treated as equals, had died with him. And the Tzanate had helped the Custodians in ending it, fearful of the demigod they had helped create.

Augardine's Tomb was a monument to error and failure. Still, they came here to pay their respects – and maybe more. The greatest Emperor could not be damned without damning his legacy, so he was officially revered, as a man. But it was forbidden to worship him as a God.

Looking down into the Processional Way, Anton feared that more than a few of the visiting tzans and altzans had forgotten that proscription. The hall, usually a bare and echoing place, was thronged. Two fleets of candles were anchored in rivers of wax on either side of the approach to the tomb. Offerings – food and wine, palms and prayer-flags – were heaped at its base.

Anton had heard whispers of a cult of Augardine within the church, who held the heretical belief that Augardine was worthy of outright worship. No one here in the reach of the Custodians would indulge in that blasphemy, but what of these visitors? Plump senior altzans, representatives of whole cities, provinces and kingdoms, stood with their heads bowed, flanked by their subordinates. They lingered, making sure all their lackeys and underlings saw them paying homage – meanwhile those lackeys and underlings put on their own displays of dignity and silence, hoping to be seen. The opulence of these groups, in their embroidered silk robes, was contrasted by the wild and solitary tzans who represented no place, and spread the Mountain's light on the roads. They were ragged and busy, flinging themselves at the sarcophagus and wailing, intoning prayers and lessons, or writhing around on the ground as if in the grips of a wakemare. *As if.* Anton had seen many wakemares in his time. The sufferers often raved, but they were marked by a fearful rigidity, their spines arching, their eyes rolling back in their heads. Not the energetic dance routines that were going on down there. Both extremes of tzanhood – the rich and the wild – were baffling to Anton. Both seemed erroneous. So what was correct? His own conduct? Was he above them all?

It struck him as unlikely. But he did have a private meeting with the altzan-al to attend.

9

INAR

The pilgrims called it the Cup of Silence. They climbed a precarious natural staircase of shattered layers of stone into a gentler world. It was a wide, curved valley, still bounded by the same gruesome peaks, but softer of line and more inviting as a path, bending steadily up and out of view. The whole natural scoop of the land was sheltered from the wind and thickly filled with undisturbed snow, which rose in blankets up the sides of the pass. After the unceasing meltwater din of the canyon, the quiet rang in the head like a peal of bells.

Pilgrim custom was to traverse this stretch in silence. Inar mentioned this to Miroslo, but did not insist on it. They were not believers, so let them prattle if they wished. But to his surprise, the usual back-and-forth, the constant shouting of instructions and warnings in Palla, naturally died away, and quiet spread down the line. The place enforced its own rules. They proceeded with only the accompaniment of the crunching of frozen snow and the rough breathing of the animals.

It was not easy going, though. The snow was thigh deep, and interleaved with crusts of ice which would take the weight of a foot long enough to make the climber imagine they had reached solid ground, only to crack and trip them. Inar and Lott had brought with them staffs and used them as walking sticks, and to probe the path ahead; the others followed in their trail.

Towards the end of the second day, as the shadows began to swell and turn bruise shades of blue and purple, they were not far beyond the point they should have stopped on the first night. Pushing through the snow had taken Inar to the point of exhaustion. The long, straggling line of the previous day had gathered itself up, keeping closer to him. His head throbbed and a sick, sucking fatigue had grown in him like a pit, swallowing every vestige of strength. When he discovered Anzola at his shoulder, wheezing and suggesting that they make camp early, he could not disagree – indeed, he was filled with relief.

"The mountain sickness," Lott said, as they all dug snow to clear a campsite. "We should not be here."

"Were you never brought up here, for the Sight?" Inar said.

Lott darkened. "It was just me and Lem, wasn't it? Lem didn't really care for the rites, he was only just a man himself, none had done it for him."

"Of course," Inar said. "Forgive me." He had never known his mother, taken by fever when he was no more than a babe, but he had known his father a time, at least. Lott had only ever had his elder brother, until he fell at Halsk Trun.

Lott's Mirolingua was basic, and he used Mishigo whenever possible, as now. But Inar noticed that his accent thickened, and he ran words together, avoiding names, as if he was trying to make his words even harder to follow for the Leaguers around them. "The lady, right? A builder, one of *their* builders. Does walls and forts – also siegecraft, right? 'S why she's a big deal with the army, and that big guy at the feast, the boss."

"Right," Inar said.

"So she would have been in charge at Stull," Lott said. He had stopped digging, and was staring at Inar. "At the siege."

"Yes," Inar said. He had been slow to realise this himself, and now Lott was putting it together.

"She would have known about the walls," Lott said.

"Yes," Inar said, his jaw tense.

"What I'm saying–"

"I know what you're saying," Inar interrupted. "When my father betrayed Stull, he betrayed it to her."

No one opened the gates of Stull, or drugged its watchmen. The capital was lost by vanity. Before the war came, King Essian decided that the ancient city's greatness – and thus his own greatness – was constrained by its tight girdle of ancient walls. Inar's father, the chief builder, was charged with laying out new walls to enclose an enlarged city, one more befitting the glorious country that Essian imagined Mishig-Tenh might become. But the king's grandiosity made him impatient, as it often is with the powerful: they confuse the wish with its fulfilment, the command and the deed, and forget that they are not the same. The quarries could only provide so much cut stone each month, and it was figured that it might take a decade to complete the walls. To speed the process, Essian ordered that the old walls be taken down, and their stone re-used – at the cost of leaving the city without walls for a time.

Before the new walls were finished, the king of Oririthen began whispering in Essian's ear. The League was plump and vulnerable, he hinted. Peace had made it weak. The hardy mountain lands should ready themselves for war. The next summer, Oririthen would humble Pallestra, and Mishig-Tenh would reclaim the lost lands as far as Matchfalls. But the walls were not yet done, there was a gap between the eighth tower and the tenth.

A secret instruction was issued: the walls had to be rushed. The completed sections were solid masonry twelve feet thick, with machicolations and archery positions all along. But there was no time for that. To give the walls the illusion of completion, the outer stonework was built between the eighth and tenth bastions, no more than a foot thick – little more than a curtain, like the backdrop used by travelling players. Behind was nothing but thick scaffolding, to prop the stone and conceal the ruse. No more than twenty senior masons knew of the wall's precarious state. Inar's father pleaded with the court to allow more time to finish it properly, but was rebuffed. He asked for men to be spared from the levy, but was refused. Essian was convinced that victory in the field was certain. The League would never come close to Stull.

The war came; so too did the League's armies, after their shattering victory at Halsk Trun. The siege, at least, was over quickly. They knew exactly where to concentrate their trebuchets and mangonels, tearing away the section of wall between the eighth and tenth towers like a cobweb and ignoring the rest. They knew. Someone had told them.

Once Otto V was on the throne and peace was made, Lord Cilma's attention turned to the matter of treachery. Inar's father knew that suspicion would fall on him, and he freely confessed in an effort to spare the others. But Cilma's rage was not sated, and every senior builder was killed. They stopped only when they reached Inar.

Camp was made before darkness fell, and with a fire burning and the prospect of a long sleep ahead, the expedition's spirits rose. Making use of the loitering light, Anzola and Kielo went to make more of their arcane measurements at the edge of the valley, with a couple of knights as bodyguard. The remaining knights cooked and laughed at the fire, and Inar and Lott reclined on sacks of mule feed and gladly talked of nothing.

Even as his mood improved, Inar's thoughts returned to the betrayal of Stull. What might Anzola know about his father? This question partly sprang from fear. Avoid a siege and save lives – that was Astar's given reason for what he did, one that Lord Cilma accepted, while still taking care to murder everyone in sight. It was a rationale Cilma could well understand, as he had driven his knife into a king while thinking similar thoughts.

But Cilma had not been at the dining table in Inar's keep all those evenings before the war, when the oil burned low, after the servants had retired, when Astar and Essian had spoken of their admiration for the League, its superior methods, the liberties it offered. There was treason, and there was *treason*. Betraying Stull as a misguided effort to halt the bloodshed was one thing; betraying Stull because Astar sincerely wished to see the League rule over Mishig-Tenh was quite another. Part of Inar's suspicion of the League, and his hatred of it, was fear of those deadly ideas, and the way they had seduced and doomed his father. And he was afraid that a careless word from Anzola might cause Lord Cilma to see the betrayal in an unwelcome new light.

That was part of why the question nagged at him – but there was more to it. Hearing a little about unseen parts of his father's life would reopen a book that was closed. In a small way, for a short time, Inar's father would live again, and he found he craved that more than he dared admit.

However, there was a way to ask about Anzola and Astar indirectly – a way to establish what the merite might know. She was seated near Inar and Lott, in the same orbit around the fire, alone with her thoughts.

Inar lifted himself from reclining to sitting, and made a big show of warming his hands. "Miss Duna," he said, keeping his tone light. "May I ask you something?"

The girl regarded him a little warily, but not unkindly. "Please, call me Duna."

Inar took this as permission to proceed. "Lott and I were talking about this earlier. I assume you know about my father. Did Anzola know him at all? Did you?"

"Assume I know *what* about your father?" Duna asked, withdrawing her hands into her cloak and furrowing her brow.

"About what happened at Stull," Inar said. What else was

there? Lott had propped himself up on his elbows and was listening in to the conversation. "About what he did."

"Oh," Duna said. Her face lost its pinch. "Yes, of course. I did meet him, a couple of times, before the war. And your brother, Essian, once. In Matchfalls. I don't know what I can tell you, we didn't talk much. I was, you know, part of the scenery." She said this with a slight roll of the eyes, and Inar had a fractional glimpse of a childhood as part of Anzola's shadow.

Inar looked into the fire, trying to form a question, but none came.

"I thought what happened to them was horrible," Duna volunteered with what might have been the slightest shudder, or might have been the cold. "I do know that no one asked your father to do what he did. He wasn't paid, or threatened, or promised anything."

"I'm glad he wasn't pressured," Inar said, with a sigh. "It was his sacrifice. Or his error. But his alone."

"And he didn't lose the war," Duna said seriously. "We were going to win. He did spare lives, and I am glad..." More was clearly intended to followed this, but the girl abruptly quieted, and Inar sensed that the subject was closed. Anzola and Kielo were crunching through the snow towards the camp.

The next day, a short hike took them to the shore of the ice sea. The snow-buried valley they had followed since the previous morning joined a far wider gulf between razor peaks, filled with a seemingly unending slope of scree. The incline was not much, but the footing was loose. Every movement sent a small slide of pulverised rock and gravel downwards, into the tread of the rest of the company, and coaxing and controlling the reluctant animals was a challenge. And here the wind blew without halt, carrying with it stinging particles, sweeping everything clear of snow.

The ice sea itself was above – it was a poor name, Inar

thought, more a fortress than a sea, a filthy blue wall taller than that he had built at Stull, cut into crenellations, with torrents of furious brown water flying from it at intervals, as if it were trying to defend itself against them. Its spring melt had begun, but it had hardly retreated from its winter maximum – in severe winters it had been known to block the pass, but Inar could still see their destination ahead, a black aperture in the sheer faces of rock that bounded the valley. Above this crevice was the stump of a tower, built by the Custodians long before the Empire came, a vestige of their own vanished realm.

"We need to head towards that gap," Inar told Miroslo and Anzola when they approached to suggest a rest break. "There's a traditional resting-place further on, you're supposed to spend the night there before heading to the outlook. We can reach it tonight, if we climb hard and don't rest."

Anzola frowned. "We have a couple of days," she said. "I'd like to see the ice sea up close."

Inar worked his jaw. The wind felt as if it was stripping the skin from his cheeks – his coat and layers of hide and wool did little to impede it. "Here?"

"If we went to the foot of the ice sea, there'd be more shelter. Don't you want to see it?"

Inar looked up to the grimy blue line far above them. "No, not really. It's – it's not a good place." He didn't have to see it. He could hear it from here – the sound came rolling down the valley, a periodic cracking and creaking.

"It's evil," Lott said, in blunt Mirolingua. Inar flashed a look at him, frustrated again that he might make the mountain people appear fearful and superstitious, but his own reluctance had roots he could not explain. When tzans brought pilgrims through the pass, they stoked the ill-repute of the ice sea, attributing to it sickness and curses, and the disappearance of whole expeditions. It was a haunted place – could they not hear its growling, like a waking animal?

He winced at his own credulity. It was ice, just ice – a hazard, but a natural one.

"Supernatural reputations are often built on sensible caution," he said. "Pallestrans revere the sea and the tides, do they not? They are the source of your livelihood and your power, but also terribly dangerous, even to those who know them well."

Anzola nodded at this, but said: "We'll be cautious. But it is a sight I would not wish to miss."

The cliff face of the ice sea was surprisingly varied up close, but no less disturbing to Inar. Ice should really be white, or perhaps pale blue, but this – an immense mountain of ice, filling the valley from side to side – had a startling variation in colour, with pits and folds that turned an unnerving dark blue, and even shades of purple, green and dirty yellow. Deep chasms and caves had been made in the ice-cliff by the action of melting water, and in places torrents burst forth hurling spray. The endless grumbling was louder here, and there were occasional loud concussions that made the whole group jump – the structure shifting and moving as it melted. Another troubling feature of the place, for Inar, was that he could not read the ice. Had it been stone, he might have been able to tell if sections of the wall were about to collapse, and detect weak points to be avoided. But although he could hear the ice and see it, it was invisible to his other sense.

Once they had made camp, with some light left in the day, Anzola stated a desire to climb the ice wall and see what was above. Inar and the League knights scouted along its foot for some distance each way, looking for places in which it might have melted into a fortuitous ramp, but nothing helpful was found. Among the baggage the Leaguers had brought with them was a heavy bundle of siege tools: ropes and hooked iron grapples used for scaling the walls of enemy fortresses. The sight of this equipment – and the knowledge of why Anzola would be familiar with its use – depressed Inar.

By contrast, the knights and the merite were buoyant. The prospect of climbing the ice wall had rekindled their adventurous spirit, which had been dampened by the hardships of the past couple of days. Wedging himself into a crevice in the ice, and using pointed axes to pull himself up, a knight named Timo was first to the top. The grapples were then thrown to him, with ropes attached, and he secured them in the ice. With these lines secured, another two knights made the ascent, followed by Anzola, then Duna. Inar was a little surprised to see the girl make the ascent – it seemed unusually intrepid for her, who preferred to drag her feet and linger near the rear of the line, who was always last to leave her tent in the morning, and who gave every impression of hating every minute of their journey. But, nevertheless, she was here, and Inar noticed that her complaining had somewhat abated in the past day or two. Instead of sulkiness, there was a kind of stormy confidence in her – more pleasing than grousing and delay, but he did not desire to be on the wrong side of it.

It was then that he decided to make the ascent himself. Anzola did have a point – they had come all this way, why not? If the women were doing it, what was stopping him? He had no desire to appear, again, as the demon-haunted rustic, cowering in camp, while the representatives of reason and order explored new worlds.

Once Inar had made his ascent, he saw that only two knights stood at the anchors of the lines – Anzola, Duna and the third knight had struck out in different direction, taking in the vast auditorium they had discovered.

It was more of a sea once you were on its surface. A rippling, unsettled sea, mirror-bright and dazzling white in places, abyssal blue elsewhere, rucked into filthy creases at its centre. It was not a silent place, like the Cup – there was that continual growling and splintering – but it wanted quiet from its guests, it wanted you to strike out and be at one with it.

A seductive and dangerous place, then. Inar saw immediately that the spring melt had cut deep, sheer-sided crevasses into the ice, which would be dangerous even to approach, as their lips could collapse. He wanted to dash after the others and warn them, but it did not seem appropriate to run and shout in this place. Instead he made a slow pace in the direction of Anzola, hoping that she had taken a staff with her and was testing each step. Even that might not preserve the unlucky – Inar expected that meltwater would cut tunnels through the ice, and the roof of those tunnels could easily collapse under the weight of a climber.

Anzola was looking up, to a point higher in the mountains. The ice-sea, up there, resembled a great worm or a white tongue, pushing down between the rocks. Above were a line of black needles against a cloudless blue sky.

"I never imagined that ice would be the master of stone," Anzola said when she heard Inar approach.

"That can be seen every winter and spring, your grace," Inar said. "A simple frost can smash a wall."

Anzola shrugged. "Strange, how something so quiet and pale and beautiful can push aside mountains," she said. "A lesson to us. And, please, no 'your grace'. I think we are beyond that."

"Very well."

"The mountains simplify human relations, I think," Anzola said. "No aristocracy here. Only mutual aid, and survival."

"I have found it is often unwise to forget one's rank, anywhere," Inar said. "As a matter of survival."

Anzola looked at him, and then away, discomfited. "I forget, sometimes, how bloody your experience has been," she said.

"We have survived, in any case," he said. It might have been an opportunity to ask about his father, but he found that Duna had sated that curiosity for now. "The most difficult part of the passage is done. The outlook is a day away, and I expect the return will be less painful, now that we know the path."

Anzola nodded, businesslike. "Good. In good time. You have done well."

Inar stared down at the snow-caked wrappings of his boots. "I am glad to have been of service."

"Would you consider remaining in the service of the League?" Anzola asked, with an uncharacteristically gamine smile. "There is so much to do."

"I expect that Lord Cilma would frown upon that." He frowned at the thought of that frown. Had he gathered the information needed to avoid accusations of treachery? He knew the League's plans: they were here to prop up an altzan-al, and then make war on the Elves. Was that enough?

Anzola's smile was now more senior and reassuring. "You should not concern yourself too much with Lord Cilma. If you stayed with us, you would never have to deal with him again."

But he would abandon his home, his role, and everything he knew, to serve an alien power. No small price, even to be rid of Cilma's tyranny. *No small price…* The words of the merite Ernesto came back to him: *Our costly friends.* What cost? There was so much danger in not knowing the dealings between Anzola and Cilma. But there was no opportunity to ask. Kielo had ascended the ice cliff, and the measuring equipment was being brought up. "You must excuse me, Inar," Anzola said. "We are going to take some readings before the light goes. Perhaps you would assist me?"

"By all means."

"Please find Duna. She appears to have escaped my sight, and I like to keep her nearby. She can't have gone far."

Duna had gone far. Inar trudged across the trackless ice for the better part of an hour looking for her, as the shadows lengthened. He cut across the ice sea, keeping the huddle of men at the ascent-point in sight on his right side, trying to identify the route she had taken. Twice he had to make long detours to avoid fissures in the ice, each time heading up and away from the camp; still she eluded him, and he began to fear that she could have slipped past him going the other way, leaving him pursuing ghosts further and further from safety.

But the landscape contained a clue. It had not been clear from the edge of the sea, but as Inar walked it became more defined. Ahead stood a colossal overhang of bread-brown rock, frosted with snow. Once, aeons ago, it had been a minor peak, a spike like the higher points that ringed the valley. But the ice-sea had rubbed away its lower portion, leaving only a ghastly fang suspended in the air, attached on one side to the valley wall. The scene was still and quiet, but filled with slow violence: beneath this overhang, the ice sheet was rucked up and filthy with the effort of gnawing away at this projection. Terrible though it was, the overhang fired up curiosity, and Inar guessed that Duna might have approached it for a closer look, just as he wanted to do.

He was right. She stood on the far side of the overhang, a good distance away from it but in its stretching shadow. She was staring up at the overhang, rubbing her gloved hands together, fascinated. Inar did not like the thought of walking underneath the overhang to reach her. His instincts told him that it was secure, that it would stand like that for another hundred winters, but those instincts were less reliable when applied to natural structures. In any case, the uneven, creased surface of the ice beneath the jut would make for hard going, so he took a long course around, calling Duna's name. It was heavy going, and although the sinking sun was taking all the warmth from the valley as it went, he felt himself breaking into a hot sweat. He called again. She did not look away from the rock.

"Duna," Inar called, for the dozenth time, irritation seeping into his voice. "The sun is setting. We have to get back while we have light."

She said nothing, and stared.

"*Duna*. The merite has asked for you."

"Inar," Duna said at last, not looking away from the rock. "I'm glad you're here. Take care. It's about to go."

"About to go? *We* have to go."

"Watch, watch," she said. She had not so much as glanced towards him. "The rock, it's about to go."

He looked up at the overhang, and realised that he had been wrong. How could he have been so wrong? The weakness was in it like a fatal dart, and multiplying faster than he could tell.

A sound, distinct amid the grumbling of the ice-sea: a *tock*. Then a dry and distant report, a heavy book dropped onto a flagstone floor several dusty rooms away.

Then the big noise, a noise without a flavour or shape, just a whip-crack direct to the insides of the ear. Duna gasped and started to pace backwards. Inar wished there was time to take more than the few paces she took, because what was happening was already happening, but he could not move at all. He was fixed in place far more firmly than the overhang, which was moving, turning smoothly to one side as the whole vast weight of it sagged and then fell.

For a second it was free, surrounded only by the cold dusk air.

Then it struck the ice sea. And the sea performed to its name: it splashed, sending up an immense blue-white crown that swallowed up the falling spire. Inar saw no more because he was knocked from his feet. He felt, momentarily, as if he weighed nothing at all, and was a money-spider falling in a blind world of blue ice; there was screaming, and other noise, but lost in the surge around him. And then he was hurled against something hard, and felt the heaviness return, bringing with it pain and fear, and worse than that the reminder, which comes at bad times like this, that he was only a tiny fragile thing, in the world-sized theatre of gigantic and unsympathetic forces.

Followed by silence. Not silence: a symphony of sounds, the pattering and sifting and trickling of powdered rock and ice finding lower levels, the dull, eerie report of the collapse itself booming around from peak to peak, and a renewed bout of shrieks and cracks from the ice-sea as it tested the damage to itself.

But no voice.

He rose to his feet, powdered ice running off him – there were pains, in his foot, in his hip, in his shoulders – but nothing crippling. (He was reminded, in a flash, of an accident that had taken place at the wall of Stull, when a crane had broken and a corbel had almost killed him – when had that happened? Months ago, it felt.)

He was alone.

"Duna?" he said, and the sound of his own voice was a nasty shock in the shattered air. "Duna!"

He turned and took a couple of desperate strides towards the rough location he had last seen here – though he could be certain of nothing, the terrain had changed entirely.

Though there was no telling where she had been, it was at once clear where she had gone. Behind him, a split had appeared in the surface of the ice, a black line in the deepening blue. A crevasse, carved by meltwater under the ice, now open to the sky. When the overhang had fallen, its roof had broken in, taking Duna with it. She was down there.

The last ember of the sun, caught in a snag between peaks, extinguished.

10

ANTON

The side entrance to the altzan-al's apartments was in a quiet courtyard on God's side of the Brink. The Zealot on guard at the heavy iron-bound door was surprised to be disturbed by a visitor. The Zealots wore bronze helmets with some of the distinctly avian characteristics of the blade-priests' ceremonial masks, but made plainer by the demands of the battlefield. There was only a ferocious slit for the eyes, but Anton had a sympathetic suspicion that the man had been dozing. In any case, it was with an air of grievance that the soldier went to report Anton's arrival. Presently he reappeared, accompanied by a wide-eyed acolyte.

"Vertzan Anton," the acolyte said, respectfully using the young priest's antiquated full title, and his eyes darted down, as if he expected to see the *ver* hanging from Anton's belt. He rubbed his hands together anxiously – his tunic had black sleeves, meant to mask ink stains, marking him as a scribe, and his face was pitted with red acne. "May I ask…?"

"The altzan-al is expecting me," Anton said, keeping his tone light. No blade-priest had been here for five years. His arrival would surely be discussed. He had to do everything in his power to appear innocent. Because he *was* innocent, he had to remember. He had done nothing wrong and was doing nothing wrong.

Why was he here, again? "I am here to borrow a book."

The acolyte accepted this, or at least had no appetite to dispute it, and gestured to Anton to follow him. They walked together through Ramnie's comfortable rooms, climbing a wide, carpeted staircase to a vaulted hallway, its walls painted with devotional scenes. Anton drank in the surroundings. He had spent almost his entire life in Craithe's Brink, never more than half a mile away from this part of the fortress, but this place had become a foreign country while Ramnie and Ving were locked in factional combat. Anton had never signed up for Ving's side in that war, but he was blade-priest, and therefore expected to be among the most reactionary of the reactionaries. Shortly they were in a wood-panelled antechamber, where two acolytes sat working at desks. Both looked up and stared at Anton as he entered, but neither offered a greeting.

"I'll inform the altzan-al that you are here," the pimpled scribe said cautiously, before cracking open a double door at the far end of the room and slipping through noiselessly.

One of the two acolytes in the room rose from his desk and went over to his colleague, who was still seated. He carried with him a thin strip of parchment covered with columns of tiny black figures, and the two young men bent over this document, putting on a great show of focusing on it while discussing in whispers. Anton knew they were talking about him. He should have politely declined the altzan-al's offer, or asked that the book be sent to his niche in the library. The thaw between Ving and Ramnie was second only to the Elves as the Brink's main topic of discussion, so wonders and novelties might be expected – but he still feared that his visit would either be seen as a betrayal of Ving, or as part of a diehard plot against Ramnie. There was a large pool of acolytes, a majority of them, who took no side in the schism, and who saw it all as a great play put on for their amusement. They were the source of all gossip, and dramatists who would put the playhouses of Pallestra out of work. If word got to them, it would spread without delay.

He should not have come. But it was easily remedied – apologise, then depart, swiftly.

The double door cracked open again and the acolyte secretary insinuated himself back into the room. "The altzan-al will see you now," he said, swinging the door wide. And there was Ramnie.

Behind him was God.

Anton had forgotten. The Brink had few openings looking out onto Craithe. The sight of God was preserved for the Terrace of the Gift, and the denizens of the fortress preferred not to catch sight of their God while going about their day. The whole Tzanate harboured a secret relief that Augardine's great rose window had never been realised. The Mountain could be glimpsed, here and there, such as from Ving's own office high in the library tower. But Ramnie had a window looking right onto it, its frame filled with thick panes of glass angled to refract and throw the view, distorting and rupturing the view of Craithe. But there could never be any doubt that the visible impossibility that lay beyond was the visible God.

The altzan-al was seated at a desk, a giant slab of Shergine ebony that made him appear even tinier and more ancient than was normal. His back was to the Mountain, and he saw where Anton's eyes had been drawn.

"The view, yes," Ramnie said, gesturing over his shoulder, but not looking. "It has been a while since you were last in this room, hasn't it? I find the symbolism a little blunt, to be frank. God is on *my* side, you see."

"Five years, altzan-al." He recalled the desk, the great crushing black weight of it, and so many other details of luxury that were rare for the Brink, such as the Estami silk carpet. He remembered the Custodian filling the room, more terrible even than the Mountain, Ramnie saying that the demigods no longer wished to receive the Gift, the chaos that followed, Leass being struck down, rolling insensibly on that fine silk.

"Please, sit." Ramnie gestured to a seat beside the desk, not opposite him. From the seat he had been offered, Anton could no longer see God. Instead, he took in the rest of the room: a high ceiling, and between stone columns bookshelves filled with leather-bound volumes, most ancient, many tethered with chains. On the desk in front of him was a newer book: Xirco, *Southern Travels*, a Mirolinian gull sparkling in gilt on the red leather cover.

"How is altzan Ving?" Ramnie asked lightly, as if it were a polite inquiry after a mutual friend, but Anton paused. Until last week, Ving had regarded the altzan-al as a titan of perfidy and lies, a sea-serpent full of heresy and chicanery. Even if they had reconciled, even if all Anton saw was a stooped old man with whiskery white hair and a kindly expression, sunk in a chair that was far too large for him, it paid to be cautious.

"He is well, altzan-al." Anton hated the hollowness and dullness of these words. Even as he wanted to stay faithful to Ving, he did want to please Ramnie. "Quite cheerful, in fact."

Ramnie pursed his lips. "He was positively exuberant this morning," he said. "I could smell the Elf-blood. He looked ready to grab a Zealot's spear and head off to the Gull Gates on his own."

"He too has God on his side." Anton tried to invest these words with a twist of irony.

"Don't we all," Ramnie said, with a small smile. "But does he have tzan Anton on his side? No more Gift, no more Holy Alliance with Miroline, how do you feel about all that?"

Anton had started to enjoy the conversation – a secret, rebellious enjoyment, but it had felt mostly innocent. Abruptly, all the innocence drained from it, taking the enjoyment too. He found himself on the boundary of betrayal of his tutors and supporters, too close to the boundary, perhaps already over it. "A blade-priest should want the resumption of the Gift," he said stiffly.

"Yes," Ramnie said kindly. "And I'm sure that you feel very

strongly that is what you *should* want. But what *do* you want?"

I don't want to kill people, Anton thought. He furrowed his brow, trying to compose an answer that combined honesty with fealty to Ving. But it could not be done.

Ramnie shook his head sadly. "You're never going to make it as a fanatic if you keep up this constant *thinking*, Anton. Blind devotion to divine purity, that was always the way of Ving and his faction. It leads to astonishing oversights. They can't see what is in front of them: that blade priest Anton is not one of them. They see only the title, the robe, the mask. Not the man."

The temptation boiled within Anton – to reject the play-acting he was forced to indulge in every day and speak as his inner beliefs dictated, to reject the Gift and human sacrifice, to renounce the blade – but he clamped a lid on it. So insistent was the screaming thought in his head, that he was sure it could be heard, even without being spoken. But he held his tongue. Perhaps Ramnie did not see the man, either. "I have told you, altzan-al, that I will not betray those that raised me."

"I have done it again," Ramnie said, with a despairing roll of the eyes. "I must apologise, young tzan, I have been most unfair to you, putting the thumbscrews to you like this. I can see the conflict it causes within you. I have no desire to cause you any embarrassment."

"Think nothing of it, altzan-al," Anton said, relieved that he did not have to answer.

Ramnie shook his head again, possibly sad, possibly amused, possibly somehow both. "I wonder sometimes that I have misjudged Ving, that he could raise such a green bough in a field of dry twigs. Maybe it was chance. Maybe not. You were a remarkable boy. We all saw it."

His eyes were sparkling, lost in memory – not happily so, the crystalline edge of tears. "It shames the Tzanate that we saw that boy and decided that he should be a blade-priest."

Anton blinked, searching for something that might comfort

the ancient leader of the faith. "It is not a bad thing to be given a purpose," he said at last.

"An awful purpose," Ramnie said, firmly. "And then we took that purpose away. But perhaps another can be found – a better purpose."

"I would like that, altzan-al."

Ramnie nodded. "Your loyalty to Elecy and to Ving is a great strength. I heard about your protest this morning – Ving has told you about my plan to ally with the League, then? And you are boycotting the Conclave in opposition?"

"Was it the wrong thing to do?"

"Not at all," Ramnie said briskly. "I wish to know if it's an outbreak of *independence of mind*. Was it your idea? Ving's? Elecy's?"

"My idea, but Ving broached it," Anton said. Not knowing the intention behind the altzan-al's questions, he felt that honesty was the path least open to later complications. "I did it mostly to support Elecy. She is very upset by the proposed alliance."

"And you are not?"

Anton still feared a trap somewhere, and realised that he had had little time to consider his own feelings about the alliance. "It makes sense," he said at last. "And Ving has approved it."

"Yes, he has," Ramnie said, his eyes narrowing. "I'm a little giddy at my own success, there. A cynic might suspect foul play, and adjust his own plans. Speaking of which…"

The altzan-al had turned to look out of the window, up, above the Mountain, checking the position of the sun. Then he pulled himself forward in his seat, stretching life back into his legs, taking up his cane from the basket it stood in. Believing the encounter to be over, Anton stood.

"Come," Ramnie said. "It is time for our meeting."

Could the old man's mind be going? "Altzan-al, was this not our meeting?"

"This? Preliminaries. The real business awaits." He limped

past Anton, approaching a wooden panel set into the wall,
carved with a design of interlocking sickles and human hearts.
When he pressed against this panel, it sprang outwards, and
swung open. A concealed door.

"Come. Come."

The door led to a narrow, windowless passage, tall and wide
enough to accommodate Custodians. Oil lamps set in niches
gave enough light to avoid stumbling, but little more. The
curved stone ceiling was black from centuries of oil-smoke.
Ramnie led the way through to an octagonal room lit by a
skylight shaft. Dusk-blue glints shone from brass equipment
arranged on a table. Four of the walls bore caged bookcases.
Between the shelves were murals. The emperor Jone providing
over the mass sacrifice of Estami prisoners. A bindling titan
laying waste to Elves. The Scourge War: magically armoured
warriors picking though a hellish landscape of disease and
famine.

"A few of my predecessors had grotesque taste," Ramnie said
in apology. "From time to time I have considered whitewashing
these scenes. But we should be reminded of the horrors of
unchecked magic."

They skirted the room and exited by an arched doorway.
Anton estimated they were keeping roughly parallel with the
fortress's outer wall. A stone stairway led downwards, ending
in another door. On the other side was a large, semi-circular
room, a room Anton knew very well. He had not often been
into it, but he was familiar with every aspect of its layout and
function. The Sickle Chamber, where the vertzans prepared
themselves for the Gift, and dealt with the bloody aftermath.
It was older than the rest of the fortress, its living stone walls
thick with Custodian runes, sepulchrally lit by braziers. In
its eastern wall, facing the Mountain, was an archway three
times the height of a man, sealed by a silver-bound door of

polished Shergine ebony. Set into the curved wall facing this door were nine niches, each containing a short, curved blade: *vers*, the sickles used for the Gift, fashioned from stone that had been fused by direct contact with the Mountain itself, with improbably sharp cutting edges that never needed the whetstone. A pair of silver basins stood to one side, and beneath them a neatly folded pile of ceremonial white linen, all in readiness to wash the sickle after the Gift had been given. Only the handle ever needed washing – the blade came away without a drop of blood on it. A material so hard, so heavy, should not be porous, vertzan Leass had said to Anton and Elecy – but it drank and was refreshed. Anton wondered, if the sickles drank, did they know thirst?

The floor was red granite, better able to disguise stains than Mirolinian marble. On the far side of the room were the vertzan's vestments, before and after. Everything was present and clean, held in readiness. With Leass indisposed, this section of the Brink was under the personal jurisdiction of the altzan-al, and to try to keep the peace Ramnie tended to it as carefully as the most obsessed traditionalist. He had no wish to be accused of blasphemy over dirty linen or cold braziers.

A rattle from the great arch made Anton jump. A small door within the great slab of ebony opened, and through came Jinnima, a small, pale tzan only a few years older than Anton, who acted as an assistant to Dreyff. Jinnima gave a respectful bow to Ramnie, glared at Anton, and departed with a word. He left the archway door open behind him.

They walked out together into the freezing mountain air.

Before them was Craithe, the Mountain itself. But it was misnamed, it could not be a mountain. It was the size of a mountain – larger than that, indeed, dwarfing the ring of peaks around it. They were painted with snow, though, and snow never settled on Craithe. Nothing disturbed the creased sheen of its surface, no mark of time. On first sight it was as featureless as the impenetrable shadows that formed in the crevices of the surrounding ranges, dark as molten pitch. As Anton looked, this overwhelming early impression receded, and more detail appeared: facets, more like a cut jewel than eroded stone, and its darkness was not absolute, it shaded and yielded into hints of many colours, all colours, rainbowed like swamp-water, trickling always upwards. It was unforgettable, but it could not be remembered: look away, or even blink, and all those facets would appear differently arranged, and no two men had described it exactly the same.

When Anton had been behind it, the fortress's ancient outer wall had felt ineffective against the power of the Mountain, a pane of clear glass held up to stop a sunray. Now he appreciated how hard it had been working to protect him, feeling the full force of the Mountain's power against him, a gale of possibility, scouring away the limitations in the world. And the Custodians *lived* up there, almost on Craithe's surface – their monastery was built on God's Shoulder, a peak of normal stone that leaned against the Mountain's side. Maybe only one man alive had visited that fastness, and Anton was standing next to him. It was the only vestige of the Custodian kingdom besides cryptic ruins in scorned and inaccessible parts of the land.

Anton looked back at the fortress wall, towering above them, its surface covered in runes. There was the circle of the rose window that would have terminated Augardine's processional way, sealed with stone. There was the window of Ramnie's study, hidden by a recess. And, he realised, this terrace could not be seen from those windows; they looked upon the Mountain but not the site of the Gift. This was the locus of their whole religion, a religion that had once covered the world – and yet it was supremely private.

Ramnie had hobbled ahead, towards the ornate stone balustrade at the edge of the terrace, letting his fingers trail against the altar of the Gift, where the offerings were held down, where Anton had watched men die. He was echoing Anton's own gesture at the lakeside temple days before. But there was nothing casual or profane in the gentle contact the altzan-al made; it was almost affectionate. Anton followed.

Over the balustrade was a sheer drop of more than a hundred feet – a natural cliff face smoothed and heightened by masons many generations ago, long before Augardine had come, long before the city of Miroline had even been founded, perhaps by bindlings, perhaps by the Custodians themselves. Before there were men here, the Custodians had found the Mountain, had found God, and it had changed them. When people first climbed into this plateau they were the latecomers, and before Augardine they had been tolerated only as long as they gave the Gift and worshipped the Custodians as the Gods that defended God.

At the bottom of the cliff, the wasteland that separated the Mountain from the surrounding peaks, an uncertain and inaccessible land of scorching vents and quicksands. The Mountain somehow angered the earth that gave it its foundation. Thin trickles of white meltwater fell from the surrounding ranges, feeding a forever-shifting terrain of silt, streams and steam. Ultimately these waters pooled and joined on the far side of the Mountain, becoming the river Sherg, which flowed into the deserts of the east.

"What do you see, tzan Anton?"

"I see God, altzan-al," Anton replied, confident in his answer. "I see the Mountain." In truth, he was doing his best to look at anything that wasn't the Mountain – if his eyes lingered too long on that immeasurable black surface, it hurt his mind.

"*Power*, young tzan," Ramnie said. "Power almost without limit – power in excess." His jaw tightened, and he gripped the stone of the parapet. Anton wondered that he wasn't colder. "Why are the Custodians the guardians of the Mountain? What gave them the right?"

It was a puzzling question – almost blasphemous. Although he felt it had given him an inadequate answer the last time, Anton again drew on the safety of pious doctrine. "The

Mountain chose them, and the Mountain has shaped them to its purpose."

"*They were here first*, young tzan. Before man, before… anyone else. We do like to attach destiny and predestination and design to outcomes, but in truth that's the whole answer. They were here first. And we should be grateful, really. They did well. They could come and go where the walking creatures could not. Fortunate for us. They never had much use for the low places, so we were permitted to dwell there."

Anton shivered, and looked back towards the door of the Brink. He wanted to return inside. The acolyte who had led them out here, Jinnima, had disappeared. He probably had his hands over a brazier right at this moment, Anton thought sourly. Another time, another place, he would have loved to listen to Ramnie reflect on faith and the history of the Custodians and the Brink, but too much had happened today already, and he needed to sit somewhere warm and order his thoughts. Hearing Ramnie speaking this way made him melancholy.

"You speak of the present as if it is the past," Anton said. "We endure with the Mountain – you, I, the Custodians. They more than any of us."

Ramnie covered his eyes with a wrinkled hand, blue from the cold, and his body heaved. Anton tensed, ready to catch the old man, who he feared might fall. He was startled. Was the old man ill? He should not be out here in the cold. Then Anton heard it – a long, mournful groan from the altzan-al. The old man had not been struck by a fainting-fit, or by sickness. He had sobbed.

"Altzan-al!" Anton said. Not thinking what was decorous, he did what came naturally, what instinct told him to do for a distraught old man: he took the priest in his arms. Beneath the folds of the robe, there was hardly anything at all – nothing but bones.

"So much needs to be done, child," Ramnie said, recovering himself. "We have sat in our hidden land too long, dwindling, withering, imagining that we are protected by the mountains, and the Mountain. We are not. It is the disorder of the world that protects us, for now. We must organise it ourselves, or our enemies will organise it against us. We need friends. We need allies."

"Yes, the League, I understand," Anton said. "Use the League to destroy the Elves."

"Just as a start," Ramnie said, wagging his finger. "Alliance between the Mountain and the Falls will grant the League legitimacy in the eyes of the faithful, and rescind Miroline's title to the world. That might bring down what remains of the old empire – in fact we must hope so, or they will rise against us."

"You wish to destroy Miroline," Anton said. The ancient empire might be no more than a rotting city and a rag-bag of warring fiefdoms, but it was still the inheritor of the greatness of the greatest age of history, and a world without it seemed impossible.

"No," Ramnie said. "Not destroy, no. Simply... tame. The imperial crown of Miroline is too useful to smash. The League's duzh would certainly find it valuable, but perhaps a more worthy holder can be found. All this is just buying us time, you see. Ving thinks I am naive about the League, but I am not – we must use the alliance to rebuild our strength, and our moral purpose. Although it is not just a question of strength, it is a question of who wields that strength. It is a question of righteousness. A test that Miroline has failed many times. The Tzanate has failed that test, too, in the past. We must not fail again. *You* must not fail."

Anton could not answer – words had abandoned him.

"It grows late," Ramnie said, pulling his robes closer over his shoulders. "It grows late for us all."

A shadow fell through the declining light.

The wind breathed cold, dry death under a beat of wings.

* * *

It was only right to be afraid, Anton told himself. We cannot worship what we feel to be our equal, only that which exceeds us.

The Custodian landed behind him and Ramnie, between them and the Brink. It stood for a moment with its wings outstretched, each as long as a refectory bench, and its beak raised, as if inviting the priests to admire its magnificence. And magnificent it was, although not beautiful or splendid – a mortuary reek wafted from its plumes and robes. Anton lived around dormitories and barracks and stables and henhouses, and he knew the odours of animals in close quarters. This was not that. It was the musk of old death, and older magic.

The beak lowered. Above its vicious point, white eyes shone.

It was the second time he had seen a Custodian in three days, yet he felt more afraid than the first time. There was none of the reassurance of enclosing ceremony. At Hleng, the Custodian had been present for the benefit of others. Here, he knew it was for him alone. He wondered if it was the same creature, and found himself certain that it was.

He fell to his knee, head lowered. Ramnie, constrained by his age, managed a stiff bow. The Custodian accepted their respect by lowering its wings, before it again wrapped them around itself.

"Deacon Cutruk," the altzan-al said warmly. "Your servants among men bid you welcome."

Bone-white eyes flickered between Ramnie and Anton.

"Ramnie," the Custodian croaked, drawing out the R-sound. Anton was already unnerved beyond words, but hearing the Custodian address the altzan-al without honorific or title chilled him as much as any other part of its appearance. *It outranks us all*, he thought. The Custodians could wield the Mountain's power directly – they breathed it, they lived in it as a fish lives in water. And they lived a long time. Great names from the histories, ancient and storied names, may have been known to this beast personally. To it, they would just have been men, part of an unceasing succession of brief, powerless men. "You assemble your pieces. Gather what was scattered like stones on the valley floor. Build an order to face the world."

Anton had not dared rise from his knee. He looked across to Ramnie, and saw his brows knitted with anxiety, his eyes imploring. "Yes, great one. The time is nearing. I present you with the vertzan Anton Shraye, who will play his part."

Anton could not control a shudder. He had the growing sense that he did not know what he had agreed to, or what his part might be.

"Anton, ver-tzan, Gift-tzan, blade-shun, can you stand?"

He doubted that he still could, but somehow his legs took his weight, and he straightened.

"Black skin," the Custodian observed.

"Yes," Ramnie said. He swallowed. "But you knew this?"

"There are few."

"There are very many," Ramnie said hurriedly. "In the south, in Yicorum and Jemestia and Baharne..."

The Custodian cut this off with a chopping *ack-ack* sound. "Few here."

Ramnie took a moment to respond. "That has been a failing of the Tzanate. Will this be a problem?"

The Custodian rolled its head, shaking away the suggestion. "You all taste the same when you are dead." It took a long, hopping step towards Anton, moving without warning, and the young tzan could not stop himself flinching. The Custodian raised its wing, and while Anton felt his body again wanting to retreat, the orders going to the limbs, he found himself frozen, all control gone. The longest feather on the Custodian's wing brushed against his cheek, cold as grave-grass.

Then the creature withdrew. "Well chosen, Ramnie," it rasped. "The Mountain knows this one. He understands?"

The altzan-al turned to Anton and addressed him. Intense focus burned in his eyes, and the younger man found himself held motionless again. Gone was the old Ramnie Thyo, the smiler and the smoother, the knowing chuckle and the indulgent roll of the eyes. Gone. The Mountain seethed in the air. "Anton. I have told you much but there is more you must know, and you must heed it well."

"Altzan-al," Anton said, bowing his head. Pathetic obedience was without doubt the easiest course. All his questions and pretensions, all his doubts, stood as flimsy and childish. He strained to listen, fearing terrible news.

"After the Conclave, you will be named as my successor."

It was far worse than Anton had imagined.

"You are young but you will be at my side for what time I have remaining, and you will learn fast. Your faction is right about one thing: there is a lot of sympathy in the wider church for the old ways. Alliance with the League, breaking with Miroline, it all risks splitting the church, which we cannot afford. Naming a traditionalist successor can keep the church whole, do you see? And who is more traditionalist than a blade-priest? And who is better suited to the task than a blade-priest who is secretly a pragmatist, a moderate, perhaps even a reformer? When the time is right you will go with Cutruk and be initiated into the mysteries."

"Ving…" Anton began. He could not imagine Ramnie's heir-apparent simply standing aside and waving a teenager into the altzan-al's chair, whatever the youth's allegiances.

"Ving has been told," Ramnie said, without patience. "Besides we three, he is the only person who knows of this decision. He must understand that I would never name him as my successor. I think he is shrewd enough to settle for having the ear of a young altzan-al with much personal loyalty to him. He will assist in your instruction, as will Dreyff."

Mention of the altzan-al's secretary caused the old priest to sigh. "It pains me to deny Dreyff, he has served me well as secretary, and I hope you will keep him in that role. He is as much a fanatic as Ving, in his own way, and the Tzanate needs unity, to avoid awful savagery. A young altzan-al, backed by both factions – do you see how that would keep the church together?"

"What about the others? Might they see me as a traitor? Ikkosh, Elecy…"

"Elecy adores you," Ramnie said. "You are her brother in all but blood. She will applaud your appointment, no? A surprise victory in the wake of defeat. And she will get a special task of her own. We will appoint her to be the Tzanate's ambassador to Miroline. Letters of introduction will go south with the Conclave when it departs. She will get to see that latrine up close. Her piety and purity will have its purpose: condemning the empire. That should settle any lingering question of the Holy Alliance."

"Miroline!" The Custodian emitted a rasping hiss – an ambiguous sound, perhaps a laugh, perhaps an exhalation of impatience or anger. "Their failure has been our most painful lesson. They took the world, and then tore it apart. Whole lands are a waste-field of our magic. Every Mirolinian we make powerful betrays us, beginning with Augardine, and still they worship him in secret. Every artefact we craft becomes a bloody squabble. They have fought among themselves for centuries and we have seen defeated enemies rise again in every direction."

"Will it be any different with the League?" Anton asked. "What if it happens again? They do not even follow the Mountain."

The Custodian swung its beak in the direction of Ramnie, who shrank back. Its tiny shining eyes were a mystery, but Anton was pleased they were turned on him.

"He does not understand."

"He will understand, great one, he will," Ramnie said urgently. "In time."

"This is the time, Ramnie *al tzan*!" the creature hissed. It turned in a surge of movement, opening its wings full stretch and beating them once, throwing the balance from Anton with a blast of corpse-scented air. Then it was on him, not striking him so much as falling onto him like an owl on a rabbit, knocking him to the ground as if he were straw, and pinning him with a foot on his chest. All the breath was pushed from Anton's lungs, and he found himself unable to refill them. Talons pierced his robe, and at once he knew how easy it would be for him to die. He knew the strength needed to tear into a ribcage, to sever all those layers of bone and muscle and sinew – and he knew the Custodian had that strength, and more, and could be into his chest as easy as bursting a ripe tomato.

The end of that long, vicious beak was inches from his nose – it was hard to see past it to the creature's sparkling eyes, rainbow-edged like the Mountain, but they were fixed on him.

"Do you understand death, Anton the Blade?" it said. An instinct, drifting in from far away, told Anton that the Custodian had spoken in no more than a whisper, but its rough voice seemed to roar in his head. "Can you feel it coming?"

Even if Anton had had an answer, he would not have been able to speak. But his life was a fragile thing, he understood that very well.

"We have made ourselves authorities on death," the Custodian continued. "We were always its watchers, from above. It is done in the dirt, and it is terrible to be rooted in the dirt. When we found the Craithe, our very first great deed was to drive away death. We made it distant and feeble. When men came to our land, we discovered it anew. Your deaths were a marvel to us. Hot and bright. You ran to them. And you would grieve with such fervour. All for a business of dirt. Taking death from a man was a mistake. Another painful lesson. One you must learn."

Every breath tore at Anton's throat. Was that it, then? He had failed a test, and was to be ended? He would give the Gift after all – so be it. He did not wish to die, but he had no great wish to live a life without purpose. Maybe the Custodian was truly a God, or a demigod. It did not matter. All that mattered was its power. These were truly the creatures that steered the world, and if one had judged Anton unfit to live, he could not challenge its will. Perhaps, in an instinct to survive, he should argue that he was worthy of life, that he could be a great altzan-al, a war leader, a wise magistrate, a guardian of the faith. But no part of him believed any of that.

"You are afraid," the Custodian breathed. "You must not be." The creature dug deeper with its talons. Anton screamed. Those talons were through the cloth of the tzan's robes and into his flesh now, scraping their way past the rib-bones, enclosing the area of the heart. One, the equivalent of an index finger, was high on Anton's chest, the only one he could see, driving in beneath the collarbone. The Custodian *grasped*, and lifted, picking Anton off the ground like a toy. He shrieked, only to find that silence came, a silence into which the Mountain roared, and he felt tissue tearing and sinews breaking and bones parting.

And the creature was off him. There had been... It was impossible to say. Time had passed and the arrangement of the world had changed. Anton was propped against the balustrade. There was no pain and no blood, and the sun had sunk behind the line of peaks, casting them all into cold shadow. Pressing his hand against his chest, probing with his fingers, Anton could detect an ache, akin to that from a long-healed wound, but no more. It was enough to have proof that what had happened had, in fact, happened.

Ramnie was hunched with the Custodian, conversing with it quietly. The pair noticed him, and approached. Anton lifted himself to his feet, not feeling the same urge to prostrate and abase himself as he had before. The beast lowered its beak, regarding Anton with glittering eyes, full of intelligence and absent of humanity.

"You doubt yourself," the Custodian said. Its words were flat, but concealed a quality of sympathy that struck Anton with peculiar force. "I could have taken that away. But I did not. You must try to rid yourself of it."

"I fear I am unfit to the task I have been given," Anton said. He felt no fear or caution. Candour seemed most natural.

"All of you are," the Custodian said. "It is the ones who believe themselves deserving of the Mountain's power that you must fear."

Before it had finished these words, the creature spread its tomb-scented wings wide, obscuring Anton's view of the Brink, and beat down hard, launching itself into the air. With three icy blasts, it had lifted far above the two priests. Anton turned to watch it stretch out and soar down into the vale of Craithe.

"Let's go in," Ramnie said, as if they had been taking a pleasant stroll. "This cold will be the death of me."

They spoke very little on their way back through the Sickle Chamber and up to the altzan-al's study. With a nod, Anton made to leave, already concerned that his long absence might have been noted by the Resumers. But as he sank stiffly back into his chair, Ramnie beckoned the young priest back.

"Tzan Anton," he said, tilting his head like a teacher. "Did you understand the meaning of the Deacon's words about death?"

"That the Custodians are masters of death, and life, altzan-al," Anton replied, an answer drawn more from his doctrinal instruction than anything the deacon had said.

"No." Ramnie shook his head. "No. The Custodians feared death, they were disgusted by it. So they used the Mountain to banish it, as best they could. But there is shape to everything the Mountain does, and the Mountain reads the purposes and motives of those that draw on it. And the Mountain forever associated them with death. That is how they became the lords of death. Do you see?"

"I think so."

"If we draw on the Mountain, we must do so for the right reasons. The whole shape of our purpose must be considered. Can you imagine that power in the hands of Ving? Or Dreyff? Elecy?"

"The Custodians will make sure it does not get into those hands," Anton said.

"We cannot depend on them forever," Ramnie said severely. "A vast war may be coming. Armies will rise on every hand. The Mountain is the greatest prize in existence, and it must be defended, not selfishly, but for the good of every living thing."

"We have defended it well thus far," Anton said. "I will do everything in my power."

"Not a word until after the Conclave," Ramnie said, businesslike. "Even to Ving – he believes you will be told later. I trust you can return without rousing his suspicions. Ah! That reminds me."

He picked something off his desk and held it out to Anton: Xirco's *Southern Travels*. "My gift. Keep it safe."

11

INAR

"Duna? Duna!"

Inar moved as close to the edge of the crevasse as he dared, laying himself flat on the ice to spread out his weight. Everything around him was on the move, he reminded himself – the consequences of the rockfall were still playing out, and it was entirely possible that the side of the crevasse might collapse, burying both of them in freezing darkness. He could see a little of the interior wall of the crack. Below the hard, exposed edges of the section that had fallen in, it was smooth and shiny, and faintly rippled, polished by water. The chasm was wide enough for a horse and cart to fall into it without touching the sides. Inar could not make out the bottom.

"Duna!"

From below came a steady sound of trickling water, and an assortment of other creaks, rattles and splashes as small collapses continued. Then:

"Inar?"

Relief blazed through Inar like a sunburst in the dusk. But it then yielded to a sickly sense of the difficulty, perhaps the impossibility, in front of them. Duna was alive – for now, only.

"Are you hurt?"

"I fell," Duna said. This answer sparked a flash of anger inside Inar – couldn't she do a little more than state the obvious? –

but he bit it back, realising that the fright of the fall might still have a hold on her.

"I know, it'll be all right," he said. "Can you stand? Where are you?"

"I'm standing," she said. "I hit my head, but it's not bad. I can see you, I can see the sky. I can see your outline."

That was something, but not much. Inar could see nothing, and the darkness was spreading and strengthening. Duna's voice was clear enough, but did not seem to be that nearby.

"Come as close to me as possible and reach up, I'll see if I can pull you out."

A bit of shuffling came up from below. "It's too far."

"Just try. Come close and raise your arms towards me."

"I am, I am!"

There was no hint of a human form in the blackness. Inar had hoped that he might be able to see her hands reaching out of the gloom, but there was nothing. She was so pale, he had imagined that she might glow, but no such luck.

There was... It was hard to tell, because of the blood beating in his ears and the confusion of different thoughts within his mind and the panic in his muscles, but focusing on her exact location made him believe that he somehow knew that she was down there, in a way beside knowing that she had fallen and being able to hear her voice – that there was a presence in his body, in the fibre of sensation, that could detect her. An instinct, that he could place exactly where she was. As if... she was a source of heat, although it was not heat, it was another quality that his body was capable of picking up.

"Can you climb up?"

He knew the answer already, because he had seen the sides of the chasm, but he was pleased that she was at least willing to try – a scuffling and a sliding echoed up from the crack.

"No," she said. "It's really steep, and slippery."

Inar thought, flicking through a succession of useless ideas.

He was forced into resting on one that had at least a sliver of possibility.

"Listen," he said. "I am going to go – to run – back to the camp. They will be looking for us already. We will come back with torches and with ropes. We will get you out."

"*No*!" Duna's voice was a shriek of undisguised, raw fear. "No! You can't leave me here!"

"I can be back very soon," Inar said, but he was not sure.

"You'll never find me!"

He looked around, trying to get a precise sense of their location. The ice-sea had become a sheet of deep-blue velvet, marbled with purest black. The sky above was another deep blue, one that made the serrated mountains and the land below appear seamlessly dark. It would be totally dark within minutes, and it was already getting colder. He tried, tried to calculate a way to know where she was, but beyond that... strange... inkling of intuition, which could not be counted upon, it was hopeless. But without torches and ropes, what could he do? Soon they would both be lost in the dark.

Duna continued shouting. "You'll fall! You'll fall too! Then we'll both be stuck! What if they're dead, Inar? What if the camp's gone? What if they're all gone?"

She was panicking. She was panicking and they were both dead already. "Shit," Inar said. "Oh, by the Mountain, by Augardine's Tomb." He scrambled to his feet. "Shit, shit shit shitting shit." He paced, head in hands, not feeling anything but a collision of all the impossibilities, a choking knot of death. "Shit."

"Inar, I can't see you any more."

He had to stop her from panicking somehow. If she became hysterical it was all over, they were both fucking dead, they were fucking dead already and it was a fucking stupid way to die, just because some fucking idiots wanted to see a fucking mountain. He had to stop her panicking. The panicking was bad, really bad.

"Inar. Inar, I can't see you. I know you're there. You can't leave me here."

Inar was finding it hard to breathe. His breaths were coming very quickly, and were very shallow. His head throbbed.

"Inar. You need to listen to me. Don't move. I can hear you gasping. Take deep breaths."

He had to stop her panicking.

"Just take one deep breath. That's all we have to do. The only thing we have to do. Just take one deep breath in, and then out. Can you do that, Inar?"

He had to stop panicking.

He took a deep breath.

"Take another."

He took another.

"How do you feel?"

"I'm better. I'm still here."

"Good. Don't move."

"It's dark."

"It's dark for both of us now," Duna said. "That's good, it's fairer that way."

Inar laughed, a high-pitched giggle that did not sound like him at all.

"What do we do?"

"I have something," Duna said. "Wait. Don't move."

He did not move, but kneeled down, taking care not to get too close to the precipice, which was now invisible.

A glimmer, in the darkness, down. A spit of spark and a tiny, persistent light. Duna's face appeared below him, picked out in a small sphere of golden light. All around her, faint glints of ice and water. He was reminded, jarringly, of the feast at Sojonost and how beautiful the hall had looked, all ablaze. It was beautiful to see Duna. A crescent of flesh had been scraped raw around her left eye, and a line of blood traced down the left side of her face, pitch-dark on her skin, like the crevasse in miniature.

She was holding one of the straw-thin taper candles that the League used for lamplighting and to get fires going. Their dirty orange flames produced little illumination and they burned out quickly, but against total darkness, it made a difference.

"How many of those do you have?"

"Two. Including this one."

"Can you see a way to climb out?"

"No," Duna said. "I think you should come down here."

Inar blinked. He was aware, painfully aware, of how short of time they were, the moments until that flame winked out, the hour or two they might have before the cold began to overcome them. He did not want to waste that time. "I think that you have been hit on the head, hard."

"No. Listen," she said. "There's a stream down here. It goes downhill, yes? Eventually it must come out of the ice sea, down the valley. We just have to follow it."

"We can go downhill on the surface," Inar said.

"Not if I'm stuck down here we can't," Duna replied. "And there's a danger we'll just fall again. Come down. The water will guide us. We can hear it, we'll know if it's going over the edge of something. If we follow it as far as we can, we can call for the others, if they're listening for us..."

She continued, giving the reasons for her plan. Inar stared at her. It was ridiculous. If someone is trapped in a hole, surely the least sensible thing to do would be to go down and join them. Could he even get down there? It was, perhaps, twenty feet from the edge of the chasm to where Duna was standing, straight down. The broken surface of the ice offered some purchase for climbing down, and beneath that it might be possible to slide down the curved wall... But there must be a flaw in her logic, somewhere. What if the stream did not lead to the valley? It must go downwards, true, but what if it just led them deeper into the ice, and then vanished into an abyss, perhaps taking them with it? What if the tunnel shrank to nothing, or there was an obstacle they could not pass?

He realised that it did not matter. He wanted to be down there. They had to stay together to survive. If they had to spend the night on the ice-sea, it was better to be together for warmth, and even to have the relative shelter of the crevasse… he only wished that he could read the ice, that he could tell if it was in danger of falling and engulfing them. This stirred the rockfall back into his mind: that he had missed the coming collapse. And Duna had seen it coming. They had more in common than he thought.

"Inar? This won't last much longer."

"I'm coming down." Don't think, act. He used his staff to score a shallow indentation near the edge of the crevasse, and then lay down on the ice and dropped the staff down to Duna. Then he swung his legs around until they were out over the edge of the crack. The pit of his stomach capsized as he sensed the nothingness below his knees.

"I'll try to catch you," Duna said.

"No, stay out of my way," Inar said. He did not want to injure them both. He found the groove he had scored with his staff and wished he had spent more time on making it deeper. It was nothing. Feet scrambling against the broken side of the ice, hunting for a hold, he lowered himself. The shapeless sheepskin mittens on his hands made grip next to impossible, and he wished he had taken them off, even if his fingers froze solid.

"That's great," Duna said. "If you – Ah!" She squealed, burned by the end of the taper. It fell from her hand, winking out before it hit the ground. And then Inar fell.

It felt as if he were falling through space for a long time, in fact only a shrunken instant. He expected the blow to come to his legs, for his bones to shatter as they crumpled beneath him. But instead he was hit in the side, hard, and the wind was knocked from him. There followed a sickening, skidding time, when up turned into down and all location was lost, and he landed on his shoulders and back, hard, again. The sound of running water was loud, now, and his face was dipped in slush.

"Inar?"

A shuffling in the blackness, and a hand on his leg, just below the knee.

"That's me," Inar said, and gasped from the savage pain that came when he spoke. "Ah! I think my ribs are broken."

"Nothing is broken," Duna said, sounding very confident. "You'll be blue in the morning, though."

"If I live to see that, I won't mind," Inar said. He sat up. His right side felt as if a cart-horse had kicked it, but she was right, nothing was broken. "I'm down. What now?"

"Can you walk?"

"Yes. I think so. Yes."

"Then we walk."

Duna had one taper left, and they did not want to use it if they did not have to. They moved forward slowly, her taking the lead, feeling the way with Inar's staff, which she seemed to have adopted. At first, once Inar's eyes had adapted, he saw that the blackness was not total: a sliver of stars could be seen above. But before long they were obscured. They were under the ice, in a tunnel cut by the meltwater. The ground was uneven but flat enough, littered with stones, most of which were small enough to kick out of the way.

"You knew what was going to happen," Inar said, after a time. They had not been silent as they walked, but all that had passed between them was warnings and questions and instructions about the path they trod. But Inar wanted some answers.

"Yes," Duna said. "You could see it as well?"

"Not before it was too late. You… see better than I do."

There was a period of quiet, with the sounds of the tunnel: rushing water, rattling stones, the crunch of their feet on the grit, all echoing weirdly.

"You've never met anyone else...?" Duna asked.

He knew what she meant. "My father, I think, and my brother. No one else."

"Of course."

"At first I thought everyone could do it. My brother told me I was wrong, and that I should never speak about it."

"I do not see better than you do," Duna said. Her Mirolingua was very good, in terms of vocabulary and grammar, but it was long on classical reading and short on contact with people who spoke it daily. This gave her speech a slight formality that could be taken for aloofness, but he now saw was just lack of practise. He wondered if *see* was really the word she wanted. It was not quite the word he wanted. "Worse, I think. We see in different ways."

"I am not good with natural formations," Inar said. It was strange, very strange, to be able to talk about his instinct. The rush of release was enough to make him light-headed, as if he was winded all over again. Or perhaps it was no more than an after-effect of being winded the first time. "Anything built by man, I can read that, but rock formations..."

"What about the ground beneath us? Could you tell if a chasm was about to open up, or if a cave was hidden below the surface?"

"No. Not really." Silence. "Can you?"

"Not really," Duna said. "It's better if there's... a shape."

"A shape. Yes." It wasn't just a problem with Duna's Mirolingua, or with Mirolingua in general. It was as if no one had talked about these matters. To bring them into words was to try to build a wall with a sewing kit, or darn a stocking with a builder's tools. "You knew? About me?"

"Yes, from the start."

"Is that why Anzola wanted me in her service?" Inar asked. Bits of machinery clunked into place. "She knows as well?" Though Inar was thrilled at being able to share this part of himself with Duna, he was less eager about the idea that

Anzola, and possibly others, might know. He already felt that Anzola knew altogether too much about him.

Duna said nothing, but did not have to.

"It's a great aid to being a builder," Inar said. "It took my father from nothing to a position of great importance. You could be a great builder."

Duna did not reply. Inar felt puzzled and a little stung. He had tried to pay her a compliment, that was all. "Women could be builders too," he said, in case she felt the suggestion was improper. "It hasn't been the Mishigo way, but..."

"Of course women can be builders," Duna snapped back. "Anzola is a builder."

"Yes," Inar said. "I'm sorry," he added, but he did not know exactly what he was apologising for. He had a general sense of having blundered, and being far from the path he wanted.

"Did you choose to be a builder?" Duna asked. She still sounded angry.

"No," Inar said. He had never *not* wanted to be a builder, but he had never made a choice towards it. "My father was a builder. His father was a quarryman. My brother and I were both expected to follow."

"We don't get to choose what we are," Duna said, sourly.

"Anzola gave me the impression that things were different in the League."

"Maybe for some," Duna said. "Like everywhere. Different for some."

Inar took his turn to be silent.

"A builder. A great builder," Duna said, giving the words a mocking twist.

"I didn't mean to offend you."

"You have not. I am sorry. I am not offended. I should like to be a great builder."

"It's good work," Inar said.

"*Quiet*," Duna replied, in a hiss.

Inar thought he might have made another stumble, and

again triggered the girl's temper. But he kept quiet, while wanting to ask what he had said wrong.

"Listen," Duna said.

He listened. Water rushing over stones, more water than before, but the size of the stream had been steadily increasing as they walked, that was nothing new. But – there was a difference. The echo had changed.

"It's opened up," Inar whispered.

Ahead of him, Duna took a couple more steps. Then she shouted, a word in Palla that he had heard used as a greeting: "Iho!"

Iho... ho... o... came the echo. All doubt was gone. They had come into a much larger cavern.

"It smells different, too," Inar said. He had thought his sense of smell to be deadened by the cold, but it was picking up something.

"You're right," Duna said.

"It smells *bad*."

"I think we should light the taper," Duna said.

The thought of lighting the last taper filled Inar with fear. As long as they had it, unlit, they at least had the option of light, and it was good to know it was there. Once it was gone, burned, then they would be permanently sentenced to the dark.

"I don't know. We might need it."

"We might need it now," Duna said. "What if we're about to walk off a cliff?"

"I'm sure we'd hear..."

But she was not listening. A flint sparked in the dark, a tiny triangle of flame appeared, and with it Duna's face and hands. It was good to see her again, Inar had to admit, however he might disagree about using the taper; it was good to see any light. "We can put it out half way," she said, in justification of her decision. "Keep some in reserve."

Inar looked around. The ceiling was higher, only visible in

tiny glints, but he was reassured to see that it was the same polished ice as earlier – they had not strayed into an actual cave. It was hard to see, but judging from the curved portion of wall that they could make out, they had found a kind of natural dome under the ice. The stream they had been following ran through its middle, carving a path through a sandy floor evenly scattered with stones. Duna walked deeper in, and Inar hurried to follow her, not wanting her too far away in case the light should fail.

"I think something has been *living* down here," Duna said. She had hopped over the stream and was examining the ground on the far bank. "This patch looks like it's been cleared. There are bones."

She was right – small white bones scattered among the stones, and Inar recognised the stripped torso of a small bird, feathers still attached to one remaining wing. "An animal..." Duna said. "Down here..."

A strange shape among the stones and bones – a dark and angular shape. Inar bent and picked it up. A belt buckle, badly corroded, decades old.

"There's more," Duna said. She was reaching the far edge of the dome, where the ice curved down to meet the ground. Inar could see what she was talking about – a pile at the edge of the chamber, not natural, placed on purpose, a collection of shapes like traders' bundles.

"It's – oh!"

Duna dropped the taper.

As it fell, its light briefly caught the pile, before it hit the ground and went out. Long white bones, a tumble of ribs, repeated many times, shadows jumping up like ghosts as the light descended.

And the dark returned.

"Oh!" Duna said again, a yelp. Inar heard her stumble. He was only a couple of steps behind her, and found her at once, putting his arms around her.

"Animals," he said, putting as much certainty as he could into the word. "Animal skeletons."

"What animals? What animals are up here?"

"We can see that there are animals here. Were. Probably long gone. Long gone." The chamber was silent, but for the running water.

"I think we should go," Duna said.

"I think that's a good idea," Inar agreed.

Inar took the lead, using the staff to feel his way around the edge of the chamber, searching for where the water made its way out. They found their way back to the stream's side and stepped along a narrow band of grit between the water and the ice wall. Once again, the tunnel had enclosed them.

"Animals," said Duna, absently, to herself.

"Long gone," Inar repeated, turning to her. And, to his surprise, his amazement, he could see her. Not all of her, and at first he imagined that his eyes, starved for light, must be playing tricks. But no: there was the faintest shine of a pair of eyes, her eyes, and behind her the tiniest hints of shifting light on the stream's somersaulting surface.

"Look!" Duna said, still looking ahead, over his shoulder.

Inar turned again, and looked. It was a gift to him that he could see anything, but what he did see was the most perfect miracle: he could see the moon and its maids.

12

ANTON

The first bell chimed at six, as it always did. Anton was already awake, as he always was. Ever since he had been given a room of his own, more than a decade ago, he had woken minutes before those first chimes sounded over the rooftops of the Brink. But these last few mornings he had been woken by the aching in his chest, legacy of the Custodian's talons.

It was a strange kind of wound. The creature's claws had pierced him, Anton was certain – they had dug deep. Ragged holes had been left in his robes, and he had spent a guilty evening stitching them by oil light before stuffing the mended garment at the bottom of his chest. But no drop of blood was spilled, and the skin had not broken. Instead, four sickly pale points had been left on his torso, like the long-healed scars of very ancient wounds, joined by a tracery of lines. And an ache, a stiffness in the ribs that recalled how he felt the day after prolonged exercise.

The ache had value, though – it was proof that his encounter with Ramnie and the Custodian had indeed taken place, and was no dream or wakemare. Besides that, he had the copy of Xirco that Ramnie had given to him. It did not have a library binding, and he feared that might draw the eye. But stashing it in his chest spoke of guilt, and instead he placed it among the few books on the sill of the narrow window in his cell, where it did not stand out. His gaze went to it as he dressed, waiting for Elecy to knock at his door, as she always did.

Anton was an orphan. They all were, all the young ones: if there was a single fact known from Pallestra to far Benzig, it was that the Tzanate took in orphans and unwanted children and treated them better than they'd fare in their slum or farmstead. "I should sell you to the tzans!" mothers shouted at their unruly ones. But the Tzanate did not ask for money. The young lives that trickled in from every part of the world were treasure enough. Almost nothing grew in the Hidden Land, recruits least of all.

Until age eight, all the children in the Tzanate were given the same basic education in the same halls and dormitories. After that, they were separated according to their qualities: the most academically promising went to become tzans, and spread the word of the Mountain to the world; the most physically gifted would be trained as Zealots, for when the word failed. The rest would be acolytes, and serve the Tzanate as workers and clerks, with later opportunities for advancement.

It was at age eight that Elecy and Anton had been taken aside, prodded and questioned by half a dozen altzans, and then informed that they were special. At age eight they had been shown the giving of the Gift, and told that this was their life's purpose.

No more dormitory. They were immediately given the title vertzan, technically granting them the same rank as altzans decades older. The blade-priests had their own complex of apartments – grand, pale, high-ceilinged rooms with grisly frescos. Vertzan Leass took over their tuition – a learned and wise priest, but Anton could never forget that on the occasion of their first meeting, Leass had killed a man in front of him. And that was not the only time they saw Leass practice his art, and the terrified eyes of his victims, and a Custodian dropping from the sky to devour a human heart.

This is you, they were told. You will do this. You are

the servants of the lords of death. You are the holders of a sacred duty older than human innocence. The eyes of the vertzans in the frescos – when their eyes could be seen at all – were not consoling. It was a burden, they said, yes. You will bear it. But what hurt the most was the absence of the other children. Those cold, echoing rooms were loneliness expressed as architecture. After the Custodians had put an end to the Gift and Leass had lost his mind, Anton and Elecy had been transferred to cells in the library complex, watched over by Ving. Once again they were near novices their own age, but their rank and their awful repute formed a barrier against friendships. Much as Anton had hated the vertzan apartments, he could not hate them entirely, as they had been where he had formed his bond with Elecy. They had spent so many years together, shunned. There had never been any taunts or cruelty from their former classmates – none of them dared. They went from being the objects of fear to being the objects of confused pity.

Anton only had to wait a few minutes before Elecy knocked at his door, as she always did.

In normal circumstances, Anton and Elecy would break their fast in the refectory. But they were meant to be keeping out of sight while the Conclave was in session, so they ate alone, at a table set up in one of the library scriptoria. The tall desks used by the acolytes had been lined up against the wall, under the high clear-glass windows. They were surrounded by shelves bearing vellum and parchment and pots of writing instruments, and the racks used to dry completed manuscript pages.

It wasn't an unpleasant place to eat, but the word SILENCE painted in huge letters above the main door cast a pall over the conversation, even if the rule did not apply. After a mere four days, the Conclave had ended; today the delegations would begin their journeys back to wherever they called home. If only that meant a return to normal, but it would not be long before the Tzanate went to war against the Elves, in allegiance with the godless League. This vast, continent-sized endeavour was dwarfed in Anton's mind by the knowledge that he was being groomed, ultimately, to *lead* this war, and then take the Tzanate into whatever world came after. It was disturbingly easy to imagine himself *losing* this war, and being put to death among the ruins by the victors or by co-religionists busily anathemising his name. Victory was too much, too fantastical, to begin to comprehend. Four days of private contemplation had not been enough to get used to the idea of himself as an altzan-al, a general, a statesman. But he had been given a decade to think himself a blade-priest of the Mountain, and even that still felt like a sham.

What pained him more than anything else was Elecy. Becoming a blade-priest had meant losing every friend he had, apart from her; becoming altzan-al threatened that last connection, especially if she had to go to Miroline. Though they had spent the last few days in each other's exclusive company, they had mostly kept private counsel. They read together, they meditated together, they exercised together, but they did not talk together. The chance was slipping away – but what could be said? The Conclave had prompted a deep melancholy in Elecy – all Anton wanted was to reassure her that there was hope in their shared future.

"Our isolation ends today," Anton remarked. "Much as I enjoy these private meals, it will be pleasant to return to the refectory."

Elecy simply scowled, and divided a slice of bacon with a practised stroke.

"I wasn't sorry to miss out on all the speeches," Anton continued, "but it might have nice to attend the banquets."

"It's just *excess*," Elecy said with a hiss. "They come all the way to the threshold of the Craithe, and then they stuff their faces. At the Tzanate's expense! I thought we were meant to be showing our poverty? Our urgent need for rich new friends? I don't understand it."

"Diplomacy demands that we indulge them, I suppose," Anton said. He tried to picture Elecy in Miroline, as the Mountain's legate in that wine-drenched court. It was the place of her birth, not that things like that mattered much to the Mountain's children. But perhaps the warm sun and the grapes and honey and all the good things of the vestiges of the Empire would speak to a native part of her. Ramnie expected her to be revolted by it all, which was probable, but Anton hoped that she took some pleasure along the way. All the time he had known her, all their lives really, she had spared herself, held herself in reserve for devoted service. What would she become, free of that?

"But this has been a sort of banquet for you, hasn't it?" he continued, with a smile.

She glared at him. "What do you mean by that?"

"A bit of persecution for our beliefs," Anton said. "Seclusion in the name of the Mountain. A martyrdom of porridge. That's a nice rich gravy to you."

She regarded him with ice-cold eyes for a moment, enough for him to feel a tiny sliver of fear that he might have gone too far. Then she snorted, and waggled her knife at him. "This is bacon, and bread, not porridge. Really, you say the most stupid things sometimes. The most stupid part is that you still haven't realised that I learned long ago to tell when you are trying to provoke me." Despite her labours, a smile tugged at the corner of her mouth.

"I have to amuse myself somehow," Anton said, returning the smile. "I've been glad of your company these past few days – and years."

"Boycotting the Conclave was the right thing to do," Elecy sniffed. "That's why I did it, not because I like the taste of bread and water." She lowered her head. "*You* were right to do it."

"It might not have changed anything," Anton said, "but we left the stage with some dignity, and seen by all."

"We did," Elecy said, satisfied.

"Our day will come, sister," Anton said. "We are young, and at the heart of power. The others are old. Maybe they've made a grave mistake in cutting us loose. We could overturn them all."

She raised her eyebrows. "First rebellion, and now sedition. Pungent talk from Anton the Timid. It's good to see you shake off some of your deference. I wish you'd come and train with me and the Zealots – I find the martial arts a good cure for inner conflict."

"We must choose what we want to do with our lives, I mean," he said. "What would you do if you ruled the Tzanate?"

She looked at him as if he was an idiot. "Resume the Gift, of course," she said, tearing at a piece of bread.

"Aside from that. What can the Tzanate do in the world?"

She rolled a morsel of bread into a pill. "Destroy the Elves," she said, with vehemence.

"That will happen anyway," Anton said. "Mountain willing."

The pill had become a neat white sphere, and she stared at it. "Justice," she said at last.

Anton tilted his head at her, not understanding.

"Justice has gone from the world," Elecy said. "Miroline is ruled by tyrants and bandits. The League cares only for money. When we gave the Gift, we sat in judgement. Only the deserving could be Given. Those that deserved to die. Even without the Gift, the Tzanate could be moral arbiters once again."

"What would give us the right?" Anton asked, suspecting he knew the answer, and that she would invoke the visible God. But he was wrong.

"What gives anyone the right?" she said coldly. "We are the ones willing to take on the job." But then she shook her head, and flicked the little bread pill into a far corner. "It doesn't matter. Ramnie has fixed himself to the throne. There's no way that he'll name Ving his successor. That was just a lullaby. It'll be Dreyff, or Yisho."

"We don't know that."

The corner of Elecy's mouth turned up, a puzzled half-smile. "Anton, what are you trying to say?"

"That I will look out for you," Anton said, embarrassed. His intentions, so clear when he started down this path, had become clouded. "Whatever happens."

Elecy shut her eyes and laughed. "And I for you, brother. You may need it more than I, if you stay on the path of insurrection."

A river of the faithful flowed across the dry floor of the Hidden Land. At its head went a squadron of Zealot rangers on horseback, led by strategos Yisho and accompanied by heralds. With them went a few of the more dashing noble altzans, who fancied the idea of riding at the head of their religion and rather thought they might commission portraits of themselves doing so when they had reached their far-flung homes. Anton wondered if their enthusiasm would endure past the Gull Gate.

That splendid, bannered band had left the Brink's main gate some time ago, and still the human torrent continued in their wake. A thousand tzans and altzans had travelled to the ancient fortress for the Conclave, and now they were departing, all at once. But many more than a thousand passed beneath Anton. Few priests travelled without at least one servant or man-at-arms, and some had brought with them great retinues of attendants, secretaries and liveried soldiers. The richest were carried in palanquins, scores more had horses or mules, but the vast majority were on foot. Alongside them marched the great bulk of the Tzanate's Zealots in two thin lines, flanking the main column of the procession. A ragged sheet of dust rose from the miles-long snake of men and women, a pale-grey pennant pointed in the direction of Hleng, and the Gull Gates beyond. It would be many days before they reached Cassodar and divided.

None of the banners hung to greet the Conclave had been

removed, and their colours had not faded. But the scene was not festive. The historic settlement of a dangerous split within the church might have been cause for celebration, but he saw many heads bowed.

"Dionny told me that few of the Conclave dared vote against Ramnie's alliance," Elecy said. "But a great many abstained. We still have support in the church."

They stood together on the battlements of one of the gatehouse towers, watching the departure. Even if one of the thousands of souls who trooped below turned back to look at the Brink, they would not be able to tell that the two fur-wrapped figures observing them were blade-priests, or any kind of priest. But few would turn back, because behind the Brink loomed Craithe, and it was better to get some distance on God before daring to glance at it.

"It is settled, though," Anton said. "Alliance with the League. That is the policy of the Tzanate from today." He had noticed that Elecy had started to bring him these titbits of suggestion and speculation that she had heard elsewhere – anything that implied that Ramnie's new order might not be as secure as it appeared. Presumably she meant to console him. Where was she getting them? Would she ever be reconciled to the new arrangement? For years Anton had been given the opportunity to study several of the most ardent and least reasonable adherents of his religion up close, and he had noticed something interesting. Their carapace of piety and certainty could not be softened over time, or chipped away. However, at times one would wake up in the morning and find that the whole edifice had moved, and now had new interests and priorities, some of which were the precise opposite of those previously held. They never noticed the change.

"The treaty isn't signed," Elecy said.

"What could stop it?"

She shrugged. "The Augardine cult? I've heard that they are not pleased."

Anton turned to look his sister in the eye. It was the kind of look that more usually went the other direction.

"Elecy," he said seriously. "You aren't talking with cultists, are you?"

She glared at him – not angrily, but with some affront at the thought. "Cultists die under the *ver*," she said. "Of course I haven't been talking with them. If I found any, I'd tell Ving, or Ikkosh."

"Good," Anton said. Worshipping a man like that was an obscenity. Worshipping any man was an obscenity. Elecy's purity frightened him at times, but when it aligned with his own instincts, he was comforted by it.

Beneath their feet, the column still marched, although the tzans and altzans had passed now and were replaced by more soldiers, guarding a baggage train.

"This is taking longer than I expected," Anton said, trying to stamp the cold out of his feet. "How many Zealots are going with the Conclave?"

"All of them," Elecy said.

"*All* of them?"

Elecy raised her brows, as if she could hardly believe it herself. "Eight thousand Zealots, headed by Yisho herself. More than three-quarters of our total strength. The Brink's garrison is down to two hundred men, and a small force of scouts and rangers. Only Mal Nulalus is keeping a full garrison, everywhere else is stripped to bare bones."

"Where did you hear this?"

"From the Zealots," Elecy said with a chuckle. "I said you should join me in training with them. You learn all sorts of things. And they're not stopping at Mal, either – no ferrying parties back and forth, they're all going to Cassodar, all at once, with the entire Conclave."

"Ramnie's mad," Anton said.

"Apparently it was Ving's idea," Elecy replied. "But the Con-clave were pretty much demanding it. Strength in numbers."

It made sense to Anton: smaller parties constantly ferrying back and forth along the Augardinian Way had made too tempting targets for Elves. But it was unnerving that the whole force of the Zealots would be away from the land they were meant to protect for so long.

It was the new shape of the world, though – the Zealots abroad, fighting. First the Elves, then perhaps Miroline. It was time to get used to it. They had been watching for more than an hour – the column would stretch to the horizon, but it was lost in the clouds of fine grey dust raised by many thousands of feet. A rearguard of rangers passed under them with shouts of command and devotion, which were returned from the battlements. The Brink's gate shut with a crash that echoed from the surrounding mountains for long minutes, like a tolling bell.

After the departure of the Conclave, the emptiness and silence of the Brink came as a shock. There was no further need to skulk around in servants' passages and hidden corners. Anton walked down the middle of the Processional Way, unmasked and head held high, and he didn't see another soul. Even before the Conclave, the ancient fortress had not been so deserted, but every spare able-bodied man and woman had gone with the immense column that had left for Cassodar the previous day.

No messengers criss-crossed the processional, and no ceremonial guards stood beside the mausoleum of Augardine. The visitors had left a drift of devotional litter by the inscribed black wall of the tomb: burned-out candles, wilted flowers and fronds from across the world, brass trinkets, ribbonlike prayer-flags stuck with splattered wax. Through many feet of stone, in spite of the Custodian runes, Anton could feel the backwash of the energies that had been spent there – a throb behind the eyes. Linger too long and it could bring on wakemares. But linger he did.

"Vertzan," said a voice at his shoulder, startling Anton. It was Ikkosh. "Paying respects?"

"Altzan," Anton replied formally, inclining his head. "I was thinking that we should tidy these offerings away."

"Yes," Ikkosh said, his sharp little eyes taking in the bric-a-brac in a judgemental sweep. "We are a little short-handed, with so many away."

"Some of this avidity bounds on heresy," Anton said, feeling that a little piety might please a reactionary like Ikkosh. But to his surprise, the priest merely shrugged.

"Harmless, I believe," he said. He smiled an unpleasant smile. "I've spent my whole life watching for heresy, Anton. It's rarely the careless ones. It's often the ones who seem most pure."

That wolfish smile unsettled Anton and he wondered if there was more to those words than conversation – did Ikkosh suspect him of something? Or Elecy?

"What can I do for you, brother Ikkosh?" he asked.

"The altzan-al desires to see you," Ikkosh replied. "With Ving, and the others, you understand."

So Ikkosh had been told. "It's not like you to run messages for the altzan-al," Anton said, cautiously, hoping for some sign of the old fanatic's feelings about the coming changes. "Things have changed."

"Ving has explained the situation to me," Ikkosh said with a sly inclination of the head. "I am pleased that the throne will soon be filled by someone we trust. This way."

A side passage – normally guarded, but not today – bypassed the mausoleum, leading straight to a series of bare rooms, ghostly white in pale marble. The vertzans' apartments, mostly empty now, except for poor old comatose Leass and his acolyte attendants. Elecy visited from time to time; Anton did not.

These rooms – of course – connected directly to the Sickle Chamber, and the Sickle Chamber led to Ramnie's study. Ikkosh gave these directions and made excuses early, saying that it was a short-cut for blade-priests alone. And so it was, strictly speaking, but Anton would have liked some company for the walk. All the usual guards and acolytes were absent, but at every step he had the eerie sense that someone had been there before him, preparing the path. Where doors were normally left locked, they stood ajar. Oil lamps had been left. Anton traversed high-ceilinged, windowless chambers half-lit by small skylights and filled with the indistinct shapes of furniture and crates left under dust sheets. He felt like a premature ghost, an unwelcome visitor from the past.

The stairway that connected the blade-priests' apartments to the Sickle Chamber was particularly disturbing. Its panelled walls had been painted with scenes of the Giving of the Gift: vertzans red to the waist with blood, lifting hearts from ruined men into skies darkened by the Custodians. Part history lesson, part instruction manual, all gruesome. The door to the chamber itself had a broken lock – recently broken, it would appear. For years the Tzanate had been slipping behind on day-to-day upkeep at the Brink: plaster crumbled, cracked glass was not replaced, the same drips appeared with every thaw, and long-disused keys were mislaid.

But in the Sickle Chamber, there were more signs of disruption. The neat stacks of white robes had been untidied and a slim metal bar – maybe the same tool that been used to pry open the door – had been left abandoned on the red granite floor. More concerning, the sacred sickles themselves had been disturbed in their niches. Two were askew, and one niche was empty.

Anton paused and considered turning back. Something was amiss, of that there was no question. But what was the sensible course of action? He felt that he should return with a couple of Zealots and investigate the signs of intrusion more carefully. But there were no Zealots the way he had come, and it seemed that someone had made certain of that. The closest guards would lie ahead, in and around Ramnie's chambers, which were among the best-protected locations in the Brink.

His mind was made up by a noise from ahead, up the staircase he had descended with Ramnie only days before. It had carried a distance, this noise, and was hard to identify, but it could have been a voice, crying out. Anton climbed the stairs two at a time, crossed through the secret octagonal room Ramnie had shown him, and only hesitated when he reached the door to Ramnie's study. His ears strained for any sounds within the room, but he heard nothing; he knocked but there was no reply.

As Anton entered, his foot bumped against a heavy object left on the floor inside the door. It was a tangle of feathers and leather straps, from which a long and curved beak of dark wood protruded – his ceremonial mask. It was definitely his, he recognised every plume and buckle on it. How could it have ended up here? A deep disquiet coiled and tightened in his gut. The mask was not kept in Anton's cell: acolytes looked after it with his formal robes, in the vestry.

He looked around for Ramnie. The altzan-al was not at his desk, but something else was out of place. In the middle of the silk carpet was what first appeared to be a pile of blankets, but as Anton approached he realised it was in fact the diminutive form of the altzan-al, fallen face down, his small body engulfed in its cold-weather robes.

With a wordless cry of alarm, Anton raced to Ramnie's side, and turned him over. The dark grey fabric of his robes was slick and black at the front, soaked with blood, and a red spray was bright against the terrible pallor of the neck and face. Ramnie's eyes stared without sight. Blood had pooled on the carpet where the dead priest had lain, and Anton now saw the sickle, which must have been left beneath the body. It was clean of blood, as was a sickle-shaped strip of carpet beneath it – the *ver* had fed, and fed well.

Anton was frozen in place. Nothing could be done to save the old man – pulling aside the stained and torn robes,

Anton found that the razor-sharp blade had made a ruin of the altzan-al's chest. This was not the result of a single strike, but a sustained and frantic assault that must have continued a time after the priest's death was assured. But where were the guards?

Just as Anton was summoning breath into his lungs to yell for help, the door to the study opened. Two Zealots burst in, spears ready, and they were not alone. Behind them came an unlikely collection of priests: Ving, Dreyff, Strang, Dionny and, lastly, Elecy.

Anton tried to think of what useful information he could convey to the Zealots, so that they could find Ramnie's killer – he had come from the sickle chamber and might yet be in the secret rooms between there and the study. But the Zealots were advancing straight towards him, spearpoints lowered in his direction.

Looking between the slack-jawed, horrified faces of the priests behind the soldiers, Anton at last saw the scene as they saw it. And the instructions died on his lips.

Dionny was the first to speak. "Anton," she said, voice pitched high with shock, "by Augardine's Tomb, what have you done?"

13

INAR

After the total dark of the ice caves, Inar felt that he could see everything in the valley, outlined in chalky moonlight. They staggered from the mouth of the cave as if drunk, overcome with elation, the noise of the stream suddenly far louder, booming between the ears as it erupted into the world with them. Without speaking, moving on a shared instinct, they scrambled downwards, away from the ice sea, putting some yards of safety between them and it. But they were not safe, Inar knew, and he was sure that Duna knew it as well: they were still alone, without shelter or equipment, wet and tired, on a freezing mountainside.

Fortunately, they were no longer lost. Once they had made their way a short distance down the slope, they were able to look back up and see – brilliant against the night – the fire of the camp. Around it, shadows moved: lines, more than one, had been raised up to the top of the ice cliff, and there were torches up there as well. But all was not as it had been. A colossal chunk of ice had broken free of the sea near the camp and lay on its side like the abandoned toy of a titan. The cliff was now less of a cliff and more of a slope, a jumble of broken ice.

They approached unseen – no one was expecting any visitors from down the valley. Four people were at the camp:

two of the knights, Kielo, and Lott. One of the knights – by the name of Thiolo, if Inar's memory served him – saw them first, and raised a cry in Palla, and the rest broke from their tasks as one. Inar was embarrassed to receive an embrace from Lott. Kielo was more emotional than Inar had ever seen him, rushing to Duna, jabbering relief at her in Palla, and taking the girl by the arm, practically dragging her toward the fire. Duna's brow creased with annoyance. And Inar, too, was also feeling discomfited by the fuss: already, hindsight was minimising what they had been through.

"Where are the others?" Inar asked, in Mirolingua, directing the question to both Kielo and Lott. But Kielo ignored him, devoting himself to clucking over Duna, sitting her by the fire and directing a stream of enquiries at her, and receiving a syllable or two in return.

"Searching, on the ice," Lott said.

"No one was hurt?" Inar asked.

"Nothing serious," Lott said. He nodded to the ice cliff, what was left of it. "It collapsed. If we had been closer we would have been buried. We lost four of the mules."

"Buried?"

"Two were under the ice. Two were made lame, one hit by the ice, the other panicked and hurt itself. We took care of them."

Inar nodded. "I'm glad. Not about the mules. That you're OK."

Lott's eyes widened, alarm showing in the firelight. He spoke in Mishigo. "She's mad, Inar. The other one, Anzola. She went mad."

"How so?"

"She was yelling at the others," Lott said. "In their language, so I couldn't say what it was, fear, lots of fear, but also anger, she was very angry."

"Only natural?" Inar ventured. "Fear doesn't like to show itself, it often comes out dressed as anger. Duna is like a daughter to her."

Lott shrugged. "Yeah, suppose. She's obviously important."

An avalanche of tiredness had overcome Inar. His head throbbed and there was nothing more he wanted to do than lie on the ground, quivering, until sleep came. And, with a further sickening slide, he realised he could not: Anzola would return soon. Instead, he sat by the fire, next to Duna, trying to work some heat back into his bones.

The merite returned within the hour, along with Miroslo and the other knights. She descended the line laid over the spilled ice at an unsafe speed and ran to Duna, who had stood, uncertainly, on seeing her. Inar, who had also stood, also received an embrace. By the firelight, Inar was able to establish the truth of part of Lott's story: there was a wild look to Anzola that he had not seen before, the look of a parent who has lost a child. Once the wordless greetings were done, an unbroken stream of commands was issued, about heating more water, changing clothes, delaying the departure the next day to allow more time to rest, keeping the fire going.

While they had all waited for Anzola's return, Kielo had conducted his own interrogation of Duna in Palla, receiving curt answers and eventually being silenced with a furious couple of lines of invective from the girl. Only the word *Anzola* was intelligible to Inar's ears, emphasised more than once, but he believed he caught the overall gist: I'll tell Anzola about it, not you. The secretary had sunk into an uncomfortable silence, and was suddenly very interested in the health of the fire. Lott had asked questions too, and Inar had tried to answer them. He gave an abridged version: a rockfall, a crevasse, omitting what they had found in the caves, and about what they talked about while they were down there.

Inar and Duna did not say a word to each other. It was not an angry silence, but a shared acknowledgement that nothing needed to be said, for now.

Anzola, once she had run out of orders to give, sat by the fire and indicated for Inar and Duna to sit beside her. Not for the first time, the merite's manner made Inar feel more a child than a man – a sensation that had to travel many years, from before the fever-death of his mother, and which came wreathed in other unwelcome and unmentionable emotions. He sat, weary, not wanting to talk.

"There was a rockfall," Duna said, when she was asked what happened. "I fell into a crevasse. Inar was there, he helped me."

Anzola turned to Inar, eyes wide and serious. "Inar," she said. "You will always have my thanks. You have returned to me my precious girl."

Inar said nothing, but shifted uncomfortably on the pack he was using as a seat. Duna rolled her eyes at Anzola's words, which Anzola did not see, and Inar believed that he was not supposed to have seen it either.

"A rockfall," Anzola said, returning her attention to the girl. She asked a question in Palla, a question with delicate pauses in it, as if an indecorous subject was being broached in polite company and the merite did not want to use vulgar words.

Duna answered with an affirmative monosyllable.

Another question in Palla, this one containing the word *Inar*, and Anzola glanced at him.

Another affirmative monosyllable, and a few supplementary words.

Anzola appeared satisfied. "It makes little difference," she said, reverting to Mirolingua. "There had to be a day for it, and tomorrow will be that day."

When Inar and Duna had stood together beneath the overhang, they had been at the highest point of their journey through the Pilgrim's Pass. Their sleep that night, what little of the night that remained, was the highest of the passage. The next morning, late, the party began to descend.

Their path was through a fracture in the mountains. A side-pass like an arrow-slit took them out of the valley of the ice sea, and into a deep ravine floored with loose rock and gravel, so narrow that they went in single file, and boulders that had fallen from the heights were often wedged between the walls far above their heads, an uncomfortable sight. The walls of the ravine appeared matched – each bump on one side had an answering niche on the other, as if they had been split apart by a catastrophe more recent than was reassuring. This feature excited Anzola and Kielo, who regularly paused to discuss in animated terms what was around them.

Before long the ravine opened up, as Inar knew it would, remembering this stretch well. They came into a roofless natural room as large as the feast-hall at Sojonost. At the far end of this "room" was the Vulture's Eye.

The rock had once, perhaps, been part of a mountain peak – it certainly belonged to the highest places. It was at least as large as the overhang that had collapsed before Inar and Duna the previous day, larger than the keep that Inar had grown up in, or the towers of the wall he had been building at Stull. It had fallen, too, but had not shattered as it fell, instead wedging neatly into the ravine like a stopper in a bottle. It almost sealed the pass tight – almost.

This rock was not the Vulture's Eye. The Eye was the way through, a chink of space between rock and ravine wall, passing under the rock. The level dirt floor of the space behind this obstruction was caused by rock and sand washed down from above, building up behind the fallen Eye-rock like water behind a dam. The aperture of the eye, where the dirt spilled out, was steep as well as narrow.

"Like being born again," Inar said, showing Anzola the route they had to take, and its military uselessness. "So the tzans say. They make a symbol of the place, of course. One must leave aside possessions, baggage, to proceed to the Sight of God. If we dug out some of this loose shingle to widen it, we might be able to get a young mule through. A starved one. But it can't carry anything."

Anzola handed the rein of her mule to Duna and approached the stone. Around it was a band of carvings: Custodian runes and knome-wards. A couple of pockets and niches in its surface were stained by smoke and traces of dirty wax.

"Prayers," Inar said. "Candles. Left by pilgrims. The Sight is just beyond. Pilgrim bands spend the night here, make a camp, and go forth without belongings."

"Why has no one removed this stone?"

Inar frowned. Anzola might be ignorant about the mountains and the mountain realms, but Inar had regarded her as intelligent. Perhaps he had been wrong. You did not have to be raised in the land of late dawn to see why this stone could not be moved, it was not mountain lore. Why it would always be here.

"How would we do that? With a couple of Titans? Even a hundred men with picks…"

"Well, maybe there's your problem," Anzola said, walking back towards them, slapping her gloved hands together to remove any stray specks of dust. "Always thinking that only men can do a job. Duna, this would be the time."

Duna looked fractionally more miserable than usual, but she handed Anzola both reins she had been carrying and walked towards the stone, avoiding Inar's enquiring glance.

"This stone," Anzola said. "Sacred, is it? Precious? Revered?"

Inar shrugged. "Not that I know of. Just a landmark. Always been here, and you can't descend to the Sight without going under it."

Anzola nodded. To Inar, she seemed to be satisfied about something.

Up ahead, Duna had removed her gloves and tucked them into her belt. After frowning at the stone a time, sizing it up, she laid her hands against its smooth surface.

"Your grace," Kielo said. He was standing with the knights

and Lott, some distance behind Inar and Anzola. "Perhaps you would join me here…?"

"Wait, Kielo, wait," Anzola said, a little tersely.

Duna had braced her arms against the stone. Her slender frame shook with effort. Inar gaped. Was she, this sickly girl, trying to push the stone? To push it down the mountain? It was fused in place by the passage of millennia! A Titan couldn't…

She relaxed, and moved in closer to the boulder, moving faster than Inar had seen, a curious, lithe, seductive quality to the action, as if pulling a lover to her.

The temperature around them abruptly dropped. Or did it rise? Every inch of Inar's skin broke out in sweat – hard, summer-toil sweat. He glanced across at Anzola, troubled. Her neck shone like glass. Her look of satisfaction had gone.

"What…" Inar tried to say, feeling a darkness coil through his innards, but all that came was a croak from a dry throat.

"Perhaps we should step…" Anzola muttered, but she, too, was unable to finish.

Then Duna spoke.

No. She did not speak. But Inar had no other word for what she did. Speaking was the only way to transmit meaning across space. Duna spoke to the stone. Her lips did not move. She did not speak. All around the mountain air screamed and was silent.

The stone answered. From within it came an awful grinding, felt as much heard, through the ground, through the bones. Thin trickles of dirt and small rocks issued down the sides of the ravine.

Then came a single shattering sound, a clap of thunder, a cry of outrage from the range itself, an instant in duration, but Inar knew he would hear it the rest of his life.

And nothing more. All was normal. Duna took a couple of stumbling steps backwards and fell, as if pushed, onto the sloping floor of the pass. Inar rushed forward to help her.

"By the tide," Anzola said. "It worked!"

"By the tide," Kielo agreed – but from him, the words sounded like a ward against evil.

Duna scrambled to her feet, shaking her elbow free of Inar's hand. He scowled at her, annoyed at her rudeness, but she was looking up at the stone. Inar looked to see what she was looking at, and froze.

A black crack, shocking in its crispness and darkness, had appeared down the stone, beginning at its summit and snaking diagonally down to one side. Perhaps two-fifths of the upper part of the stone had separated from the rest, shifting an inch or so.

Inar stared at the crack, into it. In places it was wide enough for him to insert his hand without touching the sides. He had seen the same work at the akouy shiel. It ran straight through the carvings, bisecting one he had never seen before: the polished outline of a small, slender hand. Not a carving: an *impression*.

"You did this," he said, without looking at Duna. Duna looked away, at the ground, face reddening. Then Inar turned and confronted Anzola.

"She's a scourge," he said. It wasn't a question or an accusation. It was a plain statement of fact. Duna was a scourge.

14

ANTON

Buried deep beneath the Brink, in a cell carved out of raw rock, Anton was surprised to discover that he was hot. Too hot. He knew that veins of intense heat and scalding steam riddled the wasteland that separated the fortress from the Mountain, and some were used to warm the Brink by hypocaust. But this wasn't the courtesy of a heated floor – it was torture.

The room was square and empty, but for a thin layer of ancient straw on the flagstone floor. The only light came from an oil lamp held in an ingenious recess accessed from the far side of the wall, with a cross of iron that prevented Anton's fingers from reaching it. Not that he wished to disturb it. Its small flame was delicate, and burned out regularly, leaving him in total darkness, and anything was preferable to that. The cell was too small to lie on the floor in line with one of the walls, but if he lay diagonally across it with his feet in a corner, he could just about stretch out.

But most of the time he paced, or lay curled into a ball, reflecting on the lightning sequence of events that had ended in this place. After years of successfully suppressing the urge, he found that he wept often and freely – mourning Ramnie, who had offered the hope that one day the tempest of contradictions and uncertainty within Anton might be stilled;

and also mourning himself, the young fool that he had been, slain on the same day as Ramnie's death.

It had all been set up so simply, and he had played his own part to perfection: the dupe, walking straight into his downfall, a perfect scapegoat for Ramnie's murder. He had protested, naturally, he had screamed his innocence, but at the same time he knew the magnificent damnation of the scene: the wronged blade-priest, with mask and *ver*, hunched over the eviscerated remains of the man who had thwarted his life's purpose. And of course Elecy had been there, the one who knew him best – she would have read the scene more clearly than anyone else, and her presence had made the discovery pure of any taint of faction.

And it had worked – none had said a word in his defence, although the shock of the bloody scene and the suddenness of the actions that followed might have accounted for that. Without instruction, the Zealots had seized Anton, and one laid a well-timed punch across his jaw, putting an end to the chaotic stream of excuses and pleas that had started to tumble from his lips. More Zealots had entered, and the altzans were ushered away, aside from Ving. Then, swiftly, Anton was on the move, his feet dragging along the floor, out and down, down, down, to the warren of dungeons deep beneath the Brink.

In a tall, circular chamber shaped like an upturned bucket, the Zealots again used their fists on Anton, knocking the wind from him and closing one of his eyes, before kicking him to the floor. They removed his robes, taking care to be as rough and profane as possible – but then, with Anton half-naked and half-blind on the raw stone flags, they stopped, and stepped back, as if the helpless individual before them had from somewhere acquired the means to harm them.

Anton, fearing that this was no more than a pause to gather effort before a renewed assault, did not move. When the assault did not come, he rolled onto his back, and looked up to see what had become of his attackers. Three Zealots – all drawn from Ramnie's personal guard – stood nearby, regarding him warily. Another was at the edge of the chamber, consulting with a tall, robed individual so concealed in shadow that Anton had not previously noticed his presence.

The hidden witness stepped out from the colonnaded dark that had obscured him and into the dim glow of the braziers at the centre of the chamber. It was Ving, silent and grim. No thought or motive could be read in his lined features: neither the hatred of a man in the presence of a traitor and a murderer, or the satisfaction of a plotter seeing the fruition of his scheme. He looked as he always looked, and that was terrible enough.

Once Ving had joined them, the Zealots indicated what had caused them to stop their work, and Anton at last realised what it was: the tracery of pale scars across his chest, left by the talons of the Custodian. Ving stared down at Anton, reading the marks like an entry in a ledger, and he turned back to the Zealots.

"It changes nothing," he said. "Continue."

Continue they did, stuffing Anton into a tunic of sackcloth, but the young priest noticed definite reticence compared with their earlier roughness – indeed, there was now a concealed thread of courtesy in their treatment of him. In any case, there was little left to do but to throw him into the cell in which he now lay. He had no way to keep track of the passing of time. There was no clear rhythm to the refilling of the oil lamp, or the arrival of the wooden bowls of water and corners of bread that were his only sustenance. He slept in small doses, whenever exhaustion overcame his discomfort and his racing, miserable mind.

All he could do was to assemble and reassemble the small certainties in his possession, and try to match them to a larger outline of the truth. It was obvious that he had been the victim of an elaborate snare. Who had set it up? Ikkosh had played a part, but Anton had no doubt at all that the mastermind was Ving. In one sweeping move he had removed Ramnie and deposed Ramnie's intended successor. As holder of the second highest office in the Tzanate, he would be presumptive altzan-al. All along, he had been watching the use Ramnie made of the Elf-crisis, and learning from it. He had used the cover of the encroaching threat to pretend reconciliation, and gain access to Ramnie's plans. He had used that access to ensure that the Zealots were elsewhere when he made his move. He had used one enemy to destroy another. And he had smiled at them all, and explained it, without any of them knowing. Ving had seen a path to the throne, that had been very true – not for Anton but for *himself*. A path that existed only for a day or two, and which required utter ruthlessness. But he had not hesitated. And Anton had played his own part to perfection. How well he remembered Ving's gentle suggestion that he might protest against the Conclave – everyone saw that. A blade-priest, twisted product of a savage custom, lashing out in revenge for the thwarting of his life's purpose, or in order to try and save the Tzanate from the ignominy of alliance with heathens. Trained since youth to be a killer, he made a very fitting murderer indeed.

Worse thoughts awaited, especially when the oil lamp burned out and Anton was left hanging senseless in screaming silent darkness. No plot of this kind would end with him alive. And in the spaces between the arrival of bread and water, and the rekindling of the lamp, it was easy to believe that no more bread or water would come and the lamp would not be re-lit, and that would be that. The histories were filled with human problems being sealed up in rooms until they were problems no more. Curled in the darkness, he could even imagine that death had already come, and this was it, an eternity of blackness, filled only with a parade of the mistakes he had made in his final hours.

Even more troubling were the doubts. So perfect was the snare that had caught Anton, he sometimes found himself wondering if it had been a snare at all. It all pointed so neatly to him as the killer – what if he was the killer? What if he had somehow taken leave of his senses, in the grip of a wakemare or similar, and committed the deed himself? Wakemares did not cause the sufferer to act. But the Custodian had gripped him and marked him – had he perhaps been influenced in more profound ways, or broken by the embrace of the Mountain's magic? What was simpler – that he was the victim of an elaborate plot, or that he had simply killed Ramnie?

In the suffocating heat and darkness of the dungeon, anything seemed possible. Or rather, only the worst seemed possible, as all light and hope was closed off.

The cell door rattled, and Anton stirred on his bed of filthy straw. He had been dozing, and was surprised to see the lamp had not burned out. Either that, or it had been replaced without his knowing. He expected the slot at the bottom of the door to open and a bowl of water to appear. Instead, the whole door swung wide, revealing Elecy standing in the passage. At first, he feared that she too might be a prisoner, come to join him in his confinement. But she was clean and unharassed, and wearing her usual robes.

He could not help notice the way her nose wrinkled when she sampled the air in the cell. She carried with her a wooden bowl of water, which she gave to him, and he drank from it quickly and messily, so desperate to calm his thirst he cared nothing for appearance. Elecy took a step into the cell to retrieve the bowl, and behind her a Zealot moved to follow, until he was deterred with a glance. Anton tried to stand, and she motioned to him that he should not.

"I need to know why you killed the altzan-al," Elecy said, "and if anyone else knew or helped."

"No one," Anton croaked, and he wondered how long it had been since he spoke. "I did not kill him."

Elecy blinked, but her grim expression did not otherwise change. She crouched to be nearer him. "There is to be a hearing, later today," she said. It was morning, then. "To decide your guilt, and what is to be done. You will not attend. I am to speak for you. I need to know anything that might help your cause – why you did what you did, whether there was anyone who assisted you, or told you to do it."

"Let Dionny do it," Anton said. Even in his sorrow, he could see the danger. Elecy was no juror – Dionny knew the law of the Tzanate, and she cared enough for him. Besides, Anton wished to spare Elecy the responsibility for his life. "I did not kill the altzan-al."

Elecy closed her eyes, and spoke slowly. "Dionny is under arrest, Anton – so is Strang, so are some of the others. Dreyff is dead. The hearing is Ving, no one else. He is altzan-al, in all but confirmation. There is little to be done."

The rough stone floor seemed to lurch under Anton as Elecy said these words. Cleaning up, of course. Ving was behaving as if he was rooting out a plot led by Anton – and taking the opportunity to terrorise everyone who was not part of his own plot.

"Not you, sister?" he asked. "Dreyff and Dionny but not you?"

"He came to me with Zealots, and a candorite," Elecy said. Her eyes widened at mention of the stone. "I thought them things from stories, but he had one! A little slice of milky crystal, like a coin. He laid it before me and asked if I knew of your plot, and what you had told me about Ramnie. I told the truth, and he was satisfied."

Satisfied, yes – satisfied that Elecy had not known of Ramnie's intent to announce Anton as his successor. Dreyff might have known, so Dreyff had to die.

"Elecy, there was no plot," Anton said.

"You did not ask me to join you," Elecy said, and even in the dimness of the cell, Anton saw the colour rise in her cheeks. "We were both thinking the same thing. But you did it!"

Her voice dropped to a whisper. "I understand that you wanted to spare me this fate, but I want you to know that *I would have joined you.*"

"Elecy," Anton said, feeling as if he was in a nightmare in which he spoke without being heard, "I did not kill Ramnie. Ving did. The whole… scene that you saw, it was set up for your benefit. Think! No one benefits by this crime but Ving."

Elecy shook her head. "Vengeance is not about benefit, Anton, it is in the realm of passion. I heard the things you said during the Conclave. You were a changed man. You knew your purpose. I felt it myself, but I never had the resolve to bring it about. Your benefit will be a cult in your name. Whereas I have disgraced our tradition."

"Elecy, listen!" Anton hissed. "I did not kill him! I had met with the altzan-al before the Conclave. I spent a night at Hleng with his coterie, yes? We rode back together. He wanted to appoint me as his successor. To unify the Tzanate. A Custodian came to me. They knew of the plan. The Custodians, Elecy, you must speak with them. They know the truth." He started to pull at his tunic, to reveal the scars across his body.

She was listening, now, at least, but Anton feared the effect of his words. The colour had gone from her. "Anton, please, you must understand how this sounds."

So it was hopeless. Even his closest friend – his sister – regarded him as a madman. He shut his eyes tight, and another sob rose up within him, a howl against the world, against the whole ball of stone in which he was entombed. He let go of the tunic and curled up.

Quietness passed. There was a shuffle of shoes in the passageway, as if the Zealot was about to call a halt to the encounter, but it ceased – halted, perhaps, by a gesture or a look from Elecy.

Then she spoke. "Show me, then. Show me its marks."

Anton opened his eyes. Elecy had acquired, from somewhere, an oil lamp of her own, and her face was bathed in its amber glow.

"You were told?" Anton said. "By Ving?"

Elecy glanced out into the passageway. "A Zealot told me. They whisper."

Anton raised his tunic, suddenly and absurdly embarrassed at the wretched state of his underclothes, but overcoming his fear and his shame. With the lamp, Elecy studied the marks.

"I see," was all she said. Another silence fell, and Anton replaced his tunic. Elecy was thinking.

"If it made any difference," Elecy said, "then Ving would not have let me see you. You must understand that power, the kind of power that is now raging freely above our heads, makes its own truth. It has decided that you are Ramnie's killer, and all that remains is to ratify that decision and act accordingly. If I were to stand in front of Ving and say, no, Anton is innocent, the real killer is elsewhere, we must investigate, what do you imagine would happen? I would be down here beside you within the hour, if I survived that long. You have been selected for your role, I have been selected for mine, and we must play them out."

"You must preserve yourself," Anton said, nodding. "Say whatever is necessary. If I cannot be saved, maybe you can."

Elecy stood. "Trust in me, brother," she said at last. "This is no longer a place for truth, or for honour. But they are old and we are young. We will overturn them all." She nodded to the Zealot, and before Anton could say goodbye, she was gone, and the door closed behind her.

15

DUNA

Every day, just before the great clock on Custom House Square chimed noon, it performed a mechanical dance. Three small doors opened beneath the astronomical dials of the clock face, and out came three painted figures on rails: one riding a little ship, one dressed in wools and furs, and one in leather armour. Each approached its own little bell, and they struck them in turn, making a pretty tune, before coming together and striking a larger bell, in turn, twelve times in all. Then the clock's main bell tolled the hour while the little figures withdrew. Duna thought it was the most magical thing in the whole world.

"Pallestra, Wenodar and Matchfalls," Duna's father told her, if he was not working and they could come and see the clock. Recently, that had been most days.

It was always his second visit of the day. Every morning, he came here alone. The clock stood at the corner of the House of Works, which faced the square with a wide colonnade supported by square timber columns. It made Duna think of forests, as every column was thickly covered with notices and scraps of parchment, moving together in the breeze – this matched what she had heard of forests, though she had never seen one. Long trestle tables were set up in the wide space under the colonnade, and in the morning serious men in black garb sat behind these tables, kings of the world of paper, and workers were lined up and assigned duties. If her father was fortunate in his morning meeting with these kings, he would not return to their dormitory until dark, and they would eat a good dinner. More often, since his hand had been bandaged, he returned soon after he left, stony and unspeaking, and they wouldn't eat unless they had something saved, or went to the Tide's Bounty and took what they handed out.

That had been the pattern today, and when he said they were going to look at the clock, Duna assumed she would be shown at the Bounty afterwards, and they would get some bread or a bowl of watery mutton stew. You had to return the bowl. But when they reached the square, she saw that the hands of the clock were nowhere near noon. What were they going to do, then, stand there in the midst of all those people and carts, and disappoint pickpockets? She asked her father, but his good hand gripped hers a little tighter and he said nothing.

They did not stop in front of the clock. They passed through the fluttering columns, past the tables where the kings of paper sat, though they were no longer holding court. They went through the arch in the middle of the building, into the House of Works itself.

It was another world. The noise of the square died away. Beyond the arch was a long hall, with thick stone slabs underfoot and walls of polished wood. Black-clad men crossed this space, and their feet did not clatter as they walked. Some of the men were in fact women, but if they saw Duna and her father they all wore the same frown.

Duna's father stopped in the middle of the hall, and appeared lost, looking around at the different doors that opened on to it and the steps at its end. Then he was saved from this limbo by one of the quiet-walkers, a man about his age, a king of paper, who had materialised at his elbow. Duna assumed he would ask them to leave. Instead, he smiled at them, taking time to include Duna, and spoke a few quiet words to her father.

Led by this stranger, they went through windowed double doors into a large room, startling in its emptiness. In the middle of the room was a table, and on the table was a collection of stones, mostly pebbles of various sizes, with one or two cut pieces as big as the small loaves of hard bread given at the Bounty.

Behind the table stood a beautiful woman. Her hair was short and woven with silver thread, and she wore a shining tunic of the faintest blue, stitched with ornate decorations. Her hands were clasped neatly at her waist and she beamed at them both.

"Harno, Duna, I have the pleasure of introducing the merite Anzola Stiyitta, deputy surveyor-general," the black-clad man said.

"Thank you, Kielo," the merite said. Duna had heard of merites, and seen one or two – they truly were kings and queens: extraordinary, rich, shining, clean people. "Would you mind closing the door? Thank you both so much for coming, I've been so excited to meet you."

Duna glanced up at her father, and found that he was staring down at her, and his expression was terrible, one she only saw when he thought of her mother, or in his most clouded times. The door behind them closed heavily, the noise of it echoing in the big bare room. She began to feel afraid.

"Pa," she said quietly, "I want to go back outside." "Your ladyship, this is my daughter, Duna, just as you say," her father said, speaking quickly. He had his hand on Duna's back and he tried to push her forward a little, but she resisted. "Ah, she's a good girl, very good, and smart too, her mother died having her, and I can't always get the work, what with…" He waved his bandaged hand.

"I'm told there's been some trouble at your dormitory," Anzola said, kindly. "With the other workers."

"I don't know how it started, your ladyship," Harno stammered. "These ideas, they grow like mould, but some of the others there have taken against her, with no cause, she's a good girl..."

"It's *your grace*, Harno, and please, there's no need to be afraid," Anzola said, blinking slowly as she spoke. "How awful for you both, especially your daughter. It's no place for a little girl. I expect you'd like to be out of all that, wouldn't you, Duna?"

Duna said nothing and pushed a little closer to her father.

"Duna, I'm told that you have a very special talent," Anzola said. For the first time, she unclasped her hands, and gestured to the stones arranged on the table. "Would you like show it to me?"

"I'm not supposed to," Duna said quietly. She hoped this would be accepted, but she saw the pleading look in her father's eye, and she had a feeling that whatever the rules might be elsewhere, the rule here was to do whatever the beautiful woman said.

"I would like to see it *very much*," Anzola said, in a sugary way that suggested to Duna that she didn't spend a lot of time with children. "Please show me."

Kielo, the man in black, had been lurking behind them until this point, but crossed the room towards the table. "The merite is a very important woman, Duna," he said. He wasn't smiling. "Come on, now. Show her."

Duna did not move. Her mind was roaming, flailing between the clutter of stones on the table, the thick solidity of the flagstones beneath her feet, even the tiny hard points of the gems sewn into the woman's clothes. Other places too, ones she shouldn't see, that no one should see. She could show the man in black the way she had shown that other man at the dormitory. He wouldn't like that.

"It would be very good for both you and your father if you showed me," Anzola said gently. "*Such* a special talent! And *very* rare, making you a *very* special girl. Come over here and show me."

"I think she's scared, your grace," Harno said quickly. "You shouldn't... Please, don't scare her."

"I'm beginning to think that you're wasting my time, Harno," Kielo said sharply. "What's she scared of? You should both be scared of what'll happen if this is some kind of scam. The merite doesn't just take in any waif that comes her way."

"Take in?" Duna said. "Pa, what's happening?"

When she looked up at her father, she saw his face was shining with sweat. The air tasted funny. "Oh no," he said. "Please, angel, you have to–"

"Kielo, please," Anzola said, with a calming motion. The man had taken out a small piece of white cloth and was dabbing at his neck and lip. She rounded the table and walked towards Duna, hands outstretched. "Duna, darling, you have absolutely no reason to be–"

Duna clamped her eyes shut, but still she could see. It had been building up in her with nowhere to go, even just thinking about it did that, and she could make it go away if she could be on her own with her thoughts for a while but these people wouldn't listen and they wouldn't let her go so it had nowhere to go and the only way to make it go away was–

A change, a mark between *now* and *before*. A sound like a whip, loud, and they all flinched at it.

Quiet.

"My goodness," Anzola said.

She was looking down at the floor. Right in front of her, between her and Duna, a sharp black crack ran through one of the smooth flagstones.

"How thick are these flags?" Anzola asked.

Kielo's mouth hung open. Realising that the merite was talking to him, he shut it. "Four inches, your grace. At least."

"I'm sorry, I'm sorry," Duna said, shaking with helpless tears.

"*Sorry*?" Anzola said. "Duna, you are the most wonderful little girl in the whole world."

* * *

"Does the fissure run all the way through?" Anzola asked.

Duna shrugged. She was shivering. She took a blanket from a mule's back and wrapped it around herself, then started rooting through its pack for something to eat.

"We'll be able to see when we go down," Kielo said. "It must do, from the way it has shifted. Is it stable?"

"I expect the fragment weighs scores of tons," Anzola said. "That should be enough to hold it in place. We could break it up a little more, and use the mules to haul the pieces clear – Duna, how do you feel?"

Duna found some strips of dried fruit in a folded cloth. Pulling the blanket closer around her, she shook her head in answer to Anzola's enquiry, but her eyes were on Inar. And he was staring back at her.

"She's a scourge!" he said, half-shouting.

"Duna has," Anzola said, levelling a measured look at Inar, "a very special talent."

"A *talent*?" Inar said. He was more than half-way to shouting now. "She'll kill us all! A ruin-scourge! In the mountains! She could bring an avalanche, a rock-fall–" He froze. "The overhang. That was her."

"It was an accident," Duna said. It was partly true – Inar's arrival had affected her. It had been a couple of years since the last time she had shown anyone new her ability, and she had hoped that Inar of all people might appreciate it. How could he not understand? But they were very different people, the mountain folk.

"I should have left you to die," Inar said. He said this quite matter-of-factly but that only made it worse, a punch to the gut without warning. *How could he?* was her immediate thought, but it was swiftly replaced by *How dare he?* She felt the heat rise in her neck.

Normally she was pretty quick with an answer, but not quick

enough today, a day of wonders for everyone. Anzola took two smart steps towards Inar and struck him across the face with a gloved hand – a measured, mannered blow, learned in court, not in brawls. He staggered sideways, more out of shock than from the force of it. For a second Duna worried about his response, and she felt the knights tensing, but the Mishigo simply clutched at his cheek and gaped.

"You will apologise to Duna," Anzola said. "She is my ward and my trusted friend."

Inar took his hand away from his face and looked at it, but there was no blood. He had gone red. "*Apologise*? They'll *burn* her! They'll probably burn you, too, for giving her sanctuary! Great Augardine's Tomb! You brought her into Stull, into the citadel! They'll burn us all!"

"Who will?" Anzola asked. "Not the League. True, not many know about Duna's talent. But those few see in it what I see in it: great promise."

"You're not just sheltering her," Inar said. "You're *nurturing* her. You're *training* her."

"Of course I am," Anzola said. "So she can control her gift. To avoid accidents. The better she knows how to use it, the safer we all are."

Inar appeared entirely lost. Unexpectedly, Duna felt an ember of sympathy for him – she had been talked into a corner by Anzola before, and she knew the lost, defeated feeling it caused. But she smothered that ember and chewed on a piece of fruit.

"Safe!" Inar spluttered at last. He stared around at the other faces in the party – at Anzola, who met him with a calm, neutral expression, tinged with perhaps just a dab of disappointment, at Kielo, who had the look of censoriousness and seriousness that he always got when he was nervous, and at the knights. Not at Duna. Then he turned from them all and stormed away. There were only two ways to go, back up the pass or further down it, and the path down meant going under the Eye, so he went up. This meant he could not avoid passing Duna, who had lingered near the mules. As he passed, she said, quietly but loud enough to be heard: "I saved *you*."

Anzola turned to Lott, as if she was about to consult him on seating for a banquet. The boy's mouth was open, but he did not appear angered by what had happened to his friend, or aghast at the magic he had witnessed. "Lott, perhaps you would like to follow him," Anzola said. "You don't have to bring him back, but please make sure he doesn't go too far, or hurt himself. He doesn't have any supplies, or shelter. We'll get this straightened out."

Lott nodded, and strode away up the pass. As he passed Duna he stared at her – not in fear or hatred but frank fascination.

Anzola sighed, and flexed her hand, looking down at it. Duna had seen the merite armed and armoured many times, and had seen her fencing and riding at targets, but she had never once seen her use violence on another person. She walked down the path towards her guardian, munching on the fruit, keeping the blanket on her shoulders. Anzola acknowledged her with a slight smile, and then looked up at the broken Eye-stone.

"What a mess," the merite said. "I'll fix it. You did wonderfully, you wonderful girl."

Time healed better than words, Anzola liked to say. Duna was familiar with the strategy – she had been its subject often enough, left to cool down after a row. The temper passed and people came back. But however astute it was as an observation, however often Duna had seen it working on herself and others, she had long ago noticed the satisfaction with which Anzola applied the rule. She had become very used to people blowing up, cooling off, and coming back. What if, this time, I didn't go back, Duna would think. And here she still was, at Anzola's side.

The knights made camp above the Eye, and made a fire. Once the camp was established, and everything was made inviting, Anzola suggested that it was time to find the Mishigo. She asked Duna to come with her.

"He thinks I'm a monster," Duna said, surprised even to be asked. "You might have more luck if I wasn't there."

"I have become accustomed to your talent," Anzola said, "and I think I forgot the effect it can have on others. That was my mistake. I thought it was better to show rather than tell, but maybe I was wrong. Only yesterday you were trusting each other with your lives, he knows you're no monster."

This stilled Duna's objections, and although she was reluctant to face Inar again, she went with her guardian, accompanied by Thiolo, one of the knights.

They did not have to go far. Inar and Lott were found about half an hour away, seated together on a flat stone near the point where the defile entered the valley of the ice sea. Both looked dejected, and did not brighten when they saw Anzola and the others, but did not anger or move away. Anzola indicated to Duna and Thiolo that they should hold back, and she approached them alone. They were close enough to be heard.

"I erred in revealing Duna's talent this way," Anzola said. "I thought it best to show you in the first instance, or you would not believe me. And I was accustomed to secrecy. I made too much a shock of it. I am sorry. I should not have struck you, and for that I am doubly sorry."

The Mishigo glanced at each other uncomfortably, and Inar's hand rose unthinkingly to his cheek. "It was a shock," he acknowledged.

"You should apologise to Duna," Anzola said.

Inar coughed out a laugh. "I spoke rashly, but I spoke the truth." He looked up at Duna. "Scourges *are* dangerous. If they find out about her in Mishig-Tenh they *will* kill her. These are simple facts. The name itself is a warning."

"You said you should have left me to die," Duna said plainly.

Inar reddened. "That was wrong. I am sorry for that."

"You have only known scourges from stories, and from what the tzans say about them," Anzola said. "There's little truth to be learned there, just gruesome lies. The simple fact stands before you – an ordinary girl, with a particular talent.

"I have known Duna more than ten years, since she was a child of six or seven," she continued. "Her mother had died delivering her; her father was one of my workers, and had been injured in an accident during the excavation of a dock. He could not look after her and asked for my help. He had an inkling of her ability. I have protected her ever since."

"But why?" Inar asked. "Weren't you afraid?"

"I am a woman, Inar, and I exist among men. The experience of sharing the world with creatures that might hurt me, or worse, was not a novel one. She was a frightened child. She still is. All she needed was safety, and affection."

Duna watched Inar. He was scowling down at his feet, at the filthy bindings around his boots, torn by the long days of travel.

"She can break stones with her mind," Inar said. "That is an awful power."

Anzola closed her eyes and nodded – not affirming what Inar had said, but indicating that she had heard it. "A power, yes, and a significant power – but awful? You or I could break a stone with a hammer, is that an awful power?"

"Not a stone like the Vulture's Eye!"

"True. But you or I, as builders, could order men to set about it with picks and hammers, and in time it would be gone. Is that not the same power?"

"No, it is not!"

Once again, Duna recognised in Inar how it felt to be at the mercy of Anzola's reasoning, how slow-witted and confused it left its victim. She allowed herself a tiny smirk at his discomfort – let him suffer a little in those honeyed coils.

"They were made to fight wars," Inar continued. "They serve destruction and chaos."

Anzola turned to Duna. "Is that what you want, Duna? To serve destruction and chaos?"

"No, your grace," she answered, with conviction. "I have never wanted that."

"Ruin is not like the other scourges," Anzola said, returning her attention to Inar. "Augardine made them last, and he was most proud of them. He dreamed of finding constructive uses for these powers, did you know that? Plague, blight, panic – there is no benefit to those. But the ability to break stone, we can use that! You are a builder Inar – think of it, those abilities, in quarries and mines, cutting canals... widening mountain passes!"

She had him, Duna could see it, she could see it in his eyes – that slight shine of promise. She had found the correct point to attack his wall, and aimed for it. It was a remarkable skill of the merite's, and part of how she came to be a merite. She was something of a scourge herself. If Inar was going to join the Anzola business, Duna realised that she would need to have a little warning talk with him about how that business worked. Tell him about the Anzoliad.

"Will you come back with us?" Anzola asked. "Spend time with Duna, as I have, and see that she means no one any harm, and you'll understand that I've been telling you the truth. We have learned so much about her abilities, and they have improved with time and practice."

"She's growing more powerful?" Inar asked, wary again, and Lott raised his head at this.

"Very slowly, very gradually," Anzola said. "Her strength and range seem to have reached a plateau – the Vulture's Eye, that was representative of her best. I have not seen her break a larger stone, and she must be close to it. Mostly the improvement is in precision and control: valuable areas to master, you must agree. For safety."

"For safety," Inar said, not hiding his scepticism.

"You can help with that," Duna said. "That's why you're here."

16

ANTON

Before Elecy's visit, Anton's world had shrunk to a stone egg of private misery, as if the rest of the world had ceased to exist. He had hardly given a moment of thought to what might be taking place in the grander chambers far above him. But after, he discovered he could think of little else.

His hearing, first. He was to be condemned, and then probably executed. Elecy had been quite right, and Anton found himself obscurely proud of her shrewdness: The decision was made and all they could do was perform their parts as it unfolded. His great fear was that her religious ardour might overcome the natural instinct of self-preservation and cause her to make a stand on the part of truth, dooming herself. But she was displaying impressive reserves of pragmatism.

What else? Ving was altzan-al, the Zealots were following his orders and his enemies were dead or imprisoned. If rays of light were sought, Yisho was a possibility. Anton had always admired her. On an individual level, she was the only other dark-skinned person in the Tzanate's upper reaches, and he had found her bearing and the respect she evoked in others an inspiration. As strategos she kept a scrupulous distance from factional involvement. Anton was convinced that her loyalty was to the Tzanate rather than to Ving, and she could carry the Zealots with her. Ving had struck when she and the army were elsewhere, and there must have been good reason for that. He wanted her out of the way until he was safely in Ramnie's chair and a few facts had been carved into truth with the point of a blade. She would find it hard to oppose a sitting altzan-al, drawn from the line of succession, in possession of the Brink, perhaps the most secure fortress in the world.

The other possibility was the Custodians. Their supreme policy had long been to remain aloof. Deacon Cutruk had put it plainly: they rued their past interventions and had no thirst for more. But they had made one great recent intervention: the refusal of the Gift. And they had endorsed Anton. The resulting chaos might not give them further appetite to involve themselves in the affairs of men, but that chaos was partly their doing, and perhaps they would take responsibility.

Perhaps. And what would that mean? Crushing Ving with magic? Anton installed by supernatural means, like Augardine? In the indestructible darkness of the dungeon, it seemed impossible. What happened in the halls above was as distant as the currents in the southern oceans, or the rotations of the moon and its maids. What Anton always circled back to was the much less significant business of his own death, which he was certain Ving would want to hasten.

A clattering came from behind the door, and a jangle of heavy keys, and Anton thought: here it comes. The oil lamp had burned out long ago and had not been replaced, which made sense – why waste lamp-oil on a dead man? He was lying in a curl, and the thought occurred that he should meet his doom with a little dignity. While he could not quite bring himself to stand, he could at least form himself into a pose of meditation, sitting cross-legged on the floor.

The door opened, and behind it stood Ving. Two Zealots flanked him, and Anton sensed more out of sight from the shufflings in the passage and the murmur of many breaths.

So he had come to deliver the news himself – a final courtesy.

"I am to die, then?" Anton asked, and he surprised himself with the composure he put into his words.

"There will be a hearing – I am expected there now," Ving said. "Death is to be expected. The accusation is impossible to answer, Anton, you were witnessed in the midst of the act."

Anton felt a crackle of pain across the muscles and tissue of his face, where he had been struck by the Zealots, and he feared that something had broken in him. He realised he was smiling.

"So, we must continue the charade, even when it's just us, eh?" Anton said. "Yes, I see. Death is to be expected."

This glimmer of scorn was as much a surprise to Anton as his overall calmness had been. And now it had been let out, he feared Ving might be angry. That had always been his impression of Ving: that he was a stockpile of suppressed rage, always seeking outlets for disapproval and condemnation. But Ving was not angry. The anger had always seeped out of a bedrock of disappointment – perhaps now he was sated with power, the disappointment and the anger were gone? What, then remained? He drew back, and even though he was moving from the gloomy threshold of Anton's cell into the relative light of the passage, he appeared to darken, the shadows gathering under those sagging eyes. This was not the haughty aspect of a man who has unlimited power.

And Anton realised: Ving was *wary*. He did *not* have unlimited power. Was it Anton's failure to cringe and scrape and beg for his life? His deviation from the script that had been prepared for him? And if a performance was needed, who was the audience? The Zealots?

Ving was not confident of the Zealots.

"Your crime is of supreme seriousness, Anton, you should consider your words," said Ving, and now that Anton was ready for it, he caught a whiff of bluster. "You may not have many left."

Anton nodded. "Yes, the crime was a serious one, and the criminal is present."

"You have been marked by a Custodian," Ving said, pushing on with a degree of haste. "I need to know when this occurred."

"It occurred on the day before the Conclave, when I was told – by Ramnie himself – that I was to succeed him as altzan-al."

"You accuse yourself!" Ving said with a snort. "Your own words show the delusions, the insanity, that drove you to kill our beloved father. The markings are long healed. They clearly date from a much older meeting, connected to your former role as vertzan."

An act, it was just an act. It was for the Zealots, not for anyone else.

"The Custodians do not injure those they wish to preserve, altzan," Anton said carefully, "and their marks heal with unnatural swiftness. But you would not know this, because you have not been marked. I was chosen, not you."

Ving snorted again. "Magic, how convenient," he said, though not with total conviction. "It cannot be explained, so Custodian magic is responsible. A child could see the lie."

"You could always ask them, *altzan-al*," Anton said, trying to put mockery into Ving's stolen title. He feared that the slender advantage he had gained might soon run out, or twist against him. "They will speak to you, as the rightful ruler of the Tzanate, will they not? And they will tell you the truth, in front of witnesses. Why not do that? Let them hold the hearing."

"And why not have the resurrected Augardine sit as judge?" Ving said, and a hardness in his words made Anton fear his luck had indeed run out. He stepped forward into the cell. "Madness has always been the sickness of the blade-priests. Delusions." Leaning down towards Anton, he spoke quietly, with venom. "You're an animal, unwisely elevated by fools, and the learning we tried to give you has become nothing but hatred and fanaticism. But your time has run out. What did the Custodians say to you? What did they share?"

With no more bravado to spend, Anton could do nothing but frown, overcome by fatigue. "What? I don't know."

"Tell me."

Anton closed his eyes. "I was told I would be the next altzan-al. I was told the alliance with the League would ultimately mean the destruction of Miroline."

Ving rolled his eyes. "Yes, yes. Miroline is not what it was. But what did they share? What was to be given to Ramnie, or to you, for the struggle? What did they *share*?"

"Nothing," Anton said. "I don't know. The creature said that they despaired of giving magic to men, it had caused so much harm."

"You're lying," Ving spat, and Anton was startled by the sudden crack in his stony shell. "Ramnie said that there was... he only hinted, but I know that we were being given a blessing, a power, a weapon, that we might use. What is it? *Where* is it?"

"I don't know," Anton said. "I was told of nothing like that."

There was little room in the cell, but Ving had come close to Anton, and now he withdrew a little. He was searching in the folds of his robe. "Your death might be expected, Anton, but not the form it might take. If you choose, this instant, to tell me everything the Custodians told you, then I will order a swift end by the blade, followed by the proper disposal of your remains in the akouy shiel. You will be united with heaven. However if you do not tell me, or you choose to lie, you will be buried. Alive."

Anton gasped, a gout of horror. He tried to reach back into his meeting with the Custodian to retrieve the crucial detail, the one Ving was looking for, and began to babble. "The Custodian said there was little time. It said that the Custodians were authorities on death, and they thought we needed death, when they made men immortal and gave them powers it was always a mistake, and Ramnie said that meant that if we drew on the Mountain it had to be for the right reasons, and that we had to defend the Mountain, and it... it... I don't know. That's all I can remember."

While Anton had been speaking, Ving had taken something from his robe. He turned it over in his hand and Anton was able to catch a glimpse of it: a disc of milky crystal. Candorite. "Nothing about grants to us. About weapons we might use."

Anton was at a loss, pitted in despair, unable even to understand the riddle, let alone provide its answer. "There was nothing," he said.

All of Ving's attention was on the little translucent disc that he turned in his fingers, a gesture almost idle. "I wonder what the old man meant," he said, more to himself than to his prisoner. "It changes nothing. Goodbye, Anton."

He stepped out of the cell, and a Zealot closed the door behind him with a final thump.

Burial. To be buried dead was a horrible enough prospect – a permanent dishonour to his body and his soul. To be buried alive was unimaginable. But what did it matter? He had already been buried.

If sleep came in the hours that followed, Anton did not know – it might have been one long wakemare. And at times it took on the garb of one of those visions. His mind no longer felt doubly trapped, in a filthy and starving body confined in a stone hole deep in the ground. It walked free. He fancied he rose up to see the world from above: first the jumble of roofs that was the Brink, held behind mighty walls, filling the pass that led to the Mountain. Then the wastelands and Craithe itself and God's shoulder and the abode of the Custodians, and the rest of the Hidden Land, its choking grey dust and azure lake, its ruins and unhallowed monuments. And the passes, with their fortresses, and further out there were moors and forests and deserts. But all the time Anton knew that this was not a genuine gift of sight, it was not seeing the world as a Custodian might see it, but a mere fantasy, for so much of it was ghostly and shrouded, the simplest outline, names without shapes, ideas without pictures. What he had not seen, he could not see, and he realised how little of the world he had known. A forest, he knew, was a great multitude of trees, and the Brink had a small orchard in the crystal canyon, but the descriptions of Tarch made it sound dark and terrible and difficult to traverse, and how could that be true of an orchard? And the oceans – they were expanses of water, like Hleng, but they carried on to unknowable distances, further than could be seen, and in myth and history they were given the characteristics of living things, which raged and rose up and consumed ships and men and towns. How could this be?

All he had ever known was this fortress and the empty land around it. There had been another life, once, a mother and a place that he had been born, and a journey here, but it had all been before he was old enough to know. Reaching back in his memory, he thought he could sense the terrible echoes of a great rupture, as if his earliest thoughts were finding a way to live in the wake of a great cataclysm, but whatever that cataclysm had been was lost on the mercifully spotless mind of an infant. How had he performed, in the end? There would be a place for him in the histories, even if it was for a crime he did not commit: the fanatical vestige of a violent past, who had murdered a noble and venerable altzan-al. That was not what he was. He had never wished to touch a blade, and his entire existence would be inscribed forever as a man who wanted nothing more than to carve and kill.

Anton hoped that he did not have to wait long. Would they want to execute him as soon as the hearing concluded? He guessed that Ving would be impatient to tie up his loose end, yes. And although he had no wish to die, he saw little choice, and did not want the painful eternity of a sleepless night in the total darkness. His other hope was that Ving had been satisfied with his answers and it would be the blade, not burial. That at least would be quick for everyone. Wasn't he owed that, at least? He thought back over all the loyalty he had wasted on Ving, all the effort he had put into trying to respect him, that impossible, petulant, bigoted old bastard. And what had he received? Incomprehension and resentment from a man with no idea what to do with the two young blade-priests who had ended up in his care. It was a fitting tribute to the man that Anton found it so much easier to imagine as his killer than as his father.

Although he had no way of telling how long it had been since Ving had left, he could be sure it had not been a full night before he again heard noises beyond his cell door. The door was so thick that nothing could be heard from the passageway, only the sound of a key in the lock. But this was not that – there was a loud bang, as if a heavy weight had struck the door, followed by another somewhat softer thud. For a moment Anton was puzzled. Was someone knocking for admittance? Should he tell them to come in? What was this, perverse manners towards a condemned man? But he said nothing, and in due course the key did clatter in the lock, quick and clumsy.

In the doorway stood Elecy. She was not wearing her robes but the simpler grey habit of an acolyte, and it was stained. In her hand she carried something, a sharp-edged shadow that dripped on the stone floor.

"Get up, get up," she said. "Quick."

Anton did not get up. A great gulf of horror had opened beneath him, and he withdrew at the sight of his sister in the faith. Surely they would not ask her… and surely she would not agree…? But she carried a blade, that was right, and there was a wild look in her eyes.

"Anton, quickly," she said, entering the cell and bending down to him. "You have to get up, can you stand?"

From behind her came noises – bumps and scrapes and bangs, and the gasps and cries of more than one man. A voice rang out, perhaps the first sound of a word, but it was cut short, ending in a vile gargle.

Elecy grabbed under Anton's armpit with the hand that was not carrying a knife, trying to pull him up. Anton worked himself to his feet, his legs blazing with cramps and pains.

A Zealot appeared behind Elecy, spearpoint out, and a bundle under his other arm. He threw the bundle into the cell. Anton saw fur and leather.

"Make haste," the Zealot hissed, before turning to address another in the passageway, shouting, "The door! The door!" Then he disappeared.

"Get dressed," Elecy said. "You're leaving." Anton's eyes had adjusted to the change in the light, and he could see her better. A spray of blood arced across her neck and the side of her face, and he guessed that the dark patches on her arms and across her front was the same.

"You're hurt," he said.

She smiled, a dangerous smile. "Not at all. He didn't get close."

Anton inspected the bundle – it was the garb of a Zealot scout, rugged but far lighter than armour. He made to remove the stinking rags he had been left in, and glanced up at Elecy.

She rolled her eyes. "You are a brother to me, you know," she said, turning her back.

The clothing was unfamiliar and Anton fumbled with it.

"You need to hurry," Elecy said. "We have little time. Someone may see the horses."

"Horses?" Anton said. "Where are we going?"

Elecy turned, satisfied that he was decent. "You are leaving, Anton, you must make haste."

"But where?"

"I don't know where," Elecy said. "Wherever you think there is safety, where there are those loyal to the Mountain. Go to Yisho, wherever she is – Mal Nulalus, Cassodar, I don't know. But Ving does not seem to believe in her, and she has the army. Or go to Miroline."

A scream arose at some distance, and there was a clash of steel. Elecy glanced over her shoulder, alarmed. "Hurry, hurry."

"Why would Yisho help me?" Anton said. "Ving has the throne, he has the Brink, he has everything. He must expect her to fall in line. I'll be caught and returned."

Elecy smiled, and a light came in her eyes. "No, Anton. You don't understand. Yisho will listen to you." Sheathing her knife, she reached into the folds of her rough grey robe, and produced a small red book, with a gilt gull embossed on the cover. It was Xirco's *Southern Travels*.

"Not a library binding," Elecy said, flipping the book open. "And you really shouldn't be using something like this as a bookmark." Inserted in the book was a folded square of fine parchment. Elecy tucked the book under her arm and unfolded the paper. It bore three paragraphs of close-packed, untidy writing, which in the gloom of the cell Anton could not make out. But he knew the two ribboned seals at the bottom, and the signature – Ramnie.

"It names you as successor," Elecy said. "And furthermore warns against pretenders who might claim otherwise. And I think I know who he meant."

"By the Mountain," Anton breathed. "How did you find this?"

"After you were arrested, I didn't know what I should do, and I thought you might want something to read, so I took some books from your cell. I didn't realise…" Elecy glanced around at Anton's stone pit, and did not need to finish her sentence. "Later, some Zealots came and ransacked your quarters – I wondered what they might be looking for. And as I said, this volume stood out.

"Anton," she continued, and she put her hands on his, even as they still held Ramnie's testament. "Take this to Yisho – guard it like you would guard your life. It is your life, Anton – it is the life of the Tzanate itself."

Hands shaking, Anton refolded the parchment, feeling as

if any moment it might burst into flame. Lacking any more secure place for it, he returned it to the pages of Xirco. A shouted instruction, its content inaudible to Anton, came from the passageway, and Elecy shouted her assent.

"We must go," she said.

17

INAR

"The Hidden Land," Anzola said. Inar thought she might be talking to herself, telling herself that she had arrived. But she turned to him and spoke on. "I believed that name came from its inaccessibility – it was hard to get to, an ill-omen among the few who knew of it, so before Augardine came along it might as well have been hidden, kept apart from the world. But now I see the truth – the land truly is hidden."

Below them was an ocean of cloud. The mountain-girdled plateau of Elith-Tenh was filled with white mist, like a bowl filled with milk, its surface smooth and blinding under the midday sun.

They had reached the Sight of God, a natural lookout high above the plateau. It was, in itself, a dreary place: a large jut of basalt, completely level and polished to a blade shine by the action of the seasons. Behind rose the line of peaks that they had crossed, brown as baked bread under the sun, buttered with snow at the heights. Above their position, square black openings had been carved into the rock: ossuaries for the bones of those worthy enough to be left in the Sight of God. With no shade, no water, and glare from above and below, the Sight was an inhospitable place. But there was that prospect, that infinitely nourishing prospect – though God was still far, days away across the forbidden country, there were no obstacles between here and there, and the mountain was clear on the eastern horizon, under the sun. It commanded silence, its form heavy yet curiously mobile, its inexpressive tar-like surface throwing out other hues.

Craithe's lower portions were shielded by a range of peaks, higher and more formidable than those the party had just crossed, but strangely appearing less so, surmounted as they were by God. A gap could be seen just beneath the holy mountain, and in that gap the natural tone and texture of distant terrain was a little different – there was a hint of regularity, a touch of the plumb line and the builder's square, the tiniest twinkle of glass and gilt. A citadel: Craithe's Brink. When Inar had been here before, as a child, they had made the final journey through the Eye in the early hours of the morning, while it was still dark. At the Sight, the tzans performed rites as the sun rose, and the silhouette of the God revealed itself in the burning clouds. There was no mist, and the whole of the Hidden Land could be admired – all Inar could recall was the shocking white-ringed blue of Hleng, the salt lake. A day was spent in devotions, fasting and praying; the shrouded body of a Mishigo baron was left on the carved stone slab that stood at the edge of the Sight. A sacrificial altar, Astar had told Inar and Essian, enjoying their horrified shudders. In the ancient past, living men would have been opened up there; living children, even. The Custodians would come direct from the Mountain to feast on their warm hearts. The rest might go on to make bindlings, and serve the Tzanate and Empire in death.

That rite – the Gift – had once been practised everywhere the Empire had ruled, from the land of the aurorae to the deserts of Yicorum. It had been in retreat more than a century, as the Empire crumbled. No more was it given in Miroline or Stull; but when Inar had been brought here, it was still being given at Craithe's Brink. His young eyes had been directed at the palace-fortress, and he had been told that it was a place of human sacrifice. There were knife-priests there, terrible necromancers in blood-soaked white robes, armed with sickles of Craithestone that could split a man in two.

These days, the Gift had been abolished there as well. No one outside the Tzanate had seen a Custodian in decades – no demigod had swooped down to collect the dead baron, and Inar presumed that the noble's old bones had been cleaned by venerated but un-magical mountain vultures and other scavenging birds. Because the Custodians had gone from living experience, it was becoming easy to imagine that they had never existed.

It was the Spring Rout, the day they had aimed to arrive. They kept the camp at the Vulture's Eye, as it wasn't far from the Sight and no one wanted to move equipment and mules through the Eye – another lesson about the pass was learned. On the first morning, the entire party, barring one knight, came down to enjoy their destination. A bottle of Vellene wine that had survived the journey was opened and shared. No one got more than a cup, but the knights immediately seemed quite drunk, and Inar could sniff that theirs was the dangerous male gladness that can all too easily switch to anger and violence. To them, the expedition was as good as over: the return to Sojonost would have its share of difficulty, but it would be over ground already travelled, with success in hand – there was bold talk of completing it in two nights. Inar supposed that, to them, the world must appear wide open, and the League's powers limitless – he wondered what that must be like. And he sensed the aggression implicit in that giddy liberation.

Kielo and one of the knights had brought down the measuring equipment, and the secretary, Anzola and Duna spent a couple of hours looking through the little glass at the surrounding mountains, scratching numbers and talking quietly. They seemed to be delighted with the breadth and clarity of the view. Before long they turned their attention to Craithe itself, and their chatter became excited.

"What can you see?" Inar asked them. He rather liked the

thought of peeking through that glass himself, and getting a better view of the Brink. It was reputed to be one of the greatest works of man – although, of course, man could not take credit for all of it.

Anzola beamed at him. "We've been taking readings from Craithe whenever we can, and... well, there's always the possibility of error, at this distance, in these conditions – but as far as we can tell its height isn't consistent."

Inar frowned.

"It keeps changing," Duna said, without emotion. "Higher, lower, always different."

"That certainly sounds like an error," Inar said.

Anzola shook her head. "No. That can't account for it. The difference between highest and lowest is more than a hundred feet. We haven't seen anything like that margin from the surrounding peaks. And it is consistent with what written accounts we can find: Craithe changes. Its features are never the same. And now we know: it rises and falls."

"Like it's breathing," Duna added.

Inar felt a spike of irritation at this remark, which struck him as childish. "That's what the stories have always said. The Mountain changes. It is always the Mountain but it is never quite the same." This was true, but it was obscurely disturbing to have the stuff of folklore confirmed with the equipment of natural philosophy. "It's a mountain," he continued, feeling a tetchy edge creep into his voice. "It is made out of stone. It does not breathe."

He glanced at Duna to check her reaction, and found her face wrapped with a horrible smile. "But it's not stone, is it Inar? *You* know that." She put dark emphasis on the *You*, and he could infer from it the *And Me*. "You know that, you feel it, even here. *It is not stone.*"

And she was right. There was no way for him to feel the mountains on the far side of Elith-Tenh – as was familiar, his special sense only extended a few yards around, to the ancient inertness of the dense sacrificial slab, and the cliff face behind them, all the little fractures made during the making of the carved openings, each like a bit of apple skin caught between teeth, but none of them betraying serious weakness. Beyond all that he could feel the presence of Craithe, and he realised that he had felt it all along. Gaze at a candle flame in a dark room, and then close your eyes and turn away, and the impression lingers, a red blob floating at the fore of the mind. So it was with the Mountain God, but the sense affected was not sight, it was… something else. It was there, it lingered, even as he turned his head and thought of other things.

"Maybe it has obtained the 'Mountain' from its size alone," Kielo said, using a slightly too-loud voice that came over him when he thought he was being clever. "It doesn't mean it *is* a mountain, just that only mountains approach it in scale, and we have no other language…"

Inar stopped paying attention. Duna had detached herself from the group and was walking toward the rear of the Sight, where rough steps led up to the ossuaries. *You know that.* Aye, he did, but how? Nearby lay a fallen cube of frost-shattered stone, the size and shape of a loaf of bread. A good shape, in fact, one he felt well, the kind of stone he liked to carry down from the foothills around Stull and carve. He picked it up and weighed it – heavy, as you'd expect, and dense, but had he found it on a walk he would not have thought it too heavy to carry back.

Letting the silence settle around him, he reached into it. It was stable and essentially flawless, no hidden cracks or veins of other substances that made it weaker. But within was the line and grain of it, the places the blade of a chisel would cut sweetly – and what else? A hand-hold for another power? Again, he tried, he tried to find the inner mechanism in mind or stone that let one affect the other, change the other, break the other… and he could not. He felt absurd for even trying, as if he was attempting to fly by running in circles flapping his arms. Whatever he was, he was no scourge. It was a relief – there was also the melancholy tinge of a thwarted possibility. What must it be like to possess such power?

She doesn't look dangerous, Lott had said to Inar when they were alone the previous day. Inar replied that that was true of a lot of dangerous things. To which Lott said that even if she wasn't a scourge, she could have put an axe in their heads on any one of the previous nights, which was also true, but not very reassuring either way.

There were other scourge abilities, four in all. He tried to recall the tales told by tzans. He had seen carvings and tapestries and the illuminations in books. They were always portrayed as monstrous figures: tall and robed, faces wreathed in shadow or cracked or twisted by decay or hatred, skeletal hands shattering towers or spreading sickness, some so frightful that a glimpse of them was enough to rout armies. Plague, that was the one that had caused such devastation during the war, such death that they said the world had still not recovered. Panic – the breaker of armies, the torturer. And blight, the killer of harvests and animals, the bringer of famine.

Gruesome lies, Anzola had said. And Inar had to acknowledge that the accounts were ambiguous – the tzans also warned that scourges could conceal themselves in plain sight. While the Tzanate boasted of its eradication of the scourges, of the pains that were taken to find and burn every last one of them, it also warned of hidden bloodlines, and the fact that scourgehood was passed from parent to child. Women had been burned as suspected scourges within his lifetime, but he thought that was village viciousness. After all, men were equally capable of being scourges, but it always seemed to be women who were burned. Going back to the time of Inar's grandfather's grandfather there had been a wider scourge-craze, a wave of burnings across numerous lands, accompanying the civil wars within the empire.

Duna was right there. He could speak to her, and possibly

learn what she knew about him. Now would be the perfect time, as she had strolled away on her own. But just as he had resolved to do this, he was addressed.

"Inar, let me show you why we are here," Anzola said, enthusiasm in her voice. The night before, dealing with the repercussions of Duna's demonstration and Inar's reaction, she had appeared tense and deeply tired. The tiredness was still there, showing in the lines at the corners of her eyes – all their faces were more weatherbeaten and worn than they had been when they met in Stull. But there was a deep relief there, too. Even if they were not safe – they were still in the mountains, with little comfort and few resources and days from true safety – Anzola had the look of someone who had reached safety.

She unbuckled the collar of her coat and reached in to find a breast pocket. Out came a folder of leather, and from that a folded sheaf of new vellum, a fine square from the centre of a hide, a little curved and battered by the journey. She opened it out. Inar squatted beside her to see. A flamboyant illuminated heading of greeting and titles, below which were numbered blocks of neat text in Mirolingua. Then, signatures.

"His excellence the duzh," Anzola said, indicating a tiny, shaky scratch of a name. "This is the merite Ernesto, who you met." A lazy scrawl, as if he had begun E-r-n- and then tired and finished with a trailing line, which Inar found as objectionable as the man. "And myself." A flowing and elegant mark, with a z elaborated into twisting decorative loops. "And here is space for the altzans. They will bring the Tzanate's side of the treaty for our signature."

"An altzan is coming here?"

Anzola smiled, the satisfaction radiating from her. "Yes. Maybe several. Possibly the altzan-al himself, but he is old, like our duzh. And Zealots, and Zealot commanders. It'll be quite a delegation." She glanced towards Thiolo, who had brought the League's standard with him from the camp, and Inar knew that she was regretting the poverty of their expedition.

"The most significant meeting between the Tzanate and a world power since Augardine," Kielo said. He had been standing with the equipment, but listening in on his mistress, as always. "The merite has worked most assiduously for this moment. Your grandchildren, Inar, *their* grandchildren, will talk of how their ancestor was present on this day."

Anzola laughed. "Kielo flatters me. That is part of his purpose, after all. You will write a very fine account of this day, won't you, Kielo? We will make you famous, the equal of Klintoe. Hah! Kielo, Klintoe. You even sound alike." Inar realised that he had not heard the woman joke this easily for some days. Though she rarely appeared flustered, clearly the journey had taken a toll.

"Now you flatter me, your grace," Kielo said, genuine pleasure in his smile. A weight had been lifted from him as well. "The opportunity to study this place is reward enough."

A sudden gust of cold wind, slicing through the peaks, tugged hard at the treaty in Anzola's hands, and she carefully re-folded it and returned it to its pocket. "Yes, the opportunity to survey the pass was not to be missed," she said. "They should be coming here now. They needed a Conclave of their church to agree to everything, but I was told it was all stitched up in advance."

Inar had seen an altzan, of course – the Tzanate's representative in Stull, who gave a service of devotion once a month in the high temple and who served as religious counsel to the king. He was a short, wrinkled man, and there was nothing obviously special about him. But some of them were reputed to be instructed in the necromancy of the Custodians – the subtle influence over mind and flesh, living and dead. Especially dead. As for the Zealots, surely no one in the world was unaware of their reputation: the most ferocious fighters in existence, each one worth ten Mirolinian legionnaires, or twenty regular soldiers. Death was only a temporary setback for a Zealot: first they came as men, then as bindlings.

Anzola had stopped paying attention to Inar and was looking out across the Hidden Land, eyes hunting for clues of the approaching delegation.

When he had been brought here as a child, Inar had not been allowed anywhere near the altar. But today there was nobody to stop him. It was a large and low slab of basalt, too low to be impressive from afar, but he realised – with an ugly twist in the stomach – that it would have to be low for a blade-priest to work. The flat black surface was smooth and unblemished. But the rougher sides were deeply etched with carvings: the runes of the Custodians. Basalt was a hard stone, difficult to carve, but carvings would stay crisp for lifetimes. Here, however, their edges were dulled and softened. The work was ancient indeed.

Inar reached out. He discerned the inner voice of the stone – dense and consistent. Crystalline. It had been hot, hot enough to run like water, and thick, and had cooled just right to make it such solid, pure stone.

Duna was nearby. He knew before he heard her feet scuff on the ground.

"You could put a split right through this, couldn't you?" he asked. "Easy. It's a lot smaller than the Eye-rock."

She hunched her shoulders. "Easy."

"Do you worry about the altzans coming?" Inar asked, a question that seemed to have come out of nowhere, until he retraced its steps and found it came from a tight ribbon of fear deep within. "Some of them know about these things. They might be able to tell what you are."

"Not really," Duna said. "They did too good a job of suppressing practical knowledge about the... about my kind of person. If they bring a Custodian with them, maybe, but apparently there are very few of them left. And the only people who can detect scourges are people with scourge abilities. They would have reason to keep quiet."

The sickness stirred in Inar. Because he could feel it: that warmth, that presence. The sense that mapped to none of the five senses.

"Only scourges can detect scourges?" he asked.

She smiled at him – not a particularly kind smile, the smile of an older sister to an idiot sibling. "I know what you're thinking. Don't worry, you're not. You do have... an allied ability. One that works with mine." With that, she darkened. "One a lot more helpful than mine."

Inar swallowed. "Have you ever found anyone like you?"

Duna stopped smiling. "I cannot say."

"Cannot say because you don't know, or cannot say because it's a secret?" Inar knew it was an unfair question as he asked it, because even to acknowledge that the answer was secret gave a clue as to what the answer might be.

"The Tzanate used scourges to find other scourges," Duna said, her expression darkening. "When they decided to root them out. And they used people like you as well. You should know that they killed the ones that helped, all the same."

"I'm sorry," Inar said.

"You didn't do it," Duna said, blankly.

"I'm sorry I asked."

They lapsed into silence.

The ocean of mist appeared as still as it was silent, though Inar knew it rolled with constant motion. And below, what moved there? Was a glittering party of the Tzanate's finest making its way towards them, under the cover of that white blanket?

Silence had infected everyone at the Sight. As the day wore on, the cheerful optimism of Anzola and Kielo shifted to reflection, and then to a delicate tension. Nothing happened, no servants of the Tzanate appeared, and soon the quiet was so unbearable that Inar felt obliged to break it with a question.

"'Our costly assistants'," Inar said. "What did Ernesto mean by that? Costly?"

Anzola blinked, perhaps covering a roll of the eyes. "In return for your service, the League has made certain concessions to the crown of Mishig-Tenh," she said, a little wearily. "The tribute payments of metals and stone from the mines and quarries under the crown monopoly will cease – or rather, they will continue, but the League will now pay for them. Below merchant prices, but better than nothing."

"By the Mountain," Inar gasped. "That's madness. That's… everything they want. Why would you offer that just for me?"

Anzola sniffed. "It was, in some respects, on the table anyway," she said. "The League does not have much practise at conquest, Inar. We are learning."

"We are a federation of cities," Kielo said. He glanced at Anzola for permission, which was given with an incline of the head. "The past strategy of the League has been to focus on holding cities and a few other strongholds, like Sojonost and the passes in the west. We patrol the roads and the seas and expect the hinterlands between to behave in return for markets and security. 'Ports and forts', we called this strategy. If it rhymes, it must be wise, yes?"

He looked again at Anzola, who rewarded this joke with a smile. "This policy cannot continue. The collapse of Oririthen… We had not expected the Elves to sweep in as they did. Caenon bathed in blood. Famine across a land that should be a breadbasket. Our cities surrounded by desperate people seeking sanctuary. Bandits attacking *our* patrols on *our* roads. And the Elves grow in numbers. We thought we could snatch away Oririthen's richest cities, take its forts, declare some of its roads Leagueways and leave it at that. We crippled the country, left it helpless, and it was a terrible mistake."

Anzola shook her head at this. "We snatched nothing, Kielo," she said, a note of warning in her voice. "We *freed* the cities and we took only what was essential to our security. We are not Miroline. We are not going to make everyone speak Palla and learn the ways of the Tide." She frowned, reflecting on the events, and turned back to Inar. "But he's right, it has been a – it has not worked out. Mishig-Tenh has, at least, been more peaceful, but even there the situation is not satisfactory. We cannot have a place like Mishig-Tenh, in such an important location on our border, reduced to beggary and tyranny and seething with rage. A new settlement was already needed. But we might as well get something in return, and what we wanted was you." She scowled, and made a hissing noise through her teeth, an act Inar found distinctly ill-bred. "And that swine Cilma still wanted more. The deal of the age, and he wanted more."

"He has proved a difficult customer," Kielo said, with care.

Anzola took a step closer to Inar and laid a gloved hand on his shoulder. The move startled him and, with an instinct he could not quite trace, he looked around to see where Duna might be – seated nearby, as it happened, watching the conversation in the usual mild sulk. "I am going to tell you something now, Inar, that must stay between us," she said, fixing him with a piercing stare. He froze. "It must not be repeated outside this company. Tell no one. Not even Lott."

Inar felt curiously dizzy. Kielo and Anzola were discussing the organisation of half of the world as if it was... no more than men and materials on a building site. He had believed that all countries functioned much the same way, even if some called their nobles lords and others called them merites, and some chose nobles by birth and others by ballot, and some had different views of the capabilities of women. But all countries were, fundamentally, a pyramid, with a ruler at the top, nobles in between, and the common folk at the bottom. A small country like Mishig-Tenh and a vast empire like classical Miroline were just pyramids of different sizes. But the League did not see the world as lots of separate pyramids. They saw a web, a world of connections and deals, that could be simply rearranged. He had a vision of rooms where men, and women, sat and decided these things – completely freed from the binds of birth and honour, free to say "this country is not working, let us change it". It was intoxicating. It was terrifying.

"Yes," he said. "No one. Not even Lott."

"Ending tribute is just the start," she said. "Soon – when King Otto dies – the country will become a protectorate of the League. It will have a Mishigo ruler – a governor, not a king. It will have voting rights within the Convention. It will resume the lands lost after the war, including Sojonost. Its situation within the League will be very similar to the place it occupied within the empire of Miroline. A period your people look back on with pride, unless I am mistaken?"

She was still staring at him – judging his reaction, Inar realised. And he realised that he might well be the very first Mishigo to hear of this plan. His reaction would matter to Anzola.

"I… The nobility will fight you," he said. The plan was all he could have wished for – all his father wanted, and had been prepared to betray his king for. But his father and his brother had paid for that decision, and he could not think of the change happening so easily, without more blood. "How do you expect to square this with Lord Cilma? He has spent years defending the crown, I find it hard…"

But Anzola was smiling. "The nobility in general will be neutered in the same way we dealt with our own: money, guarantees, new titles, special seating in the Convention. Lord Cilma, well…"

That smile, still. And Inar could see it, he could see the outline of the plan. He knew who would be the first governor of the League Protectorate of Mishig-Tenh: the merite Cilma.

18

ANTON

Dead Zealots lay in the passageway, more numerous than the living ones, who stood with haunted expressions, spears raised. There were more in the circular chamber where Anton had been stripped and beaten, and a couple of grievously injured soldiers, crying and spitting blood, with comrades crouched uselessly over them.

Elecy did not head for the high, arched doorway that Anton had come through when he was introduced to this hell, but to a side door. The two priests were joined by a Zealot, also wearing the garb of a scout, covered with outdoor furs.

"Anton, this is Franj," Elecy said. "She will ride with you. We have only two horses, the stables are bare."

Franj nodded a greeting. She was almost a child, younger than Anton.

"You're not coming?" Anton asked Elecy, his heart thrown to the floor.

"I must stay," Elecy said, avoiding his eye.

"They'll kill you for this."

She shook her head. "I was never here. This is a mutiny among the Zealots. No tzans involved. It is safer to stay."

"How can it be–"

"If I go," Elecy said, "Ving will suspect a wider plot. He will purge more of the priesthood. The cost will be terrible."

They had passed from the high circular chamber, through a short connecting atrium, into a long vaulted hall that stretched for further than the meagre light of the oil lamps could reach. With a shock, Anton realised he knew exactly where they were: this arcade ran the length of the Brink, directly beneath the Processional Way, and at its far end connected to the warren of buried rooms used by the blade-priests, where they kept their sacrificial victims and made the arcane preparations for the Giving of the Gift. Disused chambers, thanks be to the Custodians, but ones he knew. He had the sense that Elecy had been here much more recently than he. In any case, they turned the other way, away from the Mountain. Their footsteps echoed in the near-dark. From the distance came more sounds: the clatter of metal, thin screams. As they walked, these sounds receded.

"How many are you?" Anton asked, panting for breath. He felt pitiably weak, and if he could hardly make it across the Brink, he had no idea how he would fare crossing the Hidden Land.

"About twenty," Elecy said. "A couple more joined when we made our move. Without surprise we could never have done it."

"Not enough to take the Brink?"

Elecy did not answer, but her grim expression was answer enough. Even in its depleted state, the garrison would be a couple of hundred strong. Twenty was enough to achieve his escape, and no more. At this moment, time was being paid for with death.

"They'll all die," Anton said.

"We are ready to die," Franj said. "There is not a man or woman among us who would not gladly lay down our lives for the Tzanate."

Even in the wavering light of the oil lamps, Anton could see the ardour in the soldier's eyes, and he heard it in her voice, and did not doubt it for a moment. But it was the Tzanate they had raised their spears against, and the terrible bloodshed in the dungeons, and the bloodshed that would surely come, was all to serve something far tinier: Anton, his life and liberty. That could not be an equal price to pay. With that thought, Anton realised that in the young Zealot's eyes, he *was* the Tzanate. He was, somehow, the living embodiment of what Franj and others had sworn their lives to protect, far more so than the priests gathered above, than the man who bore the title altzan-al and the vast monastery all around them. Anton was the Tzanate.

It was a thought that made him want to stop still, to shake Franj until she saw her error, and then to return to his cell. He felt weaker than ever.

The arcade terminated in a wide spiral staircase that twisted around a stone column thick with carvings. Anton saw raised wings and sickles, flames, talons, robes, the chambers of the heart, the entwined pageantry of death. Was that it, then, the idea that he represented the power of life and death? He hoped not.

A terrified Zealot stood holding a heavy banded door on a lightless landing off the stair. To one side, briefly caught by their passing lamps, was a body, another Zealot, face-down. Not a pleasant duty, to stand in the darkness with a body. Behind the door was a communication tunnel within the Brink's fortifications, banked with massively buttressed stone. Anton realised that they must be near the immense outer wall of the fortress, having passed under the wide open space filled with barracks, stables and training yards. The warmth had gone from the air, and their breath fogged. Even under his fur, Anton shivered.

At last they reached a rust-stained iron door set within a defensive dogleg of stone – a postern gate, used to launch surprise attacks on besieging armies, but also a discreet way out of the Brink.

"The light, the light," Franj said, and she and Elecy extinguished their lamps. And suddenly they were outside, in the night-time, on the grey broken dirt of the Hidden Land. The cold hit Anton like an avalanche, and once he had breathed it in, it was as if he had never been warm. The waxing moon lay just above the black line of mountains like an anxious sentry behind battlements, and Anton counted only two of its maids, a bad omen. He wondered about actual sentries on the battlements above. Two horses were tethered by the concealed entrance to the gate, dressed for riding and tended by a groom.

"I must leave you here," Elecy said. "Goodbye, Anton. The Mountain will see that we will meet again."

"Elecy, come with me," Anton said. "It is madness to stay."

Elecy looked at her feet. "They must not believe that tzans were involved in this enterprise," she said. "Besides – the Mountain needs me. I hear it whispering. I have business here." As if jolted by a memory, she started fiddling with her belt, unbuckling and removing it, and with it came the sheathed knife she had put to work in the dungeons. "Take it," she said. "You will need it."

In the moonlight he could see the dark streaks on the hilt of the blade, and on the hand that held it.

"No," he said, his insides twisting. "I cannot." Feeling he needed to give his refusal some weight or justification, he added: "You may need it yet."

Elecy hesitated, her expression unclear, and then she embraced him. He felt the weight of the sheathed blade bump against his ribs.

"Be safe, sister," he said.

"Be quick, brother," Elecy replied. Then she smiled, a wicked smile, the smile that recalled all the best times of their childhood together. "Altzan-al."

And she returned to the shadows of the Brink.

* * *

They went cross-country, avoiding the main road between the Brink and the Gull Gate. From the Brink, the Hidden Land looked almost flat: a wide stony expanse between mountain ranges, like sand in the bottom of a bucket. This impression changed little when travelling the Mirolinian road that crossed it. But away from the road, the picture was revealed to be a lie. The horses had to climb steep ridges and negotiate loose slopes of scree. Far from taking a straight line, they had to work in careful zigs and zags, taking each furlong as it came.

It made for slow riding, especially where the shadows cast by inclines and the giant shattered rocks that littered the plain turned moonlight into darkness. The horses whinnied and complained, and the only words that passed between their riders were terse instructions given by Franj to Anton, while Anton strained every nerve for the sounds of pursuers.

"This is hard going," Anton said at last, when the base of a shallow gully gave them a stretch of natural road.

"We need the cover," Franj said. "There's a dry lake ahead that we can cross – it'll be better. But we must be across it by dawn."

"You know the land well," Anton said.

"I want to be a scout," Franj said.

"Want to be," Anton echoed.

Franj looked away from him. "I am a scout. Trained but not yet assigned. I know the land."

"I'm thankful you're here," Anton said. "I was not doubting you. You will be a fine scout."

She did not reply. Anton thought back to Ramnie's conversation with him on the ride back from the lake. How awkward he had felt. Was that the way Franj felt with him?

"Why didn't you take the knife?" Franj asked.

Anton had not expected her to speak, let alone ask such a direct question, and for a moment he could not think of what to say. "I cannot," he said, knowing the weakness of his words.

"We may need it," she said. "We will be pursued. It's danger-ous."

"I'll fight, if I have to," Anton said. "But I cannot bear a blade."

Franj frowned at him. "A knife isn't just good for fighting, it can cut a tangled rein, it can free a stone from a hoof, it can carve your meat..."

"The last time I picked up a bloodied blade, I was accused of murder."

"We may have to fight," Franj said, and Anton saw what underlay her words – not a Zealot's disdain for those unprepared to take up arms, but fear.

"I will do what I can," Anton said. "I will fight."

"I'm just surprised," Franj said. "I knew you were a blade-priest, and I expected..."

Of course he knew exactly what she expected, and a vision of Elecy flashed into his mind, the spray of blood across her neck and cheek, her stained hands. And he felt ashamed. How many lives had his scruples saved so far? The corridors of the Brink were still littered with the dead, and the killing surely went on, others killing and dying in his name. Refusing to kill might oblige Franj to take on more – was that a lesser sin? It might cost her her life.

This is the way it would have been anyway, a voice inside said. As altzan-al, he would have needed to command an army in war. There would have been killing on a scale that made tonight's deeds in the dungeon look like a children's game. Whichever way he turned, there was blood.

"I need a little time to think about it," he said at last.

Franj sniffed. "Fighting might not be necessary," she said. "Scouts are supposed to avoid and conceal themselves and withdraw alive... It's only the Gull Gates I'm really worried about. The Hidden Land is large enough. They do not have the men to comb it all. If they know we must pass the Gull Gates, that is where they will wait. But..."

She said no more, but the way that her voice had lifted on that last word had kindled a bright flame of hope in Anton's chest. "But what?" he asked.

Franj paused before replying, focused on the darkened path ahead. Anton could not make out her expression, only the puffs of steam her breath made in the icy air. "When we heard that the altzan-al was dead, the stablemaster had all available horses made ready for dispatch," she said. "Messengers would be sent, he said, carrying the news across the Tzanate and to the world. That was what he expected. But no order went out."

"Ving did not want the news to spread," Anton said. "It might have been possible to catch Yisho if he had sent out messengers immediately, but he didn't want that, he let the army and the Conclave priests pass out of the Tzanate without knowing."

"Well, yes," Franj said. "That was our assumption – that he did not want word to reach the army. We tried to think of innocent reasons for that, because it did not strike us as the act of an innocent soul. Why would you not want to tell your strategos?"

Anton considered this. Even if she had heard the news, it was unclear what Yisho would, or could, have done. The caravan of priests and their retinues she was escorting was a large, hungry, vulnerable beast. It could not be simply abandoned in the wilderness while she returned in force. The altzans and tzans could conceivably have been left at the lake or at Mal Nulalus, but they could not be fed indefinitely. They were obliged to press on to Cassodar. Nevertheless, Yisho might have been able to divide her force and send a contingent back to the Brink. To do what, though? To shore up Ving? To oppose him? The latter would be nigh-impossible. The Brink was impregnable – it was far too formidable to take quickly, even with only a small garrison within, and a besieging army could not be kept provisioned in the wasteland of Elith-Tenh.

"You're saying that we might get to the Gull Gates ahead of

Ving's men?" Anton asked. That seemed their best hope. Once there they could invent a story – trying to get a message to the Conclave, for instance – and talk their way through.

"There are very few horses left," Franj said. "Yisho took near all of them to accompany the Conclave. Today there were fewer than twenty horses in the stables, and half of them were lame, or with foal. There's a reason we are only two."

"So it's possible?" Anton said, hope again rising within him.

"It's possible," Franj said. "But the road is direct and easier travelling. Even if they left hours later, they could beat us. We must be quick."

The land fought them; fortune fought them. The riders kept to the defile far longer than either expected, as their mounts were forced to pick every step in the near dark, and every turn and dip in the terrain had to be watched for treachery. Already light was building behind the black line of mountains around Elith-Tenh when the valley splayed out into a wide, flat expanse, ringed by low hills, a kind of reproduction of the whole plateau in miniature. But they gained no speed. Though it seemed as level and firm as a flagstone court, the lake-bed had the yielding, treacherous qualities of old, frozen snow, and it kicked up thick, choking clouds of clinging dust, which Anton feared made a column of signal-smoke that would be visible from the Brink. He yearned to raise the pace, but they could not. For a couple of hours, Anton had noticed Franj's peculiar manner around her horse, the way she frowned down at it, and leaned forward to whisper in its ear, and would look around and underneath it as it walked. Once they were out into the flat, he could see why: it was limping.

Before they had gone a half-mile across the lake-bed, she stopped to examine its right foreleg.

"It's injured?" Anton asked, dismounting to give his own horse a drink from its canteen. The dust had coated them both, itching his eyes and putting a foul taste in the back of his throat.

"An old injury," Franj said, scowling. "It's why she was held back. We thought she was recovered." She clapped her hands together to shake free some of the coating muck.

"Will it get better? Can we go on?"

"Not this one," Franj said, giving it a look that combined annoyance and sadness. "Bad choice. My fault."

Days of starvation diet, and a sleepless night in the saddle, caught up with Anton all at once. He felt himself close to collapse, and lowered to a crouch, hoping that he did not appear weak.

"So what do we do? Leave it?"

Franj frowned at the horizon, towards a line of peaks now brilliantly etched in sunlight, even though it had not yet reached down into the lake bed. "Leave *her*," she said. "No, we're not going to leave her, not here, anyway. There's a settlement not far from here. We'll leave her there. They'll take her back to the Brink."

"And then Ving will know where we are."

"Not for a couple of days. Maybe longer. I'll talk to them."

"Will they listen?" Anton asked. He knew little about the Hidden Land's natives. Several times a year, small groups of them would come to the Brink in supplication and to participate in timeworn, elliptical rituals of mutual respect. They had little to offer, and once the Tzanate had the wealth of the world flowing through its halls it no longer needed the paltry barley and goatflesh they provided, so their tributes had become symbolic. Naturally, blade-priests were there to be seen and feared, not to make chitchat, but Anton had the impression that they chitchatted little with any tzan. This laconic nature was hard to read – sometimes it appeared cowed and awed, othertimes contemptuous. In an obscure and shameful way, Anton resented them, because they made him feel a visitor in the only place he could reasonably call home. They had no need for the Tzanate to know the Mountain, and who could say what they thought of its vast and gaudy temples and fortresses.

"They'll listen to me," Franj said.

"I've heard they can be difficult," Anton said.

Franj shrugged. "They are my people, so…"

Introduced in panic and darkness, Anton had seen his companion as sharing Elecy's dark hair and tanned skin, and he had assumed that she shared her origin in Miroline or Vell, or the cities of the Estami shore – after all, that was true of two-thirds of the Brink's "recruits". The Elithi who came to the Brink were elders, and he had somehow forgotten that some, most, of them must be young – but yes, she was Elithi. She knew the land, she had said. Of course she did. He covered his embarrassment with a cough. "I'm sorry. I assumed you were an orphan. Like me."

"I am. I was. They have orphans too. Come on."

19

INAR

"We give them another day," Anzola said.

"Your grace, we have already given them four days," Kielo said, closing his eyes as if tired.

"*We give them another day*," Anzola repeated, and the harsh edge of her voice silenced the secretary.

"Very well then, your grace," Kielo said. Inar had never heard such a sour tone in his voice, not when addressing his mistress. "But the men must make ready for departure. Tomorrow morn."

The dawn had come cold, and as always it took its time to reach the floor of the narrow defile above the Vulture's Eye. They sat around the fire pit, but no fire had been lit in it since the meagre pyre of the remaining wood, the night before last.

Miroslo cleared his throat. "Your grace. I fear I must reinforce Kielo's concerns. Even eating as little as we have, we have only supplies for a couple of days. It will be a hungry return journey."

"The Tzanate will resupply us," Anzola said, not looking at the knight.

"But if they do not..."

"Slaughter a mule, then!"

Miroslo grimaced. "We have no fire to cook the meat."

This seemed to penetrate Anzola's armour, and her fury

crumpled into a tired sadness. "Slaughter one anyway. Slaughter them all. We don't need them on the way back. And make the other preparations."

"Should I assist here, your grace?" Inar asked. Given the merite's mood, he felt the formal term of address was most sensible and she did not correct him, as she had on prior days.

"No, we need a Mishigo," Anzola said. "And I may need your assistance. Lott, you will stay and help break camp."

Aware that Anzola had not taken the gentlest tone with his friend, Inar added: "Is that all right with you, Lott?"

"Fine by me," Lott said, a little tartly. "I've seen enough of the Mountain for a lifetime."

Anzola strode on ahead, stormclouds above her, and none of them hurried to keep pace. Four days of inactivity and four nights of tolerable sleep had done little to abate Inar's weariness. It was as if the tension and tedium of the wait at the Sight were sapping his vigour as surely as the climbs and marches ever had. The lack of fire had beckoned the cold deeper into him, and he feared he would never be rid of it. He yearned to be back in his father's warm little keep – it was still difficult to think of that place as his – and he wondered what progress Falde had made with the wall. He lagged behind the others, and was late to notice Duna beside the path, holding back for him.

"It's changed," she said. "Did you feel it too?"

Inar didn't know what she meant. He gave her a blank look.

"The Eye-stone," she said. "Surely you felt it? A weakness in it that was not there before."

"Yes," Inar said. He had paid little heed to the stone now that it was an established part of their dreary scenery, but twice a day he was forced into close contact with it as he squeezed through the Eye. "But it's not new, it was there before. There's a flaw in the stone, a cavity. Low down. I would never have been able to tell, had you not done that damage to it."

"Had I not *caused* that *change*," Duna said, primly. "I can feel it as well, now."

Inar knitted his brows. Not for the first time, he regretted lashing out at her days before, as it was an indescribable relief to be able to share some of these sensations with another human. "I still don't know if you can... feel stone the way that I can."

She gritted her teeth. "Yes. No. I mean – you can *read* it, can't you? Like seeing, you take in the whole scene at once, and taking more time reveals more detail?" Inar nodded, and she continued. "I... It's like I have a spear, or a dirk. A weapon. And I'm blind. I can prod with the point, the blade. And that tells me a little about what I'm prodding at. Hard, soft, whatever. But only at one point. The action is just a gentle version of the *thrust* that – that causes change. So, I don't like to jab away too much."

"But if you have someone like *me* around..." Inar said. They had stopped walking at the base of the narrow-carved steps that led up from the descending pass to the Sight.

"Well, it's very helpful."

"Listen, Duna," Inar said. He clamped his arms about himself, as if trying to do something about the cold, but in truth it was because he had become very aware of his arms, and how they had nothing to do. "I know that you don't like talking about this. Thank you for sharing it with me."

She gave him a small, awkward smile.

"I want you to know that you can trust me," he went on. "I know how... I understand what it is to be unable to share." Perhaps it was the mountain sickness, but he fancied he could still feel the ringing in his ears from the blow his brother had given him when he mentioned his ability. "I hope that I can be helpful in other ways."

"Thank you," Duna said. She nodded towards the steps. "Let's go up. I hope something happens today. So much rides on it."

* * *

The mist had cleared from the Hidden Land. Now it was roamed by shoals of shadows, cast by higher clouds. The waters of Hleng, ever bright on the far side of the plateau, were by turns sapphire and violet in the changing light. The rest of the high plain was a toffee brown – not soil, but sand and pulverised rock. Look long enough and tiny scratches of green could be found at sheltered points in this cold desert, where the few native Tenhe had farmsteads.

"What do they *eat*?" Anzola asked, aghast that people might live and die here.

"They keep goats," Inar said. "I think they raise a little barley. There are fish in the lake."

"*Fish*?" Anzola said, her incredulity steepening. "How did they get up here?"

Inar shrugged. "I don't know, but here they are."

"That's, that's very interesting," Kielo said excitedly. He was digging around in his satchel, and brought out a little glass jar with a sealed top, filled with tiny white objects. "Look at this – from the dirt in the slopes just below us. Sea shells! High in the mountains! As if this whole land had once been the bottom of an ocean! Could it be that the world was subject to immense transformations? What turns ocean into mountain fastness? Once I am able to–"

Anzola silenced him with a glare. She seemed to have less patience for her secretary since the Tzanate failed to arrive. Inar could not quite discern why this might be – to him, Kielo had always appeared the model of the discreet, efficient and obsequious servant. But Inar had never had any natural skill at keeping servants. Observing those who did, it seemed that half the skill was to be annoyed with them for obscure reasons.

The ability to see the plateau only heightened the loneliness of their lookout. If there were people down there, they were too tiny to make out – besides the odd speck of green and scratch of a line that might be a dry-stone wall or a ruin, the Hidden Land might have been undiscovered by man. There was the Brink, of course, that beguiling gleam in the east, and in the hills below their position a long-abandoned Mirolinian fort, but nothing else. No clouds of dust from approaching riders, no banners, no trumpets. No diplomatic mission.

"Inar," Anzola said. He had been sitting at the edge of the Sight, feet hanging over the side of the slab, his back to the altar. The quiet had permeated every part of him, and to be addressed made him start – he feared he might have displeased the *merite*, but her tone was not unkind.

"Your grace." He climbed to his feet.

Anzola waved away the title, and gestured that he should not stand, but he was already standing. "From here the pass is easier, yes?"

"This is as far as I have been," Inar said. "But yes, that is what I understand." He indicated the foothills below their position with an outstretched arm. "They are less of an obstacle. It is not a good road, but it is more like the Augardinian Way through the Shields than the Pilgrims' Pass."

"How long would it take us to get to Craithe's Brink?"

Inar felt his mouth clamp closed. He found himself seeking out Kielo's location and, as he expected and feared, the secretary was a good distance away, conversing with Miroslo. She had chosen her moment, when she could raise this question without Kielo's voice in her ear. Her whole expression was fixed with seriousness, and although it was lined and dirty from the days of rough travel, as all of them were, her seriousness and determination made her beautiful to him. Mention of travel to the Brink had immediately filled him with trepidation, but seeing the clear purpose in her eyes he felt it ebb away as fast as it had come, to be replaced with a certainty that any distance could be achieved.

"Two or three days, maybe," he said. "I believe there are good, straight, Mirolinian roads. Provisions would be the difficult part. There are no inns, or anything close. Water could be had, there are streams and ice, especially in the spring, but little else, even as forage."

"We could go to the high temple at Hleng. There are people there."

"Yes, your grace. But remember that travel in the Tzanate is forbidden." He knew this himself, and although it did not seem to be important in the moment, he felt obligated to mention it. "If we are found by the Zealots, I don't know what might happen."

"We are here at the invitation of the altzan-al," Anzola said. "And we are diplomatic representatives of the League. I believe we will be safe from harm."

"Yes, your grace," Inar said. Myriad objections, practical and otherwise, piled up in Inar's mind, but felt insignificant. Anzola, he trusted, could make it happen.

But her expression had changed – it had darkened, and she scowled and turned away. At once, it was as if the sun had gone in, and the cold pierced through to the marrow in his bones. "No," she said. "It's a mistake. This is wrong. I'm sorry, Inar, I shouldn't have asked you like that. It's a mistake. I should listen to Kielo. I just – I just wanted so very much for things to work out differently."

Inar could hardly stop himself falling to his knees in pathetic agreement and gratitude – the party was exhausted and on half-rations. They hardly had the strength to return the way they had come, and to strike out for days across unwelcoming territory was madness itself. Why had he allowed himself to imagine differently? "Yes," he said, breathless.

"This has gone on long enough," Anzola said. She checked the position of the sun. It was behind them already, and before long the shadows would consume the Sight. "Let us return to the camp. We will rest, and at first light begin our return to Sojonost."

"Yes, your grace," Inar said, relief coursing through him.

Anzola sighed. "Ernesto will be pleased, at least. He was never enthusiastic about alliance with the Tzanate. So he will have his way."

"What is his way? If I may ask. What does he wish to do?"

"The Elves must be destroyed," Anzola said, her face grim. "We cannot move against the Elves without holding Mal Nulalus. So we will take Mal Nulalus."

"That will mean war with the Tzanate," Inar said.

Anzola shifted uncomfortably, as if trying to redistribute the weight of a heavy pack on her back, though she was carrying nothing. There was an unreadable conflict in her eyes. "Inar, there is another secret I must share. You must promise me that this, like the truth about Duna, stays out of Mishigo ears. For now, anyway."

Inar froze. "Yes."

Anzola exhaled, preparing to unburden herself. "Politics and diplomacy come quite naturally to us in the League. We have been wrangling and realigning and keeping secrets since our foundation. The Tzanate, however – it has been centuries since it engaged in ordinary diplomacy. It rots up here, and sends its representatives to Miroline, which also rots. It behaves as if the whole world still listens to what it has to say. It is consumed with petty internal disputes. The very idea of treating with us, the League, will cause appalling strife within its hierarchy. Do you understand?"

Inar swallowed. "Yes. I think so." It sounded about right – the Tzanate was a distant, supernatural thing, not a country or princedom or even an empire in normal terms. If Inar thought of it that way, it would be rational to suppose that it might believe that of itself.

"The altzan-al, Ramnie," Anzola continued. "He's an intelligent man, a shrewd man, more farsighted than all of his fellows. Really, they sound like a gang of fools and fanatics, I'm told he despairs of them at times. He is desperate to reform the Tzanate, to stop the rot, to stave off the terrible danger he sees on the horizon. But that desperation, and inexperience at diplomacy, has led him to make mistakes. One very big mistake, in fact."

Inar said nothing, but nodded, willing her to continue.

"He showed us his cards. The Tzanate is *weak*. Far weaker than people imagine. Fewer than ten thousand battle-ready Zealots, on its best day. More like seven or eight. And the Zealots are not what they were. One-third of them are kids, something like one-quarter are over the age of forty. A useful supplement to the League's army, but not a match for it."

"So Ernesto doesn't regard them as a threat," Inar said. "He can simply take Mal Nulalus, with or without their agreement."

Anzola hesitated. "Yes."

"And that would be the end of the old order," Inar said. He could see the cards laid down, one by one. "Miroline hardly challenged the destruction of Oririthen and Mishig-Tenh, its allies, and so lost a lot of its authority – but if it had challenged the League and been bested, it would have lost *all* of its authority. And that's what Ernesto wants – take Mal Nulalus, take the crossroads at the heart of the world, defy the Tzanate and the empire, reveal them as empty robes…"

"Yes," Anzola said, tense. "Well, Ernesto is very bold when it comes to war. I thought we could avoid at least one conflict, and make the others easier. Make use of the Tzanate, forge a new alliance, maybe even a new moral order." She stared across the Hidden Land, in the direction of Craithe's Brink. "I thought that the Tzanate might want that as well. That Ramnie wanted it. I was wrong, it seems."

She ended the conversation with a sharp turn, away from Inar. The builder was left standing at the edge of the Sight, further from home than he had ever been before.

Another secret, another confession. And it had had a curious effect. Inar was not left feeling that there was more truth in his relationship with Anzola. On the contrary – he only wondered what else he was not being told. Because it had been clear in

Anzola's every word that the picture that had just been painted for him was, at least in parts, a lie.

Now that Anzola had accepted the need to return to Sojonost, a cloud seemed to lift from the group, and their climb back to the camp was more cheerful than the grim silence of their descent earlier in the day. But it did not last. The merite chatted with Kielo, her manner easy and joking, a strategy of reconciliation so transparent that Inar spotted it right away – spooning balm onto a sore spot. But if Kielo knew he was being mollified, he did not appear to care, and basked in her attention and good humour. The sounds of their conversation buoyed the rest of them. But they echoed in a broader silence. They climbed and climbed, a path now familiar, without hearing anything from the camp – no sound from the surviving mules, no clatter of equipment, no shouts between the knights.

In the final yards before the Eye-stone, Inar's attention fixed on a ragged path on the cliff face at the side of the pass: not a stain, but a large pale area of exposed rock, ringed with filth, as if something had rested against that wall for many multitudes of years, and had just now been removed. Trying to figure what might have caused this mark, and why he had not seen it before, he realised what he was not seeing: the Eye-stone. The Eye-stone was gone.

Not gone: shattered. The stone, the size of a substantial building, had broken apart, separating into five or six pieces. These had fallen across the pass, almost blocking it. The Vulture's Eye, the tiny aperture through which they had all been obliged to scramble, was gone, replaced by a new obstacle. The centuries of sand, loose stone and shingle that had built up behind the Eye-stone had slumped as well, a small landslip that had part-buried some of the pieces of stone, and must have partially undermined the camp.

"Hello?" Anzola called. Silence came down in reply. "Duna, what did you do?"

"I didn't do this," Duna said. She shot a glance at Inar. "I don't think I did."

"Nevertheless..." Anzola began, in a lecturing tone.

"Quiet!"

The instruction came from Miroslo, who had been leading the party. His whole aspect had changed, from weary hiker to crouching, poised, predator. Only risking a half-second glance over his shoulder at the others, he gestured to Thiolo to join him. Then he drew his dirk. Its scrape against the metal collar of the scabbard was shockingly loud. Thiolo followed, drawing his own sword. The two knights stalked forwards.

Inar had gravitated towards Anzola and Kielo, and so did Duna, all following an unthinking instinct to cluster together. He was holding his staff, but Inar wished he had a proper weapon. Military discipline had suffered in the course of the journey over the mountains – it hadn't been that tight to begin with. The knights no longer wore full armour, just bits and pieces over winter clothes – a sensible practical decision at the time, and Inar had even wanted to jettison the mule-load of leather altogether, or leave it for collection on the return. Now he wanted to borrow some of it.

But what were they all suddenly so afraid of? It wasn't clear, but fear felt quite appropriate. The others had not responded to Anzola's call. The hush had become mocking and dangerous.

"Maybe they were caught when the ground gave way?" Duna speculated in a whisper. "The weather's been better today, maybe as everything has warmed up, there was thawing, shifting... Or a rockfall, a natural one I mean, from above..."

Inar realised that she was trying to clear herself of suspicion. She feared blame for whatever had transpired. "The stone was weak," he said, to Anzola. "There was a flaw, deep inside it – neither of us could see it at first. It couldn't have been guessed at."

"Look," Kielo said. He was pointing to the tumbled remains of the stone. "Ropes."

He was right. Ropes had been lashed around one of the smaller pieces of stone, though they were now slack and abandoned. "They were trying to clear the pass," Inar said. "There, a shovel." The handle of the tool was sticking out of the loosened apron of fallen dirt, as if its owner might return at any moment and resume digging. "Whatever happened, they were here, working, after it."

Cursing, in Palla, burst into the quiet. Miroslo and Thiolo had reached the fallen rock, and were hunched over beside the chunk tied with rope.

"Your grace," Miroslo called down the pass, a crack in his voice. "A body. You might... the others should stay back."

Anzola did not hesitate. Not for the first time, Inar was struck by her native courage, which lacked in half the men he knew, including himself. Moving fast and quiet, she caught up with the knights, and looked down into a gap between fallen stone. Then she put a hand over her mouth, and closed her eyes. A beat passed and she composed herself. She exchanged words with the knights, heads bowed, far too quiet to even tell they were speaking. Then she turned to the others.

"Inar. Come here, please."

Conscious of the example the merite had set, he stepped forward without delay. He had seen bodies – he had seen the exposed, headless bodies of his father and brother impaled above the gates of the citadel – but that had not created any wish to see this one. His primary thought, he found, was *please do not let it be Lott*.

"You have seen men killed in quarries?" Anzola asked, a warning in her voice, before he could see what they could see. He nodded assent, and thought of the vivid colours of burst fruit.

"What do you suppose..." she said, and instead of completing her question, she gestured into a narrow gap left between two fallen fragments of the Eye-stone.

Inar swallowed, again, and tasted foulness.

"It's Timo," Miroslo said.

There was little that could identify the slain knight. The remains lay on their back in the narrow space between stones, and a blood-smeared gauntlet lay at their feet. Its booted feet – it was hard to think of these leavings as a *he* – were intact, and the lower half of the legs. The rest of Timo was ribbons of cloth and flesh, and the ghastly white of exposed bone, unsavoury and unnatural like the bare patch on the cliff.

"Not a fall," Inar said, aware of why he had been summoned – clinging, in fact, to that duty, to the exclusion of all else. "And he was not crushed, they were not trying to free him. I think he must have been down here, perhaps tying the ropes, after the stone broke."

"Yes," Miroslo agreed. "He has been… but what could have done this?"

"A wolf?" Anzola asked.

Inar found that he wanted, very much, for it to have been a wolf. "A wolf, attacking five men, in the middle of the day… I have not heard the like."

"A pack of wolves," Anzola suggested.

"He was attacked," Miroslo said, "and he fell backwards into this crevice, or went there deliberately to find safety – it seems he was on his back, trying to fend off the attacker, which was on these rocks above him. It could have been a wolf. Whatever it was, it continued after he was killed – it was consuming him."

Timo's sword, unsheathed and streaked with blood, lay abandoned a short distance from the knight's body. Miroslo, Thiolo and Anzola examined it. An accident did not cover a blade with blood like that. Still without saying a word, Thiolo picked up the sword and handed it to Inar. Taking the weapon of a dead man – one spattered with gore – filled Inar with unease, but he did not complain. The sword was heavy in his hand, and he had no training in using it, but he was glad of it.

"The others," Anzola said. "We need to find the others."

The rough slope of spilled sand and rocks released by the breaking of the Eye-stone was an uneven and mobile surface, but not too steep to ascend. They did so in a blunt arrow-head formation, with the two knights leading and Anzola and Inar taking a flank each, a little behind. Inar was on the side closest to what remained of the Eye-stone. Wondering what had happened to make it shatter apart in the way it had, he studied the exposed, fractured surfaces, looking for the irregularity he had sensed in its heart. It had fissured in a strange way indeed, not what might be expected if a stone was, say, dropped from a height, or struck with a projectile. The stone had separated into large fragments of roughly similar size. The exposed faces, where they had once fitted together, were curiously smooth and regular. It resembled the coming-apart of something that had been built, rather than an ordinary and single item of solid, immemorial rock. What if the Eye-stone had not been a part of the mountain, dislodged by the work of the ages and fallen into the valley – but something that had been constructed there, for an unguessable purpose?

The stump of the stone had been half-buried by the landslip. As he ascended, Inar found his best route was to step out onto its sheared surface, where one of the men had discarded a shovel. Whoever had wielded the shovel had been digging at something – a channel cut into the stone, a straight line with a perfectly circular profile. When the Eye-stone had been whole, this had been a neat tunnel like a drain running from the buried side of the stone to its middle. It was so neat and unnatural, it was hard to know how men would have made it: very patient and precise grinding through the rock, perhaps, before the valley behind the stone had filled with debris. Which was to say, an immensity of time ago, the kind of span that made the pit of Inar's stomach drop sharply. None of this was natural – it had been built. Before Augardine. Before Miroline. Before men?

The fracture in the stone only exposed part of the hole – the chamber it led to in the middle of the stone was still complete. Inar knelt and peered in, using his staff to clear accumulated dirt. The light was failing already, and he could see little in the dark niche – but there was something there, a bundle of rags. He scraped away some more of the soil with the discarded shovel, and then fished out the object with the end of his staff. An outer surface of fabric had rotted to dust, but the inner layers were tightly and regularly bound around a hard object smaller than his fist.

"Inar. *Inar.*" Miroslo was hissing at him, quiet but urgent. Inar turned to see both knights and the merite staring at him. They had reached the top of the slope, but had not crested it – instead they crouched, looking across the campsite, keeping concealed as best as possible.

Inar stuffed the small bundle into his skins and scrambled up the slope to join them.

It was twilight in the valley already, but Inar knew that if he looked behind or above him he would see the sunlight lingering on the peaks. No lights burned at the campsite, and Inar was grateful for that, as the horrid scene was sinking into blue and grey.

The campsite was in disarray – tents torn apart, cooking pots scattered, scraps of unidentifiable garments twitching in the wind. The remains of two mules were near Inar, up against the blood-spattered valley wall: they had been stripped back to gore-twined skeletons. With a nod, Thiolo indicated a body to Inar: the head was twisted unnaturally around, showing a ruined face that would haunt the builder's dreams. It was not Lott. Another body lay a little further away, at the edge of the firepit.

"Do you hear that?" Inar asked. For the first time, he could detect sound from the camp: a steady, organic noise, many-layered, with little breaths and smacks and slaps and rips. The sound of eating.

Thiolo nodded, and Miroslo gestured. At the far end of the

campsite was a small collection of objects – Inar had believed this to be baggage, packed and piled ready for the return. But it was moving. It was a line of hairy animal backs, with sharp studs of spine and angular shoulders, clustered together in a group and hunched over whatever it was they were eating. The creatures were smaller than men but larger than children, and they were squatting like people, not on all fours. They wore no clothes but were covered in patchy, spiky grey hair. As Inar watched, a head rose up from the clutch of backs, a head with a face both like and unlike a man's, a fat squash of a nose, yellow eyes, the bristles around its wide, fanged mouth stained crimson from feasting.

A knome.

It searched left and right with its glittering little eyes, which picked up and reflected flashes of light from the sun on the snowy peaks. It knew the dark of mountain winters, this creature. And its hunting eyes came to rest, so it seemed, on Inar. They stared at one another, and Inar felt the ghastly certainty of intelligence without sympathy.

"Has it *seen* us?" Miroslo whispered, desperately.

Inar knew the answer but could not voice it. The knome did not shift its gaze, but it dropped its jaw, revealing pointed cat-like teeth, and emitted a soft chittering sound to its fellows.

The feasting ended, and head after head turned towards them, dozens of pairs of yellow eyes in the gathering dark.

20

ANTON

The village – a description that seemed too grand – was a hidden place in the Hidden Land. Its handful of buildings resembled the barrack-huts of the Brink on a smaller scale, wide trenches cut into the ground and covered by arched roofs of packed dirt. As they were the colour and texture of the terrain, they were invisible until you were on top of them, tucked into a low corner of the lake-bed. Here, in fact, the lake-bed was almost still a lake – the settlement owed its existence to a thin crescent of frozen mud and a cluster of wells. Anton was amazed to see some vegetation sheltering in this secluded spot: winter-dead reeds, beige patches of goat pasture ringed by ankle-height lines of dry stone, ridges protecting strips of cultivation covered with dew-traps. There was colour, too: bright harnesses on the half-dozen goats tethered loosely outside, and lines of prayer-flags strung between the doorways of the bothies.

"You came from here?" Anton asked.

"Not here," Franj said, "but like this."

As they approached – Anton riding, Franj leading her horse on foot – they were seen by a couple of young men who stood at a field-line at the village's outer edge. Both held long hoes, but did not appear to be doing anything with them, and Anton wondered if they were farming or guarding. They approached the Zealots (as they looked to be), meeting them some distance from the settlement. Cautious, Anton thought. Difficult, even. But their manner became perceptibly less wary when Franj greeted them in their own language, the trilling song-speak of the Tzanate's ancient past. They looked at Franj, at the horse, and – longest of all – at Anton. Then they nodded towards the village.

"Wait here," Franj said, taking the saddlebags of provisions off her horse and leaving them at Anton's feet. "I'll be back." She walked off with one of the young men and disappeared into a longhouse.

Anton was left alone with the other guard. He smiled at the man and got a wary smile in return, but a few words of Mirolingua brought no reply. Together they stood in silence a while, and Anton let the seclusion and obscurity of the settlement soothe his fears of pursuit and recapture. It was a beautiful morning, with a warm sun in a cloudless sky. The gentle sounds of life, the calling of the goats and the clatter of their bells, were restful enough for some of the clashing metal and screams of the Brink's dungeons to at last quiet themselves.

He dug in one of his horse's saddlebags, where Franj had mentioned provisions, and found soldier-cake. These hard, dry biscuits were in normal times completely unappetising, but they looked pretty good to Anton this morning, and he cracked off a quarter of one brick to chew on. It broke unevenly, into several small pieces, and he offered a portion to the villager. But the villager no longer saw him. A distant expression had settled over his face, as if he was considering the solution to a thorny abstract problem. Head bowed forgetfully, he turned and walked towards his home, with the gait of a heavy drinker, the end of his hoe dragging heavily along the ground. Anton watched him depart, puzzled at his change in manner. Quickly he was nowhere to be seen. No other signs of life stirred among the longhouses.

He was alone.

He was not alone.

While Anton had been watching the young man return to the village, he had been approached by a stranger – an old woman, who had come from somewhere out on the lake-bed, behind him. Dressed in layers of robe and cloak so ragged they appeared no better than an indistinguishable mass of filthy ribbons, hunched over and supporting herself on a staff, it was a mystery as to how the woman could have crossed such a distance of open terrain without being noticed sooner. But here she was. An initial jolt of surprise quickly dissipated, as Anton knew at once this newcomer meant him no harm.

"Tzan Anton," the old woman said.

"Yes?" Anton said. He wondered if he should be concerned that the woman knew who he was, whether that meant he was in danger, but the question seemed curiously unimportant. All the sound had drained from the air, leaving a faint buzzing in the middle of his head. Glancing back at the village to see if Franj might be coming, he noticed that it was further away than he remembered.

The woman, though friendly, was oddly difficult to register. A hood fell over her face, but beyond that her outline was indistinct. Even standing still, a cloud of dust kicked up around her feet, pulling in around her like an extra cloak. The voice, though, the voice was familiar. The voice wanted to be known, to be recognised. It announced itself before a word was spoken.

"Deacon Cutruk," Anton said, and he bowed.

"There is no call for ritual," the old woman said. "We are alone. But we do not have time. Our alone-ness comes at a price."

"Yes," Anton said. His head was beautifully clear and every word spoken to him, or even by him, had a crystalline and beautiful quality, its meaning not only obvious but faceted and sparkling.

"We dislike to intervene," the old woman said. "But we also dislike to see the Mountain taken by murder. And that is what we have seen. Your escape pleases us."

"I'm pleased," Anton said.

"Altzan Ving has explained his actions. He fears relying on heathens to protect the Mountain. We are not without sympathy. It is a policy filled with danger. But his methods fill us with disgust. Killing came quickly to him, did it not? His earliest choice. Lacking men and means, he thinks of the death-arts. In a shambles of his making, he is remaking. The slaughter of recent days does not dismay him. He is pleased. Pleased at the death of unreliable servants so he can make... more *constant*... beings."

As the old woman spoke the pillar of dust that stirred around her rose and spread out, filling the air with a hissing of loathing.

"What must I do, great one?" Anton asked, and he realised that he longed for guidance from the pit of his being. It was an all-body pain he had hardly noticed among his other woes.

"We dislike to intervene," the old woman said. "But we will, if you desire. Ving will die. Every man and woman who plotted with him will repent or die. Every Zealot that raises a spear against us will die. You can walk back to the Brink now. By the time you arrive, the gates will be open and every living thing within will be prostrate before you. Our wrath will be very terrible."

Anton froze. It was as if the sun had died and he was back in the coldest part of a cloudless winter night. What a return that would make. Another spasm of violence, this time supernatural, and the Brink at his feet: bloodied, obedient, terrified. Welcome, altzan-al.

"If you desire," the old woman repeated. The sun had not died, but Anton noted the way his companion cast no shadow.

"No," Anton said.

"If your scruple lies in having others do your work for you, we could grant you the powers. Make a second Augardine of you. You could open the gates yourself, or have them fall. And anyone who tried to stop you, make them fall as well."

A real monster, not a make-believe one. It was one way of ending the performance.

"No," Anton said. "I do not desire it."

"Is it a question of the cost in blood?" the old woman asked. Her tattered cloak whipped in the still air, fouled with dust. "Yes, there is a cost. But consider the cost of returning with an army. Or consider the cost of leaving Ving to his plans."

"We will see," Anton said. "I will find Yisho and return. Ving is weak. We can hold the Gull Gates and Hleng and Mal Nulalus. We will talk again with the League. We have right on our side."

A rhythmic cough arose from the old woman, and Anton had the unpleasant sense of being laughed at. "Your history is filled with defeated armies that had right on their side," she said. "But your belief pleases us. Ving is making the old mistake, the oldest mistake, the mistake most men, most women make with magic: that once they have it, they need nothing else. And they lose sight of other men and women. Do you see, blade-shun?"

"Augardine's mistake," Anton said.

"Yes," the creature said. It was more a creature now, less a woman. "My time is spent. You are pursued by riders and must make haste. There may be help at the Gull Gates, but do not turn towards them now. Bear west instead and turn south when you must."

The column of dust erupted outwards, swallowing up the wavering form of the old woman, and it seethed like a pot about to boil over. "The Elves, Anton," came the deacon's voice, roaring from within the column, but also thin and distant. "Beware the Elves. The Tzanate, the League, Miroline – those are quarrels. The Elves are the enemy. They are the war. And they draw near."

The pillar of dust collapsed, blasting outwards as pent-up energies were abruptly released, and grit stung Anton's face and eyes. He raised his arm into the strong, cold wind, only to find it stopped as sharply as it had begun.

Blinking, Anton saw a bright spring morning in the Hidden Land, with clear skies. Behind him, his horse whinnied uneasily, and from the direction of the village came the bleating of the goats and the clatter of their bells. And as he was looking in that direction he saw Franj emerging from a gap between the longhouses. She walked towards him, without guard or horse.

"They'll take her," she said in reply to Anton's inquiring look. "In a couple of days they'll return her to the Brink, and say they found her wandering. We'll be long gone. You take Stripe. You're weak."

The pause by the village had given Anton a chance to discover that she was telling the truth – he was weak. The fear-driven effort of his escape had ebbed and he felt the effects of days of confinement and a long, sleepless night. He longed to rest, but they had to move.

"We'll take turns," he said. "I insist."

But Franj did not answer, and for a moment Anton feared that she had fallen under the same enchantment that had so distracted the village guard. She stared at the ground.

"They were here, weren't they," she said, at last.

Anton did not need to ask who, because the veneration in her voice made it clear. Instead, he looked down, to see what had given her the thought.

A radiating pattern of runes had been etched lightly into the fine dry dirt of the lake bed – an embracing cyclone of arcane meaning, with Anton at its centre. The touch that had made such marks had been unreally light, hardly touching the hard crust of the ground beneath the surface layer of fine dust, and the gentle morning breeze was already wiping them away. Franj's eyes shone.

"Yes," Anton said. "They were here."

Once, when a lake had filled this desolate depression, there had been a beach on its western shore. Today that beach was a dead dune of sliding grey sand. Anton dismounted, and Stripe whinnied and complained as they climbed the treacherous bank. However hard the work, it was necessary – on either side of the eroding strand, the dry lake was edged with cliffs. If pursuers knew they had crossed the lake, they would know that they had come this way. It was as obvious an exit as a room with a single door. But Anton was relieved to be leaving the lake-bed. It had not been the fast route they had hoped for, and its wideness and openness had left him feeling exposed and disturbed. This feeling had grown after the visit by the Custodian. The creature had dropped from nowhere, and Anton had been gifted a vision of how he and Franj must have seemed to a bird: dark specks against a pale grey field, easy prey. And at the village, too. Predators knew to lurk near the water.

Above the shoreline was a broken landscape of sloping slabs, intercut by natural channels and restlessly crossed by billowing clouds of grey dust blown up from the bed. Near the shore was a cairn, smoothed and spilled by centuries of neglect, revealing the cyclopean blocks of a more ancient Custodian structure beneath. It was the highest point for miles, and Franj climbed its black, rune-scored stones to get a vantage across the lake-bed. Watching her climb, and then look out over the world, it seemed to Anton that he was seeing her for the first time. She had wrapped her scarf across her face, as they both had, against the choking dust, and only a slit was left for fierce, sharp eyes, fixed on the horizon. But she was every inch the born scout: observant, slight, silent in her movements, skilled in the saddle. If the Tzanate had any strengths, other than the crushing momentum of its history and accumulated prestige, it was its ability to identify talent in the foundlings that were left at its feet. It was not the first time this thought had occurred to Anton, and as ever it had a special melancholy weight – for what did it say about him?

Franj was descending.

"Riders," she said. "Four, I think. They'll be here before dark."

"So we should be elsewhere," Anton said, offering Stripe's reins to Franj. He was pleased when she took them and climbed onto the horse, with the assistance of one of the cubes of volcanic stone that had tumbled from the Custodian fane.

Franj nodded.

"West, then south when we must," Anton said.

"Yes," Franj said, but there was a cautious note in her voice. "Why do you say that? Did I say that to you?"

Anton felt embarrassed, as if he had been a novice caught peeking at another's work. He considered for a moment if the Custodian wished its words to be shared – after all, it had gone to such pains to keep its presence secret. Furthermore, Franj was the scout, and he wished he had not spoken over her own opinion of their next move. "Of course, you know the land, the decision is yours," he said hastily.

But she had drawn her inference. "Is that what they said we should do?"

"Yes," Anton said. "Is that what you think we should do?"

She appeared annoyed by the question. "If that is what they say we should do, that is what we should do."

The ground felt unsteady beneath Anton's feet. It disturbed him, this ready acquiescence, it disturbed him deeply. The scout was too ready to follow anything she saw as the word of god. He could say anything, he realised, and he feared his own power over her. Should anyone have that power? That was leadership, wasn't it?

"What are the dangers in that path?" Anton asked.

Franj turned in the saddle and scowled back over the lake-bed. "It's not a bad path. Much better for concealment, and it would rob them of their speed. The danger is that they could put themselves between us and the Gates, and lie in wait."

"But if we're expecting that, we could evade them?"

She stared down at Stripe's mane. "It's possible. If we have a little luck. If God truly is with us."

The Custodian had mentioned help at the Gates. Could it see that? Could it perceive time as it saw the land, from above, seeing what was to come as well as what had been? They were attributed great wisdom in the thousands of volumes devoted to their worship, and all wisdom has a thread of foresight, but they were never specifically held as oracles, who could see a world to come as we saw the world all about.

They would learn soon enough, he figured.

They went west.

At sunset they made camp. It was Franj's decision, made on behalf of the horse as much as anyone, but Anton was unspeakably glad of it. He had only been able to sustain himself through a full day of flight by stoking his own fear of what might happen if they stopped, and even that fuel couldn't last. Franj must have been tired as well, but she gave no sign and made no complaint.

The land showed them a little favour, at last. They had been traversing an immense expanse of shattered rock – as if a sheet of stone the size of a small country had been dropped onto an uneven surface and had broken. This broken surface made a tiring labyrinth, but it also formed many natural overhangs and shelves, sheltered spots free of snow. Franj picked one of these low-ceilinged abodes for the night and judged it so well concealed that she was ready to risk a fire. They burned a little of the tiny bundle of firewood that was in their supplies, using it to melt ice into warm water, which tasted better to Anton than the finest wine.

"What else did they say to you?" Franj asked, as they nibbled on soldier-cake and watched the embers. She did not have to specify who she meant.

Anton licked a crumb from his lips and considered his response. If she heard what they had offered, and how he responded, he did not think she would agree with his decision.

She had lost comrades and, surely, friends on the night of his escape. They had been ready to spill blood and to die for him, and he would not do the same even for himself? And he wondered, not for the first time, if he had made the right decision.

"You don't have to say," she said.

He had taken too long. "They do not like to intervene," he said. "But they said that they disapproved of Ving's conduct, and were pleased by my escape."

There was no light to see Franj's reaction. Clouds hid the stars, the weather was changing.

"By *our* escape," Anton continued. "You pleased them, Franj. You did well."

The only sound was the breathing of the horse. For a long time.

"Good," Franj said. "That's good." She could not hide the crack in her voice.

21

INAR

Moving as one, the knomes abandoned their bloody feast and sprang to face the intruders. Their motions, the way they jumped and skittered on all fours, more resembled spiders than anything with kinship to man. Then they charged.

The Leaguer knights had not waited for the charge. Pushing Inar and Anzola into untidy flight down the loose slope, the knights retreated, still facing the creatures, weapons drawn. But the terrain, the change in elevation, was against them all, with descending and broken ground behind them, and the enemy in possession of the higher, firmer ground.

"Get back!" Miroslo shouted. "Get to safety!"

Inar did not need to be told twice, even if safety seemed a childish illusion. He and Anzola began to run, retracing their steps down towards the Sight with frantic haste. Kielo and Duna, who had been left waiting, gaped up at them as they approached.

"Run!" Anzola told them. "Get down below the Sight! We can lose them in the dark!"

Even without any familiarity with the habits of knomes, Inar knew this to be untrue. The dark would not be their friend.

"Lose *who*?" Kielo asked, as if needing the detail for his minutes of the meeting.

Duna screamed. She was staring back towards the camp, and they turned to see what she had seen.

Miroslo and Thiolo had reached the bottom of the slope, and the knomes had reached the top. The creatures spilled over the ridge in a tumbling cataract of bony limbs. Their collective chuckling-chittering iced the blood, not because it was wrathful or murderous, but because it sounded almost playful. They reached Thiolo first, three at once. One got to his sword arm, spoiling his only clear blow, and gripped on, biting and scratching.

At once, Miroslo was at his comrade's defence, striking down a knome that had the knight's neck, and skewering the one that had his fighting arm. The injured beast fell away, hissing and spitting. Unencumbered at least, Thiolo was able to swipe at the third knome, which he had been fending off with his left gauntlet.

Where two knomes had fallen, six took their place. One launched a spiderlike leap at Miroslo, catching him at shoulder height and almost knocking him to his knees. It gripped on, and the knight fought wildly to shake it off as others joined in.

"Your grace," Kielo said urgently.

"Yes, yes," Anzola said. "Come, we have to go, we have to get away – let the knights deal with it, they…"

Her words trailed away. The creatures had already killed four knights, and had the best of Miroslo and Thiolo. But as they hesitated – the sword heavier than ever in Inar's hand – Miroslo freed himself from the beast that had his head, and turned to yell: "For pity's sake, *go*!"

Kielo turned and started to scramble down the mountain. Anzola and Inar made to follow, but Duna remained rooted in place – not afraid, but focused. As Inar retreated, she reached out and caught him by his fur. "Your grace, please, go with Kielo," she said breathlessly. "Inar, stay close, one moment, I had it…"

"Duna, you must come with me," Anzola said, unfamiliar steeliness in her tone. "Your safety is of utmost importance."

"I can help them, I can help them!" Duna said, her voice

rising. "But I need Inar! Let me! You go! I can't do it with you here!"

With palpable reluctance, Anzola slunk away, joining Kielo in his more eager descent.

Duna turned to Inar, eyes flashing in the gloom. "Focus," she said. "Be a still and bright flame."

She turned her attention to the fray.

Inar's picture of the scene seemed to clarify. Not what he was seeing – that was an indistinct knot of slaughter. But the mountain defile that surrounded it. He knew every ghostly solidity and weakness in the ground beneath them and the rockfaces about them. In a blink he was told a story about how the land had not always been this way and how it had come to be like this, a vision where lands floated like slices of potato in soup, and collided with one another, and forces pushed upwards and untold immensities of rock folded and rose and underneath all was unthinkable heat and elsewhere there was a vastness that was not stone…

He snapped back into the scene, though he had never been gone, and he sensed the flaws multiplying through one of the rockfaces, a cascade of brilliant and unnatural failures – and he knew of it in the realm of normal sense as well, as a gathering roar of noise and a shaking in the ground. Sweat dripped from his chin. Duna's paleness was like a lantern in a closing gyre of dark.

A wide portion of the rockface tore away from its parent mountain and rushed to the ground, breaking apart as it fell. Thousands of tonnes of stone, falling like water out of an upturned bucket, smashed across the pass, obliterating the knomes who were stalking towards the besieged knights. The rockfall came close to obliterating Thiolo and Miroslo as well, missing them by scant yards, and the thunderous concussion knocked Miroslo and his assailants to the ground. A couple of the surviving knomes recovered before Miroslo did, springing back into the attack as he struggled to raise himself and retrieve his weapon. One leaped at the knight but never completed its assault, instead crumpling to one side, shrieking and wailing. Another was on its feet, and it fell as if swept over by an unseen broom. Miroslo had risen to a crouch and was grappling with a third knome, unable quite to make contact with his blade. The creature then coiled backwards, clawing at its head, before falling, folding in all the wrong places.

Each time, Inar could not see how Miroslo had landed the killing blow – he never even made contact. And then he realised, later than he should, that he could not really see at all. Besides the dusk, the rockfall had sent up a choking eruption of dust which had consumed everything around them. With his sense for stone, Inar could still feel out the shape of the land, but he realised that he knew the location of the living creatures within it as well. Not in their entirety, but as spectral stick-figures, as if… he turned to Duna, and saw every detail of skull and spine. He sensed Thiolo too, among the fallen and broken bones of the knomes, and that the knight had ceased to stir.

"Miroslo! Here!" she called into the swirling dark.

The Leaguer almost stumbled into them, and without further words, clutching each other, they fled into the enclosing night of the Hidden Land.

Anzola and Kielo had sought refuge in an abandoned fort, perhaps half a mile beneath the Sight of God. Built of the same stone that made the landscape behind it, it made a stern square outline against the velvet blue of the sky and the emerging stars. To help them, a small light winked at its top, and as they approached they heard Kielo's voice hissing to them.

The fort was a simple keep, taller and wider than Inar's faraway fortified home but with none of the surrounding clutter of walls and buildings. Just a plain Mirolinian cube deposited on its own in the wilderness, on a ridge overlooking the trail. It was on its way to ruin. The outer shell of thick stone stood firm enough, but the roof and all the internal floors had disappeared, even the joists – robbed away for use elsewhere, or for firewood. Anzola and Kielo had sheltered in the debris-littered lower level, a square of sky above them, and had hauled a warped and rusted tank across the doorway as a barricade.

"Where is Thiolo?" Anzola demanded, but the desperate edge of her question revealed that she already knew the answer. She was more agitated than Inar had ever seen her, and it grew from something more than the fear and horror that afflicted them all.

"You should not have stayed back like that!" Anzola said to Duna, anger in her voice. "What in the name of the tide were you playing at?"

Even by the light of a single oil lamp, Inar saw Duna redden, though he did not know if it was with anger or embarrassment or a combination of both.

Miroslo stepped in on her behalf.

"She was able to cause a rockfall that disrupted the attack, allowing me to get away," he said. "It was already too late for Thiolo."

Anzola did not divert her attention from Duna. "Reckless! Completely reckless! I cannot believe you would take such a risk."

"Your grace, please," Miroslo said. "The lady Duna not only saved my life, she might well have saved us all. Those creatures would not have stopped with me, and there was a dozen of them, if not more."

"It's true," Inar said. He could not stand by and let Duna be berated. He had hardly thought at all while Duna had been doing whatever she had done, but hindsight made her bravery shine clearly. And Miroslo's defence of her, though spoken with fire, understated what she had orchestrated. "It was more than a rockfall, she was able to tear down part of the mountain."

To Inar's surprise, Duna glared at him for this. "It was a well-placed rockfall," she said. "Just that. But I had to be still for it, and to have Inar by my side."

Anzola's anger had waned. "Well then," she said, as the group took stock. "I wish I had stayed in place and seen it. I could have helped protect you."

"It was better that you got away," Duna said. She had shed her sullen tone, and switched to reassurance. "Truly. I could not focus knowing that you were at my side, in danger. You are the merite."

"But *you*," Anzola said, and Inar saw a glistening in her eyes, close to tears – tears of relief, and the backwash of retreating fear. "You are my ward, my child. And this whole enterprise depends on you."

At that, Inar wondered what was left of the enterprise. But he also felt that he understood Anzola's anger at Duna and the others, when by rights she should have been pleased at their escape. It had not come from fear, or not fear alone: she was ashamed at having left the others behind and fleeing with Kielo. On this realisation, Inar felt he understood a little of the relentless effort that had gone into hewing her reputation as a noble, a diplomat and a warrior, in the face of the objections men would raise against her sex, and how her sex would still serve to doom her for the tiniest public lapse, affording her none of the chances and forgetfulness that men enjoyed. He saw that, behind a public projection of easy command, there lay iron control, always wary, even when far from the world, among her most trusted people. He felt her loneliness.

She had missed something, though. Even within that iron control, a secret grew, and Inar had seen it now. Duna had not sent Anzola away for her safety – it was so Anzola would not see what she did. Bringing down that rock face was a far more impressive feat than splitting the Eye-Stone. Collapsing the overhang at the sea of ice, days before, had also been more impressive. But to Anzola, the crack in the Eye-Stone had seemed the extreme of her ward's achievements. The merite had no idea that Duna could do more.

Duna was concealing the scope of her abilities from Anzola.

They had no tents, no furs beyond the ones they wore, and no food. The night was short and spent huddled together in a corner of the abandoned fort, sleeping only because they were exhausted, not because they were comfortable. All awoke at first light, stiff-jointed and iced to the marrow, none eager to linger on the ground. Inar observed that a fort would have water, and sure enough they found a covered well in a stone-vaulted and rubbish-choked cellar. But its pail had rusted through on one side, meaning only a half-cup could be brought up at a time, and that only with care. Even getting that morning drink of rusty water entailed tiresome labour.

A canteen of that water had to be taken to Anzola, who had climbed the spiral stair to the topmost level of the fort as soon as she had risen and had not come down. Inar performed this duty, and found her on the battlement with Miroslo. They were looking out at the Hidden Land. The view was largely the same as that obtained from the Sight, as they had not travelled far in their escape. But the lower perspective made the land appear more expansive – and more arduous to cross.

The top of the wall was comfortably wide, but had been broken by repeated frosts into an uneven surface. One side was a ragged battlement, and on the other a sheer drop. Even exhausted, scared and very far from home, Inar could not stop his builder's eye from going over the details of its construction, exposed by the elements.

"Inar," Anzola said, on seeing him ascending the stairs. She lowered her spyglass. Her face was pale and lined with tiredness and care. "We have reached a decision – we will head south, using the old pilgrim trail, and go to the Gull Gates."

"The Gull Gates?" Inar said. "Through the Hidden Land? Is that wise?"

"Do you fancy returning the way we came?" Miroslo asked sternly, and Inar answered with downcast eyes. The knight had been hurt in many places in the fight the previous day. His face and neck were covered in scratches and gouges where the knomes had clawed at him, and one wound beneath his left ear looked deep and angry. He had also developed a limp, and his left wrist had an arc of deep cuts that had evidently been made by teeth.

"The trail is the best road from here," the knight went on, "and the Gates are the most reliable settlement. The Tzanate will have a garrison there. We will be able to resupply and rest."

"If they welcome us," Inar said.

"And perhaps we will be able to get some explanations!" Anzola said, not even hearing Inar. "We will send word direct to altzan-al Ramnie that we expect a full accounting for his failure to fulfil his commitments. What's more, I will send to Sojonost for an armed escort back along the Augardinian Way. I knew that the Tzanate was weak and its lands were slipping into anarchy, but I hardly understood the meaning of that until today."

"We are a diplomatic mission," Miroslo said to Inar. "They will be obliged to offer us some hospitality, if they want peace. Believe me, I would like to return to the Eye and gather what supplies we can, and deal with our dead, but it may yet be infested with those creatures, and reduced as we are, we cannot risk it. Besides, return via the Pilgrims' Pass would be four or five days, whereas we can be at the Gull Gates in two or three."

"What about rescue from Sojonost?" Inar asked. "They will be asking what became of us."

Anzola nodded. "That's true, a second party might already be on its way. They'll come here, and we will leave a message for them to find. But they might not be coming. And they cannot be relied upon. The passage is dangerous – we have seen that ourselves. We would have to wait here, starving, without any certainty of rescue."

The logic was inescapable. "The Gull Gates, then," Inar said.

Anzola smiled at him. "They will be a welcome sight, believe me."

22

ANTON

While they slept, fog had descended across the Hidden Land, so thick that it seemed their little niche under a flat stone was a nest in the face of a great cliff, looking out over nothingness.

Franj was pleased. "We are favoured indeed," she said. Perhaps it was a night of rest, but her attitude had undergone a marked change – her wariness and reserve had retreated and a sparkle shone in its place. In this state she reminded Anton of Elecy, and he found he missed his sister-in-faith. He hoped that she was safe. Hers was a terrible and deadly game, and he could not escape the thought that she had taken his place in the dungeon.

"Will we find our way?" Anton asked. He did not share his companion's favourable view of the fog – it seemed to him a disquieting medium in which to travel, half-blind, half-lost.

"Yes," Franj said. "Scouts would not be much use to the Tzanate if they were lost in a little mist, would they? You ride, I'll guide. Today we should find the pilgrims' way to the Mirolinian road."

"Where our pursuers might wait," Anton said. In this weather, every stone seemed to conceal a company of Zealots.

"Then we had better be careful, hadn't we?" Franj replied, setting off with a bounding gait that had few of the characteristics of care.

* * *

As they travelled, Anton began to understand part of the reason for Franj's renewed vigour. A good night's rest had made its contribution, of course, and she was no doubt buoyed by Anton's message that the Custodians were pleased with her. But it had another component, one that became steadily more clear: she was enjoying herself.

Crossing the lake-bed had been a simple matter of flight and pursuit. There had been little wit to it. Now, however, Franj was engaged in evasion. Her manner was different because the task was different.

Scouts accompanied armies, and were counted as soldiers. But scouting was not soldiering – or rather, it was a special and strange part of soldiering. Scouts made their own path, they went as they pleased. Fighting was not their purpose, but to say that they shrank from the fight was unfair, because it made them sound craven and they were anything but that. They did not aim to fight, but they did not shrink from the enemy. That was not what evasion was. Franj, Anton realised, was seeking the enemy. She wanted to know where they were. That was the stuff of her skill: not putting the maximum distance between herself and the enemy, but maintaining a fixed and watchful distance. She was not running, she was hunting, and the job evidently agreed with her.

After a hurried middle meal – soldier-cake again – Anton offered her the saddle, and she refused. "Quicker on my feet, here at least," she said. For several miles, she had been bounding on ahead, scrambling to the top of the mighty shards of stone that defined their path like buildings in a city, and trying to make out signs and clues in what lay ahead.

"The ground's rising, do you feel it?" she asked. "We're coming to the Shields. Pilgrims' path by nightfall."

"And that goes to the Gull Gates?"

"No, not directly. It's aimed more at Hleng. But it goes to the Mirolinian road between the Gates and the Brink, and that takes us where we need to go. We'll go cross country, but stay near the road."

"Isn't that exactly where an ambush would wait?"

Franj chuckled. "Why, you sound like you don't want to find the ambush!"

"And you *do*?" Anton asked, incredulous.

"I don't want to fall into it, but I want to know exactly where it is," she replied. "Safer than *not* knowing."

"If you say so," Anton said.

The chaos of broken boulders thickened and became trickier to thread through, and then it was gone. They emerged into a wide valley of loose gravelly ground, which sloped gently towards an angry spring torrent in its middle. On both sides of this expanse, huge boulders were heaped as if they had been swept aside by a divine broom. It was quicker going, but they stayed close to the rocky boundary, ready to duck into cover if the need arose.

"Elithi tales say a river of ice flowed here once, from an ice sea in the Shields," Franj said.

"Ice does not flow," Anton said with a frown. He had heard of ice seas but not ice rivers. It was absurd.

"Myth is myth," Franj said, without judgement. "The birth of God shook the world, whole lands fell into the sea, seas drained away, volcanoes spewed fire. An age of darkness and ash led to a time of shrouding ice. The ice was going when men and women came to the Hidden Land, and found that God awaited."

Anton nodded along. Elithi myth was little different to the Tzanate's cosmology.

Her telling of the story stirred up a memory.

"The Custodian told me that the last blade-priest would

shake the world," he said. "Not yesterday. A few days ago, when they laid their mark on me. I've been asking myself if they have the power of foresight – if they can see what is to come. That certainly had the tone of prophecy."

"Did they tell you of things to come?" Franj asked. "How do we fare?"

"It mentioned having help at the Gull Gates," Anton said. "I suppose that might mean it could see us getting that far."

Franj tipped her head to one side. "A midwife might say to the mother of a sickly baby – if she survives the night, she'll live," she said. "It would not mean she believes the baby will survive the night." There was no gloom in her words, just a plain pragmatism.

They rode in silence.

"The other thing, though," Franj said. "About the last blade priest. I can believe that."

Anton, abashed once again by her faith in him, could not reply.

The Pilgrims' Path was not quite what Anton had expected. He should have guessed from its name, but even that did not prepare him. In his mind's eye, he saw the Mirolinian road that ran from the Brink to the Gull Gates: straight, flat, wide, surfaced with well-fitted stone setts, and a quick passage, even though it had not been properly maintained in decades and the winter frosts and spring floods had heaved and torn its surface. Like that, he thought, but a little more humble.

Instead, he could hardly see the path at all. It was barely different to the path they had taken cross-country: crooked, narrow, threaded around obstacles rather than going over or through them. Had he been alone, he might have missed it altogether. Small cairns of pale stone marked the right gap in the valley's boundary of tumbled boulders, hung with faded and tattered prayer flags. Franj drew Anton's attention to the far side of the valley, almost lost in the mist, where a particularly massive, axehead-shaped stone had been thrust upwards by the pushing of rocks around it. It was covered in Custodian runes, scoured to near invisibility by wind and winter.

After a dicey few minutes fording the stream – which, though narrow, flowed shockingly quickly, carrying with it fistfuls of stone – they joined the path. Under a roof of fog, it was not unlike being back at the Brink, winding through corridors and passages and up and down steps. All around were titanic fallen rocks.

"A fine place for an ambush," Anton said.

"We must try to be quiet," Franj replied in a soft voice that was hushed without the sibilance of a whisper. "The fog can carry sound in strange ways."

She had ceased her bounding from place to place and instead walked steadily but watchfully, examining the ground as much as the gaps and hidey-holes around and above them. From time to time she climbed a boulder to see a little ahead – as far as the weather would allow – but now with a lynx-like stealth.

Within the bubble of wariness that she projected, Anton could detect something else: a mystery. As if the ground was not giving her the answers she expected.

For several hours they progressed in near-silence. Each birdcall came to Anton like a berserker shriek, heralding imminent attack. Even Stripe seemed jittery, and shied often. But he was struck at how quiet the horse was, how seldom it whinnied or snorted. A product of the Zealot stables.

For the first time since leaving the Brink, Anton felt the cold getting to him. Before, it was as if he did not have time for it and he wondered if he had somehow been warmed by his own fear. Now, however, he was afraid and cold at once. He yearned to find shelter, and to rest properly, and he wondered how long it might be before he was again inside a room with a bed. If ever. Thinking that activity might help warm him, and to spare the horse, he dismounted from Stripe and walked alongside her, watching Franj step on ahead.

After an age, she halted. She studied the ground at her feet, then stood and looked ahead. Then she crouched and resumed her examination of the dirt.

Treading carefully, fearful of disturbing a pattern he could not even see, Anton caught up with her.

"What is it?" he asked softly.

"I thought I was mistaken," she said. "But I am not."

She stood and gestured at the ground. It was fine grey sand, polished smooth as a flagstone by an effusion of water and then frozen hard. But the topmost dusting of material had thawed, and had been disturbed. It bore multiple scrapes and scuffs.

"Footsteps," Anton said. One did not need to be a tracker to see that. "Our pursuers?"

Franj shook her head. "Not unless they lost their horses. And there are too many – at least five. Walking ahead of us. They are not Zealots. That– " she picked out an indentation like the print of a small goblet "–is the heel of a leather boot, a good one."

"Pilgrims?" Anton said, and he had a flash of remembrance. Again, he was at Hleng, listening to Yisho telling Ramnie about the lost company of Zealots, and again he had said the first thing that came into his head and made a fool of himself. There were no pilgrims here, there hadn't been for two years. There ought not be anyone at all.

That conference at the lake had been little more than a week ago. Anton felt deeply tired, and impossibly old, though he was little more than a week older.

Franj had not dignified his speculation with an answer.

"Who are they?" he asked.

"I don't know," Franj said. She raised her eyebrows. "Not Zealots, not Elithi."

"Could it be Elves?" Anton asked, and when she gave him

a look of disbelief he added: "The Custodian told me to watch for Elves. It said they drew near."

"If they are Elves, they have found some very skilled shoemakers in Caenon," Franj said.

"Then who?"

She smiled at him. "It might be the help we were promised."

Without knowing who the strangers were – without even setting eyes on them – Anton found he was glad of them. Franj had been right, they were a help. They would wander into any traps or ambushes first, likely revealing their position. What Anton and Franj needed to do was to close the distance between themselves and the strangers without revealing themselves. Now they were the pursuers.

Dusk came stealthily. At first it seemed that the fog was thickening, until it became obvious that the light behind it was failing. The shadows filled the path like wine filling a cup, and Anton was alarmed by the utter victory of the dark. On previous nights there had been the light of the stars, and the moon and its maids, but tonight there was nothing.

The horse fretted, and once let out a piercing whinny that Anton feared must have been audible from the Brink. Walking beside the horse, he was finding the going impossible himself. Treading on a loose, loaf-sized stone, he stepped hard on the side of his foot, hurting his ankle, and he feared more serious injury.

"We have to stop," he whispered to Franj. He could no longer see the scout – she was ahead of him, and apparently had no desire to slow down.

There was silence ahead, and for a blind second Anton feared that his companion had disappeared, or been stolen away by a silent assault. Then a noise came near at hand, at the saddlebags behind him, and he jumped – but it was Franj.

"That's fine," she said, moving to Stripe's front. He heard

the horse drinking from its canteen. Rolls of furs and bedding were thrust into his arms. "Bed down. I'm just going a little further on. I think we're really close to them."

"How do you know?" Anton asked. "How can you see anything?"

She didn't answer him.

"Just be careful," he said. But she was no longer near enough to hear him.

Anton slept badly. The cold afflicted him terribly, and he was shaken by formless nightmares of the dark of his dungeon cell. All the Hidden Land felt a prison to him, with high walls and cold floors and prowling guards, and not even the promise of food or rest. He longed to be outside it, into the unknown world, Elves or no Elves.

Waking in the first stirrings of dawnlight, he found himself alone. Had Franj never returned from her excursion in the dark, was he truly alone? But she had been here. Her bedding was out, though wrapped again for travel, and a parcel of hay had been opened for Stripe. What hour was it, he wondered – early, still. The mist was lighter today, and he knew it would burn away in the sun, to be gone by middle meal. Soldier-cake, again, for middle meal, he knew, just as he chewed unhappily on a rusk of it for his breakfast. Only the horse stirred. All around was quiet. Anton wanted to be on his way.

Stones scrunched behind him, and he turned sharply, only to see nothing. Standing, he looked about, and the horse shifted and toed the ground, but he was still alone. Then Franj was at his side, materialising out of the fog. He barely suppressed a squeal of surprise.

"If I had been an enemy, you would be dead," she said. But she said it with a sly smile. She was not upbraiding him, she was enjoying herself. He thought of the play-hunting of a cat.

"I'm glad it's you," he said.

"You would probably be dead even if I came up beating a gong, right?" she continued. "On account of not wishing to arm yourself."

"I'm sorry to make life so difficult for you," Anton said. In truth he was getting a little weary of being reminded of his promise to himself, and the burden it placed on others.

Franj smiled at him. "Great difficulty is a defining feature of the great trial of faith," she said. "You know, Augardine going over the mountains and so on. If my given task was easy I might think it unimportant."

Anton didn't have much to say to this. He thought that he disliked being a task, though – a saddlebag to be hoicked to safety.

"You might not want to fight, but can you stay quiet?" Franj asked. "I want to show you something, but you'll have to be silent."

They left Stripe with hay and water and walked softly a hundred yards or so further along the kinking pilgrims' path. Then Franj guided Anton off the path, climbing up a gap between rocks filled with loose shingle, which shifted under Anton's feet with a succession of rattles that felt deafening to his nervous ears. Now they were above the path, on a natural ledge scored with numerous interruptions. Most of these could be simply stepped over, but a couple had to be jumped. Each time, as he bumped and gasped and lunged, Anton was amazed at the noiseless way that Franj was able to move. Before very long she motioned to him to crouch down, and they went the rest of the way on their hands and knees, with Franj pausing often to glare at Anton, finger pressed to her lips. And now he knew why: ahead, there were voices.

Eventually they were lying on their bellies atop an immense boulder curved like a bald head. They could see down onto the path, where a small group was packing up a miserable camp. Anton counted five, and they made a curious collection. One had the look of a knight for his spurred boots, though he lacked a mount and his leather armour was unlike the bronze plate worn by Zealots or the steel of Mirolinian legionnaires. In conference with him was a tall, striking woman who might also be a knight, but her armour was visibly superior in quality. Even at a distance, and even through days of grime, Anton made out fine decoration and the glint of gold stitches. A noble, then. The remainder – a young woman and two men, one young, one old – had the look of servants. As a whole, the group had a tired and dejected air, and they were making ready to move off without much comradely feeling.

Franj motioned to retreat, and they crawled back the way they had come. When they were far enough to resume their feet, they started to discuss, in low voices.

"Mirolinians?" Franj said, with an enquiring glance.

"No," Anton said. "I think they're Leaguers. The altzan-al said that a delegation from the League was coming to conclude a treaty. They must have come across the Pilgrims' Pass."

"But why would they come down here?" Franj said. Then she added, with a reflexive note of indignation: "It is forbidden."

"I don't know," Anton said.

Franj shook her head. "It doesn't make any sense. They came across the Pilgrims' Pass? That's a hard route to take. They are carrying almost nothing. Who would sign the treaty? You need someone important, yes? The knight? The woman-knight?"

"She looked important," Anton said.

Franj signalled her agreement with raised eyebrows and a bob of the head. "I suppose. It's just weird that they look so dirty and sad. You know, if you said 'League delegation', I'd expect something more..." She tailed off.

"Impressive?" Anton supplied.

"Yes, impressive. The League has all the gold in the world."

"It's a hard road," Anton said. "Maybe they're lost." He tried to think it through, as best he could while scrambling across rocks and jumping gaps. Ving might not want a treaty with the League, but would he attack them, and court war? It struck Anton as unlikely, especially while the Tzanate was so weak. A delegation had come, expecting to meet Ramnie, and no one had arrived. But that didn't explain this bedraggled group of five, wandering deeper into the Hidden Land.

Franj did not reply. She was lost in her own thoughts. They had reached their own little camp, which had felt sparse and mean to Anton until he had seen Leaguers sleeping on bare dirt. Now it had some of the comfort of home.

"If they're Leaguers, they might be friendly," Anton suggested. "Ramnie wanted a treaty with them. If we are to continue his work – his plan – perhaps we should contact them."

He had expected Franj to welcome allies in the wilderness, doubly so given that a detachment of Zealots was waiting for them somewhere ahead. But her face was dark and her brow creased. She delayed a reply, biting her lip, putting intense focus into the simple job of packing up their supplies.

"What worries you?" Anton said.

"There's foul magic here," she said quietly. "Can't you feel it? The air doesn't feel like the Elith-Tenh."

Anton was ready to dismiss her fears. They had the strong flavour of peasant superstition to him, but he realised there was a bitter aftertaste of truth. The air – not the air, but a quality like the air, in its invisibility and all-around-ness – had changed. He had sensed it since yesterday, but had attributed the sensation to being in unfamiliar places under terrible stress. Besides its encircling mountains, the Tzanate was ringed with powerful wards, enchantments that pre-dated the arrival of Augardine. The protection afforded by its passes resided in more than their inaccessibility. This intangible guarantee was far from intense, but its weakness, or outright failure, was nevertheless unmistakable to two young people who had spent their lives immersed in it.

"I feel it," Anton said. "We should keep our distance, then."

Franj nodded. She was separating an object from the bundle of supplies: a short bow. "A little distance." She tested the bowstring with her thumb. "Not too far."

23

INAR

Finding and keeping to the pilgrim trail was difficult enough on the first day. The pass from Mishig-Tenh broadened out, blending into the wall of mountains that enclosed the Hidden Land, but a wider way meant more choice of path, and more possibility of error. Only in one or two places were there signs of human intervention – carved steps, a cairn, a flat stone raised into a rune-scored menhir – and they were easy enough to miss. More than once, they lost any sign of anything like a trail, and had to pause and return and hunt around for the end of the thread. It took a whole day to find their way down through the foothills and onto the floor of the plateau of Elith-Tenh. From there, at least, the trail should have been more obvious.

On the second day, the fog descended.

Inar had known many fogs like it – the weather here was not so different to that of Mishig-Tenh, though it was higher, and colder. But the blinding white that filled the plateau combined in disturbing ways with its desertion and lifelessness. It was not just dead, it was death, an enclosed solitude, where even the souls about you felt distant and unreachable, where no blade of grass could be seen, where there was no horizon and no tomorrow. He imagined it had that effect on them all – it filled the spaces between the survivors of the party, blocking them off from one another, shutting them up with their own thoughts. They walked in silence, heads bowed, hungry and thirsty, and communication dwindled to occasional monosyllables of information and instruction.

Inar thought mostly of Lott. They had never been able to recover the dead, or even to establish who was dead. Unable to be certain, Inar was tormented by a pendulum of hope and grief. It was possible, always possible, that Lott had somehow escaped, and possibly others as well, and the bloody feast by the Vulture's Eye had consisted only of the bodies of the mules. This was the inextinguishable spark of possibility that rose again and again in Inar's chest. But he had seen the speed with which the knomes moved, and their numbers. He had seen the way they passed up food on the ground for food that still moved. It was hard to imagine that anyone could have evaded that onslaught, which had come by surprise, in daylight.

He knew many tales of accidents in the mines and quarries of Mishig-Tenh that had left bodies inaccessible, or worse still, living men trapped underground. His father carried those stories around with him like a hod of cobbles, an invisible weight on his thoughts. So did every man who worked to cut stone and dig ore. To lose comrades was, naturally, terrible. To be unable to retrieve them, to be unable to pay them the final courtesies, made it so much worse. It was to leave a building unfinished – or, to use an image the Leaguers would know, to leave a debt unpaid.

Nevertheless, there was always that recurring spark of hope. And Inar quickly came to hate its reappearance, the way that it taunted him with the possibility that all his grieving might be in vain, and that Lott might be safe and well somewhere. It was a chatty and cheerful visitor on a day when one would prefer to be left alone. In that respect, it was not unlike Lott, who had never been able to match the temperament of his workmates and unwilling superior, and whose deficiencies as a labourer and a mason were imperfectly balanced by the fact that he was never downcast. How that oblivious chirpiness had riled Inar, and how he wished he could have it here again. If Lott were to appear around the next turn, a smile on his face and a tale of dumb luck ready to tell, Inar was sure that he would be annoyed, as some habits could never be overturned. But he would be so glad, too, so glad.

The fog thinned on the third day, but the mood of the group was no less disconsolate. Hunger settled into them like a severe winter. Anzola and Miroslo – still working from what they had been able to survey from the deserted fort – estimated that the road could be reached that day, and the Gull Gates by nightfall, which illumined the prospect of food before sleep, and was the only thing that gave Inar strength to rise that morning. They had made camp – if it could be called camp – in a wide clearing along the path, where a carpet of broken boulders descending from the mountains above had been held behind a natural wall of unusually large stones, one the size of the fort they had left days earlier. Just as it was an obvious campsite, it was equally obvious others had stayed here before, and the stones were inscribed with runes and blackened in places by the trace of fires and candles. Prayer-flags, faded and tattered, still twitched and flapped in protected corners. None slept well, seated, pressed together for warmth.

Besides exhaustion and discomfort, the party was troubled by a growing unease. Duna broached it first, as they rose on the morning of the third day, and did so with embarrassment. When her admission was greeted with agreement rather than condescension or scorn, she was visibly relieved. Her belief was this: that they were not alone, not quite. She believed she had heard the whinny of a horse. Kielo said that he believed he had heard it as well, though he had thought it the call of a bird. Regardless of the provenance of the sound, all suspected that other humans might not be quite as far as they might otherwise be led to believe.

Inar had heard nothing, though he felt the same unease. He had attributed it to fatigue, to the eerie fog-blindness that afflicted them, and to the knowledge that they trespassed in a sacred and forbidden place. Quite aside from the tzans and their armies, what of the Mountain's Custodians? What of the knomes? The more he reflected on the possibilities, the more every shadow grew eyes.

Anzola disagreed with none of their fears, but she did not seem afraid. "Knomes would simply attack us, would they not?" she insisted, not letting hunger and tiredness intrude on her bluster. "And if it is Zealots, then they are welcome. The sooner we encounter them the better. We are a diplomatic mission. They are honour-bound to protect us."

"Your grace, we cannot rely on that belief," Miroslo said.

Anzola wheeled to confront the knight. "You agreed with me that the Gull Gates were our safest path! Food and rest, you said! Now you claim they will kill us?"

"It is not the Gull Gates that trouble me, your grace," Miroslo said. Inar noticed that he had reverted to using the merite's formal manner of address – a cautious abandonment of familiarity. "A substantial garrison, many soldiers and others present. It's out here that worries me. You must understand, that a soldier safe in a fortress has a completely different mind to a soldier in a wilderness like this. See how it has affected us? The fear it causes? We have no reason to believe it would affect a Zealot any differently. They might think it simplest and safest to kill us where no one would ever find our remains."

For a long second, Anzola regarded the knight with wide eyes, absorbing the import of what he said. Then she shook her head. "Caution is a fine thing, Kol Miroslo, but we may be simply jumping at shadows. However it stands, I don't see any alternatives to our present path. We will be at the Gull Gates by nightfall. That will resolve all these qualms."

Miroslo's jaw tightened, but he said nothing. And perhaps

there was nothing to say, as the merite was right, where else was there to go? Returning the way they had come had been impossible three days ago and had become no more possible with three days of time and distance.

"We will be on our guard," Anzola said, taking a conciliatory tone. "Your fears are well heard, my knight."

The knight nodded, curtly but with deference. Then, with a final glance up at the boulders that hemmed the campsite, he went to scout the route ahead.

All they had with them was what little they had taken to the Sight on the last day waiting for the Tzanate to make an appearance. What had saved all their lives was Kielo's motherly insistence that they would be uncomfortable sitting in the open all day – all five of them had a blanket and an extra fur with them, which had kept them from dying of cold in the night. Thirst was not a threat, as the land was alive with rivulets and torrents of meltwater from the retreating snow. Hunger was the great danger, slowing the body and clouding the mind. The expedition had been running low already, and its meagre reserves had been lost to the knomes. A few sticks of dry bread, a handful of dried tomatoes and a handful of dried sausage was all that came from the Sight, and that had been rationed down to crumbs. But when Inar accounted for his remaining possessions, he found a small and hard package in one of the folds of his furs that he could not place. For a moment he thrilled at the thought that it might be a morsel of food that he had tucked away and forgotten. But when he drew it out, he found that it was not food, or if it was it was far past eating, as it was tightly wrapped in plain sacking that was stained and decayed with great age. As he peeled away this outer layer, it crumbled in his hands, and he recalled where he had found the object: in the cavity at the heart of the Eye-

Stone, the small artificial chamber that neither he nor Duna had detected.

Duna was at his side. Only she and he were left at the campsite. Anzola always strove to keep close to Miroslo, which Inar interpreted as a proud desire to be at the van, rather than any unworthy hankering for protection. Kielo, in turn, tried to keep close to Anzola.

"What is that?" Duna asked.

For the briefest instant, Inar was gripped by an urge to keep the object secret – to lie to the Pallestran girl about what it was and where he found it. Why he should feel this immediately puzzled him – covetousness, or an instinct to protect others? What he knew was that considerable effort and artistry had gone into concealing this small artefact. Whatever it was, it was important.

"It was inside the Eye-Stone," Inar said. "I found it after the stone broke." He peeled away the last layer of rotting sackcloth, and within found a small piece of hard, glassy volcanic stone. The pebble of heat-seared rock fitted neatly in the hand with a pleasant weight. But there was nothing pleasant about its shape. It had been carved, or otherwise worked, into the form of a squatting knome, its knees drawn up to its chest, hands clutched around those knees, a devilish leer on its animal face. In each of its eyes was a tiny splinter of cut gem, which caught the light and burned a yellow spark. Inar thought of the varied and fanciful depictions of knomes he had encountered in temple carvings and illuminated books. They had been made by artists using their imaginations. Whoever had made this had worked from life.

"It's horrible," Duna said, summarising Inar's own gut reaction.

"They hid it," he said. "They hid it with care."

"Who?"

"Whoever hid it," Inar said. He had speculations, but he preferred not to share them – the idol's age, and the artistry of its making and concealment, pointed to the Custodians, or at least to a forgotten age of greatness before the time of Augardine.

"Get rid of it," Duna said.

Inar knew at once that he did not want to do that. "When we are able," he said instead, "I will return it to the place I found it."

Many assumptions and improbabilities were chained up in that straightforward sentence, and Duna gave Inar a penetrating stare that had at its origin an unmistakable suspicion, but she did not pursue the matter. "We must go," she said. "I do not wish to be alone in this place."

Inar tucked the idol back into his furs, in the safest fold he knew of, and he saw Duna watch as he did so.

Both of them made haste to catch up with the rest of the expedition, but the others had clearly found a reserve of speed, perhaps from their desire to be free from the dreary fogbound waste of the Hidden Land. They often saw Kielo in the path ahead, looking back for them impatiently and beckoning them along, but they never quite closed the distance. As a consequence, Inar found himself more or less alone with Duna.

Duna's composure these past few days had been a revelation to Inar. When he thought back to the first part of their journey it was as if he was remembering a different girl. Then, she had seemed permanently ill-tempered and sulky, and it might have been expected that the hardships and ordeals of the latter part of their time together would only exacerbate that rancour and misery. But the opposite had happened. While she was far from cheerful – it could hardly be expected of her – she had responded to their recent trials with remarkable equanimity. She remained introspective, as they all were, but that inward gaze seemed founded in a reserve of strength, rather than resentment.

"I never thanked you for what you did to the knomes," Inar said, finding that he had to give words to the sudden swell of admiration that had risen in him. "It was astonishing."

"No need," Duna replied, keeping her eyes on the path ahead. "I did what I could. You played your part."

"Nevertheless," Inar pushed on, "that was more than anything you've done before – if you could bring down that cliff face, you could certainly bring down any building or city wall."

Duna stayed silent, eyes lowered. She had reddened a little, perhaps embarrassed by the praise.

"And after that... you were able to act on the beasts directly?" Inar realised at once that he had been burning with desire to ask Duna about this latter part, which must find a reflection in his own ability, but his life-learned disinclination to talk about it – the blow his brother had struck across his head still ringing in his ears – had stopped him. "How? What were you doing? I know that the other scourge-talents can act on flesh, but I didn't realise..."

"You mustn't tell the others," Duna said. She was looking straight at him now, and her eyes were fierce. "You *mustn't*."

It was Inar's turn to redden, cut deep as he was by the passionate insistence in her voice. "I'm sorry. I won't."

The girl was grim, and returned her attention to picking her way through the uneven landscape. "It's bones," she said. "There's stuff in them – it's like some rocks. I'm not a mason, I don't know stone like you, but it's like chalk or limestone. It's not much but it's enough to act on. I can break bones."

Inar took some time with this information. She had done no more than describe what he had already seen, but it was astonishing to have it confirmed.

"When did you learn to do that?" he asked.

"You mustn't tell the others," she said, ignoring his question. "They'll... I don't know what they'd do."

"They'd be unhappy?"

She shook her head. "No." She snorted a joyless laugh. "I think they'd be delighted."

Understanding dawned within Inar. "You're hiding your strength from them, aren't you? You're showing them no more than cracks in walls and stones, but you can cause landslides and shatter castles."

"Your presence helps with that," Duna replied.

"My   presence   makes   you   stronger?" She frowned. "Sharper, let's say. Better aimed. But you need to know, the more my skills are used, the stronger they grow. I don't know where that ends."

They walked on in silence. Kielo was ahead, standing on a promontory, waiting for them. Inar knew he would keep her secret, as it was, in a way, also his secret. And he knew what she feared, because when she had told him these things, he had first filled with the awesome possibilities for engineering, siegecraft and war – and then realised that those possibilities made him a little afraid of the girl. That was what she feared: the fear she inspired in others. Fear had built the pyres under the scourges, and would burn him as well.

"I am so pleased that we need no longer fear the knomes," Kielo said acidly once Inar and Duna reached him.

For a sickening moment, Inar feared that the secretary had overheard their conversation. But no – he was simply being sarcastic.

"We are tired and hungry," Inar said in reply, not feeling particularly apologetic.

"We are all tired and hungry," Kielo said, more gently, "but it has not slowed down the merite. And I have no wish to dawdle in this vile place."

Neither did Inar, and whatever Duna's abilities, he also had little wish to be separated from the only two members of the expedition who had any training in swordplay. He had carried

Timo's sword with him ever since the battle at the Eye, but it felt more like a hindrance than a source of protection. He feared that even if he tried to use it as a club, or to block an enemy's attacks, it would end up being less useful than his staff which was lighter and more familiar in his hands. More than once he had considered simply leaving it behind, but even the thought had an air of disrespect towards the slain knight. Kol Timo was one of the knights who spoke only Palla, and lacking other tongues he had spoken little to Inar in the time they had together. Perhaps, eventually, Leaguers would make it to the Eye again and retrieve whatever was left of him. But for the time being, this sword was all that remained of that knight in the world of the living, and Inar felt he had a duty to conduct it back to its homeland – or at least back to the League garrison at Sojonost.

These melancholy reflections were interrupted by an unexpected sound from the path ahead – raised voices. Voices that did not belong to either Anzola or Miroslo.

They hurried on to find the source of the commotion. What they found was a natural amphitheatre. The path widened out into a roughly circular depression of loose dirt, surrounded by the large tumbled rocks that covered the terrain all the way back to the Pilgrims' Pass. Before them was a narrow gateway formed by two similarly sized cuboid rocks, possibly positioned deliberately – but whether they had been left there by thinking hands or by the blind workings of time, they were an effective piece of architecture. Runes covered both. Beyond lay a suggestion of flatter, more open, more welcoming terrain. But blocking the path to that appealing prospect were two Zealots. They were armoured, in loose and light bronze plate, and wore the enclosing bronze helmets that made the Tzanate's soldiery so feared. Their spears were raised and pointed at Anzola and Miroslo, and their stances showed a readiness to charge and fight. Anzola and Miroslo had their blades out as well. The encounter had a deeply unpleasant odour of violence.

Inar had missed whatever the Zealots had shouted at the Leaguers, but they arrived in earshot for her ringing reply: "We are diplomatic representatives of the League and we insist on safe passage!"

"You are intruders in a holy place!" one of the Zealots replied in churchy Mirolingua. "The entire world knows that the Elith-Tenh is not to be profaned by heathens! Any diplomat would know this!"

"We were attacked by knomes at your frontier and much of our expedition was slain," Anzola said. "We were driven into your lands by force. We wish only to depart by the swiftest possible route."

"Knomes?" The Zealot exchanged a glance with his comrade. "Lies! There have been no knomes in the Elith-Tenh since before the time of Augardine!"

The merite was having none of this, and Inar found himself thrilling at her straight back, her raised chin, and her clear and commanding voice. Only weeks before, he would have sided more with the Zealot – he had travelled far in mind as well as body. "I am merite of the League of Free Cities, surveyor-general, a commander of the League's armies and mistress of sieges! And you will escort us safely to the nearest garrison! We are here at the invitation of the altzan-al!"

The Zealot snorted. "Which altzan-al? We have a new altzan-al now, and he has promised there will be no alliance with heathens."

Anzola blinked at this news, and a little firmness went from her demeanour, but she did not back down. "Who is altzan-al, then? We have received no such communication. Might I remind you that we have an army standing at your frontier?"

With a laugh, the Zealots made a show of looking around at the empty, barren landscape. "Where, then? Will they come and help you now?"

There was a whisper of movement in the piled rocks above Inar, and the helmeted head of another Zealot appeared. So this is it, Inar thought, the attack, with one knight against an unknown number of the world's most feared warriors. But the Zealot who had risen from his hiding place did not wield a bow or loose a spear, and his emergence did not spur his comrades into action. Rather, it sent them into confused conference, and one called up a name. But the third Zealot did not reply. He was staggering, and clutching at his neck, where all now saw the fletched end of an arrow. Then he slumped over, falling ten feet or more to the path.

The Zealots reacted first, while Inar was still struggling to comprehend what had happened. They straightened their spears and charged at Miroslo, who was critically slow to respond. The knight managed to deflect one spear, but the other was driven deep into his side. He gasped in pain, a shocking high-pitched whistle unlike any sound a man should make.

Anzola went into the fray, eliciting a shout of protest from Kielo. She charged the Zealot who Miroslo had managed to knock aside, aiming an upwards slash at his arm with her dirk. The strike connected at the point of the weapon, and the Zealot cried out, but he did not drop his spear. Instead, he staggered back, putting some distance between himself and the merite.

Belatedly, as if in a dream, Inar registered that a deadly struggle was taking place scant yards away from him, and that he was armed and had to join. He lifted Timo's sword, which felt heavier than it had moments earlier, and took a few uncertain paces towards the Zealot confronting Anzola. Could he, in fact, raise his weapon and bring it down on another man? With the intent of injuring or killing? The whole notion felt unlikely, even as the alternatives peeled away.

Blood dripped from the Zealot's right forearm, but whatever wound he had taken had not loosened his grip on his spear. He had squared off with Anzola, who stood with her knife ready, and he might have been ready to charge had he not seen Inar at the Leaguer's side.

"Put down your weapon," Anzola said, and Inar was again impressed at the force she managed in her voice, when the advantage was far from secured. "No more blood needs to spill."

Before the Zealot could answer, there was a spasm of movement and a sharp, unexpected noise, a solid *thock*. The Zealot grabbed at his chest, and for a second Inar believed that Duna might have used her abilities on him – until he saw the shaft of another arrow protruding from the soldier's breastplate, above the heart. The man fell, angling round and sideways, all the up gone from him.

Inar twisted his head, trying to find the origin of the shot, but he saw only mocking rocks, rocks that now positively seethed with hostile hidden life. Anzola had moved to help Miroslo, but he needed no help. Though he was bent with pain, and had a blood gauntlet clamped to his side, he had the advantage over his opponent. The Zealot was sprawled on the ground, clutching his arm, whimpering with pain, his spear under the League-knight's boot.

"Gessel!" the Zealot called out. "Gessel!"

"Gessel is dead," said a voice above them. "He died first."

The Leaguers turned as one to find who had spoken, and saw a young woman raising herself from a concealed position in the boulders above the path. She carried a short bow and was wearing much lighter armour than the other Zealots, only a few small pieces of plate over leather riding gear, but she was clearly one of them. Inar's fingers tightened on the hilt of Timo's sword, and he saw that Anzola remained in a combat stance, but the bow and the rocks gave the girl an advantage over them all – and he doubted she was alone.

In any case, Miroslo was done with fighting. He fell into a crouch, groaned and slid further, sitting heavily on the ground. The spear had pierced him deep. As he descended, he took his foot off the weapon that had dealt him the wound, and Inar moved quickly to pick it up. Possibly he need not have bothered, as the surviving Zealot did not make any motion towards it, and looked to be in no fighting mood either.

"Traitor!" the Zealot spat at the young archer. "Murderer! You and the vertzan will burn!"

"Are any of you going to deal with that?" the young woman said, addressing the Leaguers.

No one replied – Miroslo no longer seemed to hear, and Inar did not know what she was talking about, not until it was too late.

"Very well," the young woman said, pulling back the bowstring on the arrow she already had notched and loosing it at the injured Zealot.

Anzola cried out, wordlessly, to try to halt the shot, but it came too late. The arrow struck the Zealot in the chest – it might have come from a short bow, but it was aimed precisely and at a range of only a couple of dozen yards. It pierced his breastplate and he fell back with a horrible gasp of pain and anger.

The Leaguers stared up at the young woman.

"That was not necessary!" Anzola shouted.

"That was war," the archer replied.

Anzola closed her eyes and made a visible effort to calm herself. "We are diplomatic…" she began in a high, irate voice. But the young Zealot cut her off.

"The League, yes, I heard it all the first time," she said. "You demand safe passage."

Inar thought he detected a note of unkind mimicry in the latter part of the Zealot's reply, but Anzola, the diplomat, ignored it.

"Yes. Can you provide it?"

"Yes," Franj said.

24

ANTON

"We are also emissaries," Franj said. "We are trying to reach the loyal Zealots beyond the Gull Gates. We have information about what has occurred at the Brink."

"Spies, then," the eldest of the woman's servants said, with an arched eyebrow. He had a Dreyff-ish air, a clerk, a secretary. "And this one–" he motioned to the executed Zealot on the dirt beside the expedition "–he called you murderers. Fugitives, then?"

"This is war," Franj repeated. "We do what we must."

After Franj had done what she said must be done, she had descended from her perch and signalled to Anton that he was safe to reveal himself. There was blood on her hand and on her tunic, but she was unhurt. He did not have to ask what had become of Gessel.

They had already agreed how much to say to the Leaguers. In a few curt sentences Franj told them what had happened at the Brink, none of which they knew: that Ving had killed Ramnie and seized power for himself, and that there was fighting between the usurper's collaborators and those loyal to the old regime. But she omitted to identify Anton as either a blade-priest or as Ramnie's rightful successor. It was too much to reveal, and the Leaguers might prefer them as hostages rather than guides. Anton did not fancy being traded to Ving's forces in return for safe passage through the Gull Gates. No – it was better to pose as messengers, trying to connect the loyalist forces dispersed across the world.

"If Ramnie is dead, and Ving is illegitimate, then who do you recognise as altzan-al?" the noblewoman asked. She had introduced herself as merite Anzola Stiyitta. "The vertzan, what is that? A challenger?"

"Ver-tzan means blade-priest," one of the younger servants interjected. He had not been introduced, and Anton was faintly surprised to hear he had a Mishigo accent – was Mishig-Tenh counted as part of the League, now? A guide, in any case. "They were, er, the Givers of the Gift."

Anzola's face fell in horror. "A sacrificial priest?" She fell into urgent consultation with the older servant, in a language unknown to Anton.

Franj shook her head, and circled round the party to retrieve arrows from the bodies of the Zealots she had killed. "You're wasting time," she said, gesturing at the fallen League-knight with her bow. "Your man here will die. We have to get to Mal Nulalus."

She came to the first Zealot body, the last to die, and unbuckled his breastplate, then carefully removed it, threading the arrow through the hole she had made. Once the armour was removed she pulled out the arrow, bracing a foot against the body as she did so. Something in the matter-of-fact way she approached the task filled Anton with disgust. It seemed disrespectful.

At the same time, these scruples were perhaps luxurious when the death toll in his name was rising. Until the last, he had harboured hope that they could somehow slip past the Zealots that were hunting them and make it to the Gull Gates without a spear raised in anger. But part of him had always recognised that any confrontation would have to be deadly if their survival was to be ensured, and that meant expecting Franj to kill. Even if he found himself able to countenance taking another life, he was not a practised fighter. So although he was shocked by the cool, systematic way that Franj had dealt with their hunters, he knew it was in his name, and he had to take responsibility for it, however much it appalled him.

He had heard the note of disgusted terror in the League-lady's voice when she said the words "sacrificial priest". However he behaved, could he ever shake off that expectation?

The pale, blonde girl servant had rushed to tend to the knight after the fight was over, removing his armour and trying to get to the wound in his side to staunch the flow of blood. She cut off the conference between the noblewoman and her secretary with a shout, and a few breathless lines of the League language. Whatever she said ended their debate and spurred them into action.

"Put him on the horse," Anton said, handing Stripe's reins to the secretary. "Let me remove some of these bags."

"Horses," Franj said. She had retrieved two of her arrows, and had also picked up the fallen Zealots' helmets and the unbroken spear. "They had horses. They must be nearby."

Returning to Anton, she handed him one of the helmets and the spear. He hesitated over the latter. "Disguise," she said, her voice low, her Mirolingua accented and slangy. "Including the spear, yeah? For looks. It isn't a blade, not really."

He understood what she meant: the Leaguers. If they saw him, outwardly a Zealot scout, refuse arms of any kind, their suspicions might be raised. He took the spear, stomaching his reluctance. The helmet fitted better than he hoped – it was lighter than his ceremonial mask, or at least better balanced. That wasn't for the League, but for the Gates.

The knight was conscious, but pale and sweating, his eyes lost in a private nightmare. The spear had torn a wide gash in his belly, and gone deep, and fresh wet blood had drenched the strips of blanket the young girl had used to bandage it. "I can't ride," he gasped as Anton and the Mishigo lifted him to his feet.

"Just be carried," Anton said. "We can be at the gates in hours."

He didn't protest, and let himself be led to Stripe's side, but when the time came to lift him into the saddle he shrieked in pain and began to sob.

"Listen–" Anton began, stopped when he realised he did not know the knight's name.

"Miroslo," the Mishigo said. "He's called Miroslo. I'm Inar."

"Right, thank you," Anton said, although having this information did nothing to clarify what he might say to the man. "Miroslo, listen, you just need to get on this horse and stay there a few miles. The road is close, it'll be a smooth ride to the Gull Gates, and they will have a surgeon."

This last detail was more a hope than a statement of fact, Anton knew, but he saw the dim flicker of attention it prompted in the knight's eyes. Nevertheless, it was a gamble. In normal circumstances, the Gates would have people capable of dressing wounds, but these were not normal circumstances, with the Tzanate's forces spread so far and so thin.

The noblewoman, Anzola, had appeared at Anton's shoulder. Where she might have been expected to be concerned for her knight, instead she was stern.

"Get on the horse, Miroslo," she said, sharply. "We're not leaving you here and we can't stay. I will not have it." She spoke on, barking a few further commands in the League language. The meaning of these was hidden to Anton, but one word stood out: Sojonost.

Whatever she said, between her instruction and Anton's encouragement, it worked. The knight's agony might not have been dimmed, but he had gained a feeble mastery of it, enough to allow Anton and Inar to lift him onto the horse.

It was then that Franj appeared, and with her the first really solid chunk of good fortune that Anton had experienced since leaving the Brink: four saddled horses, reined together, from the Tzanate's own stables, each with panniers of provisions.

* * *

Augardine had been Miroline's greatest Emperor, but he had not been the first. Leriden had been first, and before he became emperor he had been a minor king among the duchies and city-states of an unruly peninsula. Only a child when made king, Leriden found his reign repeatedly interrupted by barbarian invasions, as raider empires swelled in size and power in the Jesh valley and their armies looked to the south. Early one morning, as he watched over a slumbering army that waited on the isthmus to again resist an incursion, he beheld a gull over the bay. Many gulls made the bay their home, but none like this: it shone white-gold and hung motionless in the air, its eyes fixed on him, and once he had met those eyes he could not look away. Behind it, the smoke that clung to the volcanic peak of Shaddagore on the Jesh side of the bay spread out like wings, brilliant in the morning sun. A singular idea filled him, as if it penetrated every fibre of his body from the hairs on his head to the tips of his toes, an idea that he knew he was powerless to resist. Build a city on this spot, make it the ruling city of the peninsula, and make war to make a permanent peace. They called the peninsula Mirol, which was also the name they gave to the known world, and Leriden called the city Miroline and made the gull its symbol.

Centuries later, that gull soared over a mountain pass a thousand miles north of Leriden's city, between lands whose names he never knew. It wasn't quite the pure, shining emblem that he had seen. Its gold plate was streaked and battered, revealing the dull bronze beneath. But it still soared, wings outstretched, gaze locked onto the Mountain, and it was the last part of the Gull Gates to catch the light of the declining sun. Already, the road was lost in night-shadow.

The slain Zealots' horses meant everyone now could ride, with Duna on Stripe's back, doing what she could to help

Miroslo, and Inar and Kielo sharing. Anton and Franj led the party, and Franj had kept her bow out since they set off. Since the Gull Gates had come into sight, she had kept an arrow notched. But they had not seen another soul. The Gates themselves were cast bronze, three storeys high, and they stood open, a foreign night beyond. The portcullis was raised. On either side stood dark towers, each mated to the sheer cliffs of the mountains that rose on either side.

"No lights," Anton remarked.

"Why are the gates open?" Anzola asked. She had kept close behind the van the whole way, a restless and questioning presence that Anton and Franj had begun to find irksome.

"I don't know," Anton said, sharing a moment's glance with Franj. Help at the Gates, the Custodian had said. But the garrison here might have another reason for keeping the way open. Colossal counterweights meant that the many, many tonnes of bronze in the gates could be quickly slammed shut with a yank on a release lever. But opening them again was a more difficult job – it took at least twenty-two men, a nod to the size of the fellowship Augardine had led across the Mountains. If fewer than twenty-two men were present, and there was regular traffic with Mal Nulalus and beyond, they would be obliged to keep them open and only shut them in an emergency.

Such a reduced garrison would have to keep watchful, but there was little sign of that.

"It looks deserted," Anzola said.

Anton could not disagree. Only a few arrow-slit windows punctured the towers, but there were more on Tzanate side than there were on the other, and in the gatehouse there showed the tiniest ember of light. No sentries moved on the battlements or stood in the portal. The gate towers and arch had been hung with banners to welcome the Conclave, and even these were unnaturally still.

"We are not safe," Franj said, "and we must not imagine ourselves so."

No one contradicted her. The party added its own silence to the deathly quiet.

"You in the rear," Franj said to Inar and Kielo. "Keep watch behind. Don't be distracted. This may be a lure."

Anton saw the sense of this instruction, but the road behind appeared as deserted as the fortress ahead. His skin prickled, in particular where the Custodian had left its mark.

"Do you feel that?" he said softly to Franj.

She nodded in reply. "You should wait here," she said to Anzola. "Let me go on ahead."

Anzola did not appear keen on this idea, but pulled the reins on her horse and did nothing to stop Franj from separating herself from the party. The road ascended towards the gates, and then levelled off in a wide empty forecourt that had been artificially flattened. Anton knew it: it was paved in a chequerboard pattern of white Mirolinian marble and charcoal Elithi granite, but the marble had weathered badly in its centuries exposed to the elements and few of its squares were intact. The scout was now on this strange indoors-outdoors floor, a place deliberately arranged to make easy targets of anyone that approached the gate. A premonitory image haunted Anton, of Franj struck down by an arrow loosed from one of the many slits that overlooked the forecourt, but the blow never fell. She looked about, and then beckoned to Anton.

Anton dismounted and walked towards Elecy, feeling the Gates rise up over him. The light had gone from around them, though it still clung to the mountaintops and painted the sky stripes of burned orange and satiny blue as it caught the last shreds of mist. Once he was onto the paved expanse of the forecourt, Franj nodded at him to look down.

The ground was littered with broken pieces of the marble slabs that had been laid here, before the work of hundreds of winters and thousands of horses unlaid them. Those dirty white fragments had been arranged into a series of runes. From lower on the road, the rise in the land had made them invisible, and the others were unaware of their presence.

"They were here," Franj said. "Our help."

"I think we both knew that already," Anton said. A thick shroud of magic laid heavy over the fortress. With a shudder, Anton recalled the Custodian's offer to "help" his return to the Brink, with the slaughter of all that stood in his way, and he became fearful for the fate of the men that had been keeping watch over the pass.

"We should find out what has happened to the men here," he said.

"Better to keep moving," Franj said, unable to keep the fear from creeping into her voice.

"The knight needs help, or he'll die," Anton said. "And we might be able to gather more supplies."

Franj's eyes darted around, and down at the arcane symbols beneath their feet. "I couldn't say it to them, but the knight is likely to die anyway," she said. "If the spearhead skewered his guts, there's nothing any of us can do. Really we should leave him here."

"He comes to Mal Nulalus," Anton insisted. "Clearly this place has been stripped back to door-duty. But Mal will have surgeons and the means to treat wounded men. They've been fighting a war, remember? Our best chance is to get him there – if we go through the night, we'll be there before it's night again. Mirolinian road, and downhill to boot."

"Let's be quick, then," Franj said, with a sigh. She pointed at the runes with a hesitant gesture, as if she didn't want to anger them. "And let's get rid of all this, before they see it."

"No," Anton said, shaking his head. "I think it's a bad idea to disturb it."

It wasn't long before they found the first Zealot. The fortress was entered by a small arched gate on the Elith-Tenh side, an opening squeezed between man-made stone on one side and living rock on the other. The gate was unbarred and ajar, and it alarmed Anton that no one had been left on watch. Ascending into the tiny guardroom to establish what had become of the Zealots who should have been on duty, he found that one was at his post, looking out over the Hidden Land from his arrow slit. He would have been able to see the mongrel band of riders approach from some distance, let alone watch as they crept on foot around to his gate and push through it. His eyes were open and awake. But he had not stirred. He leaned on his spear, making not the slightest movement as Anton climbed the stair behind him and cleared his throat.

Another Zealot sat on a wooden stool at a small table set into a vaulted niche. He was cleaning under his fingernails with the point of his knife, or he had been. His left hand was raised, fingers folded for inspection, but his attention had been taken by the point of his knife, which had unearthed something particularly interesting or disgusting. His eyes were slightly crossed, inspecting his trophy. Both men were alive, and neither heard nor saw Anton. The faintest shimmer rose from them, like heat-haze. Sweat prickled across Anton's shoulders.

Our alone-ness comes at a price, the Custodian had said.

In the small covered courtyard behind the gate, the noblewoman Anzola and the Mishigo Inar waited. They had discovered a prize: a small one-horse dray.

"That's good," Anton said, pointing to the cart. "Your knight can travel on it. The road between here and Mal Nulalus isn't bad."

He saw the disappointment in their eyes. "There's no one here that can help him?"

"Not at the moment." If he could spare the Leaguers the sight of the magically becalmed Zealots, that was probably most simple. Certainly simpler than explanations. "But we might be able to find bandages, I suppose, and there'll be fresh water. Do none of you know field medicine?"

"Don't you?" Inar asked. "Isn't that the sort of thing a scout knows?"

"Franj maybe," Anton said, alarmed by the young man's apparent suspicion. "We're both still training. Let's just get what supplies we need and go."

"There'll be storerooms recessed into the rock behind this court," Inar said. "And branching off the tunnels that connect this tower to the other one. A well too. With Kielo and the other Zealot we can be loaded–"

Anzola interrupted the Mishigo, blinking and frowning in accented confusion. "Wait, wait, forgive me," she said. "I do not understand. This is the Gull Gates. Even when I was a little girl I had heard of the Gull Gates. An awesome fortress. The impenetrable gateway to a legendarily unconquerable land. And it stands empty and open, and ripe with plunder."

"For the moment," Anton said. He tried to put a rough, Zealot-y edge into his voice. "Shall we waste that moment, or shall we gather up what we need and be on our way?"

To his almost total surprise, they acted on his words, and resumed their work clearing the dray. But Anton knew that the seeds of suspicion lingered. And he had his own, as well, regarding the Mishigo: how did he know about the tunnels?

25

INAR

As it happened, Inar and Anzola did not have to venture into the tunnels beneath the Gull Gates. The party needed travel supplies, not sacks of dried beans, and those would always be kept closer to hand. They tried the cloistered storage bays that adjoined the fortress's little courtyard, and there they found everything they needed.

In addition, they found another one of the garrison's complement of men. He was not a Zealot, and wore a thick array of plain but warm robes, from which a pink tonsured head poked like a baby bird from a nest. Inar found him facing the shelves in one of the storage bays, where he seemed to have been looking for something, though his head was turned to look back, as if he had been interrupted.

"Excuse me!" Inar said, startled to the core to have found anyone in such a silent place. But the man did not move.

"I didn't mean to surprise you," Inar continued. "We didn't think anyone was here."

The man was as still as the barrels and bundles around him.

Inar took another step towards him. As he did so, Anzola entered the bay. She had been in the adjoining store, and she stopped dead with a scrape of boot heel against stone when she saw Inar was not alone.

"Oh!" she exclaimed.

Inar was at the man's side, and he placed a hand on his shoulder and shook him. The man swayed but did not otherwise move. His eyes were open, but nothing danced within.

"What's wrong with him?" Anzola asked. "Is he asleep?"

"Only if he can sleep standing up, with his eyes open," Inar said. He leaned in closer to the man. He had seen similarly dressed men and women around the shiels in Stull – not tzans, but in the service of the Tzanate. A steward or castellan. It was dark in the storage bay, lit only by a couple of oil burners in niches on either side of the door, but Inar could still make out an oddity in the air immediately above the frozen man – it caught the light curiously, as if it was a little thicker than the air, and flowed ever upwards. The underside of the man's chin was varnished with sweat.

"Do you feel that?" Inar said. "It's cool in here, and dry, and I'm sweating like I'm bringing in the harvest."

"Yes, I feel it," Anzola said. "The same happens when Duna uses her talent."

"A change in the air."

"You have part of her ability," Anzola said. "The scourge-sense – did you notice anything about our Zealot friends?"

The question stopped Inar momentarily. He had not thought to look at them, whatever it was to "look" with that hidden sight, and he did not quite know how he would direct it. The knowledge that there was a distinctive aura to Duna had stolen up on him, and he suspected that he had only been able to make it out at all because of her extraordinary power. It was not a glow or smoke or a pool of warmth, but a more subtle quality and one easy to confuse with natural human characteristics – for instance, Anzola's charisma, assurance and charm, which at times felt like her own motive magic. But many had that – Inar thought of Lord Cilma's distorted variant of it, the air of threat and deadly power that he exuded, even in name.

It occurred to him that he had not thought of Lord Cilma for

days, and even in the extremity of their situation, the thought
made him glad.

"Inar?"

"I'm sorry – no, they don't feel special to me."

Anzola shook her head, as if she had already known this
answer. She had asked Duna, then. "Nevertheless..." She
raised her hand at the frozen steward.

She was right, of course – it was disturbing, to be stood
here having a conversation while a third party stood magically
transfixed. And, Inar could assume, there would be others. A
whole fortress paralysed and open, just for them. But it was
not for them.

"Our new friends must have something to do with this,"
Inar said. "There is more to them than they have said. We must
be careful."

"Quite," Anzola said, making a distinctly un-noble gesture
of denigration. "Messengers, my big toe. The Tzanate might
be the barrier that keeps magic out of the world – or tries to –
but if they're fighting among themselves, could they resist it?
Could I, could you?"

You certainly could not, Inar thought to himself. You
found Duna and had been feeding her talent ever since, and
he did not think that digging canals was the merite's highest
priority.

"If they have opened their libraries and are throwing the
ancient powers about..." Anzola continued. She shook her
head again.

"Let's leave, shall we?" Inar said.

Anzola nodded. "I will be glad to put this place behind me.
And this whole godforsaken country."

Inar smiled. But the Elith-Tenh was not godforsaken.
Whatever else held the steward like a statue, it was assuredly
the work of God.

* * *

The courtyard was empty. A few sacks had been left in the dray, which stood near the gates, ready to take out. Anzola and Inar added what they had found in the storerooms, which was not much, but enough to see them back to Sojonost. Just the thought of the food they had gathered – elderly cured sausage and sliced, dried fruit and vegetables – made Inar's stomach gurgle. His hunger had become ungovernable now that its end was in sight.

Having deposited the supplies in the back of the dray, Inar moved around the shafts, ready to pull it outside. He expected Anzola to join him, but she did not – instead she wore a distracted, faraway expression, and for a terrible instant Inar feared that she might have fallen prey to whatever enchantment held the rest of the fortress in its grip. But just as that fear coalesced, she turned to Inar and held up her hand.

"Wait here a moment," she said. Then she walked towards the sentry post that the Zealot Anton had investigated when they arrived.

It was no easy assignment to wait, alone, in the gloom of that sleeping stronghold, but fortunately the merite was not gone long. Her face, as she descended the narrow stair that led up to the watch-post, was thunderous.

"Two more," she said. "Zealots – guards. Insensible, like the others. Our friend would have seen them, before he came down and told us all was well. They knew this was happening. They expected to find the Gates this way."

"Or they did it themselves," Inar said, and found himself chilled by his own words.

Anzola didn't disagree. "We have to get back to Sojonost," she said. "The merite Ernesto must know of this."

Ernesto's name seemed to rise out of another era, centuries before – but it had been only weeks since Inar and Lott had dined with the "Conqueror of the Mountain Lands" at Sojonost. And mention of the objectionable commander of the League's armies brought forth another memory, from the private conference that had followed that long-distant dinner. Anzola and Ernesto had disagreed – Ernesto had put in place alternative plans that would be set in motion if Anzola's diplomacy failed. Which was, without a doubt, the set of circumstances they now inhabited: diplomacy had failed, and failed mightily.

"The League will invade," Inar said, jumping to a guess. "You'll take Mal Nulalus and seal up the Tzanate for good. They'll starve."

Again, Anzola didn't contradict Inar, though she spoke with care. "Ernesto favours a military venture, yes. Much rests on Duna, and if she is assumed to be dead, he might pause. But he will not stop. We did not count on the Tzanate's army going all the way to Cassodar – if Ernesto has learned of that, who knows what visions of triumph have unfurled in his head. Magic is another story, though. We cannot fight a magical war, and Ernesto may be about to start one without knowing what he is doing."

Though they were still far from home, Inar's brief conversation with Anzola made him feel that they were getting closer, and that a semblance of safety and comfort might be reached very soon. The scene that awaited them in the forecourt of the Gull Gates was more than enough to disabuse him of that fancy. Miroslo lay on the splintered marble in a vortex of pain and chaos, as Duna and the Zealot Franj knelt over him, removing what remained of his armour and trying to dress and bind the wound in his side. The knight was not quite conscious, but not insensate, and he groaned and gasped in pain. All around was a mess of bloodied rags.

To this point, Inar had been approaching the difficulties facing the party in the same way he would have approached the construction of a wall: as a checklist of tasks that needed doing, each one laying the basis for the next, stone upon stone upon stone. Get to the Gull gates, get help, get home. But faced with the chaos and the dreadful imminence of death in the forecourt, it all seemed so much more slippery, more terrifying, its resolution an impossible task in which the foundations could not be laid without the upper layers in place.

"We have a cart," Inar said, tasting the inadequacy of the words. As they drew their trophy onto the forecourt, he noticed, for the first time, the arrangement of the shards of marble, that they formed lines and angles of opaque and ominous import. "We have to get out of here."

"He's still bleeding," Franj said. "We can staunch it but it's a very bad wound. We must move immediately if we are to have any chance."

"Agreed," Anzola said. "Inar, Duna, help me get him in the dray. You – Franzhe – please, harness a horse. Where in mud is Kielo?"

Inar had expected Duna to object, seeing how protective she had been of the wounded knight, but she joined in her assigned task without a word. He had also expected Miroslo to cry out in pain when three unpractised pairs of hands set about moving him, and he was deeply disturbed when the knight hardly reacted. Further and further he slipped from life. But once he was aligned on blankets, and Duna was able to resume the job of re-dressing his wound in strips of clean fabric they had found, Inar was able to sense a faint glimmer of progress.

Mal Nulalus still felt very far away.

"Franzhe..." Anzola began.

"*Franj*," the Zealot interjected.

"What is happening here?" Anzola continued, breezing past the difficult question of languages. "The Gates are held under a magical interdiction, I've never seen the like – I've never heard of the like, not outside tales of the Scourge War."

Inar's eyes went to Duna for a reaction, but she did not divert from her work.

"There is much here you will not understand," the Zealot said. "We must leave."

Anzola did not budge. "War, you said. Between the new altzan-al and those who oppose him. The new altzan-al is prepared to use the Mountain's power, then? But no – this enchantment here favours us, and you said you were opposed to the new altzan-al..."

The Zealot's eyes were fixed on the merite, and full of ferocity, but that latter fact was true most of the time. "The usurper will use magic," she said. "Necromancy. But he does not command the Mountain. The altzan-al – the murdered altzan-al, the true altzan-al – named another successor, one who commands the loyalty of the Mountain's defenders."

"The blade-priest," Anzola said.

Franj did not respond.

"Messengers," Anzola said, turning the word over as she said it, feeling it for deceit. "What message is it that you are carrying to the Tzanate's army, exactly?"

The Zealot did not flinch. "A report on the condition of the enemy's forces."

"And what form does this message take?" Anzola asked, again putting a sceptical weight on the word *message*. "Is it a verbal report or a written one? Might we see it?"

The messenger might be young, but Inar could not fault her composure. He remembered how flustered and uncomfortable he had felt when Anzola appeared in his life and asked him question after question. If the Zealot felt in any way similar, she did not betray it.

"Do the League's couriers share the content of the messages they carry with everyone they meet on the road?" Franj asked. "Is that how you win all your wars? With fine conversation?"

The merite was icy still for a moment, and then she smiled. "I have overstepped. You must forgive my curiosity – I am marvelling at the importance of a message that needs these very special arrangements for its passage." She waved towards the entrance to the fortress, where the garrison stood transfixed and silent.

Franj narrowed her eyes.

"But perhaps it is as you say, and this is all... incidental? In which case I wonder at what might be coming along the road to meet us, that needs this magical balm to ease it along. Any thoughts about that? Because you assure us that this enchantment is nothing to do with you, and yet you appear incurious as to what might have caused it, or what its purpose might be. A quirk in the weather? A sleeping draft on the breeze? So inconsequential a feature of the particular conditions here in this beautiful country of yours that it hardly deserves mention... But please indulge an interested traveller with your thoughts."

"You do overstep, Leaguer," Franj said, and her tone disturbed Inar greatly. At some point he found it likely he would have to sleep in the same camp as this woman, who had already killed four men in their presence, and he feared Anzola might be making a deadly mistake. "Immense works are under way and you are less than a bystander. You must leave this place and never return."

"We will see about that," Anzola said with damning flatness.

"Your grace, please," Inar said, urgently. "These people saved our lives and are aiding us greatly. Let us not quarrel."

"Who is quarrelling?" Anzola turned and asked him, with an expert performance of wide-eyed, injured innocence. "I am making conversation! We in the League are famous for our *fine conversation*."

To this point Inar had thought Duna completely absorbed in the work of making Miroslo comfortable in the back of the dray. But she now interjected as well, addressing Anzola in Palla. And although Inar could not follow the words, he had little trouble following the meaning, which was much the same as his own, but put more forcefully. The merite listened to her, nodding and agreeing. Without any more words she returned to making ready for departure, and at that moment Kielo appeared from the fortress, carrying a sack.

"I'm sorry," Inar said to the Zealot. "It has been a long and terrible journey, we are all very tired."

She shrugged in reply. "The journey is not over yet."

Kielo reached them, eyes wide and mouth agape. "You won't believe what I've seen!" he said. "The Zealots – they're frozen, like statues! You must come and see!"

He looked around, expecting shock and wonderment, and got only weary glances. His terrified excitement faded. "You all know."

"Where is my comrade?" Franj demanded.

"He went up to the battlements," Kielo said. As a group, they looked up, to where the pitted bronze beak of the Imperial Gull glared over once-conquered lands.

26

ANTON

"Great one."

"Blade-shun."

The Custodian stood beneath the outstretched wing of the bronzed Mirolinian gull that stood on the highest point of the Gull Gates. The immense metal bird sapped some of the awe and terror from the sight of the Mountain-keeper. He thought back to when Ramnie had introduced him to Deacon Cutruk on the terrace of the Gift, back to the mortal fear he had felt but also to the altzan-al's calmness in the Custodian's company. It had seemed astonishing then – but was he learning it? Or was another force at work on his temperament? He had known the Custodian was here, in a way that was more certain than a simple inference from the enchantments it had wrought, and he had felt no trepidation in climbing the stairs to meet it.

When it wants fear, it gets fear, he mused; when it needs calm, it gets calm. It was a strand of magic that Augardine had woven into the panic-scourges. The scourges – why think of them?

"I am considering the accidents that guide history," the Custodian said.

The casualness of this gambit disarmed Anton. "Oh?" was all he could bring himself to say, and he cursed his inability to come up with anything more weighty.

"A boy and a girl are tall, so they are made blade-priests. Augardine's empire has this bird as its symbol, and we birds look kindly on him as a result." The Custodian wheezed, a sound that could have been amusement. "Vanity. It pleased us. Yes, we shared a cause – the destruction of the Elves. The shared symbol fitted our shared desires. It augured well. Do not underestimate the power of appearances in the movement of the heart."

"We thank you for your assistance here," Anton said. Tall? Was that it? The characteristic that governed the whole progress of his life? So it went, he supposed.

"I can do no more," the Custodian said, its voice a low croak. "Once you leave the Elith-Tenh, you are beyond my reach."

Anton nodded. "I understand."

"Good. There is more," the Custodian said. It took a step towards Anton, its talons scraping on the stone flags of the battlements. A single step could not account for the stature it gained, the way it started to tower over the priest. A coat of feathers shifted and shivered, shedding the Mountain's iridescence. Men who had lived long lives of greatness long ago had been born when this beast was already ancient. Its white eyes glittered, and Anton felt the fear return. "Our abilities were useless against the Elves, so we raised up Augardine, and he was able to destroy them. More alike. The Mountain's great power is accompanied by weakness. It does not sit as one with the world. It came from without. Life does not prosper in its shadow. Where its power bleeds out into the realm of life, life pushes back, it raises up its own champions to defend itself. It turns the power against the Mountain. We fear the cycle has repeated."

High on the gates, they were exposed to the icy wind that blasted across the Hidden Land, whistling through these passes, and Anton drew his furs closer about him, listening to the creaking of the structure above them. But there was no defence against the chill caused by the Custodian's words.

"You're saying that the Elves might be impervious to magic, even if it's wielded by men?"

"Men *or* women," the Custodian said. "They were always impervious to our magic. Augardine did better. But he left Tarch stained with human magic, and the forest has learned its taste and knows to spit it out. We have seen only the few bodies the Zealots have brought back, and death undoes so much." The creature emitted a rasping sigh. "In any case – you are warned."

"What difference does it make?" Anton said, with a frown. "I have no magic to wield. I desire none." He thought, again, of being raised up like Augardine, of blazing on a battlefield with the light that does not illuminate, of bodies bursting and burning around him, and fleeing into forests that had already begun to wither and bleach. There was a wisp of desire in that thought, but it was swamped by terror and disgust.

"You do not have magic, but one of the foreigners does," the Custodian said. "Two, in fact. The young woman is a ruin-scourge, and the young man is the complimenting boon."

Anton gasped, an undignified and weak act in front of the ancient creature before him. Making any more cogent noise was temporarily beyond him. He had spent a whole day beside the girl, a representative of a race his forebears in the Tzanate had waged a world-wide war to exterminate. "A *scourge*?"

"And a powerful one," the Custodian continued. "Even without the presence of the boon, she would be the equal of any of Augardine's creations. Together, they are exceptional. We have not seen the like in many centuries. We assumed the strain would weaken over time, but, *ehhhh…*" It trailed off in a weary, would-you-believe it croak. The creature's tone overall was bizarre, to Anton – it seemed wistful, almost admiring. The Tzanate anathemised scourges, and described them with horror. Disgust and condemnation were, however, noticeably absent from the Custodian's words. It was as if it admired the emperor Augardine's craftsmanship in making these monsters.

And that was more likely to be true of a ruin-scourge than any other variety. The Custodians' own magic worked with life and death, and so plague, blight and panic were within their powers. They could do little to affect metal and stone. Their feats of construction had been achieved with bindling servants, not with the direct application of the Mountain's power.

Augardine had, in this, exceeded their greatest achievements. No wonder they came to fear him.

The boons were another product of the emperor's unique gift, but were more of a mystery. They had been made by Augardine alongside the Scourges, to bring symmetry to the whole endeavour: for every plague-scourge, there would be a gifted healer; for every ruin-scourge, there would be a gifted builder. This had made his warped creations more palatable, perhaps. But the malignancy inherent in his intentions had tainted the whole. The boons never had the dramatic capabilities of their brothers and sisters, and their presence amplified the latter's capacity for corruption and death. The Tzanate had exterminated them just as vigorously as it did the scourges, and had done more to suppress knowledge of their existence, lest others be tempted to experiment with the false promise of beneficial magic. This work had been so thorough that Anton only had the haziest ideas about them. They were a myth within a legend – although one stood downstairs.

"What do we do about them?" Anton asked, disturbed that the Custodian had not already taken action.

"She could be very useful," the Custodian said quietly.

"Great One," Anton began, hardly able to form the words. "The Tzanate regards her as an abomination. Our laws are very clear – she must burn. These are laws made with the approbation of the Custodians. Laws that you urged upon us. If I am altzan-al, they are laws I must uphold."

The ancient beast lifted its wings from its sides and rearranged itself with a little step from side to side, an act that looked as if it might be embarrassment, or a shrug.

With an unexpected spike of annoyance, Anton realised he had been treated like a child.

"You knew about her already, didn't you?" he said. Then, another shock of realisation – a piece of scenery falling with a bang, revealing what lay behind. "Ramnie knew about her. By Augardine's Tomb! She is the weapon Ving was seeking! Ramnie had hinted about her, some great power the Custodians had granted to the Tzanate, and Ving wanted to know... he tortured me for it!"

"And so you could not know," the Custodian said, with a touch of apology. "And neither could Ving. Our apologies."

"The League have a scourge."

"At least one."

Not for the first time, Anton was swept by ice. "You think there are *more*?"

Another uncertain side-step from the beast. "The girl has been in the noble's service for more than a decade. Scourges can tell of the existence of other scourges. To have one scourge is to discover more. And we may be sure that they have kept secrets from us."

"Yes," Anton said. He had become aware that tarrying up here might create questions in the minds of the party waiting below, but as the moment of departure drew nearer, he was reluctant to rejoin the group. It was thought of the mortally injured knight that jolted him from complacency. "We must away," he said.

"Tell the Leaguers: the scourge girl must not return to the Elith-Tenh. If she can be of use in the world, then so be it, but I will not suffer her presence here again," the Custodian said. "If she becomes a threat, you must see to her destruction. Go now. May the Mountain be with you, Blade-shun, even if I am not."

"Before I go – what of Elecy?" Anton asked. His sister blade-priest had been little in his thoughts for the past few days, but departure from the Hidden Land brought reminders of all he left behind, and it occurred that the Custodian would know. "Is she alive? Is she well?"

The Custodian tilted its head to one side. "She is alive, and well. She fell under suspicion for your escape, but no more than suspicion. She has been confined to her quarters. Ving has been unable to conduct the solemnities that will confirm him as altzan-al, and he is much vexed by this. Without a strategos, without blade-priests, and with many altzans dead, any ceremony would be unlikely to convey much authority. To have at least one blade-priest bend the knee is some remedy. And any such ceremony would require our presence. We have insisted that the bloodshed end."

"Thank you," Anton said with a nod. He was reminded of how he felt five years ago, when Leass was struck down and he was left with Ving as mentor and guardian. How he feared the anger and scorn of that thwarted man. He did not imagine that Ving triumphant would be any better, and he was glad that the usurper was still subject to some limits.

"Your escape was a costly business," the Custodian said. "You must make it worthwhile."

Nothing the ancient beast said was without seriousness, but this struck deep into Anton. He felt, once again, a vast and unwelcome weight of responsibility on his shoulders.

"I will find Yisho and return with the army," he said. "Ving cannot hope to govern without the Zealots and without allies, even if he does wish to use magic."

"Yes," the Custodian hissed. "This is what he does not understand."

"What of the League?" Anton asked. "These are the people Ramnie negotiated with, are they not? His treaty plans must have come with your approval? Should we resume those talks?"

"They have gold, they have fine armies, they have their own magic," the Custodian said. "Ving imagines he can treat them as equals, that the Tzanate can stand on its own. I fear he will make an enemy of them instead."

"Better to have them as friends," Anton said. He felt as if he were sitting in Ramnie's chair in that study back at the Brink, the Mountain to the rear and everything else in front, seeing the world as the old man had seen it.

"Anton," the Custodian whispered. "Our time here is spent – but you must listen. Ving is concealing something from us. He is very practised at concealing it, and may be employing a runic blind – his very knowledge of such an art makes us suspicious."

"He had a candorite with him the last time I saw him."

"This is deeper magic than candorite. We do not know what it portends. But the scourge must not return to the Hidden Land. You must make that clear."

The wind had picked up, and it carried on it a thin scream from the dying knight below.

Weeds grew thick through the cobbles of the Mirolinian road, and age and winter had buckled it in places and torn great holes in its surface, some as deep as drinking-troughs. In the dead of night, it was treacherous. But compared to the tracks and wastes of the past few days, it was like traversing the polished green marble of the Processional Way at the Brink.

Anton took the lead with Franj, keeping up the pretence that both were Tzanate scouts, when in fact the priest was as useless a wayfinder as the parlour-dwellers to the rear of the expedition. Franj had her bow out, and had found more arrows, but even with wind-cleared starlight to ride by, it was difficult to see much beyond their little bubble of movement. The road descended through the foothills of the mountain range, following the side of a steep V-shaped valley. Somewhere below them, a thaw-bloated river crashed and raged, and above rose blunt, treeless peaks – nothing compared to the ranges they had recently traversed, but high enough to surround and enclose, especially as all were etched in darkness.

This was the first time Anton had ventured beyond the Gull Gates and into the wider world, and he had expected more. Exactly what he had expected was not quite clear to him, and when he thought about it he found his imagination had been childishly crude – he had wanted the world. In his dreams, he would step through the Gull Gates and everything would be laid out in front of him like a tablecloth: the land sloping gently and smoothly down towards the moors and mires around Mal Nulalus, and beyond that the great green band of the forest of Tarch, and maybe a silver line of ocean visible in the distance, in Oririthen. In retrospect, that was absurd, expecting the whole of the heart of the world to be present in one sweeping sight, like the painted map in a book. No man could see a thousand miles. The Custodians, perhaps – but did they seem sane for it?

They. It occurred to Anton that he had only ever seen one Custodian at a time, and he was convinced that they were all the same being, the Deacon Cutruk. What of the others? They were very few, now, that much was well known. And they confined themselves to their tiny kingdom on the Shoulder of God, like very old altzans who never wanted to move from the fireside. What did they do there? If elderly altzans did give a model then the answer was bicker and reread books. The long days of inquiry and craft and learning were over. If the Mountain had new secrets to divulge and new powers to teach, they were no longer seeking them.

As soon as Anton had rejoined the group on the forecourt of the Gull Gates, he had sensed the suspicion between Franj and the Leaguers, and he saw the sharp eyes that met him. All had awaited him, eager to depart for the sake of the knight, and they departed in short order, with few words spoken. Anton and Franj could not speak freely at first, but as the party progressed it spread out, with the dray carrying Miroslo and Duna, drawn by a horse ridden by Inar, to the rear and the Zealots in the van. The noblewoman and her secretary straggled between, and for a time Anzola rode close to the front, and not for social reasons: she was watching them. But that guard on the guard could not be maintained, and soon she fell back, keeping closer to her injured knight.

"I saw one of them," Anton said to Franj as soon as he could be sure he was not overheard. He did not have to explain who he referred to – the Zealot's attention was immediate, and full. "It told me that the League-girl is a scourge."

Franj's eyes were wide, a ring of white quite clear in the starlight. "A *scourge*?" Her hand twitched to her bow. "I can have her with a single shot. If we stop and wait until they get closer – they'd have no time to stop me. We should do it now."

"No, no," Anton said. "She can't live, not for long, but the Great One insisted that she might be useful. We are not at Mal Nulalus yet – with a few more Zealots at our back it will be safer to act."

Franj grimaced, her dissent obvious. "Augardine thought they would be useful," she said. "And when it came time to correct his error, it took a lot more than a few Zealots."

She was right, of course, and it did not please Anton to be sharing the road with one of Augardine's abominations. His skin crawled at the thought of it, and every twinge and prickle beneath his armour and furs had the ominous feel of an incipient magical assault. But the thought of cold-blooded murder did not please him much either, and the willowy girl in the dray, bent over the knight with such tender, desperate concern, hardly had the shape of a deadly threat. He also knew that the Custodian had foreseen much greater use for the scourge than protection on the road to Mal, but that was best kept quiet for now. When he had refused to wield a blade, he felt that his prestige in Franj's eyes had suffered a near fatal blow, and was only just recovering. If he appeared overly tolerant of one of the faith's sworn enemies, he feared he might lose what authority he had altogether. It still struck him as hard to comprehend that she should follow him, and kill for him, at all, and he did not want to fray whatever thread held that in place. A signature on paper, the elliptical endorsement of unseen supernatural beings – it seemed tenuous even to him. As she went, so might every Zealot.

"Do not let them know we know," Anton said. "We are but messengers, remember."

Franj glimpsed back over her shoulder, checking to ensure they were not overheard. "Aye, well, they suspect us of having magic of our own. They saw what had happened to the garrison."

Despite himself, Anton coughed out a humourless laugh. "I suppose we do. Or did. Not any more. The Custodians cannot range outside the Elith-Tenh. We are on our own, until Mal Nulalus."

Franj digested this in silence. Her thoughts were not impossible to read – hostile soldiers to the rear, Elf-infested wilderness ahead, and a scourge in their party. Had she ever left the Hidden Land before? Unlike Anton, she had been born there.

No. There was more – a hesitation. Though she was silent, she twice looked across to him, eyes fearful, as if there was a question she wished to ask, but dared not.

Anton knew what it was. "I asked about Elecy," he said. "She's alive and well. She was not held responsible for the escape. She is not exactly at liberty, but she is not in the dungeon."

"Oh, thank the Mountain," Franj said with a gasp of relief. A wide and rare smile had spread across her face. "Oh, give thanks. And thank you for asking."

Anton smiled back. "It matters a great deal to me as well," he said. "She is my sister. She has always been my sister."

"Yes, yes," Franj said absently. She looked away, but the smile persisted – a smile of relief, yes, but also of a secret communion, the smile of a soul reminded of one who shares in it. It persisted, and persisted, telling of persisting thoughts.

So there's part of the mystery of her loyalty solved, Anton thought, with a little regret. I am not the one to whom she is loyal.

Dawn stole up behind them, undetected. At first Anton imagined that he was becoming accustomed to riding at night, and his eyes were finding it easier to penetrate the darkness. But then he realised that the stars were dimming and steel grey was climbing in the sky to their hind. The nights were getting shorter.

With the rising light, a detail of the road was revealed. In dells and shaded patches on each side of the raised cobbled bed, there were clusters of ghostly brightness, so clear in the lingering gloom that it was easy to imagine that they cast an unnatural light of their own. In the depths of winter, when storms scoured the Hidden Land, the fury of the wind and ice sometimes worked a strange art on the thick beds of snow, whipping them up into fields of glistening white spikes. This was what the clumps of brightness resembled: little forests of frozen white fingers.

As they passed close to one of these ominous puddles of paleness, Anton saw Franj's head turn toward it, and he looked too. They stared together, pulling up their steeds. Then, sharing the same unspoken fear, they dropped from their saddles together and went to investigate.

It did resemble a forest, on a pixie scale – a thick glade of white spikes, smoothly concave on one side, rising to a point. Their smoothness and sickly paleness marked them as a fungus, and it was a species they both recognised.

"Elfcap," Anton said. He reached out a hand towards the cluster.

"Don't touch it!" Franj said sharply.

He withdrew her hand as if stung.

"Its poisons can work through the skin," she said, leaning in a little closer. "We were taught to recognise it. Have you ever seen it before?"

"No," Anton said. "I've seen drawings in books. It's not supposed to grow this far from Tarch."

"We should destroy it," Franj said.

"How?"

She shrugged. Stamping on the outbreak, like children destroying an ants' nest, might put the deadly mushrooms beyond use, but they would grow back soon enough. They had no oil to waste on fires, and even if they did, both of them knew that this was not the first cluster they had seen, and was unlikely to be the last.

Anton's innards twisted at the thought of the necessary compromise, leaving the Elfcap be while they continued with more important tasks – this was another of the little torments of leadership, he thought, having to put aside an important problem in order to concentrate on a far more pressing matter. And exactly as he had this thought, he beheld another example of the same principle: the Leaguers. Anzola and Inar had caught up with them, and regarded the two Zealots crouching at the roadside with weary concern. Seeing them in the dawn light – knowing the powers of the boy and the secret-keeping of the noble – Anton was distinctly discomfited. Who knew what forbidden practices they were squirrelling away at in their cities, far from the control of the Tzanate. He puzzled at the willingness – the eagerness – of Ramnie to deal freely with the League, and make use of the abominations that walked among them. It had all sounded so reasonable when it had been explained to him under the blaze of the Mountain's power, but this morning he was not so sure.

"What is it?" Anzola demanded coldly.

"Elfcap," Anton said, standing and instinctively brushing his hands together, as if trying to free them from contamination. "It shouldn't be growing out here."

Anzola turned her hostile gaze to the fungus. "That's what turns men into Elves?"

Anton nodded. "We must report it to the garrison at Mal Nulalus. There are formulae for potions that can kill off infestations like this."

"Where there's Elfcap, there's Elves," Inar said. The young man was Mishigo, Anton remembered, and Mishig-Tenh had been battling the elves as long as the Tzanate, if not longer. No doubt he knew as much about Elfcap as any of them.

"Is it Elves, then?" Anzola asked.

Anton frowned. "Is what Elves?"

"The music," Anzola said. "Listen."

27

INAR

When had he last heard music? There had been musicians at the feast at Sojonost before their departure into the Pilgrims' Pass, but Inar had given them little attention. The last time he had stopped to listen to music was in Stull, with his masons on the wall who played and sang with the setting of the sun, and he found he missed it terribly. Perhaps that yearning was why he heard the harp before the others, just as the hungry man picks up the slightest scent of food.

At first he had thought it the call of a bird. It was no more than a couple of faint notes carried on the breeze. But it was followed by fragments of gentle melody – a wistful tune plucked by an idle harpist to pass the time. In another place, when it was not the first stirrings of dawn in the desolate country where mountains gave way to moor, it might have been cheerful.

Anzola had heard it as well, and was looking about for its source. When the two Zealots in the van stopped and dismounted, Inar assumed that they too were seeking an answer to the mystery. He was surprised to see them stoop to examine the fungus that grew in the roadside ditch.

"What is that?" the tall, black-skinned Zealot asked.

"You do not know?" Anzola said. "What is near here?"

"Nothing," Anton replied. "The nearest town is Mal Nulalus

– Miroline settled people here, but for a long time few have wanted to be more than an arrow's flight from the nearest legion."

"A shepherd, maybe," Inar said, as a doomed effort to reassure himself.

The Zealots were climbing back into their saddles. Inar looked back up the road and saw that the dray bearing Kielo, Duna and Miroslo was not far.

"We have to move," he cried back to them.

"Sssh!" the Zealot girl hissed back at him, eyes wild with anger. She had notched an arrow and for a moment Inar feared he might receive it in his neck.

"What?" Kielo shouted back. "Can you hear that? It sounds like music."

His words echoed across the valley, over the rushing of the spated river below.

Franj regarded the Leaguers with a murderous hatred, and even Anzola was momentarily quailed, waving to Kielo to be quiet.

The party advanced in silence, and for the first time Inar was grateful for the poor condition of the road, and the tough grasses that pushed between its stones, blunting the sound of their horses' hooves. Already the country reminded him more of Mishig-Tenh than the barrenness of the Hidden Land – though it was harsh and bare, more grew in the sheltered spots, not just the filthy mushrooms of the Elves, and there were even occasional trees, although they were storm-twisted survivors. For some time, they had been following a northwards bend in the wide valley, but ahead it swung back the other way, turning again west.

It had been this approaching turn that had concealed the source of the music. Ahead the sides of the valley dipped away, and in the dawn-light out stretched the uneven faded vastness of Culnmoor, still patched with snow where it was not scraped by the wind. Fortunately they would not spend long exposed on the moor, but merely skirt its northern edge, following the river valley down towards Mal Nulalus. Ahead, in the far distance, the horizon was a band of darkness: Tarch.

But this got little of Inar's attention. Beside the road, a man sat on a flat rock, and it had been his harp that the party had heard drifting in the last of the night. It was as if he had come from nowhere, this man: he had no horse or companions or baggage other than the instrument he played. To add to his accidental air, his clothing was a bizarre collection of mismatched fragments: the breeches of a Mirolinian auxiliary, a well-made but badly grimed blouson jacket, surely too thin for a spring night, and a floppy green felt hat with a wide brim. This assortment was untidily unified with decorations: coloured ribbons and scraps of silk, and a spray of striped pheasant feathers stitched to the hat. A travelling bard, then, or player – but they would not be here, and they certainly would not roam the Culnmoor at night.

Strangely, given that it was such an un-troubling object, it was the hat that most troubled Inar – not what it was, but what it might conceal.

The harpist heard the party approach, and he raised his head and smiled in welcome, not ceasing in his slow picking of a tune until it was done. His face was pale, and the left cheek was tracked with a pinched grey scar.

All of them took their lead from Franj, not advancing past an invisible line set by her, watching as she set two hands to her bow and tensed. The other Zealot, Anton, had his hand on the shaft of the spear taken from his fallen former comrades, and not for the first time Inar was struck by the unpractised quality of his actions. He had spent only a little time around soldiers, but he had seen how naturally they bore their weapons. In contrast, watching Anton's hand uncertainly grasping the spear as if unfamiliar with its distribution of weight, Inar was reminded – well, he was reminded of himself, and his own uncertain handling of Timo's sword. That sword was at his side now, and he moved a hand to its hilt, checking it could be reached in an instant.

"Travellers!" the harpist cried in a piercing high voice. He leaped to his feet, a rapid movement that gave Inar a horrible flash of memory of the way that the knomes moved. It was almost fatally fast, as Franj twitched in alarm and he felt sure an arrow was about to strike the stranger down.

"Stay where you are!" Franj shouted.

"Oh, for shame!" the harpist replied, more in jolly chastisement than actual reproach. He danced from foot to foot, edging slowly around the leading horses, putting Anton between himself and Franj's arrow. "No welcome for Tomilee? It's been so long since travellers have come this way, one might think the world's heart had emptied out. And such an arresting crew! Bird-brains and silky city sitters from the north... So fine!"

Inar became aware of a movement behind him. For a terrible turn he feared the unseen approach of an enemy, the closing of an ambush. But it was not – it was the dray, drawing in close. He silently cursed Kielo for making the party such a tight group, preferring that they had remained spread out. The stranger's ill-fitting jaunty manner was obscurely menacing, but he had no weapons, other than his musical instrument, and what could he do with that? And no obvious companions. Would an ambush announce itself so merrily, and give its prey plenty of time to prepare? Inar scanned the moor anxiously, looking for movement, that dull glint of iron.

Duna was trying to signal his attention, but he could not tell what she might want. When he looked at her, she directed him back to the harpist.

"We are not travellers," Anzola said, "but a diplomatic mission from the League, under escort by the forces of the Tzanate. And we will be on our way." She jostled her reins and her horse took a few steps.

"Wait," Franj said, scowling back at the merite. Then she turned to the harpist. "Take off your hat."

"No secrets here!" the stranger said cheerfully, though his high voice made Inar squirm. "Sharing is caring! There's enough for all! The hard times are over for everyone! And that means – Oh!"

He had moved along the side of the road, coming level with Inar, and thanks to Duna's efforts to attract Inar's attention he had seen the dray. In a few quick pounces he was beside it.

"This one is injured!" the harpist cried, and followed the words with a thin, high moan of artificial dismay. "Oh, poor soul! Poor blood-spill feel-ill pus-fill! So foul! But have no fear! We've got what he needs! We'll have him back on his feet and fighting fit!"

"Pay heed, stranger," Franj said, her voice also high in the morning air, but backed by a menace unsuited to her years. She had turned her horse, which was uneasy, reflecting the fear that Inar also felt. "If you do not listen to my words, I will give you an injury of your own, and you will not be back on your feet! Step back, and take off that hat!"

The harpist stilled. All at once the antic energy he had exhibited since he first rose had gone, as had his good humour. Those pale eyes turned back to Franj. "Bird brains," he whispered through thin lips, though Inar believed that only he heard.

Then he was off again, keeping some distance from the party and heading back to the flat rock he had been using as a seat. Onto this he leaped, and addressed them all like a player addressing his audience: "I forget myself! I bid you all welcome! Welcome to the Réthoielle!"

With this, he removed his hat and bowed with a sweeping flourish. Then he stood straight, eyes glittering with glassy menace, and emitted a piercing, trilling ululation, clear as lightning in the cold dawn. "Ululululu–!"

He was interrupted by the hiss of an arrow. Franj's shot went wide, passing the harpist at a distance of about a foot, but it brought his bloodcurdling cry to an end. The Zealot swore and started preparing another arrow, and Inar expect to see the man attack or flee. But instead he looked towards where the arrow had harmlessly disappeared, and then laughed.

"An arrow? You greet me with an arrow? When I bring you happy news? Well, then! Would that the arrow had found me and I could show you the truth! Death cannot–"

Franj's second arrow found the harpist's neck. It did not fell him, but brought a look of sheer amazement on his face, hands flapping ineffectually at the arrow's tail where it protruded. For the first time in all his clowning, the harpist looked faintly comical. He gaped and gasped, fingers slipping in blood.

The third arrow struck at the top of his left eye-socket, and he went down, twisting and slipping from the rock.

Franj had hit the ground before he did, knife out. But the blade was superfluous. The harpist was dead. Without ceremony, she set about retrieving her arrows.

"Was that necessary?" Anzola asked, lip curled in distaste.

The Zealot made no immediate reply, but treated the merite with a blank stare. Then she used the bloodied head of an arrow to gesture at the harpist's ear.

From his horse, it took Inar a squinted moment to see what she might be indicating. The ear, deathly white, was puckered and ugly, but Inar saw that it had been deliberately cut in the past, long enough for the wounds to have healed in wrinkled oyster-grey scar tissue. Its outer edge and top had been trimmed off, shaping the peak of the ear into a point.

"An Elf," Inar said. He had never seen one before. None of them had.

"An eléquin," the other Zealot said. The colour had quite gone from his cheeks. "Heralds, of a kind. They go ahead of Elf hordes and spread fear. Putting the countryside in panic makes the work of opposing armies more difficult."

"An abomination," said Franj, placing a shoe in the dead Elf's ribs and pushing the body deeper into the roadside gully. "And we do not suffer abominations."

These last words she spoke while staring, purposefully and hatefully, at Duna. A drop of ice fell through Inar's bowels. She knows, he knew – she knows. And ahead lay a Tzanate garrison. Duna saw the Zealot's expression as well, and her jaw dropped, and Inar felt he had to do something to defend the girl. All of a sudden he was mortally afraid for her. But he had nothing he could say that would not confirm the Zealot's inference.

Even if he had a response, there was no time to use it. For there rose from an unseen portion of the moor a sound, which in turn was answered and repeated elsewhere, and elsewhere, until it seemed that every point of the distance rang with it.

Ululululululu!

Down the moor they went, as fast as they dared. The limit was set by the dray, and even then they pushed it, twice coming close to pitching the whole thing into the ravine, and with Miroslo screaming at each jolt. Eventually Anzola insisted they let the dray move at a sensible pace, rather than risk a disaster – Inar would accompany it, and the merite would cover the road between them and the Zealots.

There was more of that road to cover. The Zealots had shown little patience for the slower portion of the expedition and had spurred their way almost out of sight. Franj would scout ahead, they said, but Anton was obviously reluctant to let her get too far from him. They were, if anything, more disturbed about the encounter with the Elf than the Leaguers, despite being warriors, despite having more experience and knowledge of Elfkin – but it occurred to Inar that their feverish unease might be from knowing more about Elves in general, and that was not a comforting thought.

An attack could come at any moment. The chain of ululation they had heard had no immediate sequel, which was disturbing in itself – every dip in the landscape, every looming ridge, bristled with imagined ambushers, and every breath contained the hiss of an arrow. The rumble of the swollen river in the valley covered the sound of laughter. They had seen only one Elf, and yet the landscape crawled with them, he was sure. And what did they have? A competent bowman, an untested spearman, Anzola's passing facility with a dirk and his own hopeless efforts to wield Timo's sword. The stories of the Elves, in Klintoe and elsewhere, did not tell of them attacking in ones and twos. They came in overwhelming numbers, and with legendary ferocity. They were immortal and invulnerable, you see – in their own minds. They did not feel fear. That was why the harpist had been so confused by the arrow in his neck. How could he die?

However much he missed the protection of the little scout's bow, it was a relief for her to be some distance from them. There had been no mistaking the hatred she had expressed towards Duna, and no mistaking its source.

Duna had seen it too – how could she have missed it? And, heaped on top of the appearance of the Elves and a sleepless, agonising night tending to Miroslo, the threat had snapped whatever thread of composure she had been using to tie together her manner. Her eyes were red and stained, her breathing high and panicky – her ministrations to the dying knight had taken on a purposeless, ritual quality, as if she might collapse if her hands stopped moving, and when she whispered "Shh, shh," to him she might as well be talking to herself.

"We do not know that she knows," Inar said, trying to comfort her. "We might be mistaken."

It was, he was sure, a lie, but he meant well with it. However it did nothing to ease her visible anguish – instead she lifted her head and gazed out over the moor in sightless torment. "I should never have come here," she said. "It was folly. Anzola wanted to show me off to their high priest, to exhibit me like a prize pet. She said it would be safe."

Kielo, driving the cart, turned at this. "The merite took every precaution," he said, tetchily. "She had assurances from the Tzanate."

"Oh, yes!" Duna interrupted, voice rising in mockery. "Every precaution! We would have a company of knights with us! We would have native guides!" She glanced at Inar a second, enough to again worry him with the red-lined exhaustion in her eyes, and then looked back to Miroslo, under his tangle of bloodstained blankets. "Every precaution!"

"Within reason, yes," Kielo said. "There will always be an element of risk in ventures of this nature – in all great ventures. It is the spirit on which the League was made rich."

"Give it a rest, Kielo," Duna said. "They have hated my kind for so many centuries. We should never have trusted them."

"You would have taken Ernesto's path, then?" Kielo asked, pointedly.

Duna did not answer. Inar felt the urgent need to move the talk elsewhere. "Maybe we should not go to Mal Nulalus," he said. "If it is in the hands of a Tzanate garrison, and the Tzanate again regards us as horrors to be expunged... we could leave the road, make straight for the Sojonost pass."

Duna shook her head. "We could never take the dray cross country. This road is hard enough. Miroslo would not make it. They said Mal Nulalus was not far. I will have to rely on my lady's rank as protection."

She had said nothing but the truth, and Inar had no answer to it. But the road was long and he felt obliged to keep talking. He told himself he wanted to calm Duna, sensing the girl's frantic fears for the wounded knight and their own safety. But he also hoped her words might distract him from his racing thoughts, from the eerie echo of those ululations in his mind.

"How did you come to serve the merite?" he asked.

"My mother died when I was born," Duna said. "My father

could not care for me – he gave me up. He worked for the company of canals, which was under the supervision of the surveyor-general. Anzola was the deputy to the surveyor-general at that time, and she made me her ward."

She paused. "She was the first person to show me kindness."

"Your father was cruel to you?" Inar asked. Within him he felt the echo of a blow struck across his head – by his brother, but he had not invented the technique, it had been taught him.

"No, not cruel," Duna said. "But he could not care for me." And she left it at that.

"What were you trying to tell me earlier?" Inar asked. "About the Elf."

Duna frowned. "Oh. The Elf – it was curious. Maybe I was too far from him, maybe I'm too tired. It's over, I don't want to think about it. Why do they cut their ears like that?"

"I believe it's a rite of passage," Inar said, aware that the subject was being changed on purpose. "They force their... converts to make visible signs of their transformation. Cutting the ears, scarring the face. The Elfcap has some healing or soothing properties, but it also compels them to cut themselves. I don't know how it works."

Miroslo groaned and tried to turn under the blankets that covered him.

"I wonder if he spoke the truth," Duna said. "About being able to help Miroslo."

It took Inar a moment to overcome the cold spear of shock that accompanied these words. "Elves lie," he said. "Elves do not help – they make more Elves, that's the only thing they do. That's what Elfcap does. They spread poison, first in word, and then in fact. They are poison."

"So the Tzanate says," Duna replied. "And it also says you and I are twisted monsters, fit only to be burned."

There was no answer to that.

* * *

Thick clouds had stolen the sun since dawn, and the day passed in an anxious contradiction – every moment ticked with nervous urgency, but time did not seem to advance. Any notion of the day's age was lost under thunderous grey. What they ate and drank, they ate and drank on the move, and when Inar stopped for relief, the others did not, and he had to spur his horse on to catch up with them.

Around them, the moor had receded and stood as a distant wall of barren brown. And the river calmed itself with a wider valley to enjoy; although it was not cultivated, the land on either side of the road was a little more green and energetic with undergrowth. In places, there could even be found vestiges of human presence: a scrap of dry stone wall, a toppled cairn, the stub of a chimney stack. Not cheering sights, as they spoke more of desertion than habitation, but it was more than they had seen since leaving Mishig-Tenh. Everywhere, however, there were spots of Elfcap.

In the distance was even clearer evidence of Miroline's past efforts to tame this desolate country. As they had built the road, they had planted rows of poplars on each side of it, in imitation of the shaded avenues of Mirol and Jesh. But the trees did not prosper here, and many had died, leaving ragged gaps in what were once neat ranks. The survivors were threadbare, bent and stunted. Beside one of these foreign trees, the Zealots had stopped – their first pause since the death of the harpist. Perhaps they finally observed the need to rest, and for their horses to do likewise – but the poplars meant Mal was near, and their manner, from a distance, did not speak of rest.

Anzola was nearer them than Inar, and she trotted on, obviously eager to see the reason for their halt. But she too reined in her horse before reaching them, and looked back to find Inar, inviting him on with fearful eyes.

When he reached her, he heard what she had heard – the

steady drone of flies. So the season was warm enough to rot flesh already, Inar thought. They had been gone a long time.

The Zealots were staring at the tree. Anzola and Inar rode on towards them, without speaking.

At the base of the tree sat a man, a man who had been dead a couple of days. His head lolled to one side, black and brown with spoiled blood and destruction, fussed over by fat flies. His arms and legs were outstretched and his palms upturned as if in appeal. A Zealot spear, broken in half, pinned him to the tree, but he was kept upright by a thin cord tied tight under his chin and around the trunk. He had been arranged like this, and left to find.

"Elf work," was all Franj said.

"A Zealot?" Anzola asked.

Anton nodded. "Infantry – the armour is gone, but the tunic is ours." He scowled up the road, looking to the next tree, and the next. "Look."

He gestured to a position thirty or forty yards ahead, between the road and the river, where thorns grew thick. A column of flies.

Anzola turned back to check the location of the dray. "I'll warn the others," she said. "Inar, go with them. Take care."

On they went, in silence. At the foot of another tree, they found a second Zealot, positioned like the first. The column of flies was over the carcass of a horse, slain and incompletely butchered.

"Another," Franj said, pointing to a third tree.

"This was not a battle," Anton said, with some confidence, but Inar heard the crack in his voice. "The Elves had been attacking patrols and scouts, and getting bolder about it."

"Bold, yes," Franj said, "but on the Cassodar road, not this side of Mal Nulalus."

"Well, now they're here as well," Anton said.

"Yes, we are."

They had been fixated on the road ahead, at the tree where

the third Zealot was gruesomely pinned, and the voice had come from behind them. In common with his kin, the Elf was unhealthily slender and pale, as if ill, but unholy vigour burned in his eyes. And he was tall, too, almost as tall as the Zealot Anton, and several inches more than his six companions, ranged behind him, carrying an assortment of spears, blades and bows and dressed in an almost random assemblage of clothing and armour, decorated with sprigs of greenery. Their leader, the Elf who had spoken and who stood a step before them, had a more composed appearance in hanging green clothes that gave him a priestly look. His ears had been cut into points, and like those of the harpist it had been done a while ago. All of them had the same cuts, but several were more recent, puckered angry red and harshly stitched. The leader was armed only with a dagger. Behind, six more surrounded the dray.

Franj had her bow up at once and an arrow notched, and Inar's hand went to the hilt of Timo's sword. But the Elf-leader raised a hand, and then turned it, gesturing behind them. They turned and saw more warriors stepping out into the road, where they had been concealed in the overgrown ditches that ran by the avenue of trees.

At least twenty Elves, and surrounding them. The leader tittered, closing his eyes as if savouring the group's discomfort. "Try, try, featherfolk, try with the bow and the blade! We cannot be harmed. Put an arrow in me, and watch me pull it out as my brethren cut you down. But why, why try? We will not harm you! We have gifts for you!"

Franj lowered her bow.

"Like the gifts you gave these men?" Anton asked, indicating the nearest impaled soldier. Inar had had cause to doubt the Zealot's mettle, but seeing him sitting straight in his saddle and speaking with a clearness that he doubted he could muster himself, he reconsidered.

"Alas, they did not want our gift," the leader said, with an exaggerated pout. "And to refuse eternal life is to beg for death – we could at least oblige them in that, poor lost children. But you bird-brains would know all about death-gifts, wouldn't you? Blademongers and blood drinkers, all of you."

Anzola had been pulled from her horse and Kielo and Duna made to climb down from the dray. Elf warriors had taken their places, and others were pushing the Leaguers towards the Zealots at spearpoint. The trap had closed, but perhaps not all the way. Inar reached out with his Scourge-sense, or whatever variation of it heredity had given him. He felt the stout bones of the horse under him, and clearer and heavier, the cuboid stone setts of the road and the packed jumbled aggregate beneath them, and the skeletons of the Zealots, and their horses.

"Duna," he called out. "Duna, now. You can do it."

"I can't!" Duna wailed.

"You can! Like you did with the knomes!"

"I can't! Inar! Look – look with the within – they're not there!"

The shell of Inar's secret sense had reached as far as the elf-leader, and he discovered she was right. Where there should have stood the skeleton of a man, there was nothing more than a tattered hole in perception, like a missing tooth. Elves could not be seen with the Scourge-sense – and so they could not be affected by it.

Duna's powers were useless.

28

ANTON

When the Elves had poured into Oririthen, they had driven a wave of refugees west towards the League-held ports and forts on the coast. All of those fleeing souls had terrifying stories of the fall of Caenon and the other towns and villages of their ruined kingdom, stories that reached the ears of the tzans and altzans of Eptim and Lagunodar and were conveyed back to the altzan of Miroline and the altzan-al himself. The Tzanate was quick to realise the value of these tales of horror in strengthening the faith of the Mountain's believers, and showing that the godless League brought only chaos and madness in its wake. For months, the Tzanate's congregations across the world heard of blood-drowned Caenon and the monstrous depravity of the Elves triumphant. But to reach those who did not routinely gather at the Mountain's pulpits, travelling tzans composed mummer-shows that re-enacted the events, with appropriate dramatic licence, demonstrating the danger of turning away from the Mountain with gruesome sprays of red silk and leering "Elves".

One of these shows had been performed inside the Elith-Tenh, at the lake, the previous autumn. The player-tzans had reached Mal Nulalus and, with the passes north closed by the League, had come to the Hidden Land for the amusement of the acolytes and Zealots. Anton had found it a crude and exaggerated spectacle, and felt obscurely insulted by the prancing, masked Elves. It was too uncomfortable an echo of his own supposed role within the Tzanate – an object of terror. He already knew he had no taste for blood, and found his resolve was only reinforced.

As he arrived in Mal Nulalus, Anton learned that the play might have been crude, but it was in no way exaggerated. If anything, it was understated.

The fighting was perhaps two days old, and where the town had burned, much still smouldered. Night had fallen and an orange glow could be seen in many of the husks that had been homes and stores. This included the shiel, one of the few stone buildings outside the fortress, which had partly collapsed. Mal Nulalus had always been more fortress than town. Miroline had intended for a trading city to arise on this spot, but it had never come to pass, and the two legions that had been quartered here had been the basis of the settlement's industry. An expansive forum had been laid out in front of the heavy stone gatehouse of the citadel, but Anton doubted it had ever seen a market day that came close to half filling it. So thin was the building on the three sides not dominated by the fortress that one could see right to the meagre outer defences – a berm and a ditch, smoothed by time, that had obviously done little to impede the Elf-horde. When it became clear that the town had been overrun by the Elves, Anton held out hope that the Tzanate's garrison held on in the fortress, and the townsfolk were sheltered there, but the defeat had been total. Disgusting trophies dangled from the stockade and the standard of the Elves – a tree bearing an offensively grinning face, painted in orange against a green background – hung from the gatehouse, mocking the forum, and from the dour block of the keep which rose behind it.

The departed empire might have made little of the Mal

Nulalus forum, but the Elves were making full use of it. All around the edge of the space were driven stakes, perhaps once intended for imperial banners, but that night they bore the twisted and incomplete bodies of men and women, some made into torches to light the revels. Most of these unfortunates had been townsfolk, but others still bore remnants of Zealot armour. In the middle of the forum, the Elves had erected a wooden stage, a sickly reminder of the re-enactments of the travelling tzans. At the start, when their victory here had been newborn, the surviving civilians and Zealots would have been gathered here as an audience for the work of the Elves, but that work was almost done. The stage ran with blood and was piled with reddened sawdust, like a shambles, and like a shambles that sawdust was filled with butchers' scraps. A handful of souls, all Zealots or former Zealots, were left unchanged. The technique was quite simple, and matched the historic accounts Anton had read. They would cut the victim's ears first, making Elf points of them, and then offer them solace: a healing poultice of dried and concentrated Elfcap, and some to eat, to heal their wounds and take their pain and give them life eternal. The poison would flow into the blood of a man and an Elf would awake, wanting more. If the victim refused, they would continue cutting. At any point, the Elf-barbers might tire of their work on a reluctant subject and deal a shrieking killing blow – but mostly they were patient. The cries from those watching and waiting and the screams from the one undergoing transformation were terrible enough, but the Elves revelled in Elf-work and jumped and clowned and yelped and tittered around the stage, skidding and frolicking in the human mess they had made. All around the stage, Elves engaged in heedless celebration and debauch in the flickering smoky light of burning human fat, gorged on Elfcap, eyes wild and unfocused, carousing and guffawing and rutting and enjoying any small luxuries they had found in the town – bottles of Vellene wine, barrels of beer, jars of preserves, flutes and paints. At a distance, behind the stage, came a lower chorus of groans of pain and delirium as new-made Elves succumbed to the effects of the profane fungus.

The whole appalling spectacle was intended to terrify, and terrify it did. Anton and his companions had been pulled from their horses and stripped of their weapons and forced to march the remaining miles of road from where they had been captured to Mal Nulalus. Confronted with the scenes in the forum, their collective nerve had broken. Franj drained of all colour and lost what soldierly mien she had acquired in the long flight from the Brink, reverting to a frightened teenage girl. Kielo babbled and begged, and Anzola did her utmost to keep her head upright and her expression firm, but the tears flowed freely down her cheeks. The impact was worst on the League girl, the noblewoman's ward – the scourge, Anton reminded himself. For a while, she had seemed close to the limit of her endurance, worn out by the hardship of the road and the emotional toll of caring for the mortally wounded knight. That limit had been exceeded. She was almost incapable with fear and grief and it was a slight marvel to Anton that she could find the reserves to place one foot in front of another – the Mishigo, Inar, had to support her. When the Elf warriors made to push their captives towards the stage, she collapsed entirely, and two of the creatures dragged her upright.

The whole company, human and Elf alike, were halted by a sudden shouted word from the green-robed leader of the ambush. The Elves had their own language, a sickly singsong confection with a little resemblance to the speech of the Elithi, but while Anton found the ancient language of the Hidden Land beautiful to the ear, that of the Elves repulsed him. Obviously, he spoke none of it – his kind had worked very hard to try to ensure that it was never heard again in the world, though tragically their efforts had failed. One word could be guessed at, though, a word they had learned from their ancient enemies: *zéloti*.

When they had all been captured, the leader had taken a particular interest in the girl Duna. He had heard the Mishigo shout instructions to her, and clearly suspected that she carried on her a hidden weapon, or posed another hazard. Which, of course, he was quite right to suspect, but Anton was relieved to note that the Elf did not seem to know or guess at the truth. He interrogated her cursorily, in the teasing, unctuous way of the Elves, and overcome by terror she had said little. While the rest of the party were searched in a haphazard way – Anton's copy of Xirco's *Southern Travels*, with its precious insert, was hardly noticed, let alone examined, and left in his possession – Duna was treated with a little more thoroughness and caution, overseen by the leader himself, who was noticeably more composed than his jittering, intoxicated troupe.

Again, it was Duna that had his attention. He separated her from the others, and after a little thought separated Anzola and Inar as well. Kielo was kept with the *zéloti*, a decision that did nothing to abate his pitiful begging – Miroslo, who had been left in the dray, was, Anton supposed, headed towards the fortress with the horses. And that now appeared to be the destination of the Leaguers, minus the secretary. The leader issued a few curt instructions to the couple of warriors left to take him, Kielo and Franj to the stage, and then left with the Leaguers and the bulk of his band of warriors, following the horses and booty towards the fortress gatehouse.

"Wait!"

This time it was Franj's voice that interrupted the Elf-work. It was high and thin and cut with desperation and it had little effect on the warriors who held her, Anton and Kielo by the arms, roughing them towards the stage. But it cut through to the green-robed leader, who turned back, again resting his pale, glittering eyes on the *zéloti*.

"You don't know what you're doing!" Franj shouted. Her tone had firmed now that she had the leader's attention. Anton thought this was a fruitless opening – they were Elves, of course they didn't know what they were doing. But he was so desperate for a change in fortune that he did nothing to intervene, and she persevered. "This man is important! This is the vertzan Anton Shraye – the rightful altzan-al! Select of the Custodians!"

We are beyond their sight, Anton thought, but he kept quiet. If Franj's gambit bought him his freedom, perhaps he could buy hers.

A thin white hand emerged from the loose robes and motioned the warriors to pause.

"The Custodians – the birds, yes?" Franj continued. "They value this one! He's worth a ransom! And if he's harmed, their rage will be very terrible!"

The leader slowly raised his arms, and with equal slowness a frightful smile spread across his face. "You think we do not wish to harm that which the birds find valuable? You think we desire ransoms? Bird-brains cannot understand what we desire, what we value – but you will! When you are opened to our truth, you will understand! The knife and the 'cap will help! The knife–"

He stopped. "Ver-tzan?" he said, his expression turned from mockery to savage cunning. "A bird-blade – a bird-barber? A knife-heartist… Perhaps there is a prize in that. Yes. We'll make a barber of you!"

The Leaguers regarded Anton with gaping expressions. The green Elf's words had temporarily cut through their own private nightmares, or added a new character to them. Even Duna had quieted while this little drama had played out. For an absurd moment Anton felt embarrassed – a near-child in borrowed and soiled clothes, he would hardly look like a blade-priest, let alone an altzan-al. He raised his chin a little, hoping that some dignity came into his figure – and then the full force of what the Elf was saying hit him, and he sagged. A barber. Not a barber – a butcher, that was what they would make of him.

"Oh, you'll thank me for this!" the Elf in green robes continued. "To go from giving the gift of death to giving the gift of everlasting life – opening eyes and bodies to the Elf-truth! Yes! You'll make a fine sight! You'll thank me!"

He concluded with an instruction in Elvish to the blood-soaked creatures on the stage, an instruction concerning Anton. It wasn't hard to intuit the meaning: *this one first*. Then he turned, herding the others, his warriors and their loot towards the gatehouse. Another scream arose from Duna as they were led away, the first of a succession that ascended in desperation even as distance made them diminish.

Franj recoiled from Anton, mouth hanging open, aghast at the effect of her words. Her mortal fear stirred up a surprising guilt in Anton. Her facility with a bow had given her a faint aura of indestructibility in his eyes, but she was no more than a very young person, just like him, and she was going to die or be consigned to a living hell. What right had he to do this to her? They had wandered around, misguidedly placing faith in each other, and here they had arrived, at the steps leading up to that gory stage.

The Elf warrior who had Anton by the elbows jostled him to the front of the pack and up those steps – in reality no more than a couple of overturned crates. Torchlight caught the red sludge that coated the boards. Fabric covered part of the platform, and although it was too sodden to tell what colour it had been or what design it had borne, Anton realised it was a banner, and that the Elves had not built this stage, it had been made for the rites attending the passage of the Conclave. At the rear of the stage, the four surviving Zealots watched his arrival wide-eyed. Three men and one woman, they were filthy and beaten up but had not been cut, and it was not clear why they had been kept until last – perhaps they were tougher than the others, though they looked pretty filthy and defeated. In any case, their transformation had been delayed another few minutes.

Anton was pushed towards the barber, and he found prayers trickling uselessly from his lips. The barber was burly, for an Elf, and stood six inches taller than the warriors assisting him. He was robed in green, like the warband leader, though only patches and creases showed pure green, as the rest of him was liberally drenched in blood. Even through the clotted black layer that coated the barber's face, Anton could make out two long scars, each stretching from a temple to the opposite cheek, forming an X centred between the eyes. This prince of torture watched Anton's forced approach with undisguised appetite, and Anton stared back at what the leader had said would be his own destiny. And he resolved, with all the strength that remained in his spirit, that he would not become the animal that stood before him. He would have to resist, he would have to withstand what they did to him until the barber lost patience or decided he was past usefulness, and then he would be allowed to die. His only hope was that it would not take too long. Maybe, he figured, maybe it could be sped along if the Elf was angered. They were not known for their even temperament.

"We destroyed you before," he said, as clearly as his dissolving confidence would allow, loud enough to be heard by Franj and the leftover Zealots. "And we will destroy you again."

The barber leered and rubbed his hands over his face, smearing in the blood and making shapes and whorls with it, marking out the carved lines of the X scar. He took a step back, to a large basket that stood behind him, and plunged his hand into it. It came out with a fistful of dried mushrooms, which the barber stuffed into his mouth, scattering them as he chewed.

"You failed before," he said, spitting bloody drool and blobs of Elfcap. "You'll fail again."

From his belt, he took a short, straight knife with a thin blade, and signalled to the warrior restraining Anton. Anton thought he heard a sob or gasp come from one of the others, but realised that he had made the sound himself. The warrior pushed him forwards and thrust him to his knees. He smelled the metal charnel-house reek of the stage.

Still chewing, the barber grabbed Anton by his hair, which had had several days to grow beyond its usual close crop. Anton gasped as his head was yanked painfully to one side, but he cut the noise short when he realised that discomfort was nothing against what was coming. But the longer he survived this, the better the chance of death. He fixed his eyes on the bloody monster that towered over him, and could not prevent the stirring of a smile. It was not meant to be like this, he thought – it was meant to be the other way around. But the symmetry was striking. He had refused the role of blade-priest, and so the role of sacrificial victim awaited.

The barber raised his knife over Anton's left ear, and paused. It was as if he was awaiting a command, but that was surely not needed, he was the master of ceremonies in this baleful arena. Still, he hesitated, a feat quite at odds with his berserker nature. A shadow of concern passed over his foul features, and he turned towards the fortress.

Given a moment to gather his nerves, Anton felt it too. It was a cold spring night, and yet sweat had spread under his chin and he felt an icy drop travel down his spine. Fear, perhaps.

A charge rose in the air, like a lightning storm impending.

Something changed in the intangible nature of the world around them. For the first time, Anton became aware of a steadily growing pressure, a great flood building up behind an inadequate dam, and the dam was the normal nature of everything and it would not withstand.

An indescribable noise, like a yelp of stone, arose from the direction of the fortress, and before Anton's disbelieving eyes a whole corner of the towering keep came loose and slumped towards the ground with an ascending roar. But the pressure was not gone with this break, it was not even lessened, it grew and grew.

Then it released. The gatehouse was three storeys tall, and it shattered all at once, from deep foundation to uppermost crenelation. It broke like a bursting sack, abruptly spilling itself, as if it had gone from solid to liquid. As Anton watched, the last thing he saw before it was swallowed up by a ballooning cloud of thick grey dust was the stone footing of the timber stockade heaving upwards and vomiting outwards, coming down like a row of matchsticks.

The dust engulfed them. The warrior holding Anton released his grip. Shouts arose from the Elves, commands and cries of panic and confusion. There had not been much light before, and now it was gone, but Anton had no intention of wasting his chance. He scrambled to his feet, almost slipping in the vile coating of the stage, and turned back to where he had last seen Franj. Shapes in the eye-stinging gloom, silhouetted against a torch at the corner of the stage, Franj held at the elbows by a warrior who had not relinquished his grip. The warrior never saw Anton coming, and the blade-priest's fist connected with the Elf's eye, sending him sprawling back. Franj was free.

"Anton!" she said. "Did you–?"

"The scourge," Anton said. "Free the Zealots, quickly."

At the fortress, whatever was happening was still happening. A small but violent storm had arisen in the collapsing wreck of the gatehouse, and was smashing outwards amid deafening concussions and shrieks of pain and fury. The dust cloud that engulfed them had thinned a little, and now it thickened again. They went to the Zealots bound at the rear of the stage, and found they were busily emancipating themselves. The Elves had vacated the stage – the shouts were continuing, a little more coordinated now but still scattered and afraid, and again Anton heard the word he knew: "*Zéloti*! *Zéloti*!"

"They think they're under attack," Anton said. "Kielo!"

The Leaguer was with them, on his feet but lost in apprehension, as paralysed as the garrison at the Gull Gates.

"Kielo, help me with this," Anton said. He was fumbling

with the bonds that held one of the Zealot's hands behind his back – he was not tied well, but gracelessly, and the tangled took some working. Kielo snapped out of his trance and tried to help another of the soldiers.

Franj was already off the stage, picking through the heap of plunder that had been left there. She took a spear, and distributed other weapons to the Zealots and the secretary as they jumped off the platform. Once again Anton found himself holding a spear, and this time he was glad of it.

"If they think they're under attack, they'll fall back to the fortress," Franj said.

"The merite!" Kielo said.

"If they were in the gatehouse, I don't..." Anton began. He looked towards the ruins. The dust around them was thinning, though it still rose in a swirling plume from where the gatehouse had once stood. The keep was still standing, but wrecked. Hope drained from Kielo's face.

The surviving Zealots were armed, and gathered around them. With a sinking sensation, Anton realised they were waiting for orders – from him.

"North," he said, before he realised he had even made a decision. "If Mal Nulalus has fallen, then the Cassodar road is gone. We go north. The League is our only chance."

He had expected an argument, but there was none. They did not even pause. They ran.

29

DUNA

"They have been most uncooperative," Anzola said, "and Kielo felt that my presence might flatter or impress them." She shook her head, pretending modesty, but Duna had spent enough years with her to recognise the pretence.

"I understand why *you* have to be here," Duna replied. "But not why *I* had to come."

Anzola's jaw tightened, and she rubbed her gloved hands together. "I thought it would be good for you. A foreign country. New experiences. New sights. Why, you've never set foot outside the League."

Duna shrugged. "I've seen enough quarries. This one is little different."

She hadn't thought much of the countryside beyond the quarry, either. It had been four days of river and road travel from Matchfalls, through steeper and bleaker terrain, with a distant blue line of mountains across the horizon. Orchards and pastures had given way to wild pine and birch and sheep-scoured uplands. The inns were dreary and the food was unspeakable. Even the name of the place was ugly: Mishig-Tenh. It didn't trip off the tongue like Pallestra or Wenodar. If this was the world outside the League, she had little use for it.

"Well, we'll be gone soon," Anzola said, with a note of forced jollity. "With barges full of stone following us, I hope.

And it's downhill on the way out. Why not find a quiet spot, and... practise."

With a roll of her eyes, Duna took her leave. But she welcomed the invitation. It was preferable to standing around looking pretty and well-raised and not saying anything. Besides, mountain people were Mountain worshippers, and she did not desire their attention. Quarries were not without their interest: strange half-natural landscapes cut into geometric mazes, the flat surfaces of exposed stone oddly pale and bright and fresh, with jungly bursts of shrubs in corners that had not been worked in years. The background of picks and chisels made a kind of music. A giant's building, but one unfinished, or ruined; an interrupted and changing terrain. The hard straight edges of cut stone and exposed faults made interesting targets for her talent.

She reached out and felt around the back of a block as large as a clothes-chest that had been half-revealed and then left in place, feeling the line of drilled holes behind it, the fern-like fractures left by the chisels. It had a flaw through it, a seam of another kind of stone, weaker, weakening the whole block, which must have been why it had been abandoned. With the tip of her strength, she found that softer stone, drawing a line through it, feeling the weakness growing. It was like running the very tips of your fingers across a carving with your eyes closed – they only picked up a little detail at a time, but slowly a picture of the whole could be built.

Then it wasn't slow. Then it was all-at-once. The fractional picture that had been building in her mind went away and even though her eyes were closed she could see and feel everything, as a whole, sight that wasn't sight. With everything perceptible, she didn't need to grope towards a good place to make her change – she could put her whole focus on the right point.

The block snapped in two with a piercing sting of noise. Duna opened her eyes and stared wildly around, fearful that what she had done had been seen or heard. But no one was nearby and the sound of stone splitting did not turn heads in a quarry.

What had happened? What had changed? Had she unlocked a new aspect of her ability? For months she had sensed that her capacity to break stone was increasing, but this was something different, like a whole new set of eyes.

The only people nearby were Anzola and her attendants. They had been joined by Kielo and a couple of Mishigo quarrymen. The merite was deep in conversation with one of them, a man with thick curly brown hair and a dark beard.

Could it be that the quarry itself was different – that it was held by an enchantment? They were closer to the Mountain, and she had read about Custodian buildings and runic arts.

Unnerved, she had no further desire to be alone. She walked back towards the merite, happy for the time being to smile and be introduced and shown off, and to say nothing while others talked. But as she approached the group, the sense of sight only brightened and clarified. It had not been there earlier – now it grew and grew. It was not caused by the quarry.

Anzola smiled when she saw the girl approaching, and the bearded man put on a polite face, but she saw the glint of suspicion in his eyes. He knew it. Maybe no one had heard, but one knew, this one.

"Duna, you're back," Anzola said, beaming politically. "Let me introduce you. Astar, this is Duna, my ward. Duna, this is Astar Astarsson, the chief builder of Mishig-Tenh."

The Elves about her moved like ghosts. She felt their rough shoving hands on her and she wanted to break and snap and burst and make them pull back and shriek with pain, but there was nothing there that could be *changed*. Just empty spaces, ones that jostled and tightened their hold on her arm and kicked at her and dragged her into the gatehouse. The unreleased change built up in her, weighing her down, and combined with the tonnage of despair that pressed on her it was too much. She fell, threw herself down, refusing to use her feet. Let them carry her.

Inar turned, throwing off the hands that held him, not seeming to care about the consequences. He knelt over her as she shrank into a ball, and she let out the single long howl of grief and rage which was boiling within. Her eyes met Inar's. He was crouched over her, closer than he had ever been, sweat dripping from his face. The Elf guards around them had hesitated, all coming to the same dim awareness of change in the air.

Particles of stone dust rose from the flags beneath them, pulling into a slow vortex around her.

Every stone of the gatehouse shone. She felt all of them, their edges and weights the different pressures within them. The crusty texture of the mortar between the stones. The fine texture of the packed dirt of the exercise ground within the gate, and beyond that the square tower of the keep. So clear, all of it within reach. She would start at the keep, because what happened closer might kill them all.

Release. Not full release – just a portion, flicking out like the tip of a whip. She did not bother to assess what she had done, but there was a mighty noise and many shouts and Elves ran and yelped. Yes, you should run. The despair was gone. In its place burned power, delicious power, power held in her grip.

She let it go.

Above them, three storeys of massive defensive structure, comprising thousands of tonnes of stone painstakingly laid by Mirolinian legions centuries earlier, split apart at every weakness and began to fall, right on top of them. If she was wrong, and this was death, at least it was a death of her own making rather than the Elves' tortures. But death did not come. She projected a whirling cone of continued change, and the giant stones that plummeted towards their soft bodies were shattered and shattered again, from building blocks to gravel to dust, and every splintering release of force pushed them outwards and around in a blasting howling tempest of shards, with her at the silent eye. The gyre of catastrophised stone carried with it much that was not stone, such as the timber beams and boards of the floors above them and the rafters of the gatehouse roof, and the broken bodies of the Elves who had been within. When it subsided, they were left in a steady rain of fine powder.

Duna dared breathe again, and got a lungful of dust. Everything was dark, all was spent. She tried to rise, but faltered and fell. Hands were on her, and she feared it might be an Elf, but she could see the bones inside those hands – it was Inar, helping her to her feet. They were at the middle of a crater, surrounded by a ring of heaped desolation. The destruction of the gatehouse had extinguished every torch nearby, and the only light came from a fire started by spilled lamp-oil in wrecked wooden outbuildings. She was glad to be spared more than glimpses of the carnage in the ruins: a horse stripped of flesh on one side by a hail of debris, an Elf-warrior speared right through the chest by a spar of wood.

"Here!" Anzola said. She was scrambling up one side of the crater. "The ditch – it'll hide us." And she started to skid down the far side, out of sight.

Without words, Duna and Inar followed. She feared the trench around the fortress might be difficult to traverse, if it was used as a drain or filled with spiked traps. Worse, it was exposed to attacks from the stockade. But it had been neglected for years, and was little more than a shallow overgrown depression.

They picked their way through brambles and long tough grass in near-total darkness, following the line of the fortress perimeter. Shouts rose up behind them, and the sliding scraping sound of warriors following down the hillside of rubble. Shouts above, too, and a falling spear, though it clattered off unseen, far from the fugitives. Still, it angered her – how delightful to be angry, not afraid – and her senses blazed again. The stockade around the fortress was made of stripped tree-trunks packed close, but it was packed with stonework and boulders at its base, hidden beneath dirt. These foundations burst like ripe fruit. The trunks of the fortress wall lurched upwards and slumped outwards, accompanied by shrieks from the defenders on the catwalk above and pursuers in the gully below.

On they went. No Elves were behind or above – killed, deterred, or called away to more urgent matters, it was not important. But at the corner of the fortress rose a square stone tower, smaller than the gatehouse, and activity twitched atop it. The defenders there might not even have noticed them. That would not spare them. She saw that Inar had already closed his eyes – he was learning. He knew.

The ground shook with falling masonry, and once more they were strafed by a gritty gale.

The ditch had carried them far enough. They scrambled up its side. The fallen town was quiet and dark, but for the fires that still glowed in some buildings. Only two Elves were seen, running towards the fortress, not paying any heed to the dusty figures scrambling out of the moat. Perhaps they took them for their kin.

Again there came a rumbling roar, but this was not her doing. It was thunder above. As they left the town by the darkened north gate, guarded only by the staked and burned forms of the souls who had once made their home here, the first fat drops of rain began to fall.

"You have been deceiving me," Anzola said as they slopped, rain-soaked, along the Mirolinian road. She said it without rancour, as no more than an observation. And there was no room for a denial. They were all too tired, and too wet, for an argument. They had come too far together.

"Yes," Duna said. "I'm sorry," she added, as an afterthought.

These were the first words any of them had spoken since leaving Mal Nulalus. They walked close together, instinctively trying for some mutual protection against the cold and the wet.

"You have become... very powerful indeed," Anzola continued. "And you concealed that. Why did you hide it from me?"

Duna's head was bowed. All of them had their heads bowed, against the rain and against a trip or fall in the near-total black of the night, seeking out the cobbles of the road as the best insurance against losing their way. Inar had put his arm across Duna's shoulders not long after they left the town, and she had placed hers around his waist, and so they walked together, Anzola beside them. The noblewoman had been pursuing her own thoughts in private, it would seem.

"What was Inar asking you to do, during the ambush?" Anzola asked. "He wanted you to attack the Elves – like you had the knomes. What was that? There were no walls to topple there, no cliff face that could be made a landslide..."

Duna let a growl of thunder answer for her.

"You can break bones, can't you?" Anzola asked. She turned to Inar. "The Tzanate tried hard to destroy all knowledge about the scourges, Inar, but we have been working hard, too. I had agents working in every port the League's ships visited – the world entire, you understand. Places beyond the reach of the empire and the Tzanate – the Shergine kingdoms, Solanya, Dvir, Far Benzig. Across desert and jungle, they hunted for scraps of knowledge about scourges. They brought back charred fragments of codices in forgotten languages. And some spoke of the ability of ruin-scourges to break a man's bones. Duna swore that was myth. But it's not, is it Duna? You have learned to do it. And you kept it from me."

"Learned!" Duna said, a word carried on a high, angry laugh. "I did not learn it! I have always known it! It was the very first of my talents – the very first thing I did in the world!"

It was Anzola's time to be silent. She had stopped, too, and did not follow them as they walked on.

Duna shrugged off Inar's arm and turned towards the merite. "You thought my father's injuries were accidents. So many crushed fingers and broken ribs on your work-sites, after all. You saw that he was unable to care for me, did you ever guess that he was *afraid* of me? I had no control of myself and I was angry, angry at being alone with him."

Again, she laughed, disliking the edge she heard in it, which reminded her too much of the cackling creatures that had overrun Mal. But it all had to be released, all of it. "My mother had died bearing me, but did he tell you why? I know that I have not told you – a broken pelvis, dear guardian, that was what happened. An unaccountable weakness in her frame, you think? I do not. The very first thing I did in the world – before I even *was* in the world."

They stood in the pouring rain, thrown apart from each other.

"I saw your father's fear," Anzola said at last. "He was afraid for you, and afraid what might happen when he could not care for you. But most of all I saw your fear. And that was very painful to see. A frightened little girl. All I wanted to do was to take that fear away. Your gift has always been... Well, just that, a gift, something in addition. The scared little girl came first, and I think you knew that. You have never broken any of my bones."

"It is a terrible thing," Duna said, "this 'gift'. I would wish it away. It has been terrible to feel it grow within me. I have become... As the Zealot said, I am an abomination."

"She didn't say that about you," Inar said, a pleading note in his words.

"Inar, please," Duna said. "I am *so weary* of lies told from kindness."

Anzola had returned to her side, and placed a hand on her shoulder. "There is wisdom in being wary of your ability," she said. "But it is terrible only if it is used to terrible ends. It is as I have said to you, over and over: together we can use it for good. And we have found Inar, a boon, who can help in that. In the hands of Miroline and the Tzanate, the scourges were terrible. But we stand for reason and liberty. That is what we wish to bring to the world."

Duna sniffed. "I would like to stand for reason, and for liberty," she said. "Bringing it to the world, that's the part that troubles me."

"You must consider the alternatives," Anzola said. "The Tzanate would burn you. And we have seen the Elves now. We must be armed against them."

"It doesn't work against Elves," Duna said. "The bone-breaking. I can't even see their bones, it's like they're not there. They're different, invisible. Maybe it has something to do with the poison in them."

"But you could still harm them. You broke their walls and scattered them."

"I am sure I killed very many of them," Duna said sombrely. "It was a very terrible thing."

"They were Elves!" Inar said. "They meant to kill us, or worse!"

"Yes, Elves, only Elves," Duna said. "It had to be done, I know. And before that, only knomes. It had to be done. And after: only Zealots? Only Mirolinian legions? Only rebels? I see now how an empire sees. I have felt the surge of power, its reach, and how enemies seem to rise up on all hands – and they all mean to kill me, so I am surely justified..."

"The League is not an empire," Anzola said.

"No," Duna agreed. "Not today. Not quite yet. But every day it has to make choices, and there is a path that leads to empire."

"The only path I wish to take," Anzola said, "is the one leading me home."

Illumined by lightning that arced across the whole of heaven, the League merite resumed her march north, and Duna and Inar fell into step behind her.

Day came without the sun. The storm had passed but the rain continued to fall, as a thick and misty nuisance rather than the hard, angry downpour that had chased them out of Mal Nulalus. But it would have soaked them just as well, if any parts had been left un-soaked. The scraggy open country around the Mirolinian fortress had yielded to wooded hills, and the road was rising again. Even in the freezing damp, the forest was a balm to Duna after the dead vistas of Elith-Tenh, even if it was more like Mishig-Tenh than home.

The scene might have cheered them all, were it not for the patches of Elfcap that waxed filthily healthy in the darker spots.

"It must be growing all the way to the gates of Sojonost," Inar said, noticing Duna frowning at the malign thickets of white spikes.

"I'll ensure we send work teams to expunge any that can be found," Anzola said. "Immediately, the instant I can give the order. Once we take Mal Nulalus, we'll drive it back to Tarch. We'll wipe the land clean."

Duelling sensations arose in Duna. She exulted in the thought of the Elves being destroyed. She had seen them now, as Anzola had said – there was no doubt as to what had to be done. But the certainty dismayed her. It made a great shadow in the future – a looming mass of death and murder, which could not be avoided.

"I suppose they don't have much of a fortress left to protect themselves," Inar said. "There'll be work for builders, afterwards."

"Work without end," Anzola said. "We'll open the heart of the world. We'll build the road the Mirolinians never finished – Mal Nulalus to Caenon. That's just the start. Roads and canals.

Mines and quarries. We'll carve up Tarch into farthing parcels. We'll turn its trees into ships and warehouses. We'll plant new cities, planned cities, symmetrical, orderly, rings of canals. We'll name them after the heroes of the coming war."

"Anzoladar," Duna said. "Ernestodar. Dunaline." She put a pointed and bleak irony into her words, making sure the others heard it, and did not laugh.

Anzola grimaced. "Well, first things first. We must make ourselves safe."

"Empires are never safe," Duna said. "What about the Hidden Land? What about the Mountain? Will we build our canals there, as well? Maybe a nice flight of steps to Craithe's peak?"

"You know I never agreed with Ernesto about all that, Duna," Anzola said. "Now I've been there, I'm all the more convinced. The Elves are the priority. Quite frankly, I'd gladly wall up the Pilgrims' Pass and the Gull Gates, post a guard and let the whole accursed place starve. Leave it to the birds."

Duna nodded at that. So did Inar, much to her surprise.

The day went, and the clouds faded into starless black. They had not seen another living soul, never mind Elf pursuers – indeed, in the dripping, whispering quiet of the forest, it was as if they were the last people alive in the world.

None of them had mentioned the others, not since leaving Mal Nulalus. Certain truths stood, shared and undisputed, in the silence. There had been no chance to try to rescue them. They did the right thing in leaving as they had done. The wrecking of the gatehouse had given the others ample chance to escape. And so the others were alive, or they were not. None of these truths needed discussion. Duna thought often of Kielo – unlike as they were, he was the only non-adventurer among the Pallestrans, aside from her. And he had guarded her secrets. They had known each other a long time. She knew Miroslo much less, but the dashing knight had seemed so indestructible before his destruction, it was a shock that was hard to bear. The threshold of death was an intimate place, and they had been there together. She could not forget his eyes, his imploring helpless eyes. They were the last thing she saw when they slept, hidden in undergrowth, away from the road.

Duna was woken by a hand shaking her shoulder, hard. She was immediately impaled on an icy spike of fear. They were found. The Elves had them. She cried out, flailing in the darkness.

"Shush!" The hand belonged to Anzola, and so did the command, delivered in an insistent hiss. Duna could see her – the first light of dawn was building in a cleared sky. Inar was already awake. They lay on their stomachs, looking towards the road.

"Horsemen," Anzola whispered. "A party. Approaching."

She listened, and he heard a clatter of hooves on the setts of the Augardinian Way. They were trotting, not galloping. "Do Elves ride?" she asked.

"They're not known for it," Anzola said. "Can you... feel them?"

Duna closed her eyes. "No. They might be too far away."

"There," Inar said.

A bright spark of orange winked in and out between the trees: a burning torch. Dark shapes moved beneath the light, unclear, glimmers of weapons.

Above them, something moved higher than a man on horseback. It billowed and flapped, a bright square of blue cloth.

The horsemen were in view. There were six of them. They were lightly armoured, and helmeted, and the horses were dressed in blue. Hope leaped in Duna's heart and she turned to say what she thought to Anzola, but the merite was on her feet already, almost falling in her hurry to escape the hollow. Duna followed, and they ran towards the road, hooting and screaming.

One of the knights bore a standard: three waterfalls joining in a single pool. Nothing could have pleased Duna more. She loved that symbol with all her heart, and its promise of safety, warmth, and home.

"Your grace?" the lead horseman called out to the women who was rushing towards him. "Merite Anzola Stiyitta?"

"Yes!" Anzola gasped. "Yes, I am the merite!" She had reached the road, and was at the knight's side. His steed stepped a little anxiously at the stranger who now seized at its reins.

"Oh, good," the knight said, without much drama. "Kol Lasono, banner of the merite Szymon. I'm glad we found you. Do you know a Kielo Kosstusi? He claims to be your secretary."

Overcome with relief, Anzola could hardly respond to Lasono that, yes, she did know the one claiming to be her secretary – she made big childish nods instead of words.

"We were not expecting you to come this way," the knight said, casting a glance southwards, in the direction of Mal Nulalus. "It's very dangerous. We heard about the Elves."

"Where is Kielo now?" Anzola asked. "Did he have anyone with him?"

"Yes," the knight said, with a puzzled frown. "He was with six enemy soldiers. They were found by a patrol protecting the work camp a way back." He pointed over his shoulder with his thumb. "They're still there now."

"Enemy soldiers?" Anzola said. "You mean Zealots? Zealots are not our enemy."

Lasono's jaw tensed. "You have been away for some time, your grace."

30

ANTON

"Are we prisoners?"

Anton considered the question, his brow furrowing. "No. In a way, perhaps. We shall see." They might be free to leave, if they tried – but where would they go? Was one a prisoner if the prison was the only place one could be? Had Anton been a prisoner at the Brink?

They had been disarmed on arrival at the camp, and had been too exhausted to resist beyond a few ritual complaints. It was Kielo, the League clerk, who argued most forcefully with the men-at-arms. They had hesitated over him, as he was not a soldier and clearly one of their countrymen, and he had scolded them and pleaded with them in their own language. It was not hard to discern some of what he told them: he was telling them of the noblewoman Anzola, whose name was repeatedly shouted into the face of the commanding knight, and of Mal Nulalus, and of the Elves. He showed the soldiers the heavy sword he had picked up in the forum. The whole time he pointed south, from whence they had escaped.

Anton could appreciate the fear that lay underneath Kielo's tirade at the men. The horde was so close, and this place was so vulnerable. The camp was an orderly but sprawling affair beside the Augardinian Way, near where it forded a busy stream. Rows of large, circular tents had been made up in a natural clearing, and that clearing had been much expanded. It was now a wide open space studded with tree stumps. When they arrived, having been detained by a mounted patrol on the road, it was long after sundown, but teams of olive-clad workers were still swarming in torchlight at the treeline, felling the tall pines, stripping their branches and loading them onto wagons. Many soldiers stood about, led by a small number of knights, but the camp had no hard defences, not so much as a ditch. A horde that had overrun Mal Nulalus would have no trouble with it.

Once the commanding knights had finished puzzling over the six Zealots, and listening to Kielo, they led their guests to an empty tent. Whatever their fear, whatever their shared and private nightmares, they slept, undisturbed even by the far sound of axeheads against wood and the splintering crash of falling trees. Only after they woke did they turn their thoughts to the future.

Their guards had roused them with a gift, a loaf of fresh baked bread, and six small tin cups of a hot, bitter black drink that Anton had never encountered before, but which had a curiously familiar smell. After that, they were left to their own devices. The bread, the first Anton had seen in two weeks, was sweeter than the finest cakes ever produced by the Tzanate's kitchens, and he ate his share with unselfconscious enthusiasm and haste. The Zealots did as well – but once their hunger had retreated a little, Anton became aware their attention was focusing on him.

Ealon, Keni, Enric and Koralina were the names of the survivors of Mal Nulalus, and they outlined the disaster in sparse terms. Yisho's main force, and the Conclave, had departed for Cassodar days before the attack, news that came as a huge relief to Anton. If the Elves were able to confront, and defeat, the Tzanate's entire mobile army, then all was already lost. But they went on their way safely, presumably watched by hungry eyes, for as soon as quiet returned to the

outpost, the Elves struck. The attack came at night. Progress
had been made repairing the stockade around the fortress, but
it still had gaps and weaknesses. (Nothing compared to the
gap it now had, Anton reflected.) The Elves were inside, in
numbers, before the alarm was raised. The garrison comprised
only a couple of hundred Zealots and there were ten Elves for
every one of them. Some – including the four survivors – were
ordered to fall back through the town, meaning to escape with
as many townsfolk as possible and raise the alarm at the Gull
Gates. But the town was already overrun.

These four were the only survivors of the garrison – the rest
were dead, or transformed. Why they had been held back, they
didn't know, but they had been made to witness the day and
night of carnage that followed, and they believed they would
have been sent to the Gull Gates eventually after all, perhaps
after they had been made Elves. They would remember what
they had seen, but remember it differently.

They were unaware of Ramnie's death and Ving's seizure of
power. But the afternoon before the night of the attack a Brink
messenger had come to the fortress, and whatever message she
had brought had provoked a storm of frowning and hushed
voices around the garrison command.

Anton pondered this last detail. It was reasonable to expect
that the messenger had brought word of Ving's accession to
the Mountain throne, and of the death of the altzan-al. That
was momentous news – why had it not been shared with the
garrison? It was impossible to be sure, but Anton thought he
could sense a commander waiting to see which way the dice
fell rather than immediately declaring his loyalty.

Anyway. It was an interesting detail, but sadly a useless one.
They were all dead, now, other than the four who sat across
from him. They had accepted what Franj had declaimed in the
forum – that Anton was the rightful altzan-al – with very little
urging. He had shown them the precious letter from Ramnie,
careful that they were not observed by the League guards, and

they had been impressed. Franj told them that the Custodians had left their mark on Anton, and they had accepted this without wanting to see. It came as a relief to Anton that he would not be inspected like a horse. And now they waited on what he had to say. Maybe they couldn't quite see him as altzan-al, high priest of Craithe, supreme authority of the Tzanate, man's ambassador to the Custodians of God, but they certainly saw him as the closest thing to a leader in that tent.

Were they prisoners? Maybe. But even if they were, they needed an objective, and that objective was the same in any situation.

"Yisho is at Cassodar," Anton said. He closed his eyes, trying to think his way into the Estami's head. She was cautious and calculating. She had not wanted to strip down the garrisons at Mal Nulalus and the Gull Gates to the bare bones they had been reduced to – that had been Ving's urging, ostensibly in defence of the caravan of priests returning from the Conclave, secretly to remove possible obstacles to his grubby little plot. "Yisho will want to regain Mal Nulalus. But she will not rush, not into battle against the Elves, not along hundreds of miles of exposed road. She will make ready at Cassodar. Perhaps she will ask for help from Miroline – she will need to resupply, at least."

He tried to picture the world as a Custodian might, from above, where he could see all the different forces and factors at once. The picture was like one of the frescoes in a neglected part of the Brink, part wiped away by leaking water or obscured by mould. Nothing could be placed with certainty. Would Yisho act as he expected? What of the League? They wanted war with the Elves, both Ramnie and Anzola had said as much, and Sojonost was a lot closer to Mal Nulalus than Cassodar. It was quite possible that they might take the fortress before Yisho got there. And what then? Would they hand it back to the Tzanate? States that had won fortresses with blood did not merrily hand them over to previous owners. It was not a mislaid hat. In some respects this outcome was as terrifying as the fall of the fortress to the Elves. With both Sojonost and Mal Nulalus in its possession, the League had its boot on the Tzanate's throat. Whether that boot was on a friendly foot or a malicious one hardly mattered – the Tzanate would be a vassal in all but name.

The Zealots sat patiently, waiting for him to continue.

"So, Cassodar," Anton said. "The Elves block our way south – but we could travel through the League, to Pallestra, and from there go by sea to Miroline. And then north to Cassodar." This proposal did not cause much in the way of enthusiasm to light up the faces around them – indeed, Anton was struck by the mounting fear that they might regard him as a madman. "But that would take a long time. Yisho would, I'm sure, act long before we arrived. So we could wait here instead, and return south when Mal Nulalus is made safe."

If they hadn't liked the first idea, he reasoned, then the second must be what they wanted. But there was no reassurance – they cooled further. What did they want to do? Neither option was perfect, he had to admit, but they must have a preference.

And then he realised: they wanted direction, not discussion.

"I don't fancy hanging around here, with only a layer of canvas between me and an Elf horde, drinking endless cups of…" He picked up his tin cup and inspected the black dregs at the bottom. It hadn't tasted great, but it had given him an unusual busy energy, and he liked that. "… Whatever this is. I say we keep moving. We go to Cassodar, even if we have to go the long way around. If Yisho has taken Mal Nulalus by then – well, good."

He looked to Franj. She did not smile at him, but she nodded, once, a small but decisive affirmation. And the others rallied. He had correctly judged one aspect of the situation: no one wanted to wait in this work camp.

Decision made, the practicalities crashed into Anton's

mind. They had no supplies and no money. Making their way across the world as beggars did not appeal. But how was money obtained? Anton had only the haziest notion of the practicalities of coin, having never needed it or seen its use. Inasmuch as the Tzanate worked in actual cash, it was left to the administration of a few acolytes. But the Tzanate had money, he knew that much. Where was it? Did he not have some call on it, as (though it still sounded a lie, even as a thought) the altzan-al? And he realised that he had to think beyond the five Zealots in front of him. He was the ruler of a world religion, and if he did not start acting like it, it would be taken away from him.

"We will make our journey a work of testimony and renewal," he said, trying to put a little more pep into his words. "As we travel we will tell the Mountain faithful that their God is fallen into the hands of a pretender, and the hated Elves are at the gates of our beloved and sacred kingdom. We will raise up an army of the righteous around us. We will begin in Mishig-Tenh – I will write at once to the altzanates of Stull, Matchfalls and Pallestra and inform them of our coming."

He stood, a little dizzy with his own sudden resolve. Writing, writing – he needed the tools. Franj had stood with him, as might have been expected, and so had Koralina – a square-faced blonde woman in her late thirties or early forties, the eldest of the four survivors. Together they went outside. Two footsoldiers – both veterans, Anton assumed from their age, although they might simply be old – had been posted outside the Zealots' tent. They carried polearms, about as long as a Zealot spear but heavy, with a blade at the end rather than a point, and it was these weapons they crossed in Anton's path as he emerged from the flap.

"I require vellum, pen and ink," Anton said, and he hoped he said it with a degree of imperiousness, as if he was accustomed to having his requests fulfilled immediately. But the footsoldiers stared dumbly at him.

"Vellum," Anton repeated, insistently. "I would write letters before we depart. We do not intend to tarry here." He noticed that, quite without conscious effort, his vocabulary had become more ornate. Where was it coming from, he wondered? And he realised: I am speaking Vinglish.

One of the footsoldiers twitched the end of his polearm towards the tent, a movement a little like sweeping a broom. He said something in an unfamiliar language. It had not occurred to Anton that the soldiers might not speak Mirolingua. Surely the entire world spoke Mirolingua?

Koralina stepped to his side and, to Anton's surprise, spoke to the men in their own language. The blonde hair, the name – she might not be a Leaguer, but she was from the north.

The men considered her words, sharing a look that combined concern and weariness. After a wordless moment of decision, one turned and trudged away with a marked lack of haste. His objective was a cluster of tents apart from the rest, and of finer quality, where the blue standard of the League was raised. A command post.

Sounds of industry could be heard drifting in from the treeline, but the camp itself was quiet. Its olive-clad denizens were in the woods, felling trees and loading wagons, and only a few camp followers and soldiers remained. The fresh air carried the warmer, muggier smell of boiling vegetables from a cookhouse.

Anton, Franj, Koralina and the League footsoldier stood awkwardly in silence a time, waiting for the return of the other man. It quickly become uncomfortable.

"You speak Palla," Anton remarked to Koralina.

"More or less," she replied with a shrug. "It's been a while."

"That could be very useful," Anton said. "Thank you."

She shrugged again, and did not look like she was going to reply, until she flicked a gesture towards the tent and said: "This is my company. Was. We lost half."

So she had led the mission, formulated in desperation at

the extremity of the fall of Mal Nulalus, to escape to the Gull Gates and alert the Tzanate. Anton found it difficult to keep the woman's gaze, but she did not appear to expect sympathy or condolence. He nodded instead.

"We'll make a success of your task," he said. "We'll raise the alarm and defend our land."

Whether this was the right thing to say, Anton did not know, but it did not seem to have been the wrong thing.

The footsoldier, who had been staring in the direction his comrade had gone, murmured a few words. He might not be friendly, but nothing in his demeanour gave the impression that he regarded the Zealots as a danger. More a nuisance or imposition. If they determined to leave whatever the League's view of the matter, could these two codgers do much to stop them? It was doubtful. But there were better fighters in the camp – knights and men-at-arms.

Koralina gave the man a short answer, and received a surprisingly lengthy and conversational reply, which she translated for Anton. "He says there's fewer people about than normal. A bigwig came through early in the morning and woke everyone up, and a lot of them have departed for Sojonost."

"A bigwig?" Anton said. "A woman?"

"Yes," Koralina said. A light came on in her eyes. "The woman you were with in Mal Nulalus?"

"Ask him if they had others," Anton said. "A young girl, and a young man, not quite so young."

The Zealot exchanged remarks with the footsoldier, who again spoke at surprising elaboration. Boredom had made him talkative.

"He doesn't know," was all that she translated for Anton.

They lapsed again into silence. Then the footsoldier broke it, asking a question of Koralina with wide eyes. She gave him a short reply, and he took it very seriously, looking out to the treeline.

Anton looked at Koralina expectantly. "He asked if there

were really Elves in the forest," she said. "That man who was with you, the clerk, was shouting about them when we arrived. I told him yes, there are Elves."

"You could understand what Kielo was saying to the Leaguers last night?" Anton asked.

"Yes," Koralina said. "Most of it."

"What did he say?"

"He told them that Mal Nulalus had fallen to the Elves, that the Elves were close, that they were coming," she said. "He talked about your noblewoman friend, that she had been a prisoner of the Elves and they needed to rescue her. He said that he was part of an expedition in the Elith-Tenh. He showed them the sword he had, he said it belonged to a League knight, who was dead. He said something about knomes as well. I didn't follow that at all. Maybe he meant Elves. Anyway, he said that they had to go and rescue this noblewoman."

"That's all true enough," Anton said.

The footsoldier had perked up. His companion was returning from the command post with the same deliberate lack of haste he had set off.

"He told them that they were all going to die," Koralina added as they waited for the other soldier to trudge the distance to them. Her expression was fatally blank. "He said that the Elves were coming and that everyone was going to die. That's true enough, as well."

After the long wait for an answer about writing supplies, the answer was: wait. Kol Lasono, the League knight in charge of the military contingent of the camp, would not be back until later. Nothing could be done about pen or paper until he returned – or rather, no one was going to do anything until they heard the command from Lasono.

So they waited. Their guards, never the most formidable line of defence, relaxed and let the Zealots out of their tent, but none of them wandered far or made much conversation. Instead they stood or sat in the outdoors in the bright spring sunshine that had followed the rain, working on private puzzles of trauma. Anton noticed that they tended to keep their gaze southward. The stream gave them clean water to wash with, but it was colder than ice. At the time of middle meal, they were each given a bowl of vegetable soup – once again, the simplest fare, but to Anton it tasted indescribably rich and delicious. It had been so long since he had eaten a proper meal. He tried to doze a little, before and after lunch, to put a few more stitches in the ragged tear a succession of sleepless nights had rent in him. But every time he edged towards sleep he woke with a ghastly skidding sensation, just like his foot slipping on the bloody stage at Mal Nulalus. That blood was still on him, on his knees and foot-bindings, smudged orange-brown by the rain.

All of them would have preferred to have a few more miles and a few more stone walls between themselves and the Elf horde. But none of them was prepared to miss the opportunity for rest, and Anton was glad they were not impatient with him. Only Franj grew surly, after middle meal, when the afternoon started to resemble the morning.

"I don't see why we can't just leave, without having to lick League boots for permission," she said.

"We're not licking any boots," Anton said. "But at the same time I don't want to tread on any toes. The League controls the next thousand miles of road, not to mention the ports. I'd rather enter on good terms and travel the rest of the way without bother than give them the slip here and have to move around like brigands and fugitives."

This she accepted, albeit without much good grace, and the matter was dropped. But as the hazy sun hung lower and lower towards the treeline, the other Zealots grew anxious. Night, of course – that was when the Elves had attacked.

Before the rising restlessness could cohere into actual complaints, there was a flurry of activity in the direction of the command post. A large number of horses had arrived, and there was a distant round of trumpets, suggesting that one or two of them had important riders. The footsoldiers who stood – or, in many cases, sat – sentry duty around the camp suddenly straightened up and started to run about busily.

The Zealots looked to Anton in expectation that he would pursue their release, and he stood and did what he could to make his borrowed Zealot uniform presentable. But he never had the chance to demand an audience with the camp commander, because before he had said two words to their guard, he saw Kol Lasono striding across the camp towards him, accompanied by half a dozen other knights and men-at-arms.

"Kol Lasono," Anton said, trying to combine courtesy and command. "We thank you for your hospitality but we ask your leave to depart for Stull. We require our weapons, and I further request some vellum, so that we can write–"

"No vellum here," Lasono interrupted, an edge of cheer in his voice, but only as a cover for its fundamental steeliness. "But there's plenty at Sojonost. And that's where you're going."

31

INAR

Anzola was an aristocrat again. Ever since the knomes attacked the party at the Vulture's Eye, it had been easy to forget her title. She was the leader of their little party, yes, but not a creature apart from them. She changed the instant she heard the astounding news divulged by Kol Lasono. The merite Ernesto was not at Sojonost. He, and the League's army, were on the move – into the Hidden Land. He had not waited for Anzola's return with a treaty but had pushed on with his own policy. The League and the Tzanate were at war.

This was alarming enough, but one detail particularly needled Anzola, and brought about her transformation into a haughty noblewoman and powerful surveyor-general. The invasion had been invoked in Anzola's name. It had been justified as a rescue mission. Her safety had been used to justify the negation of her policy – the effect on the merite looked, for a moment, to be more shattering than anything that had happened at the hands of the Elves. And at once she had set about repairing her authority and prestige, like a woman possessed by a demon.

Though Anzola's reversion to type saddened Inar in a way that he could not fully understand, his mood was buoyant. Being among League knights was a relief on its own, even if he had watched enough of them die over the past few weeks to understand that they were not invincible protectors. But it was their sheer normality that really cheered him – here were contented, well-fed souls who were not running for their lives or seeking to kill him.

The palisade cheered him even more. The League had been busy in the pass that carried the Augardinian Way from Mal Nulalus to Sojonost. The drab grey mountains were slashed by a belt of blue, a wooden wall still bleeding sap in its freshness, painted the League's colour and topped with ferocious spikes. It stretched to where the rising side of the pass became too difficult for an infantryman to climb, where it ended in a geometric burst of sharpened stakes. A rebuilt road doglegged through this wall in a bit of defensive engineering that made Inar proud to be a builder. And then, only a couple of miles further along the road, there was another just like it – a whole defensive line held in reserve. It was the very opposite of the botching and neglect that had led to the fall of Stull and Mal Nulalus. Besides the happiness of a craftsman, Inar was blessed with another sensation, one he had not felt since he was last at Sojonost: He was safe.

He was also, yard by yard, approaching his home. Even the air was beginning to smell like home. The rain had purged the skies bare and left nothing to impede glorious sun. Life was creeping back into the mountain lands. What progress had Falde made on Stull's wall? He looked forward to seeing it. Though the days were still short, Falde was reliable, and progress would have been made.

Thought of Stull brought to mind Lord Cilma. He would have to make a report to one of the Lord Chancellor's spies in the League camp. This long-feared task now seemed curiously trivial. The League had made its move and all of Sojonost, spies included, had known about it before Inar, before even Anzola. And Cilma was not the threat he had once been. Strange that a man who had loomed so large in Inar's mind months before had shrunk back to being nothing but a man. Cilma had diminished because Inar had come to realise that he would not be dismissed, not immediately. If the League was at war, Duna would be needed, and if Duna was needed, he would be needed.

This truth appeared to be pressing in on Duna as well. She had wept freely when they were found by the knights, but since that moment of salvation she had been wrapped in thunderous introspection. None of them were unaffected by the calamities that had befallen the expedition, but they had seemed to weigh heavier on Duna than any of them. And who knew what toll the use of the scourge talents had taken. Never very rosy, her skin had taken on a porcelain pallor, and dark blue shadows had gathered under her eyes. They were all exhausted, but simple tiredness and pain could not explain the deeper shadows that grew around her. While Anzola rode at the front of the column of horses, setting a punishing pace and looking only ahead, Duna hung back, and Inar hung back with her.

After a long hour of pregnant silence, listening to the effort of the horses and the great quiet sounds of the mountains, Duna said plainly: "I won't go back."

Inar nodded. He didn't need her to elaborate, but she did.

"If that oaf Ernesto has invaded the Hidden Land, he can have it. All the magic in the world, he can have all of it. I won't go there again. We should never have gone there."

Inar nodded again. "Me neither," he said.

She cast him a glance – not an appreciative glance. "You're still a novice in the merite Anzola business. She's got scores of tricks she can use to get your agreement. I've heard them all. I think of it as the Anzoliad – a little volume I've made in my head of all the things she's told me."

With a wiggle of the shoulders, she drew herself up straighter on the horse, and her expression cleared a little, as if she had had a happy thought. "I am going to sit in Sojonost and look out of the window. If I see a pointy ear coming from one direction, I'll drop a mountain on it. If I see a beaky helmet coming from the other direction, I'll drop a mountain on it. And if they try to get me to do anything else, I'll crush their precious fortress to dust."

Inar didn't reply. Duna had spoken jokingly, but with conviction.

"When Anzola comes back from Ernesto's war, we'll go back to Pallestra. If she doesn't come back..."

She trailed off, not ominously, but in thought. "I don't know. Go back to Pallestra, I guess."

Inar understood, or thought he did. The girl had always followed the merite. She did not know what form her own will might take. He was beginning to appreciate the terrible paradox that bound her, and the root of all her philosophical grumbling about empires. Her immense power was not really power at all, in the sense of sovereignty or liberty – it was a kind of slavery. She had to be obedient, she had to go where she was told, and that obligation only increased as she became more powerful, because the very instant she ceased to be obedient to the League, its armies and its surveyor-general, she became a threat to the League, its armies and its surveyor-general. What could she do, go and live on a farm? What could *he* do?

They reached Sojonost after dusk. A bed was pointed out to Inar and he fell into it. Only in the morning did he note what a good bed it was: small but comfortable, with clean linen covered by a patterned Wenodari woollen blanket, and in its own room. It was a small room, only big enough for the bed and a chest, but it was warm and had an arched niche containing a bowl of fresh water.

This room was on a wide spiral staircase rising from the courtyard, and a few steps further up was the panelled, mahogany door of Anzola's rooms, among the best the fortress had to offer. He had been promoted – or the room had been vacated. Indeed, the whole fortress felt emptier than it had when he had arrived with Lott weeks before. But it was no less busy – servants, soldiers and olive-clad workers still scurried about without pause, the smell of cooking rose continuously from the kitchens, and the courtyard rang with shouted instructions and the clatter of tools and crates. It was all the rattling of chains, and the far ends of those chains were attached to a vast and hungry beast, out of sight: an army on the move.

The thought of Lott made Inar disconsolate. If the League army had reached the Vulture's Eye, then perhaps his remains had been recovered, and Inar could bear them back to Stull to be interred in the catacomb of the shiel.

With that thought, the cosy room felt suffocating, and Inar had to leave it. The clothes he had arrived in had been spirited away – to be burned, he hoped. Replacements had been left for him, and Inar wondered at how well they fitted, until he realised that they were his own possessions, left behind when the expedition departed. It was as if they had belonged to someone else.

Stepping out onto the spiral stair, Inar heard shouting. The door to Anzola's rooms was thick and well-fitted to its frame, but even through that barrier he could tell it was Duna's voice he heard, raised in anger. Intermittently there was a lull for a quieter interjection, but Duna's replies were loud, forceful and definite. They were concluded with a sudden shattering concussion and a tuneless chorus of broken china or glass. The door flew open and Duna burst out of the room, red-faced and tearful. She shoved past Inar and disappeared down the staircase. She had tried to slam the door behind her, but it was too heavy and slow on its ancient hinges, and it hung half-open. From the room within came the tinkling of shards.

Anzola was crouching near one of the room's casement windows, gathering splinters of Benzigo porcelain into a cloth. When she noticed Inar, she stood, brushing her hands together.

"Inar. Good morning. I'm sorry about that."

Anzola's appearance had caught up with her return to aristocratic manners. She was wearing a leather riding habit embroidered in a pearlescent silk thread that was either a pale blue or an unearthly white. Over the fitted trousers of the habit was a surprising decorative touch, a sash of deep blue and glowing white, tied at the waist. Her hair had been cut back to a close, shaped bob, which – another jolt of majesty – was woven with a thread of silver wire. Inar could not guess when she had found time for the barber but his hand self-consciously went to the days of beard on his chin. He felt quite intimidated at her presence.

But if she looked the part again, at least some of the haughtiness had gone. She bade him enter and sit, and offered him a hot drink from a silver pot on the table. It was the bitter black drink of the Leaguers, which perfumed the air of the room. He declined, preferring the smell to the taste.

Anzola took up her own cup like she was greeting a lover. "It's good to be among comforts again," she said. But she did not sit. "I have seen Kielo, and he is well. He gave me this."

Inar had been distracted by the finery of the room, letting his eye wander from the dark wood panelling to the Estami carpet and the Mishigo tapestries. When he turned to see what the merite was referring to, he was surprised to see her carrying a sword, a sword he knew.

"It's Kol Timo's sword," Anzola said, unnecessarily. Inar had spent enough time in its company. "Kielo was able to retrieve it from the Elf-plunder during his escape. He felt that perhaps it should be returned to Timo's family, but Timo didn't have much family, and I thought you might like to have it. You bore it faithfully out of the Hidden Land, after all."

"I…" Inar began. He stopped. "I hope that my days of sword-wielding are over, your grace." The honorific came automatically to him in the refined atmosphere of the room. This was not a morning chinwag between equals. "I am unsuited to it."

Anzola smiled. "It is a League sword, made for a League knight. Would you feel suited to it if you were made a League citizen?"

A mysterious lump had found its way to the back of his throat. *A few score tricks*, he thought.

"You have been in the League's service," Anzola said kindly, but the kindness was a balm, an oil, smoothing the way. "You have served the League with distinction – indeed, with exceptional bravery and resource. One might say with heroism. You have more than met any requirements for citizenship. It is yours if you wish, and the path is open to further preferment."

Inar found it difficult to speak. A new life blossomed before him. It was hard to refuse – if it even could be refused. But it carried a high price – it would be a boundary between him and his old life that would be hard to cross, and surely came with an obligation to ride with Anzola again, this time to war. Yes, a few tricks. You did not walk away easily.

"I would be expected to return to the Hidden Land," Inar said. "This time, to make war."

"You could not be forced," Anzola said. "But, yes, that is what I would expect. You must understand that this is a war I have tried to prevent. If you help me, we can make it a good war – one to remove a usurper, and place the rightful altzan-al on the throne."

"The young blade-priest. You believe his story?"

"He has proofs," Anzola said, raising her eyebrows, as if she didn't entirely believe it herself. "Ernesto was wrong to start the war, but I can steer it to a just conclusion – with your help."

"And Duna's help. If you need me, you need Duna."

"Yes. And she is reluctant, it's true. But I think she will agree."

"She has been through a great deal of suffering," Inar said, neutrally. "We all have."

Anzola closed her eyes and nodded. "And it causes me suffering to ask. But I have been forced by Ernesto's recklessness. I believed that it was impossible to wage war on the Tzanate without knowledge of the pass, and without Duna's abilities. A prolonged siege of the Brink – it's a nightmare of supply, the expense is monstrous, two mercenaries for every League soldier. But he has charged ahead. And now we must make a success of it, otherwise our army will be freezing in its boots in the Hidden Land while the Elves make merry. Will you help me?"

While he thought on the question, she placed her hands on each side of his head and kissed him on his forehead. He had been unsure of his answer, and this act left him unable to speak at all.

"I have been very grateful for your presence at my side these last weeks, Inar," she said, smiling. "And I hope you will be there in the days to come. Take the sword. The armoury has provided a new scabbard."

The sword's new sheath was blue-stained shagreen, to match the binding of its handle. It was not highly ornamented, but beautiful nevertheless. Inar flushed with embarrassment at it.

"How will you convince Duna?" he asked. And he realised he was now on Anzola's side of the equation, which brought forth a pang of disloyalty towards the girl.

"She will be with us," Anzola said, without any trace of doubt. "Make the barber your next call, would you? A beard does not suit you."

So he was dismissed. His cheeks burned as he stepped into the cooler air of the spiral stair. Inar had never known his mother, but he found he missed her terribly. And he saw a little more of the hold Anzola had over Duna, and over him.

Inar had left Anzola's rooms feeling curiously deflated. The possibility of rank left him feeling ungroomed and unworthy rather than a better kind of being. So he made his first stop the barber, and, once he had shed the thin beard that had accumulated over a couple of weeks, he went to the bath-house in the gloomy, smoky undercrofts beneath the hall. Six heavy wooden tubs banded with iron were set in its arched vaults, and mid-morning was its least busy time, so only one of the tubs had been filled with warm water. But the water was at least fairly clean, and soothing once Inar had sunk himself in it.

There he rested for some time, enjoying the quiet and the solitude. When the door banged and he heard the sound of wooden shoes on the flagstone, he assumed it was the servant who wielded the kettle of hot water. But it was a woman, short and busy, wearing an apron over her olive tunic and with her hair pulled back under a headscarf. Inar assumed she would attend to a task and ignore him, but she made straight to his side, and he covered himself uneasily.

"Anything for the washerwomen, sir?" she said. Her Mishigo accent was a comforting reminder of home – his old home, anyway.

"No," he said, glancing to the clothes folded on the bench. "No, thank you. Those are clean."

She smiled and nodded, but did not depart. Instead, she looked towards the door, then back to Inar. Her eyes had changed – they were hard and full of purpose. "Anything for Lord Cilma?"

It was as if she had dumped a bucket of crushed ice into the bathwater. Inar was momentarily unable to speak. So here was one of the Lord Chancellor's loyal spies.

"The League has entered the Elith-Tenh," he gulped. "They

had meant to make a pact with the tzans, but it failed. So they make war."

The washerwoman took another look towards the door. "That's known from here to Far Benzig, young man," she said, all the humble charm gone from her voice. "What doesn't Cilma know, that he should know?"

He doesn't know about Duna, Inar thought. Or about Inar's own abilities. But Inar realised that there were some secrets he didn't mind keeping, even from Cilma, if it meant keeping Duna safe. There was no knowing what Cilma might do with the knowledge that the League had a scourge. Fortunately, he had something else to share.

"They have a captive," he said. "A young tzan, a blade priest, who claims to be the rightful altzan-al. The League endorses his claim – apparently he has proof. So they will have a puppet."

The washerwoman considered this. "Very good," she said at last. "I had heard tell of captured Zealots, but not that." Without a goodbye, she turned to leave.

"Am I still in Cilma's service?" Inar said urgently to her back, the water slopping around him as he sat up.

"I've never heard of a man leaving it," she said over her shoulder, and the next thing he heard was the door.

It might have been a satisfactory report, but the incident left Inar shaken and sorely in need of solitude, so he went to the library. And it was there he encountered Kielo, bent over the small reading table under one of the high windows.

Never having seen another soul in the library, Inar regarded it as his exclusive sanctuary, and was mildly affronted by the secretary's presence. This affront was only increased by the sour expression that appeared on Kielo's face when he realised he had been disturbed, as if Inar was the intruder. Then he nodded, and Inar nodded back, and they accepted one another.

"I understand you are to be one of us," Kielo said, without

rancour but without enthusiasm. "My congratulations."

"It has been offered," Inar said, feeling the swirl of conflicting loyalties within him. "I hope that you are being considered for reward as well? You summoned our rescuers."

"She had no need, for me," Kielo said, casting his eyes modestly down onto the papers that were spread out in front of him. "I am already in her service."

Inar was beside the table, and he looked at the papers arranged there. Many were small, stained, tatty pieces taken from a pocketbook and covered with microscopic scribbles, but at the centre was a large, smooth piece of pale paper on which Kielo was drawing a decorative pattern of interlocking triangles. There was no symmetry or regularity to this pattern, and indeed it was hard to call it a pattern at all. It more resembled the kind of doodle a bored apprentice might make on the chalk floor of a mason's shed before his master told him to clean it up and get back to work. Forgetting he was not alone, Inar found himself fascinated – he leaned in and saw, besides the triangles, numbers, annotations and little drawings. Kielo was plotting the design out in a lead-point, making calculations as he went, then filling it in with a metal-nibbed inkpen. But in places he had fouled it somehow, and the pattern was blotted out with angry scribbles.

"A very rough first attempt," Kielo said, noticing Inar's interest. "The readings are very unreliable – the equipment, the conditions. And they're more or less useless when made with reference to…"

He moved a couple of scraps of notepaper aside, covering a book and exposing the right-hand side of the big sheet of paper which, Inar now saw, had been made by pasting several smaller sheets together. The right-hand side was relatively uncluttered, with fewer triangles, but a few marked points. All the inscriptions were in Palla, but Inar suddenly realised what he was looking at. There was a large oval, which had a single point marked on its edge; much further to the right was a cluster of other points, most of them just dots, but one a crude little picture of a castle, and another a triangle with two upper points, one higher than the other, inside of which was a little skull device. It was this latter point that Kielo had indicated, and a child of four could have seen that it represented a mountain. Not any mountain – The Mountain. Kielo was drawing a map.

"The peak just to the south of the tzans' palace was visible a lot of the time, and not so hard to look at," he continued. "Plus another peak to the south of the lake, and the lake temple, here and here. All our equipment was lost to the knomes, of course, but fortunately I kept all the readings we had taken. And of course a lot of those measurements are wrong, probably all of them, but by cross-referencing and with a bit of educated guesswork we can still begin to build up a picture..."

"Amazing," Inar said, unembarrassed in his breathlessness.

With the secret of the design unlocked in his mind, it all slotted together and Kielo's tiny illustrations sprang to life. There was the Sight of God, there was the ice sea, there was Sojonost. The Pilgrims' Pass was a thick maze of triangles, plotted in detail, and the rest of the terrain was more notional, but it was all there, the whole Hidden Land, with measurements marked. Most maps were just diagrams showing the rough dispersal of locations relative to a particular spot – this is in the north, this is to the west, and so on – or pictures telling a story. But this was more. It hinted at the possibility of a more useful kind of map, one that made sense whatever your location, one that could relay all kinds of valuable information about roads and areas and distances. Inar could plan out a building before it was built with string and floorboards and chalk-dust. He could measure out a plot of land and calculate its extent, with ribbons and angles. He could do the same for volume, assessing a block of stone in a quarry. These were the essentials of the mason's craft – the parts that looked a little like magic when observed from a distance, but which were simple maths. If you had an angle and two measures of length, you could infer the rest of the triangle. What Kielo was doing here was the same, but on a vaster scale. He was taking a straight-edge to the whole world.

"Elevation is the devil," Kielo said. He had picked up on Inar's interest and was enjoying it. "We are forced to estimate. Our philosophers have many ideas for ways to measure accurately how elevated one is – using frogs, or taking blood from mules and tasting it, or with balancing apparatus, or boiling pots of water – but none of it is very convincing. The mountains do make some things easier. Among the peaks you have all these handy points of reference that can be seen from far away. On the estuaries and in Wenodar, the hills are little more than ash-piles, you have to use a tide-spire here, an old fort there, the mast of a moored ship. Speaking of ships, we tried it with ships on the ocean, trying to get a distance between the Golth headland and Serpent Stack – you know you can't see one from the other? – I suppose you don't. Anyway, you get the damnedest results. As if the sea slopes, even when we know it cannot. But I daresay we will master it eventually."

And Inar could believe it. There was a hunger in the way Kielo spoke similar to the hunger some men used when speaking of women, and it suggested that none of the world's mysteries were safe from him.

"It's remarkable," Inar said. He wished he could form a more useful response. "I was so impatient with you, when you were fiddling around with poles and spyglasses and so on, and night was coming... Had I known..."

"I would not have explained it," Kielo said, ruefully. "It was a state secret, then – and I suppose it still is. You can see the military advantages of a survey of this kind. But you are a Leaguer now, aren't you? Almost. Our secrets are safe."

Inar snorted. "Well, this one certainly is." He could readily imagine Lord Cilma's impatience and reluctance to understand the import of what Kielo was doing. Nevertheless, this is exactly the kind of detail Inar would previously have been anxious to include in any report to Cilma – and now he thought he might keep it to himself.

"We are similar people, Inar," Kielo said, with a smile playing across his lips. His glorious, world-reducing triangles seemed to dance in his eyes. There was a boyishness to him that Inar had not encountered in their long shared days and nights of travel. "Titles aren't what you seek, are they? You prefer the deeper satisfaction of reason. Discovery, that is my reward."

"I'm beginning to understand the way a merite operates," Inar said. "Appointing and directing according to talent... I can see why she values your services."

He had intended this as a heartfelt compliment, and was crestfallen to see Kielo's smile fade and his expression darken. "Not all of them work that way – and not even..." he began, then paused. "What do you suppose is Anzola's great talent, Inar?"

"I don't know," Inar replied. "She's a builder, isn't she. She builds quays and digs canals."

"Yes, but that's not the skill that has made her a merite and the surveyor-general of the League," Kielo said.

"Siegecraft. She took Stull, and Eptim."

"She was merite and surveyor-general before the war," Kielo said. "And Stull – forgive me – was taken by treachery, not strictly by siege."

Inar needed no reminders of that. "Yes, but..." he began.

"*Promises*, Inar," Kielo interrupted. "Anzola is a master craftsman when it comes to promises. She can make a promise that will get you to give her anything. She will promise that quay done in half the time, or Stull taken without a siege, or even the Brink taken without a siege. But any fool can make impressive promises – people stop listening when those promises fall flat. Anzola's promises have a habit of being delivered. And how does she do that? She walks paths that others cannot see. And, to be blunt, she uses people. The promises are paid for with more promises – promises to you, to me, to Duna. Promises, I'm afraid to say, to your father. They do heap up. All the time."

Inar digested this in silence. His eyes still rested upon Kielo's extraordinary plan of the Pilgrims' pass. Reason, applied to the whole world. Perhaps Anzola was only seeking status for herself. But when it led to roads and canals and wharves and wonders like that map – however embryonic it might be – who could resist her?

"Anyway," Kielo said, growing a little uncomfortable at the gawping young man at his shoulder, "what brings you here?"

It took Inar a moment to remember. "I was going to do some reading about…"

He trailed off. The word that was going to finish the sentence was Elves. But as he spoke he turned to the shelf where he had last seen the library books on that subject, and he beheld that it was empty. Someone had beaten him to it.

Much had changed. A messenger camp had been established further up the Pilgrims' Pass, with shelter and water and horses, so it was possible to ride into the mountains right up to the point where it became too treacherous. "*My* idea," Anzola said defensively when she heard of it. "All part of plans *I* made." But it was Ernesto who had ordered it. On the day that Ernesto was expected to arrive back at Sojonost, they all rode to this camp: Anzola, Inar, Kielo, Duna and as many knights and servants as Anzola could scrape together. There was no need to ride out to meet the commander of the League's armies, but they had to ride somewhere. Anzola was insistent that they be on horseback when Ernesto appeared on foot. It was much more impressive that way. So, to the camp they rode, in the service of petty power-plays. And they remained there, getting chilly under the League's banner, not talking much, as their horses grew restless.

Returning to the pass had not prompted much warm

comradeship between the four survivors of the diplomatic expedition. But Inar was at least pleased to see Duna again, and she treated him to a glad and genuine smile. Over the preceding three days, he had seen little of her. She had been sulking, or resting, or simply keeping herself to herself, and after visiting her a couple of times and being pointedly told that she was fine, Inar had decided to leave her to it. The previous day, Anzola had tried to inveigle Duna and Inar into practising their skills together on one of the boulders scattered in the valley below Sojonost. They waited almost an hour before Duna and the merite made an appearance, both scowling. After an unsightly display of bickering and condescension between the pair, Duna turned her glare on the largest boulder within range and turned it into gravel with a single sickening *change*, showering them all with stinging flakes and splinters. She was halfway back to the fortress before the concussion of this act had finished ricocheting between the mountains. This was not the sullenness of their first acquaintance. She was angry.

He wished he could speak with her but Anzola left little opportunity, filling the time with complaints about Ernesto's conduct of the war. It had taken three whole weeks for the army to move through the Pilgrims' Pass in its entirety, and it was still moving. They could watch it now, still on the move, a constant steady stream of footsoldiers, bearers and mules trudging without pause into the defile between the mountains, and even a trickle of olive-clad workers and unburdened mules returning. The footsoldiers were mostly clad in tunics of burned orange hue, or other scraps or touches of orange, and were quite unlike the League levies Inar had seen so far – mercenaries, Anzola explained, although she called them auxiliaries. Hirelings from Oririthen and Ashony. And men were just the start: tonnes of food needed per day, only a tiny number of horses, no wagons, no siege machinery because they couldn't take any timbers longer than a mule, precious little firewood. The League's army would be under-equipped and in poor formation in an alien and hostile terrain, and the enemy would have leisurely opportunity to prepare whatever response it wanted. A small, mobile force of Zealots could perpetrate a terrible massacre. It was madness. But what an achievement, even if it was madness.

Anzola watched the pass like spring thunder. The wait had been like torture to her – given the freedom, she would have departed for the Hidden Land the morning after their return. Indeed, it had initially struck Inar as bizarre that Ernesto should want to return to Sojonost – surely the commander of the League's armies would want to stay with those armies while they traversed enemy territory?

Anzola's explanation was simple: the Zealot, Anton. The vertzan, the rightful altzan-al, or so his strange, intense female companion had claimed to the Elves at Mal Nulalus. The great prize that their disastrous exhibition had managed to salvage. Ernesto was coming to see this treasure for himself. And Inar fancied he knew why that was: disbelief, at Anzola's luck if nothing else.

So she contained her impatience and waited at Sojonost, but her eyes rested on the thin, straggling column of men filing into the pass with something like jealousy.

"He has committed the whole eastern army," she said at last. There was no sign that she said this to anyone, but Inar and Kielo turned to listen. "The whole army, and the mercenary companies. For a rescue operation? Why would he move our whole strength, with no scouting?"

"Perhaps they found another guide," Inar said.

"Inar, we tried to find guides, but the best we could do were old men who had been through as pilgrims long ago," Anzola said. "There were a few tzans who knew the route, of course, but they would never help us. No guide, and no idea if we were alive or dead."

The discussion had drawn the attention of the horseman beside Anzola, a herald from the messenger camp who was serving as standard bearer. A frown had creased the young lad's brows as he listened, unseen by Anzola but observed by Inar. He clearly wished to contribute, but was wary of addressing a merite without leave. So Inar looked him in the eye, summoned up whatever authority his new rank gave him, and said: "Yes?"

"Forgive me, your grace," the herald said, "but the merite, the merite Ernesto, he did have a guide, and he knew that you, your grace, was alive, your grace. That the knomes hadn't gotten you, anyway, your grace."

Anzola stared at her standard-bearer in frank astonishment, mouth hanging open. All she could say was: "But *how*?"

But the herald had no time to answer. A blast of trumpets came down to them from the pass, so distant it was more echo than salute, and he raised his own trumpet to his lips, sounded a bright response. The trumpets in the pass replied, closer.

Amid the drab brown, orange and olive of the figures filing up the pass, they now espied a beautiful cluster of blue and silver, surmounted by the neat blue square of a standard. The trumpets sounded again, in dialogue, hailing each other across the furlongs that still separated them.

Inar never had any time to enjoy the mystery of how Ernesto had had the confidence to move his army through the pass. It briefly teased his mind as he watched the other merite's party pick its way along the pass, footsoldiers and workers squashing themselves against rockfaces and almost throwing themselves into the valley in order to get out of their way. But as the approaching group grew closer and clearer, Inar discovered – with a thrill of impossible joy in his heart, and tears starting in his eyes – that he knew the answer.

Walking beside the merite, clad in League leather with a neat blue tunic, was Lott.

32

ANTON

They were now prisoners, that was clear. On arrival at Sojonost, Anton and the five Zealots were led to a small room in the main tower and left there. Food and water was brought twice a day, and twice a day they were led to use a garderobe not far from the room. Guards stood in the stair outside at all times, and firmly rebuffed any effort to leave. Requests for audiences with whoever was in charge were listened to with sympathy and, it seemed, ignored. On the second day, this confinement led to a volcanic confrontation between Franj and Enric and two of the League soldiers, and Anton and Koralina had to physically intervene before it turned to violence.

After that, the mood became resigned. Every day, Franj would chide Anton for not doing more to secure their liberty, and he would go out and demand to see the merite Anzola and to be given pen and ink and vellum so he could write to the altzans of Stull, Matchfalls and Pallestra, and he would be told, sure, we'll get right on it, and nothing happened. For a couple of hours, the act of demanding would satisfy Franj, but the more time went on and the more that nothing happened, the more she seethed. Meanwhile Koralina mediated the grumbling of the survivors of Mal Nulalus.

The other Zealots were at least content to be safe, even if they would prefer to be free. Franj was still ablaze with the need to continue her holy mission, which was to deliver Anton to... well, to somewhere. Anton feared his own inner fire was dimming. When he was fleeing across the Hidden Land, whatever his exhaustion, terror and hunger, he did at least feel himself to be special in a way, even if it was only to be the victim of a special kind of persecution. But here he was, still in borrowed Zealot garb, cooped up and forgotten. His copy of Xirco's *Southern Travels*, with its priceless letter from the late altzan-al, had been purposefully confiscated at the Sojonost gate. He trusted that it had not gone straight in the fire, and was still exuding whatever power it had, wherever it was. Surely he was a more valuable hostage as vertzan and nominal altzan-al than as just another Zealot? But the League was at war with the Tzanate – so they had been told – and perhaps that simply meant he would be first for the axeman.

Robbed of action, he sank into passivity. He ate, he dozed, he stared from the small window, he gave curt replies to Franj's impatient queries, and he contemplated the future, which was as blank as the freshly whitewashed walls of this fortress.

And then, after three nights of stewing in melancholy and resentment and sweat-smell, Anton was called upon. A guard beat against the door before opening it, an uncharacteristic courtesy in itself – he demanded Anton by name.

"The merites wish to speak with you," he said.

Mirolingua was not the man's first language, and Anton could not guess Palla's various declensions. But he could have sworn that the man said *merites*, plural.

Anton insisted that Koralina and Franj accompany him, and was mildly surprised when this condition was accepted without argument. Were they so negligible a threat? The three of them were led down the tower, out into the castle's courtyard, and through to a feast-hall, filled with servants and workers stuffing their faces in an atmosphere of steamy day's-end noise. Statues of Mishigo kings gazed down on their usurpers with dismay. Though most of the diners in the hall were too busy eating to notice them pass, several stopped and stared: Zealots, the enemy, here, at Sojonost.

They were directed through a back door to a smaller room, one so heavily carpeted and cushioned and lined with tapestry that the noise fell to the slightest murmur. Six day-beds were arranged in a circle around a sunken brazier, and two had pretty little tables arranged next to them, covered in fine food: cuts of beef and chicken, slices of fruit, golden crescents of bread, snowy cubes of white cheese and a carafe of red wine. The food brought to the Zealots' quarters had not been ungenerous in quantity, but it had been spartan in preparation, and the sight of so much variety and fine flavour made Anton's mouth water. Sadly he and his companions were directed to sit away from the tables.

A wait followed. They did not fill it with talk. Few topics suggested themselves, other than the food, and talking about that would only make its presence more punishing. The comfort made Anton deeply uncomfortable. He was acutely aware of the inadequacy of his efforts to clean himself and his clothes since – well, since he had been seized in Ramnie's study, what felt like an epoch ago. Sojonost might not be the dungeons of the Brink or the forum at Mal Nulalus, but what was there to look forward to here? He had already been offered death, and a choice between death and life as an Elf torturer. He was not exactly excited to learn the League's bid on him.

The tapestry before him depicted an ancient Mishigo king kneeling in front of Augardine, with a fanciful version of Sojonost rising behind the Mirolinian, the sky filled in with wheeling Custodians. All around the Emperor's head were crackling spears of radiance, picked out in thread that had once been silver but had tarnished to black. Behind his dominant form were lined Mirolinian legionnaires and black-robed, beaked figures – tzans and altzans. There was history: greatness bowing to greatness. Presumably, at the time of those vast events, there had also been bad bets and duds and dead-ends like himself, but no one made tapestries of them.

Anton squinted at the scene. Mishig-Tenh was Augardine's first conquest after making his pact with the Mountain. But it was not a conquest. The Mishigo, primordial devotees of Craithe and the Custodian cult, had immediately accepted Augardine as a demigod and yielded their realm to Miroline without raising a sword. The tapestry depicted a moment of submission – of surrender, almost. And yet in the story the Mishigo told about themselves it was a triumph. They saw the winning side, enlisted themselves without delay, and called themselves winners for the next six hundred years. They made the best of it.

The hangings parted on the other side of the room and a brace of servants entered, holding back the heavy and ancient weavings to clear a path for their masters. In walked two of the most gaudily dressed people Anton had ever seen. This was not a high bar to surpass. The Brink was grand in architecture but austere in fashion, and its altzans were quite content to totter around its halls in ancient and fraying wool robes faded from black to slushy grey. The man and woman who entered the small dining room were alike in splendour, and both wore heavily embroidered and adorned variations on the League's leather armour. The man was tall and paunchy, with greying hair and a twisted, unkind mouth to which Anton took an immediate dislike. He entered a step ahead of his companion, making fullest use of every servant in the vicinity, distributing cloak and gloves and commands. It took Anton more time than it should have to see that the woman who followed him was Anzola. Her hair had been cut and decorated with silver thread and she too wore a riding habit, but was less road-stained than the man. The merites were followed by four men-at-arms, who distributed themselves evenly through the room. From seeming empty moments before, the room now buzzed with servile activity.

Anton, out of courteous instinct, stood to greet the dignitaries, and Koralina and Franj rose as well. Anzola met Anton's eye for a moment and looked away. Taking her place at the other merite's side, she spoke to him in Palla, indicating Anton and Franj with a slender, outstretched hand. The man took in the priest and the scout with a frown, and turned his attention to Koralina.

"You must be the boy's mother," he said, and then roared with laughter at his own joke.

Anton's jaw clenched, and he felt the frost on either side of him.

"Ernesto," Anzola said, with a note of polite caution, "Anton and Franj were a great help to us while we were stranded in the Hidden Land. Without them we would not have been able to pass the Gull Gates; we might well owe them our lives, if not our freedom."

"I'm sorry, I'm sorry," Ernesto said without obvious contrition, his face still creased with mirth. He sat on the day-bed beside the food and poured himself a glass of wine, batting away a servant's efforts to help with the same impatience he had displayed when issuing commands moments before. "You cannot blame me for finding some amusement in the situation, Zo. Not least at your remarkable luck. Scourges, helpful traitors, rightful rulers – these people just fall out of the trees around you, don't they?" He drank and chortled to himself, and Anzola sat in icy silence.

"We are grateful for this audience," Anton said, taking advantage of the opening. "I am vertzan Anton Shraye, named successor to altzan-al Ramnie. We desire safe passage across the League's lands so that we can join the Tzanate army at Cassodar. In return for this service, as altzan-al I would like to revive the treaty that my predecessor and the merite Anzola had negotiated. This war is a terrible mistake. Surely we can agree that the Elves are the true enemy, and we must cooperate in bringing about their defeat."

Anzola looked at Ernesto, hopeful for an answer. The other merite had turned his attention to the food in front of him, and was cutting a slice of sausage.

"Yes. No," he said, without looking up. "None of that is going to happen. That Tzanate army is going nowhere. It probably never will. No leadership, no supply – how many Zealots slip away every night, do you think, now they're not walled up in that ghastly prison you call home?"

He mimed "walking away" with his fingers, a look of mocking sadness on his face. Then he continued. "Don't worry, you do have your uses. We were going to win this war anyway, but having you in our pocket is a real bonus. It gives everything a delightful air of legitimacy. Restoring the rightful altzan-al to his throne! Marvellous. What I need from you is some nice signatures on some nice guarantees – free passage throughout the Hidden Land and free use of Tzanate defences and facilities. The Cassodar army is to be placed under my command. We'll disarm and dissolve it. And a permanent grant of Mal Nulalus and its surroundings to the League. I don't know if that fool Ving and that fanatical strategos of yours will listen – I doubt it – but it should at least sap their will to resist. And then we'll have a lovely big ceremony somewhere to appoint the League as 'Protector of the Holy Places' or somesuch, and *you*, my lanky friend, will bow to *us*."

He turned to Anzola. "There's your fucking treaty. That's the one we should have gone for all along."

Anton realised that he had slouched, and he straightened his back. On the tapestry behind Ernesto, the Mishigo king knelt before Augardine. What was the king's name? Anton forgot. But he knew that once he had finished kneeling before Augardine, he stood up. And Mishigo legions fought alongside Mirolinians as they conquered the world, before Pallestra even rose from the mud. He did not stay on his knees. Augardine might have wanted his submission, but he did not rob the Mishigo of their dignity, and that was why they still yearned for Miroline.

"No," Anton said. "I will not grovel before you, now or later. I am the chosen representative of God. We will make a treaty on equal terms, or not at all."

Ernesto's knife clattered onto his plate. He looked to Anzola and emitted a frustrated laugh, gesturing towards the Zealots. Then he snapped his attention back to Anton. For the first time, he looked him straight in the eye.

"We're going to crush you, do you understand?" he snarled. "We've got fifteen thousand men in the Tzanate and we haven't encountered more than a handful of Zealots. And now we have the scourge girl back as well, thanks to you – we can grind the walls of the Brink to dust. The war is already over. I'm not negotiating, these are our terms, and they will be accepted."

"The scourge girl will die first," Anton said, trying to keep his tone cool. "I have been told as much by the Custodians of the Mountain. She is not to set foot in the Elith-Tenh. But I am glad you have seen her, because she is an example of the power we have at our disposal. Ving is ready to use magic. You should ask your fellow merite about what we found at the Gull Gates. Picture your armies frozen in place while Ving's bindlings cut them down."

When Anton began to speak, he had been trying to control his fear. But as he went on, he realised it was not fear he was keeping in check, but fury. "You cannot conquer God. Even Augardine learned that. He made an enemy of God and its Custodians, and he came into God's home with an army and he was cut down. That was Augardine, and you are *not* Augardine."

Over the course of this little speech, Ernesto had turned a pretty shade of crimson, and his mouth had blurred out into a shapeless expression of disgust, as if the fine food in front of him was rancid. For a moment Anton thought that the merite might actually be cowed. But then he exploded.

"I will not be hectored by a filthy black kid on my own stronghold!" he screamed, jumping to his feet and knocking so hard against the table bearing his meal that it almost overturned. Even the servants and guards flinched. "We don't need you! You're nothing! Weren't you listening? We've already won!"

"Ernesto," Anzola began, full of weary conciliation, "we don't know…"

"No!" Ernesto barked at her. "We don't need him! The war is won! I won't have terms dictated to me!"

Franj had coiled herself, ready to jump at the enraged merite, but Anton laid a hand on her shoulder. "You do need me," he said calmly. "Maybe you did not, before you knew I existed. But here I am. Lock me up in a cell if you wish, treat me with the hatred you obviously feel towards me, but how does that make me appear to the world? I am the true altzan-al, and if you want the world to believe that, if you want to make war in my name, then you'll have to treat me like an altzan-al."

Ernesto snorted, and in another burst of movement he snatched up the knife from his plate and lurched forward, holding it point-out at the tzan. Franj and Koralina tensed and almost rose, ready to meet him in unarmed combat, and all around the room the men-at-arms put their hands to the hilts of their swords. Anton placed a hand on Franj's shoulder, willing her to sit.

"I could slit your throat here and now, you cur," Ernesto said. "Isn't that your way? The blade, the killing blow? Your fucking ugly harem, too. It would cost me a carpet, nothing more."

Anton raised his chin. "Do it, then," he said. "I will die, and Ving will be rightful altzan-al. But you will not be able to stop with me and my sisters in faith. We are not alone."

"A couple of mangy Zealots…" Ernesto said, but the pillar of his rage had cracked.

"How many Mishigo do you have serving you here?" Anton asked. He opened his arms to the room, bringing attention to the shadowy figures at its perimeter, bearing cups and cloths and trays. "How many from Oririthen and Ashony? How many Mountain faithful from Pallestra and Matchfalls and Wenodar? How many in this room? This is how myths are born."

The merite wavered, and he flicked his eyes from side to side, as if noticing for the first time that there were servants present. He turned stiffly and dropped the knife back on its plate. Then, dissatisfied with the aesthetic effect of knife on plate, he pushed over the table, so that it shed its delicious cargo with a polyphonic crash, and stalked out of the room.

Servants, until this moment frozen in place, rushed in to clear up the mess. As they worked, Anton noticed their eyes on him, rather than the calamity on the floor.

Anzola's eyes were on him as well. She crossed her legs.

"The Custodians will kill Duna if she enters the Hidden Land?" she asked. She did not appear afraid.

Anton nodded. "I was told to tell you. Her power shines like a beacon to them, Anzola, they will know."

Anzola returned the nod. "Ernesto underestimates the forces he is dealing with. As you said, he has not seen what I have seen. I hope you understand that I was against this folly."

"*Was* against," Anton said, with emphasis. "Not any more?"

"It is done," Anzola said, with a sad shrug. "We must adjust to it. All of us. It's my hope that Ving will consider the forces arrayed against him and surrender without a siege or an attempt to storm the Brink. If you were to help us – or to accept our help – by playing your part, our chances would be greatly improved."

All of Ernesto's threats and bluster were gone now, and Anton realised that the negotiation had begun. He found himself wondering if the frenzy and fury he had seen from the commander of the League's armies might have been a planned part of what was happening now. No, not planned –

but he could see how the merite double-act worked, now.

"If it prevents bloodshed in the Elith-Tenh," Anton said, "and if the Tzanate can retain its army and its independence and work as the League's ally, rather than its vassal, then I will do what I can."

Anzola gave a single, solemn nod. "Then you must tell me what you need."

33

DUNA

The other Leaguers called it a city, but Duna thought they were being overly polite. She knew cities. She had been born in Pallestra, maybe the chief city of the world, given that Miroline was not what it was. She had been to Matchfalls and Wenodar, and those were cities worth the title.

Stull was a dump.

They stood together on a bluff overlooking the valley, Anzola splendid in blue leather battle armour, Duna feeling road-worn in riding habit, Kielo in his dreary clerk robes. Around them was a loose ring of trusted League knights from Anzola's banner, under the command of Kol Miroslo, and beyond that a small company of men-at-arms with the horses and standard. Miroslo kept the defensive ring wide, and the merite and her ward could talk without being overheard by their protectors. Summer had come, but on this exposed headland a chill wind snapped at their heels.

"What do you think?" Anzola asked.

"That's the new wall?" Duna replied. The city on the far side of the valley was wearing a belt several sizes too big – a pale scar running through the drab open country around it, outside the tight cluster of buildings at its heart. Bright new-cut stone. Outside this boundary, at regular intervals, scratches of smoke rose into the sky from League campfires. The siege line was almost complete, and trebuchets were being assembled.

"That's it," Anzola said. "Fourteen bastions, not counting the citadel. We'll break it, eventually, but it will take time. Meanwhile the eastern army will be tied up here. The sooner we take the city and head west, the sooner the war will be won. I have promised the duzh that we can take Stull within a month."

Duna glared icily at the merite. She had heard the strategic summary many times, but had not heard what Anzola had been telling the duzh. *That's your problem, not mine*, she did not say. For one thing, it was not true. Anzola had just made it Duna's problem.

"What do you want me to do?" she asked.

"Find a weak spot," Anzola said. "Or, better yet, make one."

"Remember the way we practised at Tempi, Miss Duna?" Kielo put in, his tone oily. "Repeated, uh, uses of your ability weakened a three-foot-thick wall to the point of collapse. This wall is thicker, and newer, but..."

"I *remember* that took hours," Duna said. "And I was standing right next to it. Wouldn't they be firing arrows into me the whole time?"

"You would be armoured, and accompanied by men-at-arms, and we will rig up some kind of screen or shield..." Anzola began, spinning a hand as she conjured new structures and rationales out of nothing. "We could have decoys... we could do it at night..."

"Am I the only option?"

Anzola frowned. "If you're thinking about – it has taken a great deal of time, and a war, for merite Ernesto to get used to the idea of you, let alone... For now, yes, you are the only option."

Duna looked about at the armoured backs of the knights who stood around them. What did they think of a reconnaissance expedition centred on a teenage girl? That the merite was training her ward in the art of war? Only a couple knew the truth. *You are a treasure*, Anzola had said, aiming to reassure her. *A treasure that must be defended. I will not let you come to harm.*

Treasures did not get much say in how they were kept.

"You would be revealing me to the world," she said. "To our enemies."

"Yes," Anzola replied. This, at least had the tang of honesty. "It's possible."

"What if the wall is magically protected?" Duna asked. "These are Mountain worshippers. We know they have boons. They might know I'm here."

"I don't think they know they have boons," Anzola said. She ignored the first part of the question.

"It's cold," Duna said. "I've seen it now. A wall. I understand. I'll think about it."

She turned away from the valley and from the merite and started to walk back to the horses. Anzola said nothing more, and neither did Kielo. But even though her back was to them, Duna saw the way they turned to each other, and could guess the tolerant, impatient roll of the eyes contained in that movement of the head, and she hated it. Of course she would do what was asked of her. But she would make them wait a little before they knew that, and let them sweat.

In the end, though, she was deprived of this youthful pleasure. Once they had returned to the League's command post at Stedmur, couriers and anxious men were waiting for them, and immediate conferences took place behind tightly closed and guarded doors. In the evening, horses left at speed, bearing orders. Anzola emerged exultant, and the firelight reflected in her eyes and on her armour shone with victory.

"You are safe, for now," she told Duna in a whisper. "Stull has been betrayed."

How many battles with mothers and fathers and guardians were lost through boredom, Duna wondered. When she was younger, her capacity for sulking had seemed limitless. Now she tired of it so fast. Her determination had not dimmed, but her willingness to stay shut up in her bedchamber without speaking to anyone was ebbing away, and only a day had passed. Perhaps this was maturity, but it seemed more like weakness.

The bell for middle meal had sounded, and was followed after a few minutes by a knock at her door. A servant, bringing something to eat, Duna assumed, and she did not answer the knock, even though her stomach growled at her about it.

Then the knock came again. "Duna, it's me," came Anzola's voice through the light inner door of the chamber. "I've brought your middle meal."

"I don't want anything," Duna lied.

"I'd like to talk to you," Anzola continued. "I'm not trying to push you into anything. I have news about Inar."

Find a weak spot. Or, better yet, make one. Duna suspected a ploy, but she also saw an opportunity for a face-saving exit from her self-imposed isolation, and a bite of food. She had been lying on the room's comfortable box bed, above the furs, listening to the sounds of Sojonost's courtyard below the tower and the pigeons scraping around in the eaves. This did not seem a dignified place to be discovered, so she climbed out of the bed and went to sit at the little writing table under the window. "Enter, then," she said.

Anzola came through the door with an ungraceful bump. She was carrying a wicker tray on which sat objects covered by a cloth, and carrying a tray through a door was not something she often did. Perhaps Duna was supposed to be softened by this personal ministry. The merite could be transparent at times, not least when feigning homeliness.

Duna's guardian took in the room with a practised sweeping gaze, assessing the condition of the enemy's defences. "You've got the window open. You'll catch cold."

"You had news about Inar," Duna said, hoping she sounded cold.

Anzola set the tray on a chest and closed the door. The room had two curule seats, and Duna was sitting in one. Anzola took the other. "Inar, Kielo and Lott have left with Ernesto for the Hidden Land," Anzola said. "They will join the army massed at Hleng. Ernesto delivered an ultimatum to the Tzanate before he came here. Maybe they will surrender."

"You'll be wanting to join Ernesto at Hleng, then," Duna said.

"Yes," Anzola said. "But I can afford to tarry a few days."

"I won't come with you," Duna said, trying to be plain in her words. She was deploying Anzola's own lessons in manners, being forceful without being emotional.

"I know," Anzola said. She smiled a smile of regret. "I must say, though: by the tide, we could use your help, now that I've seen what you can do. What you can *really* do."

"Now that you've seen what I can really do," Duna said, keeping a tight rein on her temper, "you'll understand why I don't want to do it."

"I do, I do," the merite said, with a sad nod. "If you change your mind, then–" She caught the girl's eye. "No, of course not."

"Don't you care at all about the men who came with us, and didn't come back?" Duna asked. She wanted to stay statuesque and aloof, but her voice shook and she felt the heat in her face. "Thiolo, Timo... They were *your* men, sworn to *you*. I had to sit in Kol Miroslo's blood... I will never forget that, the way he looked at me. We had to leave him behind!"

"Their memory will live with me forever," Anzola said, her tone grave, her hand on her heart. "My utmost wish now is to avoid more killing. That was why I wanted your help. But I didn't come here to argue with you – all I wanted to say was that Inar will help us. His ability might be more than enough on its own, he might be able to find a vulnerability or a postern or something."

"If that's all you wanted to say, then you've said it," Duna said, looking out of the window, keeping her head high and her neck straight. "Perhaps I'll see you at dinner."

Anzola lowered her head. "That's not all. I do not want to go back into the Elith-Tenh with bad blood between us. I would like to spend a little time repairing that rift."

Duna did not reply. There was a polished silver looking-glass on the writing table, the handle of which she had been idly toying with. She glanced at the plate and was disturbed by the hard eyes that glanced back.

"You concealed yourself from me," Anzola said. "I am coming to understand that. You feared my knowing."

"All you want me to do is destroy, destroy, destroy," Duna said.

"That's *not true*," Anzola said, with a breath of sincere emphasis on the words that Duna found false and grating. "Remember in the pass, we talked about all the ways we could widen it, improve it?"

"To move armies," Duna said.

"For now, to move armies, but later, pilgrims, traders, philosophers! All we have to do is win this war…"

Duna chuckled. "You said that about the last war."

Anzola stopped. "Yes, I suppose I did," she said, shaking her head as if disappointed in herself. "I promise I didn't come in here to revisit old arguments. I just wanted to be reacquainted, while we have a little time. Let's talk about something else. Why not have something to eat? I'm told you haven't touched anything since breakfast yesterday."

"I'd like that," Duna said. She rose from her seat and picked up the tray from where it had been left on a chest. "What is it? It smells good."

"Soup," Anzola said. "I made it myself."

34

ANTON

The altzan of Stull was a short man with a lined, weatherbeaten face and sunken eyes that at times seemed shrewd and other times gave him the appearance of being half asleep. His arrival at Sojonost had been a surprise to Anton, who had expected him to be on a ship somewhere off Vell, weeks away from Mishig-Tenh. He had been caught off-guard, and was glad at least that he had proper rooms in which to meet, rather than receiving him in a sweat-stinking dormitory cell.

After his confrontation with the merites, Anton had been given the quarters of the chaplain of Sojonost, including the fortress's tiny shiel. They were small rooms, but there were several of them, enough for a tzan and staff. Anton also had a compact study, which had been left in a mess by the former occupant in their hurry to decamp, and which Anton had invested effort into tidying and making a place fit for an altzan-al in exile. He was pleased to find, among the goods left by the chaplain, a few tzan and novice robes in charcoal grey – a little short for him, but they would do. At last he could shed the borrowed Zealot garb. At the Brink, he had never thought much of the robes he was obliged to wear. Not that he disliked them: they weren't particularly uncomfortable, or particularly ugly, or particularly impractical. But he simply never thought much of them. That was the point. They were dreary and monotonous and devoid of vanity and wouldn't distract him from his devotions. It had only ever been a costume, and he disturbed that when he donned it again, he felt more like himself.

Nevertheless, the altzan's arrival was a shock. It was, he realised, the first time he would address a priest from the wider world while in the role of altzan-al. How could he rid himself of the sensation that he was addressing a superior? Or the dread that he would be instantly laughed into obscurity? Writing to the altzans of Stull and Matchfalls was his first act in the new rooms. But he had expected several weeks of silence while they made their way around the world from Cassodar, followed by some delicate correspondence. Not the altzan of Stull in person, showing up at Sojonost four days after the letter had been dispatched. The very immediacy of it boded ill. It had the smack of disciplinary action, an ambush to expose an imposter.

At least his copy of Xirco had been returned to him, and with it the letter from Ramnie – although, taking it from the lockbox under the table, it felt a flimsy shield against accusations of fraud. He hoped he would not have to show his chest. Why could the Custodians have not marked him somewhere more visible? But as the thought occurred, he was glad they had not.

The altzan had brought a retinue with him – an acolyte aide, a junior tzan and a couple of guards. But he was a shrewd enough man to see that the office could accommodate two comfortably and no more, and he motioned that they should stay outside, in the shiel. He sat opposite Anton and regarded him carefully, his eyes embers set in wrinkled beds.

"You do not look like an altzan-al," was his opening.

Anton tried to retain his composure, and not begin a series of gibbering pleas. He had to be assured. "Brother, I am more the altzan-al than the pretender seated in Craithe's Brink," he began, opening his copy of Xirco. "Here I have a letter from my predecessor, formally granting…"

"Yes, yes," the altzan of Stull said. He paid half a moment's attention to the letter, but hardly enough to read a signature, let alone anything else. "You are the altzan-al." He inclined his head, a tiny bow that might have been seen as mocking, but the quick smile that came with it was reassuring. "I mean your robe. You found it here, I suppose? My secretary dresses better. That ass Halsted took all the quality with him when he left. He had a cartload, I am told, with all the plate from the shiel, and I expect he sold it as soon as he got to Cassodar. We will bring you some vestments from Stull."

"That would be most generous of you," Anton croaked.

"Very good," the altzan said. "I am Krig, and the altzanate of Stull is at your disposal, altzan-al. What do you require?"

For a time Anton could not speak. He was dimly aware that his mouth was open, and he shut it. What *did* he need?

"Were you expecting more of a debate over your credentials?" Krig asked, tapping Ramnie's letter with two fingers. "They are either legitimate, which is excellent and I salute you, or illegitimate and I don't wish to have that confirmed with my own eyes, thank you very much. What really matters is that you are the League's chosen candidate, they are at war with your opponent, and Mishig-Tenh is a League satrapy. I could dress this up with a lot of soul-searching and theological argument and close questioning, if you want, but fundamentally that's the bread on the plate. My erstwhile brother Halsted did the whole pious 'I will never serve under heathens' performance, shortly before he took everything that could be melted down and scuttled off to the brothels of the Empire. You might decide for yourself which of us is the more principled."

"I am more than the chosen candidate of the League," Anton said. "I am chosen of the Custodians. I want you to trust that I hold in my heart the interests of the Tzanate, and the Mountain, not those of the League. It is my intention to pursue the policy of my predecessor Ramnie, and form an alliance with the League on equal terms."

Krig murmured, or growled, a sound that did not have the air of an endorsement. "Perhaps not with Ramnie's blindness, though," he said. "I mean, behold where Ramnie's policy has arrived – murdered by a rival, betrayed by his treaty partners, hostile armies in the Elith-Tenh, Elves at the Gull Gates, the Zealots indisposed, and the rightful altzan-al is being held hostage in a cupboard."

Anton frowned. "You don't like this room? It was the chaplain's – brother Halsted's – study. It seemed appropriate."

"A study is for study, not for audiences," Krig said. "You should hold your audiences in the shiel."

"But that is the shiel," Anton said. "It is sacred. It should be reserved for holy purposes."

"You are the altzan-al. Everything you do is holy. Holding audiences there will help impress that message. You must act as if you have the Mountain at your back, at all times."

Do not underestimate the power of appearances in the movement of the heart. The Custodian's words. How Anton had hated that mask he had been forced to wear.

"I believe that you are doing holy work here yourself, altzan Krig," Anton said.

Krig raised both his eyebrows, and for the first time Anton saw more of his eyes than a withdrawn gleam. They were as grey as the ice-sea. "Oh really? That's reassuring. I can assure you that my intention was wholly profane. Backing a side, doing what I can to make it the winning side, trying not to get my throat cut. These are worldly concerns."

"Well, I value your pragmatism," Anton said, venturing a smile for the first time. "And since everything I do is holy, you may consider your worldly concerns blessed. Your throat now has whatever protection the Tzanate-in-exile can offer it."

"I am most grateful, altzan-al," Krig said, with a gracious inclination of the head.

"I hope your advice will help me win over the other altzans of the north, once they have returned from the Conclave,"

Anton said. "Which reminds me – how did you return to Stull so swiftly?"

Krig shook his head, amused. "Foolery, really," he said. "Why turn a journey of a hundred miles into more than a thousand? I thought the talk of Elves was exaggerated. Home was close enough. A few of us abandoned the Conclave caravan and went north alone. A stupid risk, in retrospect – I suppose every Elf was preparing to assault Mal Nulalus and too busy to bother with banditry on the north road. We didn't see a soul until we got to League territory."

Anton nodded. "I am glad that you did, and I could benefit from your advice," he said. "I hope that the other altzans prove as reasonable."

"Oh, I'm sure most will," Krig said, with a theatrical toss of the head. "The ones in League territory will all make the same calculation. They might not be as clever as me, but most altzans have the same animal instinct for self-preservation. That's how we end up altzans. You should work on nurturing yours."

He stood and stretched. "Another useful altzan skill is knowing when to end a meeting," he said. "In high office, that's *after* you've said your piece and *before* the others present have worked up the courage to ask favours."

Anton stood, realising that he should be annoyed at an inferior standing ahead of him, but helplessly impressed by the altzan of Stull. "Altzan Krig, thank you for your time, and for your guidance. If you did have any favours, now would be an excellent time to ask."

"Oh, not really," Krig said. He winked, or possibly it was no more than a twitch, it was hard to tell. "I'm certain I will, in time. So try to stay alive for that. And you should…"

He trailed off. Anton cocked his head, waiting for him to finish, but nothing came. For the first time, the altzan appeared embarrassed.

"Yes?" Anton prompted.

"Your gratitude," Krig said, uncomfortably. "It's very

welcome, of course. You're all warmed up and encouraged now, aren't you? Ready to trust me."

It was Anton's turn to remain silent. This was an unusual thing for anyone to say – too familiar, even if they didn't hold office.

"The ones that seek to destroy you, that's how they'll make you feel, at first," Krig said. "They'll come with kindness and candour and ask nothing in return. And the next time you'll welcome them in, that's when they bring the knife."

The days were staying light for longer but they still waned fast in Sojonost's steep-sided valley, and even faster in the chasms of the fortress itself. Franj had volunteered to fetch the evening meal for the six members of the Tzanate-in-exile, as she did every day, and Anton had gone with her.

He had to insist. The food and drink for six people was provided in a large basket, and while it was not defeatingly heavy it was cumbersome, and there was a distance between the shiel and the kitchens, with steps. But fetching the meal was a job that Franj seized for herself early on, and she resisted all help. Anton had let her do it. There was very little for the Zealots to do, and Anton did not want to simply employ them as servants, no matter how willing they might be. They had arrived at Sojonost as equals, and he believed it would be arrogant of him to start using them as lamplighters and washermen when he could light his own lamps and wash his own clothes. It was not as if he was overloaded with responsibilities, for the time being. But – but, but, he could never help do anything but seesaw on the issue – were they true faithful, and would they stay so, if he gave them nothing to do, never acted as altzan-al for them, and let them grow bored and purposeless? They had been given clean clothes, but he noted they still wore what bits and pieces of Zealot garb they had if at all possible. He asked Koralina about the dilemma and she instituted a little daily training and drilling. But Anton worried about her as well. It wasn't the present that concerned him so much as the future – how long would they have to wait here?

Franj, meanwhile, had resisted falling in with the other Zealots, and Koralina had not tried to assume command over her. While at first she had stayed glued to his side, a permanent watchful bodyguard, Franj was spending more and more time on her own, and Anton was worried for her. And so he walked with her, through the colonnade that skirted the shiel's courtyard – a place that reminded Anton strongly of the Brink, and made him lurch with homesickness on a regular basis, but it was impossible to avoid. He had hoped to strike up conversation with Franj to discover what was bothering her, and if it was anything he could help with, but as it was she spoke first, and she came straight to the point.

"We should try to send word to Elecy," Franj said. "Let her know where we are, and that we are well."

A host of difficulties shouted for attention when Anton thought of trying to pass a message to the Brink, but he suppressed them. It was not the time. The principle was correct, the cavils could wait. He was here to give Franj hope and purpose, not to squash her initiatives.

"You're right," he said. "I daresay they'll learn of our survival from the League's army soon enough, but we should have our own line of communication. But I don't know how it can be done."

She did not hesitate. "There are Mountain faithful in their army, and even more in their supply train. The Oriri mercenaries almost all follow the Mountain. They know who you are. They can help us."

Anxiety wormed deep in Anton's gut. "This is what you've been doing, is it?" he said. "Spreading word about who we are."

She halted and glared at him. They were in a deserted stretch of vaulted passage connecting the shiel-court with the fortress's main courtyard. No lamps had been left in its niches and the dying blue light at each end did not reach far into its shadows. A place for conspiracy.

"I did not have to spread word," she said, crossly. "Word spreads itself in an army. The League is making no secret of you, you are very valuable to them in keeping the Mountain faithful in line. They have been coming to me, when I go among them, which is what you should be doing."

"And what have you been telling them?" Anton said. He was torn between anger and fear. "What would our hosts make of your activities?"

She laughed a bitter laugh, and it echoed in the tomblike stone hall. "Our hosts?! Our gaolers. I did not slaughter a path for you out of the Brink and out of the Elith-Tenh in order to grow fat in another prison. We both have a holy purpose here, and I am afraid you forget yours."

"I have not forgotten it!" Anton said, and he was shocked to hear his affronted tones ringing back at him. "I am merely aware of the need for delicacy. There is not just the League to consider. What if some of these Mountain faithful are most loyal to Ving? Our whole purpose could be put to an end with a night of knife-work."

Even in the dark, Anton could sense Franj rolling her eyes. "If they're loyal to Ving, they're in the wrong place," she said. "And as I say, our presence here is no secret. It's all the more reason to go out among them, and so they see a man, not a blade-priest or a cowardly pretender. Be that man. There is much they could do for us."

Anton resumed walking. "You must be cautious, Franj," he said. "The League might view your activities as sedition. We survive here at their sufferance, and our lives are only worth so much."

"With the Mountain faithful in their army loyal to you, they would find a thousand knives at their back if they lifted one to your throat. The mercenary armies outnumber theirs."

Knives, knives. Always knives. Franj's reasoning was sound, but following her course would require ice in the veins. He shook his head sadly. "I am afraid, Franj," he said. "I am afraid I do not have the Mountain-stone in my heart to see this through. To stomach such risk, and the probability of death and failure."

What Franj did next stopped Anton in his tracks. It did more to unman him than any complaints or accusations that he had lost his purpose. She grasped his arm above the elbow, and squeezed, and she smiled at him.

"It's the Mountain's power that makes Mountain-stone," she said. "Let that burn in your heart and the strength will come."

For a moment, Anton was so overcome, he feared he might spill hot tears into the courtyard of the fortress. He mastered himself. "I cannot tell you how much your faith means to me, and how grateful I am for your sacrifices," he said. "I owe everything to you, and it is why I fear I will not be worthy of your trust."

Franj shrugged, and gave a further half-smile. "Then be worthy," she said. "Be the man I freed, not a man happy to stay in captivity."

"I will," Anton said. He had meant to say, *I will try*. But trying was not enough.

From the courtyard, the kitchens were reached by a wide flight of descending steps, from which rose a permanent plume of warm vapour. It was welcome after the chill of the walk. So great was the heat from the kitchen-fires that the heavy double-door was propped open, despite the cold. Inside was a melee of activity. Kitchens were busy all day long, but the bell for evening meal had struck and a garrison clamoured to be fed. Olive-clad bearers and orange-clad mercenaries were gathering at the doorway, ready to take food out to anyone who was not eating in the great hall above their heads. As the Zealots approached, eyes turned to them. Anton supposed they might have made an exotic sight even if his identity was not as widely known as Franj claimed it was.

"I'll wait out here," Anton said. "It looks busy."

"You've come this far," Franj said. "You don't have to speak with anyone. We're just fetching dinner. Really, I don't see how you are going to lead our faith into war if you're nervous about going into a kitchen."

She was chiding him, but she did so fondly, and he abruptly felt a fool for being nervous. Her manner was so like that of Elecy that he abruptly missed his sister-in-faith most terribly, and desired nothing more than to communicate with her. And he knew that Franj had the same pain in her heart, and perhaps more acutely, as his love for Elecy was something that had grown to its fullness, but Franj's was a seed that awaited becoming whatever it would become. It was decided.

"We will try to get a message to Elecy," Anton said. "We will write it together."

Entering the kitchens was to walk into a wall of heat and noise. The large arched space had been recently repainted and its white walls ran with condensation. The far end of the space was filled with a range, and down its middle was an immense slab of a table, at which cooks worked. Bearers dashed around them with the high dignity of urgent purpose. Platters of meat and vegetables and bread were being readied to carry up to the hall. Their entry was not immediately noticed.

"We have to make plain that you have not compromised your intentions," Franj said to Anton. "Your loyalty is with the Tzanate, not with the League – your intention is still to reach the army, by word if not in person. And we must find support in the mercenary armies."

"I tell you, Franj, we must tread carefully in this," Anton hissed. The kitchen was noisy, but it was also full of ears, and servants who ran to every part of the fortress and the army. "I am happy to make myself a symbol to the Mountain faithful in the League's service – it is my job to be that symbol, that leader, and to act appropriately. But if we are seen to be driving a wedge between the faithful and their masters in the League…"

"This is exactly why you must speak with more of your faithful!" Franj said. "Our vulnerability comes from our isolation – with support in their armies, we would not be so vulnerable. So many of the mercenaries and slaves they rely on are Oriri and Mishigo, Mountain faithful for whom defeat and humiliation at the hands of the League are a recent memory. Did they admire the Tzanate for sitting in silence in the Elith-Tenh while their defeat was unfolding? They did not. They do not. The sight of an altzan-al out in the world is a powerful one, brother Anton."

"Do not underestimate the ruthlessness of an empire," Anton said. "I am sure, faced with the possibility of mutiny in their armies, they would not act kindly."

"We will form cells of support in the mercenary armies and the baggage train, and they will circulate your words," the scout continued. "I already have names…"

"Franj, please!" Anton hissed. He had huddled in closer to her, partly to be sure to hear her in the din of the kitchen, but also to try to block her from being heard as the dangerous, treacherous, promising words spilled from her lips. "We can talk about this, but not now, not here, where we risk making enemies!"

"You already have enemies, and you will make more," Franj said. "That's just the way of power. What you need is friends. And they are waiting for you – you need to look around."

Anton became aware that the noise around him had fallen back to nothing, and the kitchen was as close as it could get to silent, save the bubbling of pots, the rub of feet shifting on the rush floor, and the steady drip of moisture from the vaults. He turned, thinking that they might have been left alone, but there were as many cooks, servants and bearers as ever there was, stood together in silence, looking towards him.

35

INAR

How could a place remain much the same, and yet be utterly changed? The same location, the same disposition of stone, the same contents, but unrecognisable. Inar remembered walking the rooms of his keep in the days after the execution of his father and brother. Every floorboard, every stick of furniture, every half-burned log in the grate was as it had been left when Cilma's men came, and none of it was the same. He stumbled here and there, picking up pewter plates, lamp-flints, his own carvings, as if they were inscrutable artefacts he was seeing for the first time.

So it had been with the whole length of the Pilgrims' Pass. It was hard to believe that he had travelled this way before. The League had swept away snow, cleared rockslides and bridged gaps with boards. Pinions had been driven into the rockface and rope strung between them, providing handholds. They made it to the ice sea in less than a day, and slept in the permanent camp that had been established there.

At the Vulture's Eye, all trace of the old campsite was gone. With the Eye-stone broken and tumbled out of the way, League engineers had dug into the packed dirt that had built up behind it to make a wider slope where the steep, narrow path had once squeezed. This entailed burying the lower portion of the stone, and with it the peculiar cavity where Inar had found the idol. Inar had initially intended to return the idol to this spot, but when the time came to leave, he had recoiled at the thought of bearing the little stone statue back through the pass, and had left it behind. Seeing that the spot was now gone, he felt vindicated in that choice. The rest of the Stone, the fallen upper portion, had been dragged further down the pass, out of the way.

It did not displease Inar to find the Eye transformed in this way. No fond memories attached to the place. Such human remains as had been found had been spirited back through the pass. The League practice of burying its dead still struck Inar as unseemly, but he was pleased they would not linger here. Was it better to be a dinner for worms, or for birds? Inar knew which he preferred, to be with the soaring creatures in the union with heaven.

He was more troubled by the permanent camp at the Sight of God. Its tents were packed so tightly on the outcropping that it reminded Inar of the massed, steep roofs of Stull: a small canvas city wedged into what had been a solitary, holy place. For a time he could not even orient himself – where was the altar of the Gift, which had formerly dominated this natural platform? Lott told him: Ernesto's command tent had been erected over it, and it had served within as a table for charts and strategy. The desecration swirled uneasily in Inar's stomach and, for all his reformed attitudes towards the League, Lott seemed uneasy about it as well. The ossuary caves around the Sight – natural openings enlarged and shaped by generations of Custodians, tzans and Mishigo – were being used as stores. Rightfully, they were places for the dead.

Inar wished that Anzola had been with Ernesto when he came here. She might still share some of the brashness and profanity of the League, but he saw that it was now tempered with a hard-earned respect for the Hidden Land. It was difficult to imagine her being so blithe about the altar or the ossuaries. It was the same when they reached the main League encampment, at the high temple at Hleng – a devotional city made into a wartime garrison. But whatever the sensibilities it trampled, he could only marvel at the League's capacity for organisation. It made him feel obscurely embarrassed as well. The ominous reputation of the pass had loomed so large in his mind, and now it seemed a trifling superstition. Did it have to be such heavy going the first time around? Had he somehow made it more difficult than it needed to be? And he had at his side someone who had traversed the pass alone, backwards, at night, before any of these improvements.

Lott was just the same, splendidly intact and unharmed, and yet he was utterly changed. He was the same height as ever, but had grown all the same. The slouch was gone, the babble quieted.

"This is all right, isn't it?" Lott said, sipping Estami wine from a pewter goblet. "If this is war, clearly the Late Dawn was fighting it all wrong. No wonder we lost."

The sun was setting over the blunt pyramid roofs of the temple complex, and the shadow of the marble colonnade in front of them was creeping closer, bringing with it a chill. But for now it was just warm enough to sit outdoors and listen to the waters of the lake lapping gently against the wall beneath the terrace. Behind them, the sacred mountains were bathed in peach light, but that way lay the Mountain itself, and it made a less calming sight than the jumbled marmoreal heap of the temples, sinking into blue night.

"It's too easy to forget it is war," Inar said. "They might not have had a fight here, but they're going to get one eventually, I should think."

The League had taken the temple at Hleng without raising a sword, days before Inar had arrived. Not a single Zealot or tzan was found within, only a handful of caretakers. Also left behind were food and drink, the vestiges of the banqueting afforded to the Conclave, including a room filled with bottles of wine. A trap had been suspected – poison, or a scheme to get the invaders drunk – so the stash was guarded. But a couple of bottles, vintages with ancient wax seals that could reasonably be considered untampered-with, had been opened, gingerly tested, and then enjoyed more liberally by higher ranks. One of those bottles had found its way into the hands of Inar and Lott, who had been quartered in a palatial guest wing of the complex. While thousands of men slept under canvas, they had real beds under painted ceilings in attractive rooms opening onto this lakeside terrace.

"You want to be careful," Lott said with a sly smile. "Now I've had a taste of being a *hero of the League*, I'm not sure I can see myself back on your work-site. Don't get me wrong, I enjoyed being shouted at all day, but this is kind of agreeable as well." He swirled the wine in his cup and took a drink from it.

In the past, Inar might have frowned at this, but he had not yet tired of the sight of the apprentice, alive and well. He believed he never would.

Lott's account of his escape from the knomes had been light on heroic detail. After the Eye-Stone had fractured, the knights at the camp had busied themselves trying to get the fallen fragment out of the path. "They didn't want my help, did they," he had said to Inar on the day of their reunion at Sojonost. "The only one who knew anything about stone-lugging. I left them to it." When the knomes attacked, he had been on the far side of the camp, and he did what came naturally: he ran. In the Cup of Silence, he was found by League scouts. After that, he had been drafted into a rescue effort. The rescue party had found the message left by Anzola at the abandoned fort below the Sight of God.

"I'm not sure I can see either of us back in Stull, to be honest," Inar said.

"Do you think we'll have any trouble back home, after all this?" Lott asked, waving his free hand to indicate the temple and the vast military camp that lay around it. "If we wanted to go back, I mean. There's plenty who'd be against us, knowing we were tangled up in all this. Leading a League army into the holy places? I thought it was just a rescue."

The encounter with the washerwoman at Sojonost swam back into Inar's head, and he frowned. They were not free of Cilma's influence. "I don't know," he said. "Have you told anyone about Duna? Anyone who didn't already know about her?"

"No! Not at all," Lott said, with a gasp of affected horror. "Anyway, I was kept busy by Ernesto the whole time. I wouldn't dare talk about it."

He leaned in closer: "Remember what the camp at the Eye was like on those last couple of days, while they were waiting for the tzans? Lots of whispers? They're crazy about the scourge-girl, the ones that know about her anyway. Most of them have no idea about her, only a few at the top. That's why our expedition was so small. But there are rumours, which they're always trying to shut up. A lot of the auxiliaries are Mountain faithful, and they're edgy enough about marching into the Elith-Tenh. I think they would have killed me to keep it secret, if I looked like I might blab. So I made myself useful, and I kept my mouth shut, wanting to keep my head on my shoulders. But they warned me: not a word about the girl, to anyone."

"She was the key," Inar said. "A siege weapon that they can get to the Brink. They've based their whole strategy around her."

"But no one can know," Lott said. "Remember how we felt when we found out about her? Imagine that feeling spread across a whole army."

"Yes," Inar said. "It's a pity – once you get to know her..."

But that was Duna's curse, Inar reflected – armies and kingdoms would never get to know her. They would never recognise her individual wishes or concerns. She would always be a scourge before anything else – either a precious weapon to be guarded and used, or a threat to be destroyed. From what he knew, she desired none of that, but he could conceive no way out for her. And what applied to her also applied to him. Craithe's Brink was less than a day away, and all around these comfortable rooms was a city of tents, containing seven thousand League soldiers and twelve thousand mercenaries and auxiliaries: a vast massing of purpose, and to be a bubble of leisure within that body was a disturbing state. His presence could be explained: Duna or no Duna, Inar was needed to survey the walls of the Brink. But this cosseted separation from the rest of the army was more mysterious. Was a secret being held from them, or were they the secret?

Inar thought that a little wine might ease some of these concerns, but he wasn't used to wine in normal circumstances, and hadn't touched it at all since the feast at Sojonost before the first expedition. It made him woozy. As the sun dipped behind the mountains, a bank of fog could be seen rolling in across the lake. The night arrived as a solid force, with a thickening of the air and the dying of all distance. Where on previous nights the arc of the heavens, and the moon and its maids, made a crisp black line of the mountains that surrounded them, and the smooth surface of the lake carried that light under their feet, that night they were lost in depthless, opaque darkness.

Disturbed by this change in the weather, Inar retreated to bed. There might not be many more opportunities to sleep on straw and under furs, and he could at least enjoy that. But even though sleep came quickly, it was light and uneasy. The room swirled around him, and troubling snatches of dream came and went. He forgot where he was, thinking himself sometimes still at Sojonost, other times under a hostile sky in the Hidden Land – but never home, never safe.

Not asleep. He opened his eyes, or they were already open,

or not – the room was dead dark, but he knew its outline, there must be light from somewhere, even if only starlight. Or the stranger carried a light, though he did not have one, but there was light with him, the man in the room, standing over the bed.

More alert. There was someone in the room, a dark cloaked figure, standing over the bed like an assassin in a story, but not an assassin. No harm would come.

It was Kielo. How had that not been obvious before? Wine was not his drink. He felt devilish slow. Lott was in the bed on the other side of the room, a dark line of hills, completely motionless, in a sleep halfway to death.

"What is it, Kielo," he asked, faintly annoyed at having been woken.

"The scourge," Kielo said. "She is not with you."

"No," Inar said. "Don't you remember? We were told she couldn't come. She didn't want to come, anyway."

"That's good," Kielo said. "The land is large, I cannot see it all, but you both shine like beacons, and only you are here." Was it Kielo? There was no way of telling, which was odd. But even asking the question was absurd. Of course it was Kielo, who else would it be?

"Sojonost," Inar said. "She's at Sojonost."

"Why are you here, if not her?"

Inar laughed, but the sound was strange, like an echo heard from the depths of a shaft, long removed from the original. "That's what I've been wondering! I wish I knew what I had to do."

"All you have to do is sleep," Kielo said.

That sounded good, and Inar did.

Then he was awake. He could hardly have slept long, but at least it had been dense and dreamless sleep since the interruption. The heavy furs that hung across the doorway had been pulled back, but beyond was a thickly misted darkness. Inar had been shaken awake, and standing over him was Kielo. Lott was waking as well.

"What do you want this time?" Inar said.

"'This time?'" Kielo said, with a frown of confusion.

"What is it?" Inar asked. "You're as white as milk."

Kielo rubbed his hands together anxiously, yanking on one of his thumbs like it bothered him and he wanted rid of it. "Inar, you need to be in your armour," he said, ignoring the question. "Lott, please, assist him."

Neither of the Mishigo moved. "What is happening?" Inar said, more firmly than before.

"The merite Anzola has arrived and the army is moving to attack the Brink," Kielo said, only making eye contact with Inar for a moment. "We need you to assess the walls for mining."

"The whole army is moving up?" Inar said. "Mining takes time, Kielo, you know that, Anzola knows that. It's better the army stays encamped."

"You're moving in the fog, at night?" Lott put in.

"Ideal conditions, apparently," Kielo said, but his hasty manner did nothing to invest his words with confidence. "Lott, you'll come with me, we'll be moving as well, with command staff."

"Is Duna here?" Inar asked.

"No!" Kielo said, and with this denial he did meet Inar's gaze and held it, but his eyes were filled with trouble. "It'll be dawn by the time we get to the Brink anyway. The fog's fine. Unless you want their archers to be able to see you? Armour, *please*."

From behind him came the muffled sound of trumpets, and a strange steady murmur of noise which was steadily growing stronger. An army, stirring to life.

An advance party had planted torches along the road that led between the temple at the lake and Craithe's Brink, but the

League army exceeded any road. Instead it spread across the rough but open terrain to avoid forming into a tightly packed column that would make an easy target for attack. Torches had been issued to every twentieth man, and they were instructed to move fast, but silently. Outriders were marking the flank, making sure that none strayed too far from the main body, as if they were a herd of cattle. Inar never saw them – he had been assigned the company of half a dozen League men-at-arms, and told to stay with them.

They moved in an unreal landscape, and Inar was tempted to imagine that he had gone to bed after all, and all this was a dream. But the cold, the difficulty of the ground, the fear gnawing at his entrails and the hard focus of the men around him kept him reminded that he was for the time being awake and alive. He was glad of the armour, though it was barely half-armour: a shirt of chainmail and, over that, a metal chestplate and spaulders to protect his shoulders and upper arms. This was accompanied by a helm, with a hinged plate that could cover the face. None of it shone – it was well made, but plainly, with no decoration, and a dull dark blue stain. While it was not exactly the stuff of dreams of chivalry, it had provided a means of filling the time during the six long days at the lake, practising getting in and out.

One of the men-at-arms in Inar's party had a torch, and it cast the seven of them in a murky underwater light, revealing just enough of the scraped, broken ground to be able to walk fast without fear of falling. They had not been told of any hazards, and gullies or pits of swamps that might swallow them up, but they had not been told much of anything at all. He found himself falling back on his boon-talent, sensing the shape of the rocks ahead, to try to reassure himself that the ground was firm. Natural dangers were more than enough to preoccupy Inar – when he recalled that they were an invading army, traversing sacred land within a handful of miles from the enemy's innermost stronghold, he felt the possibility of ambush or attack as an impossible surfeit of fear.

No attack came – but other terrors hid in the mist. Beyond the puddle of light cast by the nearest torch, there swam the swaying glows of other torches, which carried with them a phantasmal host, the moving, stumbling, whispering shadows of more League soldiers. Unnatural sights reared out of the blind night. Inar was confronted with the battered, fallen torso of an immense statue, followed seconds later by its head, lolling on its side, nose scraped away, scarred pits for eyes. A short while later they came across another defeated monument, the skeleton of a capsized ship, bleached and fossilised in its impossible final resting place.

Shouts went up from time to time, as men tried to locate each other and regroup their parties; some were cries of pain or alarm, never sustained into evidence of an attack, often followed by hissed exhortations to stay quiet. But they were not quiet. Sound travelled strangely in the haze, and alongside the shouts and hisses came the tramp of feet and the rattle of weapons and armour and the whispering combination of many far sounds, each individually too hard to make out, and together the sound of a mighty creature on the move.

A yell of fear or affront went up from one of the men in Inar's own party, several yards ahead of him and the torchbearer and almost lost in the murk, where a wide, dome-shaped rock loomed up to block their way. The man jabbered in Palla and the others hurried to him, bringing the rock into the meagre flickering light as they did so. It was carved into the shape of an immense scowling toad, its hands crossed on its belly in a pose of monstrous divine complacency, its warty hide coarsened by the removal of the precious stones that had once been embedded in it.

Meeting this ghastly apparition had detached the man at the fore from his reason, at least temporarily. He raved and gibbered at it and at his fellows, being comforted by them. Before long he regained control of himself.

"A dead god," Inar said. "A dead god from far away."

The torchbearer – the only man-at-arms Inar knew to be able to speak Mirolingua – listened to these words but did not reply. Inar saw none of buoyant arrogance of a conquering army in his eyes, and that was just as well.

Inar had no way of knowing how long they walked that night – three or four hours, perhaps – but it was an age to him. The darkness and the enfolding fog swallowed up time, just as the constant concentration on avoiding a fall meant that he could never allow himself to forget where he was. At times, though, any sense of a destination wavered and melted away, and he found himself fearing that he might be trapped in a purgatory, condemned to walk forever in darkness with other damned souls. And against that thought even a battle was preferable.

No light had entered the sky when the shouts from ahead changed, and became a series of calls and responses, relayed commands rippling back through the vast body of the army. The torchbearer in Inar's party heard them, and they changed course, turning south towards the road, until they encountered a torch-carrying herald who directed them again east. The road, with its fixed line of lights, could at times be made out, and the throng of knights, men-at-arms and mercenaries was thicker than it was before. Some were even on horseback. Quickly, a clutch of three lights appeared ahead, and then the shrouded blue of a banner. A shining golden gleam of polished armour: Anzola, and a select bodyguard of knights, one on horseback. No Kielo, no Duna.

"Go no further," Anzola said, without greeting. Her brow was creased with worry. "The Brink is near. They've shot arrows at lights not much further on. We are waiting for protection."

"What do you need me to do?" Inar asked. Every breath in the mist sounded like an arrow.

"I need you to wait," Anzola said.

They waited, in silence. Around them came more shouted commands and responses, Most in Palla, some in Mirolingua and even Oriri and Mishigo. Companies regrouping, the army forming up. Hooves drummed in the darkness on the road, not far away – they were at the end of the line of torches – and a messenger appeared on horseback, leaning down to whisper into Anzola's ear. She nodded, once, and spoke a soft reply to the messenger. He disappeared the way he came.

Then she shook her head, as if rousing herself from a reverie. "Inar, I apologise," she said. "It's good to see you again. I have been preoccupied with the war, you must understand."

"I understand," Inar said.

"Shortly – before it gets light, I hope – I need you to go forward," she said. "Approach the wall, and use your abilities on it. See if you can find any points that might be susceptible to mining. You'll be protected."

Inar nodded, but he was not content. The wall was still far beyond the edge of his perception, but he could feel the ground under his feet, and all around. "Your grace, this is solid rock," he said. "Ancient and hard. Digging into it will be almost impossible. It will take a great deal of time, at least. Meanwhile you have an army to feed – surely that would be easier at the lake?"

"The army is here now," Anzola said, as if she had not really been listening. "Maybe it will be useful to you, a diversion, shielding your presence."

That seemed doubtful to Inar. Of course, Duna could not be here – but how much easier the job would be if she were. *You both shine like beacons*, he thought. Who had said that to him, and when? How did he know that his ability made him so visible to whatever powers resided at the Brink, and the Mountain? He knew it, it had been said to him, but when, and how? The Mountain was close, he certainly knew that much. It tingled at the edge of all his senses, but not least his talent for stone, which stirred and strengthened as if it had received its first ever proper meal. How Duna would have shone here – a beacon indeed, a terrible one.

"I will do what I can," he said.

But Anzola really wasn't listening. She was fixated on the road, where more hooves sounded and a party of men approached – more men-at-arms, like Inar's accompaniment, in the same half-armour, but with bearers and three horses. Each of these horses had strapped to its flanks large panels of tight-woven branches, willow or rush, each longer than a man was tall and bent at one end. Once these arrivals had drawn near to the merite they burst into activity, unloading the panels and standing them up so the bent end was now the top. Using the straps that had attached the panels to the horses, they began to tightly bind them together. They worked with practised efficiency.

Inar knew at once what he was looking at: a screen, almost a mobile palisade, that should shield attackers approaching a wall from view. It would not offer much lasting protection, but would deny the Brink's defenders clear targets. This would be his protection. It was better than nothing, for sure, but he had more faith in darkness and fog.

Like beacons. Inar shivered. The Tzanate had resiled from magic, so he had spent his life believing – but he had been at the Gull Gates, and he had seen what had happened there. Other creatures used magic, even if men did not, and what did *they* think of his presence here?

Anzola had broken away to speak with a couple of the men-at-arms who had arrived with the screens. She returned quickly after.

"We will proceed immediately," Anzola ahead. "We must beat the dawn. Be ready."

The shields were bound together, making a flexible screen wider than the road, carried by a line of men-at-arms. More were gathered behind it. Inar saw how alike they all looked in their drab tunics, helms and half-armour – just like him, of course. An anonymous band of decoys, to deny the bowmen an easy target even if they saw over the shield.

"It's open terrain between here and the wall," Anzola said

to Inar, her word fast and hard, laced with urgency. "They will listen to you. Get as close as you need to be but no closer."

"Yes, your grace," Inar said.

"Go," Anzola said, clapping Inar on the shoulder with a gauntleted hand. "Go."

There were no torches now, and no light at all beyond a sourceless glow in the swamp that had replaced the sky. The men-at-arms who held up the shield walked in step with each other, keeping a steady and practised pace over the rough ground. Inar struggled to keep up within the clutch of soldiers that followed, and he caught his feet and kicked heavy stones and feared he might tumble – or worse, that the shield-bearers might, and he would be left exposed. Could a bowman find him? He could hardly see his own hands.

All around was silence. The great creature that was the army was no longer at his side. They were alone.

Inar reached out with his secret sense, feeling the shape of the ground around him to help his feet stay planted, seeing without sight the variations and layers of the stone beneath them, the hard uniform shapes of the broken rocks scattered in their path, even the ghostly suggestions of the bones of the men around him. He tried to push out the radius of his perception, and to find the wall of the Brink. He preferred to get no closer than was necessary.

The lack of light helped him. He could better disregard the input of his other senses. As his sense of the stone around him sharpened, he found he could even close his eyes and walk without stumbling. He ignored the busy, jumbled, phantasmal shapes of the men-at-arms, a confusing tangle, and reached ahead.

A regular observer, on a bright summer's day, would no doubt see the terrain around them as a wasteland, untouched by man. But as Inar concentrated he saw everywhere the signs of past human activity – forgotten paths, stones that had known the chisel, filled-in post-holes. The trace outline of a building, long demolished, just a vestige of foundations. A ditch, smoothed away by time; a heap of offcut stones made by hand, not by nature; to one side, far from their position, a vertical shaft, also choked with debris, that might have been a well.

And ahead, an edge, stretching in both directions. A carved ditch, then a verticality, a pure interruption, the empty waste replaced with a colossal barrier, its mass registering on Inar almost as the change in the air that portends a storm. The outer wall of the Brink, less than a hundred yards ahead. He fought the urge to tell the party to stop, so he could clarify it in his mind. And for all his fear, an inner instinctive mason urged him on, for the wall was so beautiful. He felt the mass and the precise carving of each cyclopean stone on its outer layers, and the solidity of the rougher matter within – he knew it to be centuries old, and carefully maintained. He saw the ways the largest, lowest stones in its building interlocked with the bedrock beneath – splendid, magnificent, a work of art. Quite impossible to mine, unless you had a decade to spare, but that hardly mattered to him. His senses flared, brighter than he had ever known them. Maybe it was the proximity of the Mountain, maybe it was the wall itself, but never before had he been able to feel with such range and such definition, as if it was all bathed in the most glorious light, so bright indeed that it produced distortions, illusions, spectres in the near, just as it revealed the far. He could see inside the wall now. He could sense the passages and stairs and guardrooms of the defenders. He could see the far side, and at one edge of his perception, the bulk of a huge gatehouse. Even the defenders themselves could be made out, moving suggestions and bone and armour and arrowhead – they were close, close enough, too close.

"Stop," Inar said. He opened his eyes, and realised they had been screwed shut so tightly they ached. Sweat dripped from his chin, despite the cold.

A shout sounded ahead. With his eyes open, Inar could see that more pale light had come into the sky, raising total blackness to a deep gloom.

Enough, anyway, for the trained eyes of a night-watch archer. A whistle in the air that became a sharp *thwack* as an arrow struck the screen. The men around Inar tensed. Another arrow struck the ground, far off its mark, yards to their left. But they would not always miss.

Shouted commands along the wall. An oily yellow dart cut through the murk and thumped against the screen, sending up a lick of fire. A flaming arrow. The men-at-arms carrying the shield didn't flinch, but those around Inar instinctively ducked and crowded in closer.

Enough of the dawn had gathered to give the fog a curious, diffused inner light. The men around him were part revealed. A second flaming arrow zipped over their heads trailing the scent of pitch, falling far behind. Another hit the screen, where flames had caught and were playing across the folded lip at the top. The fire would make a target for more. They couldn't linger. What did Inar need to do? He had lost his focus. Again he closed his eyes and tried to feel outwards. There was the wall, in all its beauty, and he pushed and tried to outline a wider slice of it, sensing out weaknesses, once again sensing that miraculous boost to his abilities, and feeling with it – because there *was* something there, a weakness, a crease of potential all along the structure, deep in its very fabric, one that he had not sensed before...

Because it had not been there before, and it was there now, and it wasn't stable, it was growing, a force was pushing into it, prying at it, spilling into it from one edge of Inar's perception to another – drawing on the vast reservoir of power that was the Mountain, flowing through him, finding out all the corners and details he had revealed, yes, but from without, from someplace else, *someone* else...

Abruptly fearful, Inar tried to withdraw. But it was as if the sun had come up – he could not tell his inner eye it was night again. It could see everything and it would not be shut. But where was it coming from? The men-at-arms could sense it as well now, it was too vast a change in the world to be invisible even to them, could it be coming from one of them? Surely he would have been able to feel it? But he had only been searching for a presence, and he saw now, too late to do anything about it, that they were accompanied by an absence, a blind spot, a missing patch where a man-at-arms clearly stood, but the boon-sense showed nothing, no bones, just a blankness.

He was unarmed, this one. Right behind him. Right behind, all this time.

The man-at arms flipped up the faceplate of his helm. Her helm. Her face was plastered with sweat, and her eyes were red and wild, and a nightmare grin twisted her mouth.

"Surprise!" Duna whispered. She raised a finger to her bleeding lips. "Shhhhh…"

She made a *change*.

36

ANTON

Four days after the visit by the altzan of Stull, a cart came to Sojonost under the flag of the Tzanate, driven by the acolyte who had attended Krig on his visit. The cart carried three chests, two filled with clothes and the other with Tzanate banners and flags. Mishig-Tenh, a kingdom that prided itself on its holy proximity to the Elith-Tenh and the fact that it had worshipped the Mountain long before Miroline and its Empire came, tended to emulate the asceticism of the Brink. Though they were often dissolute, Mishigo priests were nowhere as gaudy as the altzans of Miroline, Vell, or even Pallestra. They eschewed crowns and gold thread. Nevertheless, the vestments supplied by Krig were finer than any Anton had worn before. Even his white ceremonial robes at the Brink were plain linen. Opening the first chest, Anton was hit by the traces of many perfumes: incense, camphor and sandalwood heavy among them, trailing many others he did not recognise. The robes were all black, and mostly silk, weighty and slow-moving, shining like oil spilled on water. There was little in the way of ostentatious decoration, no lavish embroidery or precious stones, but the quality was easy to see, even from a distance. So was their age. Many of the garments had the hard creases that showed they had not been taken out in many years, and their craftsmanship spoke of an earlier time. It had been years, probably decades, since the tithes of the Mishigo faithful had been spent on such luxury.

This last fact made Anton feel a little better about taking delivery of the new robes, although they still struck him as almost unseemly. Nevertheless, Krig's words had stuck – he had to make the right impression, or he would not be taken seriously. When receiving important visitors, or conducting the ceremonies of the faith, he would dress appropriately. At other times, he saw little reason to deviate from familiar plainness.

Anton did have ceremonies to conduct, after all. After going with Franj to the kitchens, he realised that he had been neglecting his responsibilities towards the Mountain faithful at Sojonost. The League had made no provision for them to express their faith, and had forbidden tzans from attending its armies – that was why the shiel was unused. They had been making do with clandestine, ad hoc meetings overseen by laypeople. He had met one of these volunteers, a young Mishigo washerwoman, and had attended one of her services. To Anton, whose thrice-weekly holy rites had been overseen by the altzan-al himself in the astonishing grandeur of the Brink's shiel, these meetings had a poignant simplicity that he found almost shaming. He had lived his whole life at the foot of the Mountain, he had felt the wakemares and known the altzan-al, he had seen the Giving of the Gift and the Custodians – the Custodians had left their mark upon him. And he felt he treated his faith with half the seriousness of the small gathering of devout workers that he met.

And so he instituted a timetable of worship in the shiel – three services of thanks to the Mountain a week, including one on the highest day, and a quieter meeting of contemplation and prayer every morning. Though he had never led worship, the basic ceremonial motions were drummed into him, as they were into every tzan. But he felt uncomfortable about supplanting the humble yet sincere rites the faithful had arranged for themselves, and so he offered Melecin, the Mishigo woman who had led those congregations, a presiding role at the morning prayers, and at his side during the thanksgiving rites.

Just setting the timetable lifted Anton's melancholy. After he had conducted his first service he began to feel useful again, and wondered why he hadn't done it sooner. Twenty-two people, servants from the fortress and workers from the League army's baggage train, attended, only about a third of the small shiel's capacity, but more than enough to make the enterprise seem worthwhile.

The war seemed very distant, but a steady stream of news still reached Sojonost via the supply train through the Pilgrims' Pass. They heard of the fall of the temple at Hleng between Krig's visit and the arrival of the cart. It was greeted with a mixture of jubilation and awe, as the imagination of the common Leaguers held the temple as a sheer-sided citadel of black glass surrounded by a moat of lava and populated by blood-crazed Zealots. Anton knew it as an unfortified heap of buildings, unused most of the year and more-or-less useless in military terms. Nevertheless, Anton noted that the porters of the baggage train, who had seen the truth of the temple with their own eyes, did not rush to correct the misconceptions of those who heard their stories, enjoying the enhanced splendour that reflected on their small role.

So it was with war. The mythmaking began sometimes before the events it described. Anton bore this in mind as he listened to the man Franj had brought to him, an Oriri porter who had recently returned from the lake, on the introduction of Melecin. He was an underfed, haunted man with thin red hair, who spoke with a quiet, rapid insistence that came across as seriousness. In the past few days, Franj had been carefully exploring ways of getting a message across the Hidden Land and into the Brink, and this man might have found the key: a few Tzanate acolytes had been captured with the temple, and imprisoned.

There were, of course, secret routes into the Brink, postern gates and such, specifically for passing messages and supplies in times of siege. Anton had escaped through one, and he suspected there were others. But he also knew very well that they would be sealed tight and watched closely, and the acolytes left at the lake would not know any way of getting in. No commander would leave that information where it could be prised out by torture. But, at the same time, a commander expecting a long siege might want a conduit to communicate beyond its perimeter, and so that commander might have made provision for secret signals that could be made from outside, and those instructions might be in the hands of one of the servants at the lake... It was a lot of mights, but it *might* be a way to get a message to Elecy.

Had the acolytes been tortured, Anton asked? The porter did not know for sure, but thought not – they appeared well, and were not even that closely confined, as if the League was not overly interested in them. That was strange in itself. As if they were not really making ready for a siege. But he was pleased the Tzanate's servants were not being harmed.

"So what do we tell her?"

The porter had departed. They had turned their attention to the content of the message he was to carry.

"Give an account of our escape," said Franj. "The intervention of the Custodians at the Gull Gates, the fall of Mal Nulalus, our situation here."

"She may know much of that already," Anton said.

"Not if she is imprisoned," Franj said. "And it will mean more, coming from us. From you."

From us. Anton eyed his companion, remembering how important the message was to her.

"Implore her to remain faithful to our cause, and that we are working on securing her safety and liberty," Franj continued, voice a little strained. "You might name her as your successor – so that if disaster befalls you here, the legitimate line can continue, and will not revert to the usurper."

So used was he to *being* a successor, Anton had not given any thought to naming a successor of his own. But Franj was right, the line had to be secured, and why not Elecy? Dreyff was already dead, and if Anton ended up dead as well then clearly the days of moderation were over.

"We must remember the dangers here," Anton said softly. "If the message is intercepted by the League, it could mean the death of this porter, and grave trouble for us. If it is intercepted by Ving, we might endanger Elecy."

"You don't want to do it?"

"I do. But, whatever we write, we must imagine it being read by eyes other than Elecy's."

Franj nodded, a little sadly.

"You should write your own message," Anton said. "I'm sure that she would like to hear from you."

At last he had said the right thing. Franj smiled. "Thank you, I'd like that," she said.

"How did you come to know Elecy, anyway?" Anton said, and he wondered that he had never asked it before. "Obviously you did not meet the night of our escape. Did you train together?"

Franj pinkened slightly. "No. That is, yes, we all saw Elecy training. But that wasn't where I spoke to her. In the stables, if you... As a punishment, you're sent to work in the piggery, cleaning and so on. She was there."

"Practising," Anton said. "With the blade."

"Yes. And it sickened me, to be honest. Although I suppose pig blood is cleaner than pig shit. I hadn't seen much of the real thing, and I thought she was a berserker, like the Elves, sprayed with blood. She has these eyes – well, you know her. And she had this reputation... You know, of course. Sorcery, necromancy, human sacrifice. And now I've killed more people than you, how about that?" She laughed, but it was more like a bitter cough.

"I would not have wished that for you, or for anyone," Anton said.

"So she said," Franj continued. "She – Elecy – had slaughtered a pig in the shambles. The blood on her was so fresh it steamed. I had only heard the act, and that was enough. But there was bliss in her eyes. I was revolted. I didn't intend to speak with her, but my words sprang from me before I could stop them. I asked her if doing that made her happy. I wanted to shame her. But she answered me straight away, no shame, no pride – she said she was happy, but not because of the killing, because she had served the Mountain. The unpleasantness of the task, its shunned nature – those parts of it only burnished the service that she felt she had rendered.

"I grew up the shadow of the Mountain, I know its power as much as any tzan, but I have never found it easy to serve, and in Elecy I saw someone who could show me how to find what she had found, that bliss, that connection."

She lapsed into silence, staring down at the scored, polished surface of the table between them, where there lay an unmarked strip of parchment, ready for a message.

"We are alike in that," Anton said. "I always wished I had Elecy's ardour, her conviction."

"It was a mystery to me that you did not," Franj admitted with a sideways glance. "I believed that the blade-priests would all be the same breed." A shy smile formed at the corner of her mouth, and she avoided his eye. "Although no one is in the same breed as Elecy."

They spoke no further, for at that moment the door to the little office opened with a bang, revealing Koralina, fierce and urgent.

"The marshal and the castellan are here," she said. "They are not pleased."

* * *

The castellan was scrawny and almost completely bald, with a worried expression that looked as if it might be habitual rather than prompted by the circumstances. The marshal was close to being his opposite: well-padded, red of face, with a thick head of curly hair mirrored by a bushy beard. He did not appear worried. He appeared furious, and it was he who governed the fortress garrison, and enforced its laws.

"We believe that you have given some religious tasks to one of our washerwomen," the castellan said, once Anton and Franj had come out into the shiel. This was not going to be a sit-down meeting, for once.

"Yes," Anton said. "I have put in place some basic hours for the Mountain faithful in the community here, and she has been assisting me."

"She has other duties," the castellan said, anxiously.

"What right do you have," the marshal interrupted harshly, "to command our servants?"

I am altzan-al, Anton thought, and he might have said as well. A week earlier, such a challenge might have filled him with fear. Today it did not. He noted that change with interest, and decided on a more diplomatic course.

"Perhaps she could be released to the Tzanate's service," Anton said. "For some of the time. If she so desires. She is not a chattel. It would be a gesture of goodwill towards the faithful here. She has been leading some of the other servants here in worship, completely on her own account, for some time."

"We're aware of that," the marshal snapped. "A gesture of goodwill! Your whole existence here is a gesture of goodwill. You eat our food and use our rooms when good men shiver under canvas. Now you are calling our servants away from their work and stirring up rebellion. We should have used this place as a barracks." He cast an arm angrily at the shiel.

The castellan shot an anxious glance sideways at his

colleague, before saying to Anton: "Working hands are in short supply here, with a baggage train to feed, and the absence of men from their duties is not just noticed, it is suffered by others."

"It's not my intention to stir up anything," Anton said, addressing the marshal first, as his was the most dangerous grievance. "On the contrary – showing your workers that you respect their faith will surely lessen the possibility of rebellion, will it not? With a League army in the Hidden Land, using the shiel as a barracks might have made a provocative symbol of it."

The marshal obviously had a reply to this – his increasingly strained outer surface reddened and darkened – but the castellan jumped in before it could explode from him. "Yes, absolutely, and this is a matter that we both have already agreed, which is precisely why these rooms were left empty," he said quickly. Then he spoke a few words in Palla to the marshal, whose colour diminished a little. "I will speak with the master of the washhouse about Melecin, and we will make it known that workers may attend, let's say, one of your sessions of worship a week."

Anton nodded deeply, close to a bow. "I would be very grateful for that. And I would be glad to speak in detail with you and vary the times of our meetings so that they interfere as little as possible in the functions of the fortress and the baggage train."

"And I," the marshal said, a high sardonic note in his voice, "will ensure that your devotions here have at least one extra attendee, one of *my* men. I will not have mutiny preached within this fortress, do you understand? And if I hear so much as a word of it..."

He let the threat trail off, but it had been delivered.

Anton ended the day exhausted. A deep fog had rolled in with nightfall, and he knew its type from his years in the

Hidden Land – it would shut out the world tomorrow, and leave Sojonost as isolated as a ship on the ocean. He feared for the League bearers in the Pass. Winters were hard up in the Mountains, but often it was the autumn and the spring that were deadliest. That was when the weather whispered that all was well in the world, luring you out, only to betray you, and you wouldn't know it until it was too late.

The tzan's rooms were kept warm in the modern way, with a fireplace and chimney rather than a brazier. It burned coal, dug out of the black veins that could be found exposed in Mishigo valleys. Some of that hard, black fuel found its way to the braziers and ovens of the Brink, though it mostly depended on peat and charcoal brought in from Mal Nulalus. How were those supplies holding up, he wondered? How much was left in store after the winter? The fortress made use of the hot water that bubbled up naturally from the deep fissures in the rock around it, but its Mirolinian aqueducts and hypocausts were cracking and failing. We presume to govern the conscience of the world when we cannot even manage the heat under our beds, Anton thought morosely, lying in his bed, watching the orange glow of the coals.

The fireplace was built into the corner and it opened on two sides to heat two rooms, the one Anton and Franj slept in, and one used by Koralina and Keni. This opening in the wall allowed sound to travel between the rooms. So it was that Anton was roused from the uneasy doze he had drifted into by the rattle of the latch on the door to the other room, footsteps and sudden conversation, low but intense.

In the cot on the other side of the room, Franj sat up. She was awake and listening.

He sat up as well. Franj was tense, he could sense it, and it made him alert.

"Trouble," she said, swinging out of her bed. "Get dressed."

Floorboards creaked on the other side of the wall. Was it the marshal's men? Surely if men were coming to arrest them, they would start with Anton. But there wasn't a confrontation in the next room, just an urgent conference, and it sounded like Mirolingua.

Franj had on her leather tunic and breeches in no time at all, while Anton was still pulling on a plain but thick robe. If he was under arrest again, he wanted to have some clothes this time. The scout went to the door of their room and cracked it, looking out into the loggia that connected the rooms. The loggia was open to the air and unheated, and thick mountain cold pushed in through the gap she made. Anton put his feet into his wool boots. Franj had picked up the dirk she kept by her bed and kept it by her side, out of sight of anyone who might be outside.

A Zealot, not wholly dressed, was in the loggia. Ealon, Anton thought, from his low voice. He had come out to investigate as well, or had been roused. Seeing him, seeing that the loggia was not swarming with League soldiers or Elves or knomes, Franj opened the door.

"Enric woke me," Ealon said to Franj. "There's an intruder in the shiel."

With that, Enric emerged from Koralina and Keni's room. He was in armour, having been on guard duty – Koralina posted two shifts a night. He had a torch in his hand.

"Intruder," he agreed, in accented Mirolingua. "I do not know how they got in. Not through the main door. Must be another way."

"There'll be another way," Anton agreed. "This place is a warren." He put a fur over his shoulders.

"Just one intruder?" Franj said. "Or more?"

"I don't know," Enric said. "One or two? It's dark, I didn't go in."

Koralina came out of her room. She had donned armour and carried a short sword.

"Everyone up?" she asked, more making comment than asking. Everyone was up. "Enric, where is your spear?"

"At my post," Enric said.

The commander glared at the Zealot but did not say anything. "I will lead, Franj, you follow; then you, Enric. Altzan-al, you should remain here with Ealon and Keni."

"I would like to come down," Anton said. "If it's the marshal's men, I would like to be ready for diplomacy rather than war."

Koralina did not argue but led the way down to the shiel. Most days and nights the loggia looked out over the little courtyard in front of the temple, but tonight it looked out into nothing at all, just a solid darkness, deeper than night but somehow not as black. Enric's torch picked up on the fog, casting out a dismal halo of orange, making the world seem weirdly small and close.

A tight doglegged flight of steps descended to the courtyard. To the right was the colonnade that ran beneath the loggia, and a series of arches. The nearest had no door – it was the guard post watching the stair and the shiel, just large enough for a chair and a tiny hearth, which filled the niche with an indistinct red light. Enric ducked inside to fetch his spear, which was propped against the wall. Next to that arch was the door to the little office. Anton tried it – it was locked, just as he had left it. What might intruders want?

"Thieves, maybe," Anton wondered aloud. But it was doubtful. Perhaps the purpose was intimidation, or to profane the shiel, to send a message.

Koralina was at the shiel's tall door, and she eased it open. No lights showed within. She stepped across the threshold, and then sharply back. Staying at the door, she beckoned to Enric to bring the torch, and then to Anton.

The torch did little to illumine the interior of the shiel. Anton saw a few of the closer benches used by the congregants, and a dim constellation of glimmer where the flames were reflected back from bronze and brass further in. But Koralina drew his attention to the floor just inside the door.

A symbol had been scratched on the worn flagstone beyond

the doorstep. It was a Custodian rune, perhaps carved with the point of a knife, but sloppily, in a rush.

"A ward," Anton said. "Did it hurt you? It shouldn't have." If this imprecise symbol was able to yield any force, it would be weak.

"It didn't do anything to me," Koralina said. "I just thought it was best you saw it."

Without waiting for permission, Anton crossed the threshold and the design. The Custodians' runes couldn't be used by just anyone – if this had been placed by an unbeliever it would be as harmless as any child's idle scrawl. Even if it was connected to the Mountain's power, it would be unlikely to affect a Custodian-marked vertzan. As it was, he felt nothing.

"It's safe," Anton said. "Enric, would you follow me?"

The torch-carrying Zealot entered the shiel, and the whole space filled with jumping shades and shadows as the wavering flame moved and steadied. The shiel was square in plan, with walls that slanted inward, rising to a square skylight about thirty feet above the centre of the space. Directly beneath that stood the altar. Benches stood in ranks around three of the four walls. Against the fourth, the *mirab* facing the Mountain, were seats for altzans, tzans and acolytes, and assorted ritual equipment.

A shape was piled against the altar, substantial and dark. It could be a man, wrapped in many layers of robes. But the torch's light did not carry far enough to show more, and the view was part blocked by benches and the altar itself.

"There's someone there," Enric said.

Anton inched closer. He expected – indeed, part of him hoped – that at any moment Koralina or Franj might tell him to stop and get behind them, but for once the boldness was left to him.

As he drew closer to the altar, he sensed a change in the air – a charge quite apart from the buzzing energy of his own trepidation. And more, a scent, one he recognised, one strange and also intimately familiar.

"Wait," he said to Enric, who had been keeping close behind. "Stay here."

He covered the last of the distance alone. The shape was still not clear, disguised by the lurching shadows cast by the torch against the benches. It was not a man, it was larger than a man, though it was wrapped in a robe – one of the new robes, from Stull, out of a chest nearby.

It was a Custodian. It lay on its side, one wing folded beneath it, the other curiously kinked upwards, with its head and beak tucked under. A bony, gnarled foot, with yellow talons the length and viciousness of daggers, was kicked outwards. Nothing about its position was comfortable – it looked as if it had fallen, and Anton wondered if it was dead.

But as he approached, there was a small movement from the creature's head, exposing a white eye.

"Anton, blade-shun," the demigod croaked, its voice barely audible in the dark. "I am afraid."

37

INAR

The wall did not break or collapse. It erupted.

The defenders along and within the wall would never know what had happened. Within seconds they were dead. The League army never knew, either – the dawn was too weak and the fog too strong for them to see. They would only have heard the unforgettable death-scream of the structure, a shattering blast of pure concussive noise, followed by a prolonged, anguished roar that filled the Hidden Land like wine filling a cup, echoing from mountain-range to mountain-range for what seemed like an age. In years to come, veterans of that day would claim they could hear it still.

Inar alone perceived what Duna had done. Everything she had learned in a lifetime honing her abilities, all the strength she had gathered in that time, all of her rage and frustration, had been channelled into a deep seam of awful possibility along a hundred-yard section of the wall's foundation. It was a crisp and pure creation, made using the clarity provided by Inar's own abilities, lit by the light of the Mountain itself. It was scourge *art*, and Inar was the only person who could appreciate it, for the fleeting moment in which it existed. And then it was gone, and so was the wall.

How did Duna do what she did? Inar could intuit some of it. He knew, for instance, that within uniform and irreducible matter, there was a different realm, smaller than could be seen. And even when the surface of matter was dark and still, that inner realm roiled with energies. What Duna did was supernatural, for sure, but it worked on this undetected secret realm. Ants. It was like a million million ants, all scurrying about at random in every direction, so that all their frenetic activity came to a cumulative nothing. Seen from a distance, this field of a million million ants might appear an unmoving patch of ant-black. Duna's intervention made every ant move in the same direction at the same time. This was to dabble in the impossible, and the stolid material of the world did not care to be impossible. It preferred to tear itself apart.

Resolving itself from impossibility back into possibility, the wall erupted like a hundred-yard geyser of obliterating stone, belching upwards into the occluded dawn, then falling back down and pancaking out.

Inar was too shocked by the scale of Duna's assault to shout a warning to the men. The pulverised stone hit them like a wave. Fortunately the men-at-arms retained their hold on the wicker screen they had used to protect Duna and Inar, which saved many lives. The bombardment knocked them back and off their feet. Men collided, sprawled and screamed. Now it was raining, raining stone, mostly a steady patter of rice-sized particles and gravel, with some larger, deadly chunks thrown in. Inar felt a fist-sized rock bounce off his helm, filling his skull with pain. Had it not been for the armour he might have been killed. A couple of yards away, a two-foot section of carved corbel smacked into the sacred land, and Inar was reminded of a previous brush with death, a month before, when the world had been different.

Duna alone stayed on her feet. She was laughing, listening to the after-effects of her achievement as they ricocheted around the mountains. Yells and cries of panic and pain came from every direction, invisible in the billowing chaos of dust that had mingled into the fog. The advance party had been part-buried by the rain of shattered stone, and as men staggered to their feet, cataracts of dirt poured from them. One was shouting, unhooked with fear, and Inar did not need to know Palla to understand what had affrighted him so: "*Skurzhe! Skurzhe!*"

For a second Inar feared that the man might attack Duna, but instead he backed away, and then turned and fled towards the rear. His comrades seemed less perturbed, or were simply too shocked to grasp what had happened and who had done it. Still the sounds of destruction rolled around the plateau. Duna had stopped her laughter and stared ahead, panting, pale features streaked with mingled dust and blood and sweat. Then she filled her lungs, and shouted.

"Charge! *Charge!*"

All of a sudden, Inar was acutely aware that he was standing between an army, and that army's objective. Shouts and commands started to rise up from the League lines.

Duna spun on her heel towards the Leaguers, her exultation turning to rage. "This! Way!" she yelled, her thin voice splitting with effort. "This! Way! Now, now now *now*! Charge, you fucking cowards, *charge, kill them all!*"

Inar put his hand on her shoulder. "Duna..." he began.

She whipped back in his direction, pure loathing blazing in her eyes, a droplet of fresh red blood on her bottom lip where she had bitten into it. Within, Inar felt the deadly point of her power rove across all the small bones in the hand he had placed on her, up his arm and neck and into his skull, around the base of his spine. But she didn't break anything, she had seen it was him.

"Surprise!" she said again, sending herself into a fit of giggling. She bowed her head and scratched furiously at the skin behind her ears, under the helmet, like an animal plagued by fleas. Her fingertips came away bloody.

"What's happened to you?" Inar asked, fearing even to express his horror at the change that had come over his friend, as if acknowledging it would make it real and irrevocable.

"Can you feel it?" Duna asked, eyes wide. "The pulse on the horizon? We have to go to it."

Inar didn't feel anything. The insides of his head rang with shock and fear. Behind them, from the direction of the League lines, the shouts of command continued but were lost in a deeper, louder, uniform noise, the hammering of feet on the ground and weapons against shields and thousands of voices raised in battle cry.

Duna heard that too. She glanced towards the lines, still lost in fog, then back towards the Brink. "Come!" she said, taking Inar's hand. "We don't want to miss it."

"Our work is done," Inar said. "We needn't go further. Come with me. We need to get you some help."

"Help?" she laughed, uncomprehendingly. "We've come all this way, and you want to leave? Are you afraid? Just stay close to me – no harm can befall me."

Her hand slipped out of his, and she was away like an athlete, bounding over the splintered and abandoned palisade, towards the devastation she had made. Within a second she was lost in the fog.

Truly lost – once again, Inar realised that he could not see Duna with his inner sight. Fearing that she was in the grip of a mania that might lead her into fatal danger, he raced to follow her, but quickly discovered that he was marooned in an emptiness of fog and drifting stone-dust. Behind came the gathering thunder of the League army; ahead were isolated cries of alarm, inquiry and command, more all the time.

It was the dust that provided the clue. He pushed onwards, eyes stinging with sharp particles of crushed masonry, tasting it rough and bitter on his tongue, and he became aware that his inner sight could perceive the drifting cloud as an even haze in the air. And in that haze there moved an absence, just up ahead, a gap the size of a slight young woman, ascending a ridge of rubble. Tacking towards it, he saw the gap stop moving, and for a moment it disappeared to him, lost in the falling stone-sleet. Then he saw her – she had turned and come back towards him.

"What are you waiting for?" she asked, again taking his hand and pulling him forward.

The rubble ridge was all that was left of a wide section of the wall. It was a mixture of fallen chunks of cut stone, some of them very large, and pulverised debris. Though it was not stable, and their ascent set off slides of tumbling stones, it was not hard to climb. At one point Inar stepped over what he believed to be a fallen statue, only for it to flex as the stone around it shifted, revealing a black-red stain across its cheek and neck – a broken body, coated in fine dust.

At the summit of the ridge, Duna paused and looked about. There was little to see – the fog had thinned as the light had come up but still hid most of the surroundings. Inside the wall was an open area of packed dirt, and further on loomed the bulk of the fortress itself, a towering darkness in the diffuse illumination of the far, weak sun. Inar had seen no Zealots yet, apart from the crushed corpse mixed in with the wall rubble, but he could hear them: panicked shouts in Mirolingua, some urging a retreat to the fortress, others insisting that the wall be held, that the breach be defended. The breach – that was where they stood. Many Zealots, regaining their composure, would be racing towards them.

With that thought, a Zealot footsoldier appeared below Inar – just the one, either very brave or very lost, an accidental advance party. He was a young, dark-skinned man, maybe Estami, and he gaped with horror at what had become of the Brink's outer wall. Late, he saw the two Leaguers standing atop the rubble, and he took his spear in both hands. No way was he going to charge up a loose slope while he was outnumbered two to one, and no way was Inar going to run down to fight him, so for a few strained seconds they stood and stared at each other, as if sharing a recognition that fighting was an absurd formality and best dispensed with, but unsure what came next.

Then he fell, screaming. Inar knew what had happened only after it had happened – the Zealot's left femur had exploded just below the hip. He saw the action as an after-image, the heavy bone, thickest in the body, shattering into matchsticks. It would never heal, and if the Zealot lived he would never walk again.

"You can finish him off, if you like," Duna said, absently.

The next defenders to appear would be too late. Already the most eager of the League's fighters, those hungriest for glory, had arrived at the breach. Two knights on horseback were at the foot of the rubble ridge, hollering commands and encouragement, which mingled with the screams of the crippled Zealot. Not far behind were scores of soldiers on foot, a mixture of knights, men-at-arms and mercenaries.

"So slow!" Duna yelled down at the men, who were scrambling up over the ruins of the wall. "Waiting for a girl to do your job for you?"

The knights and soldiers stared at her uncomprehendingly, apparently as surprised to see a young woman in the midst of the destruction as the unlucky Zealot had been. Very few of them would have had an inkling as to what had befallen the wall, Inar realised – he might have become accustomed to the company of a Scourge, but outside Anzola's coterie they were still the stuff of legends and the dismal past.

As the League's soldiers swarmed around them, Duna resumed her awful giggling, and bent over and scratched angrily behind her ears. Then she lifted off her helm and tossed it aside. Her long blonde hair was tied up behind her head, showing where the scratching had torn the skin and left matted blood.

"Dead weight! A nuisance!" she said, observing Inar's worried glance at the helm. "Just for show. I cannot be harmed!"

The air hissed and a man-at-arms beside Duna shrieked, an arrow skewering his forearm. Inar and Duna looked up to where it had come from, the immense squat cube of the Brink's gatehouse, which had partly revealed itself in the shifting mists. A company of Zealot archers had recovered their senses and had taken to the parapet, sending arrows down at the many targets pouring through the breach.

Duna didn't even gesture. There was a blast of noise and half of the top tier of the gatehouse disappeared, replaced with a ghastly grey flower of dust and sundered stone, which as it fell into the invaders crushed as least as many as the Zealot arrows had taken.

From below came the sounds of battle, a jumbled chorus of metal and shout and agony. Little could be seen beyond milling chaos, but there was seemingly no end to the torrent of men through the gap in the wall. The garrison here was supposed to only number a few hundred – victory was surely certain, a titanic and famous victory. But Inar was overcome by foreboding. Dread overcame him, affecting him physically, filling his belly with caustic bile, and making him weaken at the knees.

He had hardly noticed that Duna was no longer beside him. She had rushed down the rubble slope with jumps and kicks, like a small child playing with heaps of autumn leaves. Inar ran to keep up with her, almost falling more than once, and he marvelled at the speed she had made over the broken surface. When he reached the packed dirt of the fortress yard, he lost her again, ignored in the running fury of mercenaries and men-at-arms. The battle had been in progress for ten minutes at most and already the mood had shifted. The first fighters to come to the breach had been full of ferocity, but also the seriousness that came with harnessed fear and clear purpose. With later waves, these qualities had gone, and as the invaders scented victory, frenzy had taken hold. The mercenaries who ran past Inar now had an urgent, careless thirst about them, a desperation to taste combat before it was all over, to get their blades wet and have a story to tell.

A flying pennant of blonde hair showed itself in the rush,

and Inar jogged towards it. Bodies were scattered on the ground he covered, not many, some sickeningly lessened and painted by violence, others simply still and quiet, as if they had lain down to sleep. There were wounded, too, all of them Leaguers – no Zealots had been left to suffer. A hand clawed at his leg, and he did not turn to see what had befallen its owner.

The main battle was elsewhere. Duna had been drawn to a sideshow, a squat square tower that stood apart from the main body of the fortress. Archers had its roof, and were firing down at the League. A score of soldiers were trying to break in a heavy banded door at the tower's base, and more were pouring around it, trying to find another way in via a colonnaded building abutting it.

Duna had stopped some distance from this tower. "Get away from there!" she shouted to the League knights trying to break in the door, her voice filled with glee rather than warning. Only a couple of them heard her, and hesitated.

She gave them no further warning, and no time. The tower split open at the base with a dire cough of tortured matter, and all the balanced forces that had kept it standing for centuries flew to the winds. This time her work had been hasty and messy. The tower lurched, vomiting structural stone from the ragged wound in its side, its internal buttresses exploding. For a horrid moment Inar feared that she had made a mistake and killed them both, and they would be crushed by the avalanche she had unleashed. But having made a drunken slump onto one knee, the tower twisted and fell backwards onto the colonnade that abutted it. Debris pancaked outwards, and Inar screwed his eyes shut a fraction of a second late against another shower of razor-sharp splinters. The men who had been clustered around the tower had gone from sight in a maelstrom of destruction. Inar heard cries.

Duna squealed with delight at what she had done, and her childish, unthinking pleasure snapped Inar out of the trance of horror that had held him. He grabbed her by the shoulders and shook her, hard, once. That broke her out of her spell, too, and she stared at him abashed, dust-smeared face drained of colour. She was so slight, so much smaller than him, and seeing fear again in her eyes he at once felt ashamed to have put his hand on her.

"What are you doing?!" he demanded. "There were men there! Our men!"

"Not mine," Duna whispered. Then she batted his arm away, and strode off, heading towards the sounds of fighting.

When he tried to follow, he found that he was incapable. It was the sound. It had thickened and grown new tongues and they whispered in clashing metal and the screams of dying men – a memory. He was back at the fall of Stull, listening to the League's armies surging through another broken wall. How he had hated the League back then, little more than two years ago, and here he was helping their Scourge-adorned army into the fortress guarding the greatest treasure the world had to offer. What was he doing? Was he simply weak, and eager to serve?

So don't serve the League. Try to do the right thing for Duna. Even if she could kill a man with a glance, and level his city, she was vulnerable. Once she had been able to see this danger herself, but now she had lost sight of it, wrapped up in the berserker fury that had her, and he had to try to remind her of it. But what if that fury *was* her? What if that was revealed when her reserve and caution was stripped away?

The bailey that separated the Brink's outer wall from the palace itself was crossed by a wide avenue, which ran from the part-ruined gatehouse to the main ceremonial entrance. Parties of League soldiers were trying to storm the gatehouse from the rear, climbing the rubble-piles that were heaped against it and trying to force their way in. It was not clear if they were succeeding, but they were keeping the defenders there busy, and no more arrows were being fired from that position. Meanwhile the body of the army was assaulting the main entrance of the inner fortress. This was a vast set of bronze double doors, as tall as four men, at the top of a wide, shallow flight of steps. At least, Inar assumed there were steps from the white marble balustrades – the steps themselves were submerged under a heaving throng of men, a pushing mass of armour bristling with polearms. Unbelievably, one of the doors was open – not fully open, but half-way, and what looked like every armed man in the League was trying to push it wider, while defenders inside tried to stop them. It was a messy, ugly battle, and farcical in a grim and unfunny way – two armies concentrated in the tiniest space, the threshold of the door, two giants struggling for command of the head of a pin. Meanwhile, the surging throng behind the sharp point of the battle looked as if it might kill more men through asphyxiation and crushing than ever met a Zealot's spear. More defenders, positioned in the battlements and windows above the bailey, were loosing arrows down into this heaving scrum, where they could not fail to find targets.

Duna had stopped just short of the melee, yards away from where the pushing grew dangerous, in the lea of a stone pillar topped by the blackened metal cage of a beacon, one of several that lined the avenue between the gatehouse and the palace. She was still invisible to his inner eye, a deadly numb patch of nothingness where an unmissable banner of bone and magic should be standing, but as he approached her he felt his boon-talent flare as she channelled it, feeling her way around the Brink's gate, seeking the most spectacular way to bring it down.

"Please, don't," Inar said once he was at her side, as gently as he could while still being heard above the battle. She broke off her probing in the structure's foundations to listen to him, but her expression was impatient and unkind. "If you bring down too much, you'll kill more Leaguers than Zealots. There must be five hundred men there."

"Why should I care about that?" she snapped. "They want me to win their fucking war, I'll fight it how I please. Do you think Ernesto would hesitate if five hundred men stood between him and victory? Or Anzola?"

"They'll kill *you*," Inar said. He was pleading. "You have to see. You said this yourself. If they believe you're dangerous, they'll kill you."

She laughed, a bright parlour laugh completely out of place amid the chaos and carnage of their surroundings. "Inar, you really do need to listen – I cannot be harmed! Let them try to kill me. My life is without end. I am free now."

It was talk Inar had heard before. He stared at her and he faced the conclusion he had drawn earlier, the one suggested by her invisibility to his secret sense, but had desperately put aside, hoping besides everything that another explanation was possible. "You sound just like an Elf."

This reached her. She had veered between ecstasy and rage since the first moment of the assault, but now Inar saw a hint of doubt in her pallid, blood-streaked features. Then it was gone.

"I'm not frightened of them, either," she said. "Not any more. Look around you, Inar. People dying. Happens everywhere, every day. Please, let's just win this and end it."

Inar nodded. "The door jambs and hinges. We can bring down the doors without collapsing the whole front of the building."

"Very well," Duna said with a shrug. "But it would have been more fun my way."

Relieved, he reached out towards the doors with his hidden sense, but he was too slow. All he got was a flash, a fraction of a fraction of a second, more after-image and impression, and the doorframe was gone. The thought had been the act for Duna. The cyclopean blocks on either side of the bronze doors disintegrated like a pair of dropped crystal goblets. For a longer moment, which after the quickness of Duna's strike felt like an age, the immense doors teetered unsupported, battered by smashed masonry pouring onto them where their hinges had been mounted. Then they started to fall inwards, crashing down with a titanic succession of resounding metal booms that seemed to have sprung from the world's primordial past. Neither fell neatly; behind them were scores of Zealots and hurriedly erected props and barricades, and they toppled back onto those, the fortress killing its own defenders.

Once again they were caught in a flurry of billowing stone-dust. The League army had reeled back when the door-frame had been broken, as best it could against the pressure of soldiers pushing in from behind, but the whole host appeared to grasp that it had not cleared the way with its own efforts. There was an interlude of purest, ghastly chaos as League knights tumbled backwards down the steps and others were shoved over them, and the doors continued their clangorous descent to the ground. Duna giggled delightedly at this disarray and confusion, her disappointment at not tearing a larger hole in the Brink apparently forgotten. The League army did not surge forward, as Inar expected they might now that the way into the fortress was clear – evidently the vanguard was trying to understand what had happened, and was wary of a trap. No more arrows were loosed from above, either. A startled calm prevailed.

But before very long, the leading League knights climbed carefully and cautiously back up the last few steps, onto the shattered threshold of the Brink. They were met there by Zealot spearmen, shrieking battlecries and leaping over the fallen doors and the crushed bodies of their comrades. This bravado did not hide their desperation. For the first time, Inar saw actual combat – blade against blade, spear against armour, dirk against flesh. He was glad to be out of it.

"Last stand," Inar said, to himself as much as Duna. The Tzanate had magic, he thought, it had forbidden knowledge, it had magical defenders – where were they? Without meaning to, he looked up, but the sky was still thickly occluded.

Duna was not watching the fighting. Her attention was

fixed behind Inar, back towards the breach, the way they had come. She was frowning. Inar turned and saw what she saw – a magnificent company of knights, blue banners flapping, and a dozen horses, armoured battle-chargers. Anzola and Ernesto, arriving just in time to seize the Brink in the name of the League.

"My victory," Duna said, her voice a rage-filled whisper. "My victory! I'll not let them claim *my victory*!"

With that, she strode towards the Brink, and Inar had to follow.

The defenders at the doorway were overcome, and the League was forcing its way through. Still a great suffocating crowd pushed in towards the steps and the entrance, a bear trying to push into the neck of a bottle, and for a hopeful moment Inar expected that Duna would be forced to hang back. Men twice her size were struggling to elbow their way into the Brink and he did not expect her to do better. She reached the rear of the pack and was assessing the problem for herself when a footsoldier – an orange strip tied around his arm marked him as a mercenary – laid a hairy hand heavily on her shoulder. Inar, a couple of paces behind, did not think the act was aggressive, more concern for an unarmed, unhelmeted girl trying to push her way into the thick of battle. But Duna clearly took a different view and wheeled about. The man yowled in pain and snatched back his hand, clutching at it, tears jumping to his eyes.

Seeing this reaction, Duna smiled. Others had seen as well and shrank back, eyes more fixed on her than the battle raging yards away, gripping their swords and polearms with white knuckles. Consternation rippled through the line. They had all seen what had happened to the door, and to the outer wall. They had all heard the cries of *scourge*. And now the inchoate fears that those acts had birthed had a focus, a form.

A path melted open in front of Duna. Only the dead blocked her way, heaped up on the steps. She picked her way past them, finding exposed marble, once snowy white, now red with blood. Inar followed, feeling as if he was following the devastation left by a storm.

The dead had fallen in the greatest numbers around the broken doors. On the steps it had been just about possible to pick past them, but there they had to be climbed. This Duna did without pause, but Inar found it the slow work of a nightmare. They found themselves in the largest enclosed space Inar had ever seen – Stull and Sojonost had nothing to compare to it. It was a colossal colonnaded gallery, its vaulted roof higher above their heads than the chief tower of Stull's citadel, its floor a shining canal of swirling green marble. The columns that lined the hall sparkled like snow, and Inar recognised them as quartz. In the far distance, the gallery terminated in a black basalt wall, lifeless and dreadful against the opulence of the rest. So this was the Processional Way, spoken of by builders in awestruck whispers, the utmost achievement of their craft.

That awe seemed to have quieted the battle, too. League knights stood around, tense and wary, weapons drawn and many gored, but the fighting had stopped. Inar feared that they might have been transfixed by the same enchantment he had seen used at the Gull Gates, but they were not motionless or insensate, they had simply stopped fighting. Were there no more Zealots to fight? Or was it Duna – had the whole army realised, as one, the power of the magic that walked among them, and the form of the one who used it?

Sure enough, they watched her, and Inar, as they walked the hall, and they did not shrink back or try to stop them. But something else had caused them to cease. The last Zealots were dead, or had retreated, yes, but the Tzanate did have some magical resistance to offer against its invaders.

In the distance, close to the black basalt terminus of the hall, there skulked a small number of robed figures, surrounded by

clutter and paraphernalia. Between them and the foremost
League knights stood just four defenders, ones that did not
fear death as they had already experienced it. They were four
skeletal warriors, ungainly yet appalling, heads hanging at
grotesque angles and jaws swinging open, pale bones bound
together by brown thongs of tanned flesh, swords knotted to
their hands by the same method.

The Tzanate had revived the art of making bindlings.

38

ANTON

To lay hands on the Custodian seemed blasphemous, but it had to be done. Even so, they dared not move the sacred beast very far. Enric and Koralina fetched furs and blankets, and with those they made a rough bed on the flagstones behind the altar, hidden from the main door. All the while, Franj stared at the creature, dumbstruck with horror, although Anton could not tell whether it was the creature itself that had induced this, or the miserable condition in which they had found it. The Custodian itself said nothing more and moved little, though Anton hoped it knew it was among its servants and friends, and whatever extremity had driven it here had ended in a safe harbour.

Once the rough bed had been made behind the altar, the time had come to move the creature. Anton, Koralina and Enric arranged themselves around it, judging their positions as best they could in terms of how to handle the beast, with Franj too stricken to assist. But her assistance was not needed. Although the Custodian stood taller than a man, it weighed less than one – no bird is as heavy as it appears. With little exertion, they carried the curled form to the soft surface they had made and set it down. It rewarded them with a perceptible relaxation and straightening, and they laid a blanket and a fur over it. Anton suggested that a jug of water and some food be brought, although he did not know what a Custodian would want to eat, other than human carrion. For now, none of that was available. Raw meat, he suggested.

There was no more that could be done. But Anton could attend to nothing else. He sat on the dais that surrounded the altar, the great hunched form of the Custodian at his feet, and leaned on his knees. He was overcome by a familiar sensation of alone-ness and abandonment, and he was profoundly grateful when Franj bridled her shock and came to sit beside him.

Silence filled the shiel. The other Zealots had withdrawn, some to catch up on their rest, others to watch the closed and barred door to the temple. The square of the skylight at the apex of the pyramid, high above the altar, showed the dullest sign of dawn, but no light reached down into the building. Anton knew these foggy spring days, where the sun was never seen.

"You said that they never left the Hidden Land," Franj said at last.

Anton nodded. "That was what I was told. They needed to stay close to the Mountain. I don't think one has been seen outside the Elith-Tenh since the Scourge War."

Together they regarded the shrouded demigod, the same questions on their minds.

"It must have been driven by the greatest urgency," Anton said. "It said it was afraid."

"Afraid?" Franj asked, a desperate edge to her voice. "What could a Custodian possibly fear?"

"I don't know," Anton said. "But it must be related to the League's invasion."

"If *it* is afraid," Franj said, "What can *we* possibly do that it cannot?"

Rather than say again that he didn't know, Anton stayed quiet. But he shared her fear.

"Is it the one you spoke with before?" Franj asked.

"Yes," Anton said. "It knew me by name. I'm sure it is. Its name is Deacon Cutruk."

The Custodian shifted uneasily beneath its layer of furs. It emitted a low unconscious whimper, disturbingly like the mewl of an infant suffering a nightmare.

"I hate to see it weakened like this," Anton said, knowing that he spoke for them both. "They are gods. They should be powerful. How does one care for a sick god?"

As if in response, the Custodian woke, and the sight was terrible. It suddenly straightened out of the curled ball it had become, afflicted by an agonising rigidity. Its long beak, which had been tucked under one of its wings, was thrust straight upwards towards the patch of sky at the temple's summit, and it cried out, a shrill and wordless whistle of pain. Then it subsided, but not into repose, as it still kicked and thrashed.

Anton knelt at its side, as close as he dared, hoping that he might be able to comfort the beast, but nervously reminded of the awful strength he had felt on the Terrace of the Gift. A stray talon could easily open his neck. But a white eye gleamed steadily at him, and the fit quelled itself.

"Great One," Anton said, unequal to the task of reassuring a god. "You are safe. You are among faithful friends. We will bring you whatever you need."

"The girl," the Custodian croaked. "The scourge. She is not here."

Anton was momentarily on the wrong foot. Was this a statement, or a question? He had not seen the girl since the merite Anzola had left the fortress, but he had seen her little before then. She kept to herself.

"I... believe she is here," Anton said. "I told them that she was not to return."

"She is not here," the Custodian repeated. "I suspected. I thought they were heeding my warning but I could not be sure, for nothing else made sense. I could not search the whole land and my suspicions grew. And now I know."

"Perhaps she was sent back to her homeland," Anton said hopefully.

The creature's beak tilted sadly. "She is at the Brink. She is invisible to me, but… I know what she has done. The deed echoes within me. She has broken the Brink. It has fallen."

Franj gasped, the sound terminating in a stifled sob.

"When?" Anton asked.

"Now," the Custodian said. "It is happening now. While I am here."

It groaned, another unholy sound, itself very like a sob. "I saw that the girl's guardian, the League noble, had arrived at the Brink, but I could not see the girl. Where was she? I could not tell. I had to know. It is worse than I feared."

"The League has taken the Brink?" Franj asked, distraught, crying out for the creature to contradict what they had all just been told.

"She was invisible to me, Anton," the Custodian said with deadly focus, its eye a frozen star. "I could not sense her – even if I had seen her, I fear I would not have been able to stop her. Do you understand?"

The stone floor of the shiel seemed to tilt under Anton. Nausea rose in his throat. "They would not do that. No people who valued reason would do that. They told me she would not go into the Hidden Land."

"They lied to you, and worse."

This was no more than the truth, Anton realised, grappling with the sheer scale of the League's treachery – their betrayal of him personally, of the Tzanate and the faith, and their treachery against every living man and woman. There was only one way that Duna could have been concealed from the Custodian. She had been given Elfcap.

"I am supposed to be in alliance with them," Anton said. "Their use of scourges was hard to stomach – but if they are using Elf poison as well, then our alliance must end."

The Custodian closed its eye, an action it filled with aeons of sadness.

"You must tell us what to do," Anton said. He swallowed hard. "Not long ago, you offered to clear the path to the Brink for me. It was a price I was unwilling to pay. I now see the price of the path I chose instead – perhaps we should look again at that."

"That time has passed," the Custodian said, without opening its eye. "I am sorry. Your answer was the correct one, the one I needed to hear. Now it is too late."

Anton was bereft. He had no desire to make himself altzan-al by means of magical slaughter – he had little enough desire to be altzan-al at all. But he had also found a dark ember of reassurance in knowing that supernatural beings stood ready to commit mass-murder on his behalf.

It was too late.

The Custodian opened its eye again. "I am sorry. In fact, things are worse than they appear. And I am very tired."

After that, the Custodian slipped into semi-consciousness and spoke no further. They kept the shiel closed and locked. Fortunately there was no service that morning, and they would have no visitors. The thick mist had quieted the fortress like the Custodian's enchantment had stilled the garrison at the Gull Gates. Tomorrow they would have to think of a reason for its closure, and if what the deacon said was true, in four days or so word would come that the Brink had fallen to the League, and with it a host of new difficulties.

It was disturbing to know of a distant event as it was happening. When word spread in the usual way, events were only known of after they had occurred, as was only right. Hearing of a disaster as it took place a hundred miles away gave the false impression that Anton was somehow involved, that by action or inaction he could influence it in some way.

He could not, of course, so the instinct twitched and flailed hopelessly, spreading restlessness and despair in the soul.

Anton sat in the little study, pretending that he had everyday business to deal with, but only able to think about the Brink and the ailing demigod on the other side of the wall. Had Franj's porter been able to deliver the letters to Elecy? If there was fighting, he hoped that she was safe.

After a couple of hours, before middle meal, Anton abandoned the pretence of work and returned to the shiel to check on Franj, Koralina and the Custodian. He discovered the Custodian on its feet behind the altar, wrapped in the furs. His heart thrilled at this sign of health, but he disliked how geriatric the thing appeared as it scratched about. Franj and Koralina looked on, wide-eyed.

"Great One," Anton said. "I am glad to see you risen. Can we fetch you anything?"

"The deacon has refused all our offers," Koralina put in.

"I need nothing," the Custodian rasped, almost too quietly to be heard. "I will not be long."

"You must return to the Brink," Anton said with a nod.

The demigod raised its beak at the priest, and stared down it, eyes as pale as the ash in the grate on an icy winter morning. "No," it said. "No, I fear not."

Anton's mouth fell open. Behind him, Franj made a small sound of dismay, a swallowed gasp.

"I knew the end was near," the creature continued. "It was just a question of what I did with the time and effort that remained." It wheezed, a pained sound that nevertheless could have been expressing amusement. "That is the question that is before all of us, isn't it? I told you we had spent centuries trying to learn again how to die; now I am out of the Mountain's shadow, I see the trick to it. It is easier than I thought."

"What can we do?" Anton asked. "There must be something we can do."

The beast turned its fur-clad back on Anton and shuffled

away towards the rear of the shiel, talons scraping on the stone flags. There, it peered up at the banners Anton had hung, the largest of which was the crimson symbol of the Tzanate, a human heart superimposed on the outline of the Mountain.

"Are there others?" Anton asked, following the creature. "Could we summon others of your kind, to help you home?"

"I am the last," the Custodian said, keeping its back to the humans gathered nervously in the shiel.

Anton discovered that he had expected this answer, but he was dipped deeper into sorrow all the same.

"Then the Mountain is undefended," Anton said. "The greatest prize in existence, free for taking."

"Yes." The word hissed half in the ear and half in the heart. The beast turned to Anton, but it acknowledged Franj and Koralina as well, standing taller, stretching out its neck and for a moment returning to a form close to the glorious terror it had once embodied. It stretched out its wings, calling them to heed. Wordlessly, Franj sank to her knees, an act not of fear or abjection but frank reverence. Koralina followed with a hesitant sideways glance. Impressed at the rawness and honesty of the Zealot's awe towards the beast, Anton joined them.

Cutruk lowered its beak and closed its eyes, apparently abashed by the gesture. "You must rise from your knees," it said. "That is the message I have to deliver. We, the Custodians of God, are almost gone from the world. The race of men and women will inherit the Mountain."

Anton forced himself to speak. "We cannot be trusted with that power. We will not use it wisely. We will make a wreck of the world."

The Custodian raised the long feather at the tip of a wing. "Believing that – knowing that to be possible, even probable – is the first step to the necessary wisdom. We learned from Augardine that the users of magic become reliant on magic, and as the rest of your race starts to fear and despise them, their reliance increases, and turns to disaster. I fear that is the road chosen by Ving, and by the League. The temptation is very strong. But not irresistible. I have offered you that power, Anton: I offered to sweep away your enemies, and to make you a god. You refused me. You preferred to use human means. You would make a fine Custodian."

"I cannot imagine," Anton whispered, lowering his head.

"You must," the Custodian said, an edge of command in its faltering voice. "You must all rise up. There is no more time. The Mountain must be in the hands of the righteous, or it will fall to the Elves, and the world will fall. And there is worse than the Elves."

Its voice had risen to a whistling scream, awful not because it was strident, but because it betrayed vanishing strength, a last great effort made to transmit this vital information.

"Worse than the Elves?" Anton said, not comprehending.

"Ving says he knows how to defeat the Elves. I cannot see the secret. But I see the shape of his mind. He does not deal in creation and novelty. He returns to the ancient. Do you see? What defeated the Elves before?"

"Augardine," Anton said. The thought dawned without light. "Ving is a cultist."

The Custodian's ivory eye closed, exhausted. "They must be stopped. *You must all rise up.*"

39

INAR

The skeletons twitched and swayed, their heads gaping and lolling. But their weapons stayed straight, directed at Duna and Inar. Their bones did not have the desiccated quality of ancient remains – instead they were moist and dabbed with pink, closer to the butcher's shop than the crypt. Inar was aware of a line of League knights somewhat behind him, but no one had been as rash as to advance as far as Duna.

Inar slid his foot backwards. The polished marble floor was covered in a thin layer of stone dust, and it scratched under his sole. To have come through fog, through the chaos and horror of battle, and into this silent, grand place, to be confronted by the messengers of death – the sequence had the cadence of a dream, and he wished he would wake.

"My lady..." one of the knights behind Duna said at last, his tone cautious, dried to a croak, but he did not complete his warning.

One of the middle pair of the four bindlings took a lopsided step forward. Duna did not flinch, and regarded it with a curious tilt of her head. To Inar's stone-sense, the bindling looked like every skeleton did, though its joints – where the strips of cured and enchanted flesh bound it together – were oddly blurred. The skeleton's jaw flopped open but no sound emerged, with no flesh or breath to make it. It lifted its tied-on sword and lurched towards Duna.

She raised an eyebrow, as if at a presumptuous servant, and the dead thing's sword arm snapped clean through, just below the elbow. Carried by the weight of the sword, the sheared-off section of arm twisted over and clattered noisily to the ground.

The skeleton did seem not to notice the loss of its weapon and pressed on, closing the distance with Duna. She stepped to one side, easily dodging a blow that would have had little effect even if it had landed, and shattered both the creature's femurs in a flick of her talent. It collapsed, its upper portions skidding away on the shiny floor, carried by the forward momentum of its ungainly charge. This took them close to the feet of a knight, who flinched backwards. Duna sneered at him.

"It's *harmless*," she spat. "A conjurer's puppet!"

The ugly smile of scorn on her face withered away when she saw Anzola push her way through the line of knights. Splendid in shining half-armour, the merite's expression was hard to read – seriousness and worry, as might be expected in the dangerous circumstances, but Inar wondered if there was more to it than that. She met Duna's eye, that changed eye, and did not quail. A moment passed in watchful silence, until there was again the scrape of bone against marble.

"Duna!" Inar shouted.

The other bindlings had begun their attack while she was distracted. This time they advanced as one, swords raised, with a little more certainty than the first. Duna wheeled to face them, and the head of the nearest creature snapped neatly from its sloping shoulders. Then she turned her focus to the second, exploding its sword-arm in a puff of bone. But the headless first bindling had not stopped its advance. It raised its sword and brought it down.

Inar had moved. He thrust Timo's sword dangerously into the dwindling gap between the bindling's weapon and Duna, clumsily blocking the blow. Though the hazard had been knocked out of the attack, both blades still made contact with Duna, and she was bumped backwards. Inar regained his grasp on the heavy sword's hilt with both hands, raised it above his head, and brought it swinging down onto the headless monster. It made contact with nothing but splinters. Duna had burst every vertebrae the bindling possessed and smashed its pelvis like a snowball. With nothing to stop it, Inar's blow scythed down into the floor, sending a painful shock through his arms and shoulders and cracking the corner of a green marble slab.

One bindling was left, and it had tarried. Duna turned on it with bored annoyance. She popped each one of its ribs in rapid succession, and they fell to the floor with an obscene musical scale. This made her giggle as she took two brisk steps to the side, dodging the creature's lunge. For her next act she broke the moorings of the bindling's jaw, letting it clatter to the ground. Pacing backwards as it continued its increasingly pathetic advance towards her, she began to make the small bones its feet crack one by one like knots exploding in a fire. She was taking her time, measuring the exact moment the creature was disabled.

A shout of something had come from the small group huddled near the end of the great hall, and there were sounds from the League ranks as well, cries and oaths.

The bindling had lost too much of its feet to keep walking, and had fallen to its knees. Nevertheless, it strived to get close to the girl, crawling forward.

"Stop this," Anzola said, her voice loud and pained.

Duna glared at the merite, and every remaining bone in the bindling's body splintered at once, with the exception of the skull, which dropped near Duna's feet. She nimbly kicked it towards the merite.

"A trophy for you," she said. "To remember your victory."

Anzola gaped at Duna in horrified dismay. But the scourge was not watching. She had swung towards the priests who skulked at the far end of the hall. They cowered at her attention.

"Old magic," she said, addressing the altzans. "There were bindlings before Augardine, weren't there? Before scourges. People like me were made to destroy things like that."

"*Things* like you," shouted a high voice from the end of the hall.

The air itself seemed to hiss.

"Duna, *stop*," Anzola commanded. She was striding down the Processional Hall, far beyond her vanguard of knights, trying to reach the girl. Inar saw that Ernesto had arrived, and one of the mercenary captains, a man he had met long ago at the banquet at Sojonost.

"Yes, please stop," said another voice from the group of altzans, steadier, without fear or rancour. One of the priests stepped forward, a wizened ancient, with bags under his drooping, bloodshot eyes. The others around him stirred anxiously and one raised a hand, trying to stop him, but he brushed it away and quieted them with a glance.

"I am the altzan-al," the elderly priest said. "Please, let us put a stop to this. We are defeated, and it seems we have been deserted by our protectors. So be it. You have our surrender. All I ask is your audience – there is much of importance you do not know."

Now that he was closer to the basalt terminus of the Processional Way, Inar could see it in more detail. He knew what it was, the mausoleum of Augardine, but he had only read about it, never seen it. It was covered in Custodian runes, more intricate and elaborate than any he had seen in the past. But the patterns were interrupted. At ground level, several of the basalt slabs had been prised away, and were stacked neatly at one side. This removal exposed the solid masonry within the wall, which was scarred and pitted with tool-marks. The priests had been trying to break in. Ritual clutter was arrayed around the gap they had made, its purpose unclear. But the mausoleum was powerful. Inar's stone sense could not fully penetrate it. Once again, like the bindlings, it wasn't because whatever was within had been made invisible. It was because it was weaving its own magical effects, enchantments woven into the structure and rougher power coming from within, and they drowned the fine touch of his perception.

Duna did not pay any attention to this. "You're in charge?" she demanded of the priest.

"I am," the altzan-al said, with a respectful inclination of the head. "It is a genuine pleasure to meet you, young lady. You are a child of Augardine. We too are his disciples, for you see…"

He stopped his monologue with an unholy squawk of surprise, and his eyes bulged. Inar perceived what Duna did to the priest's skull only in the simultaneous instant that it happened, and it caused him to retch. And this time the change was clear to everyone else as well. The altzan-al's head burst apart like a fruit struck by a hammer, becoming first an awful pink cloud filled with dancing carnage, and then pattering to the ground as scarlet rain.

The priest, gone from the neck upwards, sank with grisly slowness to his knees, then fell forward. Inar almost fell too, and he emptied his stomach onto the marble, dizzy with disbelief. Screams and shouts of horror arose from the altzans and the League armies alike. Cries of anger, too, in Palla and Mirolingua: *Kill her. Kill the scourge.*

Duna turned slowly to face Anzola and the League armies. The murder of the altzan-al had misted her with blood and particles of gore, completing her transformation into a creature of nightmares.

"The war is over," she said. "Behold. I am the spirit of victory."

A communication passed in a glance between Ernesto and Anzola. The merite nodded, and motioned to the knights of her retinue. Six of them drew in to form a bodyguard around her, three on each side, at last overcoming the paralysis that had held them. Together they advanced towards Duna, not without trepidation, but without delay.

"The first man to come within ten yards gets his back broken," Duna said plainly. "Nice clean break. He'll live, as a cripple. He, or she."

Anzola raised her hand. The knights halted.

"You cannot break every bone in the world, Duna," the merite said. "It has to end."

"Who says I can't?" Duna replied, with a smile.

"Duna, please," Inar said. He had approached her as well, and had been closer than ten yards when he began. When he spoke, he was within arm's length. But he was able to approximate where her talent was focused, and it was very much on the knights, not his spine. And there was something else, too: she was visible. Not as clearly as she should be, but his stone-sense showed the faintest suggestion of a skeleton where she stood.

"They have to learn, Inar," she said, without facing him. "I've done what they wanted, but I won't be their slave. *They* have to do what *I* want."

"You can't oppose an army, Duna, not on your own."

She laughed, a brittle and tired laugh, and raised her arms. "Look around you!" she said, eyes sparkling glassily. "Look where we are! The heart of the world, and I put us here! I destroyed an army this morning, and there's the afternoon to come!"

A transformation was spreading across the League troops, unnoticed by Duna, but Inar knew it. Since the appearance of the bindlings, they had milled about, wary and uncertain. But now they were becoming an army again. Swords and polearms were being held more firmly, directed with more purpose. Ranks were forming up. He heard the quiet ripples of command and saw faces harden. How many knights, men-at-arms and footsoldiers were there in the hall already – a few hundred? And thousands more behind. A whisper of activity reached his ear. Men were stealing up along the colonnade on either side of them.

"Duna, you are not yourself," Inar said, dispensing with delicacy. For the moment, Anzola was doing nothing, letting him talk, but only for the purpose of buying time and dividing Duna's attention. "You've been given something – Elfcap, I think. It's what hid you from the Tzanate's magic, but it has made a berserker of you. None of this is you, none of it is your doing, not truly, but the work of the poison in you and the poisoners who gave it to you."

Duna faltered. "Elfcap?" she said, looking at Inar for the first time, her bloodshot eyes without bloodthirsty gleam, just tired and sad.

"I don't know," Inar said. "But you're not the Duna I know. The Duna I love."

Tears pooled in her eyes. She closed them and the falling drops cut streaks through the blood and grime that layered her face. "Is this true?" she demanded.

The question was not directed at Inar. Anzola stepped ahead of the knights that flanked her, her head held high but anguish in the expression. "It was for your protection," she said. "In your food. So you could be brought here safely. I only wanted to keep you safe."

Duna laughed bitterly. She seemed to have shrunk a little, to have diminished from the terrifying sorceress that had held the world in its talons just moments before, back to being a young woman. "For my protection," she said, acidly. "Yes. Everything is always for my protection."

"For pity's sake," came a loud, harsh voice from the League's lines. Ernesto strode forward, polished armour clanking, a plumed helmet under his arm. "Anzola, bring this pathetic display to an end, please, one way or another."

Inar flinched, expecting that the merite had spoken his last words, and fearing what kind of an example Duna might make of him. But she had hardly registered him.

"Yes," she said, thoughtful. "An end."

Stepping around the headless body of the altzan-al and the

red pool it had left on the charnel-littered marble, she paced towards the handful of priests at the far end of the Processional Way. They shrieked and cringed as she approached, and several fled through side arches. The remainder cowered before her, creeping back towards the shining columns flanking the hall.

"The Mausoleum of Augardine," she said. "Augardine's in here, yes?"

None of the altzans were capable of forming a spoken answer, but one managed a nod.

Ernesto emitted a grunt of annoyance and issued a command in Palla, raising his voice to cover Anzola's objection. Behind the columns on either side of the hall, swords were brandished.

"And he made the scourges, didn't he? He made my ancestors?"

The altzan who had recovered enough to nod nodded again. "It's sealed!" he bleated.

"Old, tired magic," Duna said, almost to herself, and Inar thought he was the only one who heard. She had reached the mausoleum, and she raised her arms and pressed her hands against the exposed inner masonry where the outer basalt slabs had been removed. Inar felt the change she made, marvelling at how restrained it was when he had half expected her to tear apart the whole black cube. Fissures radiated out through the stone from the points where her hands made contact, racing down to the ground and inwards and upwards and together, riddling the thick wall so thoroughly with weakness that it was crumbled into a rough gravel, which poured down like spilled grain, part burying Duna's feet. She kicked it out of the way. Before her was a tidy arched doorway, and she stepped through, even as the altzan shouted at her to stop.

"She mustn't!" the elderly altzan said thinly. "It's dangerous! The ground itself is poisoned!"

No one moved. An uncomfortable silence opened in the Brink. Nothing could be seen through the doorway, but Inar fancied that it was not wholly dark within the mausoleum chamber, and that a dim red luminescence could be detected.

"This has gone on far too long," Ernesto said, striding up the Processional Way with a bodyguard of knights. "Witchy madness. A whole army, afraid of a girl."

"You stop her, then," Anzola said as her fellow merite passed her.

"She was *your* responsibility, Anzola," Ernesto snapped. "If she was all banquet manners you'd be claiming credit right now, wouldn't you? Well, you have to take the bad with the good. But I will stop her."

He had drawn close to Inar, who was ten feet from the aperture in the tomb, trying to see within. Inar found – with a distant, odd sensation – that he was not entirely in control of his body. It was almost as if he was watching himself turn, step into the merite's path, and raise his sword.

"Don't be a fool, Inar," Ernesto said gruffly.

"Don't hurt her," Inar said.

Ernesto sighed. "She's a danger to us all, Inar," he said, taking another step towards the Mishigo. "Don't let her drag you into her death wish."

"She hasn't got a death wish," Inar said. "She thinks she's invulnerable – that's what Elfcap does. She thinks she'll live forever. She has forgotten danger."

A sound came from within the mausoleum – a resounding, echoing clang, the fall of something heavy and metal against a stone surface. Inar glanced back to see if Duna had reappeared, and Ernesto did not miss his opportunity. He struck Inar's wrist, hard, with the mailed fist that held the hilt of his sword. With a cry of pain, Inar dropped his own sword, which clattered onto the marble, and clutched at his wrist. Ernesto's elbow struck him in the face, just under the left eye, and Inar buckled. Then, Ernesto's right arm was around his neck, and he was being pulled upright, facing the tomb. He felt the point of a dagger under his jaw.

"If she kills me," Ernesto said to his bodyguard, "kill him first, then kill her."

There was a scrunch of stone chips. Duna stood in the rough archway that had been made into the mausoleum. She had picked up an ancient sword, a weapon blackened with age. Calmly taking in the scene in front of her – Ernesto with a blade to Inar's throat, Anzola behind them with an expression of terrible loss, and behind them an entire League army, just for her – she brushed dust from her armour with her free hand.

"Nothing," she said. "No dead god. Just old bones and burned-out magic."

And with that, she stalked away, leaving through one of the side-arches through which the priests had fled, moving with the confidence of someone who had lived her whole life in the Brink.

Ernesto released Inar and, with a push, sent him sprawling onto the marble floor. "Hold him," he barked to the two nearest knights, who helped Inar to his feet and kept a grip on an elbow each. "You others, get after her! Priests – what lies that way?"

Anzola had approached him. Her eyes were red with tiredness and strain. "It's not necessary," she said. "The Elfcap won't last. It'll wear off and she'll recover her senses. Or she'll come back for more."

"How could you?" Inar said, the words more a howl than a question. "After everything we endured! After everything she endured! How could you!"

Anzola's jaw tightened and her mouth became a thin line. "There's more at stake than individuals, Inar," she said. "I made a calculation. Duna lives – you live – we all live. I know that I've wronged her, and you, but I hope you'll come to forgive me."

"You're going to have a lot of forgiving to do, your grace," said a loud, familiar voice from the League lines. Solbey Neathe, captain of the Company of Caenon, was striding towards Anzola and Ernesto, and he did not look happy. "No one mentioned to me that the League would be using scourges. No one said anything about Elfcap."

"One scourge, captain," Anzola said, closing her eyes. "The Elfcap was just – just a ruse, a one-off."

"It always starts as a one-off, your grace," Solbey said gravely. "No one wants to be an Elf. Folk take it for strength, or for courage. Then they take it because they want more. And then they're cutting their ears off and massacring my wife, and my boys, and laughing as Caenon burns."

"I'll destroy what little I have," Anzola said. "That's the end of it."

"It's not the end of the scourge, though, is it?" Solbey said. "This is just the beginning of it, your graces, if you're not careful. My men have enough questions about being here as it is. Come sundown they will all have heard about what happened at the walls, and here." He glanced down at the headless body of the altzan-al. "Have you ever tried to stop an army talking? Can't be done."

Inar could see that he was telling the truth, and more. The great crowd of men in the Processional Way did not have the collective demeanour of conquerors. There was no chatter or singing, and nothing could be heard from the larger part of it, outside the fortress. Mistrustful eyes glared at the clutch containing the high commanders.

"We'll find her, Solbey," Ernesto said, with a cheerful pat of the mercenary captain's shoulder that Inar recognised at once as a political falsehood. "We'll find her and tuck her away. And there's a bonus payment coming your way, remember? We have the Brink. Your men don't have to linger here. Straight on to the next act. We've got to take the Gull Gates. Take their surrender, I expect, when we drag some of these priests there to explain things. And then it's on to Mal Nulalus. Teach those Elf bastards a lesson, eh?"

"Aye," Solbey said reluctantly. "Listen, I'm just telling you.

They won't like it. No scourges at the Gull Gates, all right? No magic."

Ernesto laid his hand on his heart. "No magic. I promise. We need that gate, don't we? Keep this place safe."

"Aye. 'Specially with a bloody big hole in the Brink." He nodded. "Right then. We'll move the auxiliaries to the Lake today, they can rest a night, and to the Gull pass tomorrow morning."

"Good man," Ernesto said bluffly. "Go and break the good news to your men, about their part in our victory here this morning, and their payment. We're on our way to Caenon."

"Aye," Solbey said, and without further pleasantries he left, taking the other mercenary captains with him. Ernesto watched him filter into the League lines, the bonhomie gone from his expression.

"We do have to find her, Anzola," he said once the captain was gone. "The fortress has to be secured. It's huge, and there may yet be Zealots who haven't accepted their defeat. I'll not have her running around causing trouble as well. What if Solbey and his men come across her?"

"We'll find her, then," Anzola said.

"How, though?" Ernesto asked.

She didn't answer, but she looked, and the look contained the answer. Ernesto followed her gaze, and also looked at what she was looking at. It was Inar.

40

ANTON

"We must tell Melecin," Franj said. "Whatever we decide to say to the others, she deserves to know the truth."

Anton bit his lip. "I am fearful of the effect this might have," he said. "A dying Custodian – it is worse than an ill omen. The garrison is so tense."

They stood in the quiet of the shiel, considering the question. It was dawn two days after the Custodian's arrival, and soon the faithful would come, expecting to praise the Mountain in the small temple, little knowing that it hosted the last representative of the defenders of their God. Two braziers had been lit, and some grey illumination fell through the skylight onto the altar, but it was almost as dark as night. The fog had not lifted, and Anton knew it might not lift for days. In fact he prayed it would not, so that communications through the Pilgrims' Pass would be slowed and word of the fall of the Brink might be delayed. He did not like the thought of being at Sojonost when that news came – the jubilation it would cause for some, the despair for others.

"You're a natural priest," Franj said with a sly smile. She had spent all day yesterday with the Custodian, but had been persuaded to rest after the evening meal, and was better for it. "Always keep the mysteries, eh? Smoke and curtain."

Anton frowned at this – not because it displeased him,

but because the gentle mockery reminded him so strongly of Elecy. He and Franj sat together on the dais of the altar, facing the curled form of the Custodian. Only the beast's great beak showed, cracked slightly open. It lived – the continuing presence of its life filled the temple like incense – but it had not stirred since the previous morning. "Think of it as a military problem, then," Anton said. "The death of a commander, or a monarch, during a campaign. That could break the fighting spirit of an army. So it might be with the faithful, especially as we know that news will soon come from the Brink."

"Melecin can be trusted not to make rumours," Franj said. "She's been running a secret religious order for more than a year. Besides, the creature's presence here shows that we have the endorsement of the Mountain's keepers. It is miraculous. Nothing is more certain to cement her faith, I am sure, and she will pass on that fervour to her flock."

"Very well, then," Anton said. He had learned to recognise when an argument with Franj had been lost. "We will admit her. But we cannot hold our usual service. We were able to cancel the last gathering without suspicion, but another? We must think of a reason to close the shiel, temporarily. I won't make a spectacle of the creature, and the League must not know of its presence."

Franj lowered her head. She did not have a ready answer to that. Neither did Anton. Having argued hard with the marshal and the castellan to open the shiel, it seemed back-to-front to be searching for reasons to close it. As that thought occurred, so did another.

"We could say that the marshal ordered it closed," Anton said.

A mischievous smile played across Franj's face. "Why, Anton, that's almost *devious*. I wasn't sure you had it in you. Blame the heathens! It's perfect."

"It's far from perfect," Anton said, suddenly alarmed at the success of his own idea. "Besides being dishonest, it's deliberately stirring up ill-feeling between the faithful and the League. It could cause a lot of trouble for us."

"You're too afraid of trouble," Franj said with a shake of her head. "The people need some blood running to their faith. See the world, Anton. Armies clash, citadels fall, Elves rampage, old magic walks again. Gods die. The faith needs a leader who thinks of more than inkpots and meetings."

"Then perhaps it does not need me," Anton said quietly. "I have spent my whole life running from blood. And what has been gained? I have undone the Tzanate. It is destroyed. I would have done better dead."

Franj glanced across at him, then unwrapped a hand from the furs that swaddled her and laid it on his shoulder. "No, no," she said softly.

"We helped the scourge out of the Hidden Land," Anton continued. "She made it to Sojonost, and then she was able to attack the Brink. Without us they might have been stopped."

"And what if they had been stopped?" Franj asked. "Maybe the Gull Gates would be in ruins now, and then where would we be?"

Anton shrugged. "If I wasn't *here*, the Custodian would have stayed at the Brink, and she might have been stopped there."

"It said itself that it could not see her," Franj said. "If she was full of Elfcap, then the Custodian would have been powerless."

"Not powerless," Anton said. "It could have opened a rift under her, or affected the League army somehow, or used any kind of forgotten magic."

"The time and place to stop her was at the Gull Gates," Franj said. "And it let her go."

"It said that she might prove to be useful," Anton said.

"There you have it," Franj said, raising her hand from Anton's shoulder in a decisive gesture. "We all make mistakes. Even gods."

Anton smiled at this, and placed his hand on her shoulder, returning the comfort she had given him. "Thank you Franj," he said. "I don't know what I would do without your counsel."

"All I do is ask myself 'what would Elecy do', and I do that," Franj said, with a shrug.

"What would she do here, do you think?" Anton said, making an effort to straighten his back. "Faced with this?" He inclined his head towards the stricken demigod.

A moment of silent consideration passed. Then Franj rose, wordlessly, and approached the custodian. She took her dagger from her belt, and for a terrible, baffling instant, Anton feared she was going to attack the great beast. But instead she held out her left hand and, without giving herself time to doubt, drew the dagger's blade across her palm. With a suppressed gasp of pain, she closed the slashed hand and kneeled beside the Custodian, letting the dark trickle of blood fall into its beak.

The horsemen arrived after dark the following day, thundering from the fog-bound pass. The persistence of the fog had started to trouble even Anton and Franj and Koralina and the others who had knowledge of the mountains and the Hidden Land. It continued to squat in the valleys, unchanging, waiting. It was as if the elements themselves were trying to hide what was taking place in the holy country.

The riders did not stop at the camp around the fortress's base, but instead rode hard up the long ramp that led to Sojonost's gate, shouting all the while: "Victory! Victory!" This commotion roused both the camp and the garrison, who had been waiting on edge for news. Every League soldier and mercenary rose as one and followed the horsemen up to the fortress, just as the cries of triumph brought down the guards and workers inside the citadel itself. The messengers had not chosen their moment, instead travelling as fast as they could to arrive as early as possible – but they could not have chosen better. The evening meal had not long finished, Sojonost's residents were mostly free from duties, and had had their measure of wine and beer.

Anton was alerted by Enric, who had heard the shouting from the main courtyard, and seen servants and soldiers running. At first he had no desire to go and hear of the capture of his former home and the abasement of his religion before the League. Then he realised that it was a momentous hour and it was best to be there and to be seen, rather than to skulk in his lodgings.

The Zealots came with him. However, they found it difficult even to get into the courtyard. It was not a large space, and it was so thickly thronged with people that they backed up into the passage that connected it to the shiel-court. But workers and mercenaries outnumbered Leaguers two to one, and when the former saw the priest and his comrades, they allowed them through.

"... the mightiest castle in all the world, and its walls tumbled in a single day!" a herald among the horsemen was saying. The messengers had stayed on horseback, to keep above the throng that pushed around them, and their steaming horses pressed together uneasily in a tiny circle. "Truly there is no place that the League's armies cannot go, and no force that can withstand them! The very heart of the world now beats under the waterfalls of our free and peaceful union! Terrible bindlings, ghoul warriors foully stolen from the grave, had been raised up to oppose our legions by the depraved necromancers who have usurped the sacred places, but they were nothing before the might of our reason and justice!"

"Bindlings," Franj muttered. "Can it be so?"

"Ving had threatened as much," Anton replied. He looked around at the crowd, trying to judge its mood. The League soldiers were enthused and ready to celebrate, cheering along to the herald's words, rocking together in song and laughter, sending belligerent eddies of movement through the crowd. Many of the mercenaries joined them – victory meant pay, safety and rest, so Anton couldn't blame them. The workers were less visibly delighted. Many stared at him, and at Franj, and whispered. Yesterday's closure of the shiel, "by order of the marshal", had been the cause of a good deal of resentment among the faithful, but had not yet prompted any reaction from the authorities. Anton kept his back straight and his chin up, trying to appear serious, even grim.

"Today a holy place is cleansed of evil!" the herald was shouting, struggling to make himself heard. "The cabal of necromancers who had usurped the Mountain from the faithful have been deposed! Their leader, the pretender who called himself altzan-al, is dead, struck down in battle by one of our own soldiers!"

The crowd bayed, a sound that alloyed approval and shock, depending on who was shouting.

"Ving dead," Anton muttered, his throat tight.

"You'll be King Bird, then," roared an unkind voice from his side. In the heaving of the crowd, Anton had not noticed the marshal approach, accompanied by a small band of soldiers who seemed to be cronies rather than a retinue. "On a short leash, of course. I'm just glad you'll be out of my fucking castle."

He lurched to one side and wiped some spittle from his mouth. If he had started drinking in celebration of the League's victory, he had achieved prodigious results in a few minutes. It occurred to Anton that he never usually saw the marshal in the evenings. The clutch of red-faced men-at-arms around him all had flagons of wine, and ugly expressions filled with the cruelty of triumph.

"I will be sad to leave," Anton said. "You've been a gracious host."

"And what do we get for our hospitality?" the marshal slurred, lurching closer to Anton. "Slander and sedition, that's what. We should have kept your fane closed, if you were just going to try to shame us about it."

"That's close enough," Franj said, her right hand at the hilt of her dagger, the bandaged left resting on its sheath.

"Dogs," the marshal said, waving his pitcher of wine unevenly at the Zealots. "Dogs and bitches, yapping about blood and magic." With this, he leered especially at Franj, eyes on her bloody bandages, and she recoiled in disgust. "Don't know why we need you – Don't need you, it seems. We've conquered your shithole, we should have it for ourselves."

Too afraid of trouble, Anton thought. He took a step towards the marshal and leaned into his face, close enough to smell the wine fumes. The marshal was a stocky man and bulked out by armour, but Anton had several inches of height over him. When he spoke, he did not raise his voice, but he spoke clearly, clearly enough to be heard by the halo of people around them who had fallen silent at the sight of their confrontation. "Augardine thought he was a god, and his army perished in the Hidden Land. Are you a god, little man?"

The marshal went a peculiar colour, not far different to red wine. His mouth mashed and twisted, forming up a furious reply.

Anton leaned back, and before the marshal could fart out his rejoinder, he raised his hand, palm out, as if he was a sorcerer about to deliver a fireball. The marshal shied back, not a huge movement but a noticeable one, and almost choked on his tongue. His thunderous complexion darkened yet further, while Anton kept his own expression carefully neutral, and his hand raised.

The men-at-arms around the marshal tensed. One flung aside his near-empty wine flask and bared half of the dirk he had sheathed at his belt. They hesitated, taking their lead from the marshal, who was obviously trying to bend his fogged brain around the question of whether Anton actually possessed any supernatural powers, or whether it was all a bluff. This deliberation went on far longer than it should have and Anton almost pitied the man, left flapping and robbed of bellicose momentum. Then one of his confederates intervened, one who had not shown a blade, gripping the marshal's arm above the elbow, and drawing his attention to the nimbus of silent, watching faces around the confrontation.

Anton lowered his arm. He was aware how quiet and volatile the mood in the courtyard had become, thanks in part to his own actions, and that it could be tipped into real bloodshed with very little effort.

"Trickery," the marshal muttered. Then, without warning, his battered pride flared back. He shook off the restraining hand of his crony and pulled his dirk all the way from its scabbard. "I'll not have it! In my own fortress! I've stood it long enough! I'll not be made a fool! I–"

Whatever he meant to say next, no one ever learned. A bristling night-black shroud fell in a silent movement from the roof above the shiel-court arch. It landed behind the marshal with a rasp of sharpness against stone, separating him from his companions. The scent of an opened tomb filled the air, and a terrible charge of supernatural power.

Robbed of the ability to make any sound beyond a croak, the marshal started to turn to see what had landed behind him, although from the look of terror on his face, he already knew. He got to see nothing more than a flash of talons.

The Custodian's blow passed through stout body and bulky armour as if it was the sweetest, softest League pudding. It struck at the right shoulder and exited the body at the left hip, making two heavy pieces of the marshal. Sliding awfully together, these halves fell in a cascade of gore.

All around was a cathedral of silent horror. Basking in the gaze of hundreds of terrified eyes, the beast stepped forward, pinning the remains of the marshal to the ground, and thrust into the Leaguer's chest with its beak. With a practised twist of its head, and a cracking of ribs, it emerged with a bloody morsel held delicately at the apex of that killing instrument, which it raised aloft, as if showing the marshal's heart to the crowd before swallowing it.

And then, with a mighty beat of its wings, the creature lifted up, rising out of the courtyard, completing a long lazy circuit above the aghast horde beneath, and powering away, above the fortress, out towards the mountain ridge.

"We must follow," Anton said urgently.

"Follow?" Franj said, exultant. "It's going to the Brink!"

"No," Anton replied. "No, it isn't."

The air was chill, with a tang of moisture – this room had been carved into the mountainside itself. An ancient black door set into an ornate archway led outside, to a narrow defile and a rising flight of steps. Bodies were meant to be borne this way, from the hall out to the union with heaven, but the black steps, many carved into the living rock, were worn glassy smooth by time and were slick with damp from the engulfing mist. Once they had reached the ridge, the ziggurat form of the akouy shiel was hidden in the fogbound dark until they were at its entrance. A spectral silence held the mountains in its grasp. Passage to the upper platform of the tower was made easier, at least, by a flight of steps around its central column, thrown into dancing shadows by their torches.

The Custodian was waiting. It hung in the air above the shiel's upper platform, beating its wings slowly to stay aloft: sinking and then rising with each heavy, effortful beat, like the rhythm of a slowing heart. They emerged from the steps behind it, and it did not acknowledge them, but Anton knew it knew that they were there. For long moments, nothing happened other than the steady tempo of those wings, and Anton wondered if the creature's strength really had returned, as despite the clinging gloom of the fog, it seemed bathed in lambent light. But the light was not coming from the Custodian – it came from the stars. As the ancient demigod beat its wings, the mist parted, receding in every direction, revealing the still and frozen night sky above and the band of heaven. Above the shiel, above the Hidden Land, rose the moon, and all five of its maids could be seen, rainbow hints in their glistening whiteness. It was the moon that the Custodian faced, its head raised, and Anton fancied its eyes were closed, as it bathed in the revealed light.

Then it fell. It did so lightly and silently, but it did not land, it fell. Meeting the stone surface of the akouy shiel platform, it crumpled sideways, curling into a ball, all the light gone from it.

For further long minutes, neither Anton nor Franj moved, held in awe by what they had seen. There was no urgency. It was as if a great and joyous music that they had heard without knowing since the creature's arrival had suddenly ceased, leaving them in silence. The Custodian was dead.

Anton did not know how much time had passed. He had slipped into a trance, or perhaps simply dozed. After the death of the Custodian, Franj had returned to their quarters and fetched furs and a sheet to lay over the creature's body. Then they had sat together on a folded blanket, pressed together for warmth, near-buried under furs of their own, to keep vigil. Neither wanted to venture back to the fortress. The courtyard had been cleared by League knights after the slaying of the marshal, without violence, but violence stayed in the air like the flammable vapours that rose from marshland, waiting for a spark. Few slept below – men talked quietly, drew lines of loyalty, and kept weapons close. Anton half-expected arrest, or worse, but it did not come. That would be a spark. None of the other Zealots joined them, though they would have been welcome. They guarded their temple and quarters, and tried to rest.

What had woken him? Anton did not know. He did not

know what he was waiting for. No other creatures had yet come to investigate the Custodian's remains. They likely would not do so until the humans had departed. Was the remnant of the divine beast even subject to the corruption that came to other dead things? Would the scavengers that feasted here be transformed by its flesh?

The fog had returned with haste after the Custodian had fallen, and the torch they had left lit had burned out. Barely any light filtered through from the full moon above. But Anton knew that something had changed. He shifted, shocked at the stiffness of his limbs, and groped for another torch and the bundle containing tapers and flint. His movements woke Franj.

"What is it?" she asked.

"Something has happened to the Custodian," Anton said. A breathless bubble of hope was held within him. So many religions had tales of resurrection at their heart, why shouldn't the Mountain faith? Franj seemed to pick up on this hope, and helped him with the torch. Once it was lit, they approached the spot where the great beast had lain.

A bird – a mountain vulture – wheeled into the sphere of torchlight, and out again. Then a second. Crows, too, and others, gathering above them, not alighting, but circling, watching. It was night-time. This was not normal behaviour.

The Custodian was gone. It had not succumbed to corruption – or if it had, it had done so with remarkable completeness in a very short time. There was no carcass, no bundle of bare bones to take to the ossuary. In the middle of the circular space was a tangle of death-scented shrouds, and nothing else.

"I had hoped for more," Anton said.

Franj gave him a sympathetic smile, but said nothing. They approached the empty spot.

"I knew it was dead," Anton said, "but the sight of its remains... I don't know."

"It's not as if you need proof of their favour," Franj said.

"You have the mark. It struck down your enemy in front of the whole fortress." She nodded towards the twisted sheet on the flagstones. "The shroud should be preserved, at least. The last thing touched by a god. It is a relic now."

Anton nodded, and Franj bent to gather up the sheet. He watched a moment, and then turned his attention to the swooping vortex of birds above them, plunging in and out of the fog. *They were here first*, Ramnie had said. That was how they became gods. They were not found to be especially noble or deserving – they were simply there first. So what was he waiting for?

He lowered his head. "I think I understand it now," he said. "All this time, I have been worrying about what gave me the right to lead. I wanted a sign to convince me. And it doesn't matter. Any man could do it, because it is an act, not a state, and what matters is to act righteously."

Franj wasn't listening. She had paused in her gathering of the sheet and was rummaging about in it, trying to fix a snag. And then she drew out her hand, revealing what had caught in the linen folds: a charcoal-grey feather as long as her forearm, gently curved, its thick barbs slightly ruffled, but alive with a strange Mountain iridescence.

"By the Mountain," Anton exclaimed. There was no disputing that the feather had come from the Custodian, miraculously left behind by whatever unseen process had spirited away the rest. Only an object touched by the Mountain's power could carry in it those strange, hypnotic glistens.

"You desired a sign," Franj said, holding out the feather towards him. "And here it is."

Anton was amazed to find that hot tears were running down his cheeks. The deacon had not been a kind or loving creature, and had hardly even been helpful or wise, really. But Anton had recognised in it the deep weariness that came with unrequested power, and he detected how sad and reluctant it had been to pass on that burden to as erratic a creature as man. It had understood, and he had felt at last that he might understand it. And he missed it.

"Perhaps it has powers," Fran said, studying the feather in wonder.

"We must not rely on magic," Anton said. "The Custodian warned me about its lure, and it has been right all along. The possession of the scourge has brought out all the League's recklessness, and made it thirsty for conquest where once it was cautious. Ramnie wanted the scourge on our side, and that desire steered his dealings with the League. Ving didn't even know about it, but he knew there was secret power somewhere and he knew he wanted it. He thought that bindlings could stand in place of soldiers and allies, and the Custodian said he intended worse. All of them placed their faith in magic first and people second. Even the Custodian, who we imagine to be above temptation and error, thought the scourge might be used to our advantage. And I believed it. I let myself believe it."

"The scourge helped us escape from Mal Nulalus," Franj said.

"An accidental product of her own escape," Anton countered. "An escape that had terrible consequences for the Tzanate. But I believed she could help us, all the same. What does a ruin-scourge do but shake the world? And that is what the Custodian said the last blade-priest would do. 'The last blade-priest will shake the world'. I thought that might mean the scourge would end up aiding me – not smashing the Brink."

Franj was frowning. "'The last blade-priest will shake the world'. You said that before."

"Yes," Anton said. "That was what the Custodian told me, that I would shake the world."

"But you renounced the blade," Franj said. "You are no longer a blade-priest – you are altzan-al, not vertzan, but I think you stopped being vertzan long before you became altzan-al."

Anton stared at her. He could not answer. The air had frozen into a block in his throat. How could he have been so vain, and so wrong?

"You ceased to be a blade-priest, and there is another," Franj said, even though he had already reached the conclusion she was pushing him towards. "You are *not* the last blade-priest."

"Elecy. Elecy is the last blade-priest."

Franj stared at him, eyes wide, amazed that he only now understood. "Men think they're the hero in every story. *Elecy* will shake the world."

41

INAR

A scream rang across the polished marble and the line went slack. Inar's stomach lurched. Above him, a bronze representation of the slain Emperor Augardine wobbled and tipped, as if leaning in for a kiss, and for the length of a missed heartbeat Inar fancied it would fall and crush him. Many thousands had been killed by that Emperor in life, but it would be unlucky indeed to be killed by him hundreds of years after his death. Then the other lines snapped tight. Some men were pulled from their feet, but others held firm with a chorus of grunts and curses. The immense door ceased its lurch to one side and righted itself.

"Not another one?" Inar shouted, rushing to the scream's origin as the soldiers around him ran about, trying to keep the door upright. A League man-at-arms, one of the work team moving the door, had fallen to the green marble slabs, and was pitching and raving, his back horribly arched. Spittle foamed at the corners of his mouth. Men stood around him in a loose circle, uncertain of what to do.

"Another one," Kielo agreed, with a frown. "You there – get him out of the way. Make sure he doesn't bite his tongue off. He can join the others."

"Flesh! Flesh for the feast of the reborn god!" the man ranted. "Laughing faces on the still water!"

Two of the soldiers dragged the man away from the work site, a job made easier by the polished floor. The man's ramblings receded from the hall. Kielo looked around at the others in the company charged with moving the giant door. "All the more reason to get this job finished," he said, loudly. "Come on – it's not as if we can sleep with it half done, is it? We all want it done."

Fatigue was written into every man's face, but none grumbled. They resumed positions and took up lines, and resumed the long and arduous work of heaving the door down the Processional Way. At least there had been no shortage of volunteers. Within hours of the League's victory at the Brink, a wave of Wakemares, seizures and visions had torn through the conquering army. Even the surviving altzans said they had never seen so many in such a short time. The men charged with clearing debris and dead bodies from the Processional Way had been worst afflicted, and their already grisly work had turned into a macabre farce as soldier after soldier was overcome and collapsed into delirium. A night of terrors had passed – it was said that not a man in the whole host slept without being visited by terror. All through the next day, and the next, an unrested army struggled with its tasks while the nightmares were succeeded by wakemares. The unshakeable conviction among the League soldiery was that this fever of the spirit was the result of Duna breaking into the Mausoleum of Augardine.

Ernesto and Anzola had put the matter to their captured priests with threatening urgency, and were rewarded with puzzlement and fear. The priests simply did not know, but they admitted that it was possible. In the absence of other solutions, Ernesto ordered that Anzola, Kielo and Inar halt the hunt for Duna and seal up the tomb. They decided to use one of the giant bronze doors that Duna had torn from its hinges as a temporary barrier, laid on its side and propped with mighty timbers taken from the wreckage of the tower that Duna had demolished.

Between hunting for the missing girl, and repairing the damage she had done, the name of Duna hung over the army. A great shudder of fear and superstition had passed through its ranks. Everywhere her name was muttered, and less kind terms for her, and Inar felt hard eyes on him as well. So, when a messenger came and informed him that the merites desired his presence, his annoyance at being torn from a building job was tempered with relief.

"Why is the tomb not sealed?" Ernesto demanded. "It was ordered a day ago. Why is it not done?"

He spoke deliberately and slowly, without raising his voice, but he didn't need to rave and scream for his anger to fill the room. On another day, in another life, Inar might have quailed; he might have been terrified. He was not. His own anger smouldered within him.

"The men – your men – are tired and afraid," Inar said. "The door is solid bronze, weighing many tons, and has to be carried more than two hundred yards. Only Augardine knows how it was mounted when this place was built."

"Fascinating," Ernesto hissed, with a cruel twist of the lip. The high commander of the armies of the League of Free Cities had commandeered the altzan-al's personal office as his own. It had windows that looked out on the Mountain itself, but after just a few hours in a room with that view, Ernesto had ordered that a League banner be hung behind his desk, blocking out the prospect and most of the natural illumination. Even during the day his conferences had taken place by candlelight, and now it was past midnight. "Kielo can handle the rest, I'm sure. I want you back hunting for the girl."

Inar narrowed his eyes. "In the morning, yes."

"Now!" Ernesto said, with a chop of his hand. "I don't want the search to so much as pause until she's found, night or no night."

Inar said nothing – he felt no need to justify himself – and so Anzola spoke in his stead. "This fortress is a labyrinth, Ernesto," she said, impatiently. "It's more like a city than a citadel, and Inar says there's more underground than above."

"But I thought that didn't matter!" Ernesto insisted. "Thanks to our friend here, and his ability to see through walls!"

That's not how it works, Inar thought, but he recognised that the merite wasn't trying to be fair, he was trying to wound. He found the strength to be patient. "There is much about this place that I do not understand," he said. "There are enchantments woven into its structure, and exotic materials, and I don't know what else." Even trying to perceive the structure as a whole was almost impossible, and the distortions it created gave him a low but nasty headache. So much for the surge of potency accorded by the Mountain – it had cancelled itself out with juddering side-effects. He was little more use than an averagely sighted man or woman.

This explanation did nothing to appease Ernesto, but had the effect of shifting the focus of his rage. He turned to Anzola. "She'll come back, you said. The mushroom will wear off, and she'll come back."

Anzola paused. "So I misjudged," she said, without any suggestion of apology. "It may yet be true. Elfcap's effects are short-lived, and when they fade, a great sickness and craving takes hold. She must be experiencing that by now. It will drive her back to us."

Inar glared at Anzola, and so did Ernesto. Then he rubbed his eyes. Even in the half-light of the altzan-al's office, the dark circles were clear. Little had been done to make these rooms more homely. It had been found in disarray, heaped with evidence of frantic work and sleepless nights, and those books and papers had simply been swept off the desks and left in piles at the edges of the room. The merite was sleeping nearby, Inar knew, on a cot in a side room – if he was sleeping at all. Who could sleep, knowing that he might wake to find his guards dead and a Scourge standing over him? This thought, at least, gave Inar cause to smile a caustic little smile.

"Is it possible that she is no longer in the fortress?" Ernesto asked, almost hopefully. "She made quite a gap in the outer wall, and the guards may have missed her, especially in this damned fog. And there may be other ways out."

"If she keeps to the road, she'll be seen by our men," Anzola said. "Cross country, it's days to the passes, with no food, no knowledge of the land, in the fog – a death sentence. I'm sure she wouldn't risk it, not alone."

"Alone," Inar said. "Desperate. Betrayed by people she trusted. You might have left her no choice."

Anzola did not meet his eyes. "She would still be stopped at the passes–"

This was interrupted by an ear-splitting bang, the sound of Ernesto's fist hammering the desk in front of him with bruising force. "*We* should be at the passes, Anzola! We should be out of this mud-damned place! Only three days here and the whole army has gone to rot! That is why the girl must be found! We have to garrison the Brink and move on! I have had no word from the auxiliary forces we sent to the Gull Gates, we haven't even had a resupply caravan from the lake!"

"The fog is..." Anzola began.

"The fog is *not a sufficient excuse*," Ernesto said across her. "The men are uncomfortable enough as it is. If they start to miss meals, we could face mutiny. I need you back at Hleng, coordinating supplies. What if the Elves get to the Gull Gates before us?"

"The Gates are impenetrable," Anzola said. Inar saw the flicker of uncertainty that accompanied those words, the memory of how easily they had passed that obstacle. She pushed on, to avoid questions. "So we'll find Duna. It has to be me, doesn't it? Your men won't go near her! And I don't want them near her, anyway. They've invented her into some kind of monster."

Ernesto raised his eyebrows. "*They* didn't invent her, Anzola," he said. His tone had eased. Perhaps his fist was hurting. "This enterprise of ours is still a success, for now. But if we tarry, our triumph will slip away. We have a responsibility to our men, and to the whole League, to press on."

"Leave me behind, then," Anzola said with a pained sigh. "Surely you don't want a scourge running wild in your rearguard? You don't want to risk her turning to our enemies? Leave me."

"I need you, Zo," Ernesto said, without much in the way of kindness, but even Inar was able to recognise a deliberate show of vulnerability. "We are embarking on war with the Elves. Our victory here was swift – the next war will be more arduous. We have always achieved the most when we work together."

To Inar's surprise, this plea reached Anzola in full force. She visibly softened, and Inar was reminded, as a child might be, that the two people in front of him had a relationship that long predated his acquaintance, and which contained many secrets and hidden mechanisms.

"Give me tonight," she said. "Tomorrow we can make plans."

Ernesto regarded her, motionless, for a lengthy moment, and then nodded once. "Very well. It's late already, later than you think."

"I was surprised you gave yourself so little time," Inar said, after they had left the study behind. "He's right, it's late already, and we won't achieve much at night."

"Sometimes a negotiation is more about saving face than achieving anything," Anzola said wearily. "I know Ernesto – he'll be picking up and leaving as soon as he can anyway, with me or without. He didn't have to ask me along. And he's right, the longer we delay, the greater the risk of the war slipping away from us."

"Do you really think we can find her before tomorrow morning?" Inar asked.

Anzola tightened her jaw. "No, to be honest, unless she wants to be found. And I think we both know that she does not want to be found."

They walked in silence through the grand sequence of rooms that connected the altzan-al's office with the processional hall – high-ceilinged spaces shining with marble and gilt, but none of the lamps and braziers had been lit, and even at the height of the day, all was sunk in gloom.

"I truly am sorry for what I did to Duna," Anzola said quietly. "I thought it was for–"

"I've heard the reasoning," Inar cut in, with an exhalation of annoyance. "You can keep it."

The noblewoman held her tongue. "Yes. I'm sorry. That's it, that's all: I'm sorry."

Inar nodded. "Thank you. It's really Duna who needs to hear that, though. That's the only reason I'm helping you here, so you can make it plain to her that you regret what you did."

"I do," Anzola said. "And let me tell you, in future–"

"In future you need to listen to what she wants and think about that before you get her working on what you want."

In the half-light, Inar felt Anzola's cool gaze on him, and he wondered if he might have strayed beyond the licence afforded by this little window of candour and acquiescence. No matter – it all needed to be said, and heard, even if it did end with a rebuke.

No rebuke came, not really. "I get less of what I want than you imagine," was all she said.

Dawn had come, but not the sun, which was still no more than a suggestion in the western fog. But with the light came Anzola's punctual fulfilment of her promise to Ernesto. She and Inar reported to the altzan-al's office to confirm that they had once again failed to find Duna.

They had truly failed. Few of the other search parties would go out after dark, and so it was left to the merite and the Mishigo and a couple of knights in a reluctant bodyguard to roam alone. Even the passages and rooms they entered felt barely half-searched, the light from their lamps hardly touching anything, doing no more than carving total darkness into a thousand conjoined shadows. As Anzola had said, and Inar knew already, if she did not want to be found, the Brink offered endless opportunities to remain lost. And although Inar did not have forgiveness in him for the time being, he had reached a temporary peace with the noblewoman. She was not searching hard, he saw – that is, she was not tearing open every possible hiding-place they passed. Instead she was simply moving from place to place making herself seen, calling Duna's name from time to time, kindness and concern in her appeals. If Duna did not wish to be found, Anzola would not find her. If she wanted to be found, Anzola was there.

The night was fruitless, and neither of them were surprised.

What was more surprising was the disappearance of Ernesto. The high commander was not in his rooms, and neither was most of his retinue. His secretary and a lone guard were in the scribes' antechamber outside the rooms, drowsing on a settle. Anzola clapped to wake them, and swept past, into the altzan-al's study, which was empty and unlit. Through a narrow door half-hidden in the panelling was the small room Ernesto had been sleeping in, and the cot there was unused.

"The merite is at the gatehouse, your grace," the secretary – a young man named Silvio – said, stepping in behind her, irritable from having been woken. "A rider was sent to the temple at the lake last night, to check on the delays in supply – he has been impatient for word, and wanted to wait in the open air."

"I don't blame him," Anzola said, wrinkling her nose. The office had the staleness of a sickroom. "I will find him there."

* * *

Not only had the fog not lifted, it had hardly thinned. Leaving the Brink by the shattered gulf where mighty bronze doors had once stood, descending cracked steps washed clean of blood and cleared of bodies, Anzola and Inar could only just make out the wounded silhouette of the gatehouse. The former centrepiece of the Brink's outer defensive wall was an impressive structure in its own right, at least as large as the keep at Mal Nulalus. But now its imposing outline was lopsided where Duna had torn at its upmost level during the battle. To the right, where the line of the wall should have carried on, there was only rubble and whiteness, and work teams digging and heaping while bands of knights watched and patrolled.

Ernesto was on the highest battlement, keeping to the un-ruined side of the tower, accompanied by a small coterie of knights from his retinue. They were looking out over the Hidden Land, or what little of it could be seen – the edge of a scoured, grey pit, with the straight pale line of the paved road directly beneath.

"Nothing," he said to Anzola, without pleasantries, hardly turning to acknowledge her. "No word from the Gull Gates, not a stick of supplies from the lake. I've sent riders. We can't delay."

"We have not found her," Anzola said, but her fellow merite was not paying attention.

She approached Ernesto, and Inar followed. The high commander looked better for being outside, but was still more grave than Inar had seen before. His usual bellicosity was gone, and his face was grey and shadowed.

"Watching for them won't speed their horses," Anzola said. "It's early. To reach here at this hour, they'd have to ride through the night."

"Exactly what I told them to do," Ernesto growled. "What I

ordered them to do. Ride *at once*, regardless of hour or conditions, and bring word."

"When did you last have something to eat?" Anzola asked, catching Inar unawares with the gentleness of the question. "You'll not serve the League if you make yourself ill."

"I hate it here," Ernesto said, breaking his gaze from the point where the road was lost in the fog, and casting it around at the roof of the gatehouse and the dark bulk of the Brink behind them. "We had to come, but now we have to go."

"Yes," Anzola agreed. "By all means."

Ernesto turned to face her. "I'm sorry about the girl. We could not have succeeded without her, or you, and perhaps any difficulties we face in future from her are a fair price, to be paid without comment. But I hope that she does return, for you. I know what she means to you."

"Thank you," Anzola said. "I just hope that she is not harmed. I don't know the full effects of ceasing to take Elfcap – I know that they can be agony, as ceasing to drink is agony to the drunkard, but none of the knowledge we could find said it would be crippling or deadly."

Inar frowned. "The knowledge you could find," he said. "In the library at Sojonost, yes?"

"Yes," Anzola said. "There were books there on Elves and Tarch and the campaigns of Augardine – some had pertinent information about Elfcap."

"Well, there's another library here," Inar said. "A much, much larger one, one that has specialised knowledge, not to mention *suppressed* knowledge."

Ernesto had been listening to this exchange with some interest. But his attention was drawn away by a commotion among the knights who watched over the road. He rejoined them, and they urgently conferred and then there was a quick burst of shushing. Silence fell.

Inar strained his ears. Despite the deadening effects of the fog, he could make out what it was that had alerted them:

horse shoes on the road. Just the one horse, at a gallop.

"About time," Ernesto muttered. "Someone still listens to orders."

The horse and rider were not yet visible, and all that could be heard was the steady drumbeat of hooves, carried through the white. But then there was something else: a cry, a thin shout from the rider, a single word.

One of the knights asked a question in Palla and Ernesto gave an I-don't-know shake of the head. Inar turned to Anzola to ask what had been shouted, but the question died in this throat. She was as white as the snow on the mountains.

The rider was getting closer, close enough to be seen. It wasn't a messenger, it was a knight in half-armour, on a pale horse. With his destination now in sight he began to shout, louder and more urgently than before, mostly the same word, sometimes a couple of others. A warning, unmistakably a warning – a call to arms.

"What is it?" Inar asked in a whisper, but he knew the answer from the frozen faces around him.

"Elves," Anzola said. "Elves in the Hidden Land."

42

DUNA

Nothing but rooms connecting to more rooms. Marble floors, square-vaulted ceilings, high or no windows, painted plaster, cold braziers. Half these rooms appeared to be without any purpose, or had fallen into disuse – either shockingly bare, or heaped with dusty furniture and other junk under sheets turned stiff by years of stillness. Pallestra and Matchfalls had been full of rooms as well, many of them grand and opulent. But those rooms were always busy, always full of men and women and servants. There was never enough space, never enough seats, never anywhere to hide.

Here, she could hide.

It was cold, though, and almost always dark. On the first night, she had almost frozen to death trying to sleep uncovered under a table on a marble floor that might as well have been a slab of ice. She was gripped by bouts of shivering so severe they felt more like full-body spasms, and an ancient ache entered every one of her bones. Despite the penetrating cold, she was still tormented by fits of fiery heat, which made her run with sweat; then the fire would die and the sweat would frost and she'd be quaking again. How much time passed in this fashion, she didn't know, though it felt like a millennium. It was enough to convince her that even exhaustion was preferable to trying to sleep, and she had continued her slow movement from place to place, from corner to corner, always listening for pursuers.

League soldiers were everywhere. In the hours following the battle, they had been gathering up tzans, Zealots and acolytes, and then later on they were clearly looking for her. But neither job was done with much effectiveness. She felt she had seen more of the fortress on her own than the whole League army had collectively. She had seen the cells near the refectory where some of the older altzans had hanged themselves, apparently preferring death to the new reality. In the catacombs beneath the ground, she had come across a sizeable group of Zealots, leaderless and demoralised but still armed and armoured, missed by the League and hiding out. They did not notice her, and she had passed by like a ghost.

Near the kitchens and the glass-covered gardens, it was warmer, even though the servants had been rounded up and were under guard elsewhere. That meant there was less risk of being disturbed, so once again she had tried to sleep, burrowing into a pile of laundry beneath a stone shelf. Once again she was stricken by the alternating bouts of freezing chills and boiling sweat, and deep pain in her joints. Thrashing about, unable to rest, she briefly considered that it might be preferable to be found, and to return to Anzola. But even in her fever, she was under no illusion that a knight would see her and gently take her by the arm and lead her back to the merite, and everything would be as it was before. That was gone now. She had seen the look in the eyes of the soldiers around her, and she feared what they might do if they came across her without Anzola present – and what she would have to do to them in order to protect herself. Even Anzola might not protect her, not any more. Perhaps the fateful balance was weighing in Anzola's mind, the balance between Duna's usefulness and Duna's potential danger. How could she trust any reassurance from a woman who had secreted Elfcap in her food?

Could the Elfcap explain this fever, this accursed shaking?

Illness was no surprise, on the road, with an army, in sometimes harsh conditions. But her skin itched and itched and hungered for the tear of nails or the cool touch of a blade, and there was a thought, a persistent and sometimes overwhelming thought, that if she could just have a touch of the power she had felt over the past few days, the power she now knew came from Elfcap, she would be the better for it. Just a taste of it. Her mouth watered at the idea.

Either she slept, or she lost hours in shivering and sweating and running over the same thoughts time and again. She did not know. The light had changed and hinted at evening, and she became afraid that she had been woken by a sound, the sound of soldiers nearby. She tried to stay motionless and silent, listening. Footsteps, quiet voices. Receding. An age of waiting passed, and she wondered what strength she had left to fight or flee. It had been some time since she had eaten or drunk anything, and she recalled the reason she had been drawn towards the kitchens. Was it better to stay where she was, now that a search party had passed by, or move to a new place?

Quietly, she picked up the sword she had taken from the tomb and stole towards the doorway of the side-chamber where she had been hiding. It connected to a vaulted passage that led to the immense kitchens. That was where the men were, she could hear them, and even see them, pick up snatches of their conversation. They were gathering all the food they could find. But while they were occupied with that, she could creep away unobserved.

Keeping her eyes fixed on the kitchen end of the passage, she stepped out, and then turned to see a League soldier standing between her and escape.

He was young, not even a man-at-arms, just a squire or a foot volunteer. He had no armour and no helmet covered his blond hair. The only weapon he had was a dirk, which he raised, sticking its point in Duna's direction. But he said nothing, his face frozen, lips slightly apart. The end of the dirk waggled comically as his hand shook.

Just a child. A terrified child. He had not raised the alarm.

Duna stilled the wavering dirk with the tip of the scorched blade she carried, slowly directing its point downwards, gazing into the boy's fearful eyes. He did nothing to stop her. So this was scourge-power, this was what it was to be a witch. She raised the index finger of her free hand to her lips, and said "Sssh." And then she slipped past the soldier, and was away.

Via a concealed servants' door, Duna found herself in a series of grand state rooms, deserted but better kept than many she had seen. They were swept of dust and the braziers held recent ashes. A private dining room was followed by a small library, and then a bedroom. In the bedroom there was a bed, and in the bed there was a priest.

She could tell he was a priest from the robes that hung beside the bed – the usual dark grey, but also white, which she had never seen before on an altzan. The robes were clean and unworn, and from the look of the bed's occupant he had not worn any for a while. He was an old man, and he lay on his back, arms at his sides, straight as a corpse. His eyes were open but stared insensibly at the ceiling. Only the soft sigh of his breath spoke of continued life, and the unpleasant sweet smell of declining flesh in the room. Next to the bed, on an aged rug, was some clutter left by whoever had been taking care of this invalid – a silver dish of water, a jug, a bowl containing traces of porridge, towels and bandages, and a small, sharp-smelling wooden chest containing medicaments. There was a cushioned chair by the bedside, and another in the corner. Peat still smouldered in the brazier at the foot of the bed, with a sprinkle of incense to mask the less pleasant smells in the air.

To find this comatose priest left in lonely grandeur in the midst of a nightmare palace might have been upsetting. But

Duna felt more calm than she had since leaving Sojonost, as if she was in the stilled eye of a storm. The signs of care around the old altzan comforted her, and told her that the Brink was more than a necropolis of superstition and bloodthirsty ritual. The room was warm and quiet and the breath of another living soul, however frail, was comforting.

The only really disturbing feature of the room was the far wall, which the bed faced. While the other walls were faced in icy pale stone, this one had a fresco – a twelve-foot figure clad in white, one hand clutching a curved red blade, the other raised aloft, holding a human heart. Blood ran down the upraised arm, and stained the other to the wrist. The figure's face was idealised and beatific, and behind it rose a dark, winged shape.

It could be ignored, especially as the shadows advanced. The chair in the corner had its back to it. Duna took a blanket from a neatly folded pile left on top of a chest, curled into that chair, and fell asleep. She slept longer and more soundly than she had for days.

When she awoke, the light through the high windows suggested the dawn. She was not alone.

The old priest had woken, and sat on the side of the bed. Duna could see that he had once been physically impressive, before he had been struck down by age and illness. Beside him was a young priest in plain black robes, also tall, with the shaven head of a novice. They were conversing quietly, but when Duna started in surprise at their presence, they turned their attention to her. Duna noticed a sharp metal glint at the young priest's side, but the elder smiled reassuringly.

"My apologies," he said. "We have startled you."

Duna gathered herself. "I should apologise to you," she said. "This is your room."

"Oh, it's nothing," the ancient priest said with a courteous wave of the hand. "I am glad you're here. Your presence is an elixir. Really quite amazing. Like the dawn, after years of night. Are there many like you?"

Duna didn't know how to answer. She felt the priests' eyes on her, and she feared betraying a secret, but she also understood, on an instinctive level, that one particular secret was not a secret in this company. "I'm the only one here," she said carefully.

"My name is Leass," the old priest said. He moved his bony shoulders, and Duna was reminded uncomfortably of the bindlings, no more than a skeleton bound with a vestige of flesh. The thin night-shirt he wore had been cleaned often, and was mostly clean now, but told of many venerable stains. Ugly sores streaked what little of the lower part of his legs that was not covered by nightshirt or bandages. "I have been... asleep. But you have brought me back. I met one of your kind once, in Yicorum. A long time ago, many years. A blight-scourge. I'm afraid to say... that nothing good came of it. Tell me, how did you get here without being sensed by the Custodians? Have they left the Mountain?"

"I don't know," Duna said. Lost in the horror of escape, and before that in a haze of bloodlust, she had hardly been conscious of what *had* happened, let alone thought about what had *not*. But mention of the Custodians made their absence suddenly obvious, and aberrant. They had loomed so large in the secret discussions that had taken place at Sojonost, before the berserker veil had descended and she no longer cared if they existed or not. "We haven't seen them. My people feared that my power would draw their attention, so they gave me Elfcap to mask it. Without my knowing," she quickly added, seeing the scowls cloud the priests' faces. "I hate the Elves. I hate the people who gave me their poison. But it has worn off now, I think."

"The poison, you mean," Leass said.

"Yes."

"Not the hate."

"No."

"So it's true," the ancient priest said with a troubled glance at his young carer. "The Elves have returned. And the Elfcap, you want more, I daresay?"

Duna thought that maybe she should lie, but she was tired of all that. She nodded, and her eyes stung.

"You must not take more," the priest said, fixing her with a piercing stare. "For your own sake, but also for us all. Do you understand?"

Again, Duna nodded, feeling the tears run hot down her cheeks.

"You went into the tomb," Leass said. "The mausoleum."

Another nod. The old man was surprisingly well-informed.

"What's within?"

"Nothing," Duna said, then shrugged. "Some scattered bones, armour, weapons. Nothing that looked like a dead emperor."

The priest and the novice looked at one another, with matching frowns.

"Is that bad?" Duna asked.

"It's unexpected," the priest said. "Did you get that from the Tomb?" His eyes turned to the plain black sword, which Duna had laid beside her chair.

"Yes," Duna said. It struck her that this might be seen as grave-robbing, and wanted to justify taking the weapon. "I was unarmed, and upset. It was just lying there. Everything else in there reeked of old magic. Was that wrong?"

"Not at all," Leass said. "Keep it safe. Let no one take it from you. Tell me – why did you go into the tomb? You knew that Augardine created your kind, and thought there might be a way to… What?" He saw the suspicion on Duna's face. "Several altzans and novices were there, they heard what you said, and word travels, even in these conditions. Not every brother and sister has been confined by the invaders." Again, he shared a glance with his young helper. "You wanted to be rid of your Scourge-power."

"I am a monster," Duna said, casting her eyes downwards. "The people who nurtured me are afraid of me, of what I have become. Their whole army is afraid of me. I have hurt people. Since before my first breath, I hurt people, and I fear I will never be allowed to stop. Your church burns people like me, and I fear it is right to."

To her amazement, the ancient priest chuckled at this, although his companion showed no emotion. "A monster!" he said. "I quite understand – Look what they made of *my* kind!"

He raised an emaciated arm and pointed at the wall behind her. Duna recalled the ghastly fresco, and did not desire to look at it again.

"You're one of them?" she asked. "A blade-priest?"

Leass nodded, eyes closed. "One of the last. Which reminds me – Anton, the young vertzan – he lives?"

"Yes," Duna said. "He is a captive of my people. They intend to install him as a puppet here."

"That would not be desirable," Leass said. "Do you desire to revenge yourself against your poisoners, the people who made you into a monster?"

"No, not really," Duna said, with a shake of the head.

"But you want to be away from them. And away from the Elves. And perhaps you'd like to be in a position to hurt them if they tried to come for you?"

Duna thought this over, shifting her glance between the ancient blade-priest and the novice. They returned her gaze with equanimity. An understanding existed there that had no name.

"Yes. I'd like that."

"Good," Leass said. "Then we know what must be done."

It was a long walk – impossibly long, it seemed to Duna, covering more distance than could be contained within even the Brink's walls. At first their route took them through catacombs and dungeons, and then into a narrow, sepulchral tunnel. Even Duna, slim and small as she was, found she could not walk through this tight space without brushing one wall or the other, and the arched ceiling was close enough to make her want to duck. On and on the tunnel went, sloping down and then up. Sometimes its walls were faced with cut stone, but mostly it was just the living rock itself, still marked by the tools that had dug their way inch by inch centuries before.

"Your assault collapsed one of our postern gates," the shaven-headed novice explained. "Another has been found, and is guarded. But they haven't found this one. Too deep."

The party comprised Duna, the priest, and eight Zealots. All were armed, the Zealots with spears and bows, the priest with a long knife not unlike a League dirk. Duna had the sword from the tomb, and was mindful of Leass's instruction to keep it safe, an instruction that puzzled her. Besides its obvious age, there was nothing obviously special about the weapon. It was simple in design and devoid of decoration.

At the end of the tunnel was a shaft, and Duna was struck by the uncomfortable sensation of being at the bottom of a well. Iron rungs were set into the wall of the shaft, and one of the Zealots climbed to the top, which Duna was relieved to note was only twelve feet or so above the floor. With some difficulty, the Zealot pushed up the heavy cover that capped the shaft, and then whispered down that their path was clear. Already Duna could feel the cold breath of the outdoors, and despite her warm clothing she suffered a new bout of queasy shivering and shaking.

The Zealots around her were dousing the oil lamps they carried, and reluctantly Duna did the same. She heard the scrape of the cover being lifted again, and the crunch of it being moved aside onto dirt, but even with the shaft open, the darkness did not yield. Duna had to find each rung by touch and scourge-sense. Near the top, a strong hand grasped her under the armpit and hauled her out onto the scree of the Hidden Land.

There was light – only a little. Somewhere, the moon and its maids were out, but the fog still lay heavy over the land and the little luminosity they cast was diffuse and eerie. What had blocked it from entering the shaft was a bizarre overhanging shape, an immense curved disk, like the circular cover of the shaft but much larger.

"What is this?" Duna asked, looking up at the disc, feeling as if she stood under a plate dropped by a giant.

"It's a mirror," the young priest answered quietly. "It was the sacred object of a dead religion. Just junk, now. How are you feeling?"

Duna was suddenly aware that her face was slick with sweat, despite the cold. "Not my best," she said.

"The Elfcap?"

Duna nodded.

"We have a long journey ahead of us, and we must make haste – will you endure?"

Duna nodded again. She liked the young priest, who had the aspect of a born carer.

She was rewarded with a warm smile. "I know you can. We'll get away from here, from all of this."

"Where are we going?" Duna asked.

"Miroline!" Elecy answered.

ACKNOWLEDGEMENTS

As ever I am immensely grateful to my agent Antony Topping for his advice and his work on my behalf. It may have come as a shock when one of his literary clients suddenly produced a fantasy novel, but he barely flinched. Thank you to Eleanor Teasdale and Simon Spanton for signing the book to Angry Robot. At Angry Robot, my thanks go to Gemma Creffield, Caroline Lambe, Ailsa Stuart and Desola Coker, all of whom helped put the book in your hands. Alice Coleman designed the cover. Andrew Hook provided vital edits.

A brilliant insight from Jo Fletcher made this book hugely better than it was. Adam Roberts, James Smythe and Sam Byers provided invaluable feedback on early drafts, and I am grateful for their moral support throughout. Thank you to Paul McAuley for his generous words. And to my family, who put up with a lot.

ANGRY ROBOT

We are Angry Robot

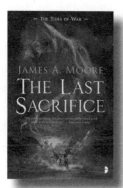

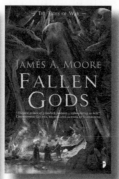

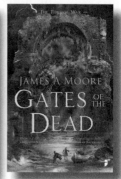

angryrobotbooks.com

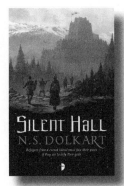
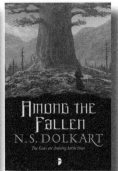

We are Angry Robot

angryrobotbooks.com

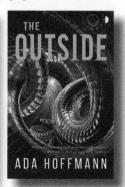

Science Fiction, Fantasy and WTF?!

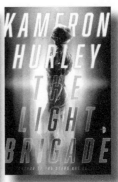

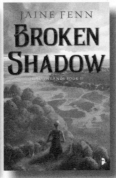

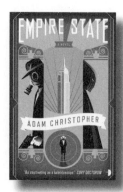

We are Angry Robot

angryrobotbooks.com

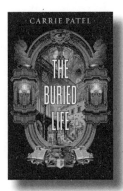
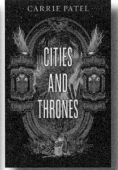

We are Angry Robot

angryrobotbooks.com